Bare

Lynn Kelling

ForbiddenFiction
www.forbiddenfiction.com

an imprint of

Fantastic Fiction Publishing
www.fantasticfictionpublishing.com

BARE
A ForbiddenFiction book

Fantastic Fiction Publishing
Hayward, California

© Lynn Kelling, 2016

CREDITS
Editor: Rylan Hunter and D.M. Atkins
Cover Design: Siolnatine
Cover Art: Adapted by Soilnatine from photo © Mayer George at Shutterstock.
Production Editor: Kaye O'Malley
Proofreading: Kailin Morgan
Font: Wellrock Slab, by Manfred Klein

SKU: LK1-1.000287-01 FFP
ISBN: 978-1-62234-310-2

Published in the United States of America

In the far corner of the room,

a door opened and closed. The click of booted footsteps peppered among the charcoal's scratching. He wanted to look, but without breaking his pose Ev could only just make out a man's form at the back wall. The man seemed to be speaking to the teacher. They shook hands and lingered closely. Another set of eyes was added to the mix. The additional scrutiny tightened Ev's skin, making his hair stand on end from his calves to the top of his head.

When the man walked closer, toward the platform, Ev swallowed hard and told himself not to move. He walked into Ev's line of sight.

When their gazes met, a strange jolt hit Ev. Right away, he knew why.

Ahh, fuck, Ev swore internally, glancing away. His face heated and he feared a blush so powerfully, his balls drew up. Dread and discomfort twisted inside him. It was just like when he'd accidentally catch John's eye in the locker room while they were both naked and no one else was around. It was exciting but there was danger there. Ev couldn't run from it this time. There would be no fleeing the awkward moment by grabbing his bag and jogging for the exit. He was stuck in place for scrutiny.

The guy had dark auburn hair, vivid, sky blue eyes and was probably the most attractive man Ev had ever seen. He made John look like a troll. The redhead came even closer, staring up and down Ev's body.

The blush came with whispers he may or may not have imagined. The redhead circled the platform, taking in every angle. Never had Ev been more aware of his nakedness or felt more self-conscious.

With a honeyed tenor, the redhead called, "Hey, Günter, it's okay if I walk around awhile, right?"

Don't get hard, you dipshit. Don't you fucking dare.

Also recommended...

You may also enjoy these other ForbiddenFiction works:

Loving the Master by Lynn Kelling

David Davenport is, by most standards, a very successful man. He has money, influence, and the Manse, his private gay club. Still, that's not enough to make him happy. Despite all his privilege, David is a lonely man. While at lunch with an old friend, David finds himself enchanted by the charming young waiter, Shea Whittier. Unlike David, Shea does not have wealth or influence. He does have problems, though, and David is more than willing to help. As the men grow closer, Shea's submissive nature responds to David's dominance, bringing a powerful intensity to their relationship, and leaving them vulnerable to an unexpected danger. (M/M)

Leather Wishes by Julian Keys

Mason, the leather top known at the Cockpit Bar as the Fancy Man, loves to create BDSM scenes for people—the more unusual the better. Charles brought him one of his tougher challenges, and the two have been together since. It hasn't always been easy, as they work out what they are to each other, both as dominant and submissive and as lovers. Now Mason and Charles work together to create BDSM experiences of intense emotion. As they help other people deal with broken hearts and long-buried desires, they also confront the possibilities in their own relationship. Partners in the scene and in the bed, the two men come to appreciate that they could be so much more together. (M/M)

DISCLAIMER

This book is a work of fiction which contains explicit erotic content; it is intended for mature readers. Do not read this if it's not legal for you.

All the characters, locations and events herein are fictional. While elements of existing locations or historical characters or events may be used fictitiously, any resemblance to actual people, places or events is coincidental.

This story depicts fictional BDSM; it is not intended to be used as an instruction manual. It contains descriptions of erotic acts that may be immoral, illegal, or unsafe. The characters are not models for the Safe, Sane and Consensual forms embraced by most current practitioners of BDSM. The author takes license with the use of BDSM for dramatic effect. Do not take the events in this story as proof of the plausibility or safety of any particular practice.

Such content should not be read as a depiction of the desires, opinions, or fetishes of the author or the staff of ForbiddenFiction.com.

*For all those struggling to own their truth,
with hope, encouragement, and love.*

Contents

Chapter 1

Secret Show Off

"What are you doing, man?" Leo stood at Ev's side, looking as if he was trying to stare Ev down or intimidate him into walking away. It wasn't going to work. Though Leo was built and broad-shouldered, he ran track, so his physique was more lean than big. Ev still had plenty of size advantage on him. After so many years playing sports, Ev was used to being surrounded by guys who determined worth based on physical accomplishments and whether people were cool to hang with. Leo still had some of that, but Ev could usually count on him to balance things out with a more well-rounded type of common sense.

Leo looked back over his shoulder like he was making sure no one saw him standing next to a guy who was reading this particular flyer tacked to the dormitory bulletin board. Ignoring him, Ev re-read the flyer again, though he'd practically memorized it by now.

"This is a joke, right? Please don't tell me you're actually thinking about it."

"What business is it of yours, anyway?" Ev leaned in, using his size to his advantage, wanting Leo to back off.

"I have to live with you. My reputation hinges on not bunking with the nude model for the life drawing art freaks."

"Nice." He gave a shake of his head and readjusted his pack, heavy with three massive and expensive textbooks. Each one of them felt as though they weighed the same as a cement block, but the cost weighed even more heavily on his mind.

The genuine, if selfish, worry painted over Leo's face spurred Ev's regretful but deep-seated need to pacify or deflect critics. It was an instinct ingrained from a childhood spent lingering at the side of a career politician. Instead of walking away, like he should have, Ev answered in a way that he knew would appeal to Leo's practicality. "I need the money, man. So unless you're gonna pay my bills for me, maybe lay off, huh?"

His gaze skimmed the listing once more, looking for whatever was hidden between the lines. He didn't need to write down the phone number for the model sign-ups. He'd already written it down the day before, just in case. Now it was just a matter of finding his balls.

A couple of blondes passed close enough to brush Ev's arm. Leo grinned and said, "Hey."

"Hey, Ev," one of them said with a flirty smirk, ignoring Leo entirely.

He gave her a half-hearted grin. It was the best he could manage under the circumstances. She seemed to notice the paper he'd been examining and turned to whisper to her friend as they continued into the stairwell.

"God damn, Myers," Leo groaned. "You're killing me. This can't be your best option." Shrugging off most of the uncomfortable expression on his face, Leo turned his attention back to his roommate. "I get it, a'ight? Money woes and shit. But you already have a job."

Ev had to admire Leo's persistence, both with the blondes and the pestering. That morning, Leo was dressed in his typical attire of a plain, V-neck t-shirt that was pulled tight across his chest but hung loose and low around his hips, with a pair .of exercise shorts; both hands plunged deeply into the pockets. As thrown together as his outfit was, Ev had seen Leo take a full hour to style his curly black hair, arranged in perfect little twists that stuck up all over his head, and his thick but short beard.

"No, I don't think you do get it. Yeah, I have a job—a shitty one that pays exactly minimum wage and only gives me three hours a night, max. This pays more and it's not a huge time commitment. You know my history textbook alone cost two hundred and fifty dollars? That's like what I make in a month, and I have a whole stack of other bills waiting in the pile below that one. My loan only stretches so far and my parents aren't helping. They won't give me another dime for random expenses. They hate that I picked this school and they're not gonna let me forget it. I can't go to that well anymore."

The job he already had was in the registration office, mostly filing paperwork and other mind-numbingly boring office-monkey tasks. He didn't hate it, and it could be worse. Those poor bastards in the café looked like they swam in grease all day. At least in the office he had a padded chair and air conditioning.

Though his parents set up a hefty trust fund for his tuition, and had agreed to take on dorm and meal plan expenses, too, anything and everything else was on Ev. He'd been fairly spoiled his whole childhood, so it was painful to make so little at his job while watching his credit card balance get bigger and bigger. Since a school back in Kansas had given him a chance at a full ride, and he'd turned it down, this was his payback.

Ev turned and finally walked away from Leo, who just quickened his step to catch up. Ev pushed out of the dorm building and crossed the road separating it from the main campus. Leo was right at his heels.

"Leave me alone, dude. Come on."

"You know it's not just girls in those classes, right?" Leo jogged to catch up but wasn't winded at all, thanks to being a runner. Ev was also doing fine, thanks to too many years in varsity football and baseball, trying to live out his old man's dreams. "You really want some creepy dudes looking at your junk?" Leo made a V with his hands in front of his crotch and Ev had to roll his eyes. "You know the arts majors are more likely to be… you know."

"Oh, I do? Come on, I'd be getting paid for nothing. To just stand there or something. Seems like easy money to me."

"Why don't you just be a stripper then? Lots more money." He actually sounded angry, which was so funny, Ev tossed him a grin and shook his head.

"What are you, my mom? I can't dance. If I could, yeah, maybe I would strip. Who cares?"

"I care, 'cause it's fucked up. I know you've been ragging on your folks, but come on. Don't you have any damn principles for yourself? Some self-respect? You're in fucking commercials that play regularly out in cornfield country. A poster boy for the future of conservative America, standing next to your pops in your polo shirt and flag pin, big old goofy grin on your face. I've seen that shit on YouTube. And now this."

Ev rolled his eyes again. He thought Leo knew him a little better than that, but maybe not. Maybe Ev had been selling the family brand for so long, and gotten so good at doing it, he'd even convinced his best friend he was a cardboard cutout instead of a real person.

Ev's neck itched where the gold crucifix used to hang around it. He scratched absentmindedly as old echoes of sermons in his family's Southern Baptist church rang in his memory; condemning him for all the ways he knew he was a goddamned liar. He'd fled halfway across the country but it still felt like everyone was watching him—spies for the church and disturbingly devoted constituents of his father.

The restless discomfort intensified, darkening his mood.

"Yeah, I get it. Thanks." Ev slammed through the side door to the large brick building where his Behavioral Theories in Management class was held. The door ricocheted off the wall and Leo caught it before it could whack him in the face. Then he turned down the hall that led to his class. Knowing Leo was headed the other way; he glanced over his shoulder and said, "Luckily, it's still not your problem! Later."

"Myers!"

"Bye!"

Getting lost in the small crowd filtering into the classroom, Ev kept his head down and slipped into a desk near the back. The coffee he'd had with breakfast in the cafeteria hadn't been enough to wake him up. A run in the brisk fall air would have done the job, if it weren't for his unfortunate early Monday schedule. Letting his bag slide to the floor, he rolled his shoulders to stretch the knotted muscles, then rolled his head too to work some kinks out of his neck. That eerie, imagined weight of the crucifix was still there, taunting him.

His sports days were over. School and work took up all of his time, but he still tried to keep in shape. He'd grown proud of his body. Staying trim, working on his definition and strength were a top priority after a childhood spent as the chubby, short kid who always got laughed at. Now, he was six feet tall and just managed to squeeze his wide shoulders and broad chest into size large shirts.

Pulling off his knit hat, he ran his hands through his dark blond hair, smoothing it back as it threatened to fall into his eyes, then tucked the hat in a pocket of his jeans. Though his hair was on the lighter side of the color spectrum, his eyes were a dark, chocolate brown and their naturally half-closed state tended to make him appear sleepier than he was.

The last drowsy students trickled in, filling the few remaining desks. Some of them wore sweatshirts with Lehigh University stenciled across the chest. Others were still wearing pajamas, their hair un-brushed and no hat to mat it down. In his opinion, that was a little too pathetic for being still so close to the start of term. It usually took a few solid months for people to start giving up at that level.

He opened his notebook, grabbed a pen and got ready to take notes. Not cooperating with the game plan, his thoughts shifted sideways.

It wasn't that he hadn't heard what Leo was saying, it was more that Leo didn't understand the context or the twisted mess that was Ev's psyche. Memories of the locker room in high school after football practice came back to him. Back then, he'd gotten really good at keeping an eye on everyone from the edges of his vision. He could tell if someone was looking at him and could size up the other guys, too. It had always seemed a defensive maneuver more than anything. He was watching out for trouble, staying alert. It wasn't that guys like his teammate Shaun, for instance, looked bad. Their bodies were amazing, especially Shaun's. While some guys were too skinny or too barrel-chested, Shaun was slim with broad shoulders, a narrow waist and a tight, round ass. A single glimpse of that ass was enough to rouse the overpowering temptation to give it a hard slap or snap a towel against it, in a totally sportsmanlike way, of course. Shaun wasn't the most facially attractive guy, but he had a lot going for him otherwise.

After those practices, at home, Ev would look at himself in the mirror, trying to compare what he had to what he'd seen. Did he measure up? Was he too bulky? Not bulky enough?

He wasn't into guys or anything. It was more figuring out his place in the scheme of things. If his gaze lingered on Shaun's ass when he dropped his towel and bent over for his boxers, it was perfectly normal curiosity. If a naked person bent over in front of you, you'd look whether they were hot or not. It was human nature.

The professor welcomed the class and began scrawling some key points on the board. Ev automatically moved to copy them down into his notebook.

Ev caught one guy looking at his body in the locker room on multiple occasions. Ev had always been really careful not to let on that he could tell, because he secretly liked being looked at that way. It gave him hope that he had something worth looking at. It thrilled Ev in a way that made him want to smile, and got him standing a little straighter or maybe even flexing slightly as he moved.

The guy's name was John, and he was actually kind of handsome, though a little scrawny. He had one of those faces the girls seemed entranced by. They'd gather in packs, whispering to one another as he passed, maybe calling out to him to get a hello or a smile back.

Ev had always been kind of proud that John snuck looks at him when he got changed. If John watched, Ev would take his time and let John look a little longer. Those locker room interludes had taught Ev he didn't have to worry about measuring up when it came to what hung between his legs, either. If John went home and beat off thinking about Ev's dick, it was fine with him.

That was why the modeling gig didn't seem like such a big deal. Sometimes it was nice to have people give your body some attention. Why work so hard to stay in shape if you couldn't show off once in a while?

"Evelyn Myers?" the teacher's booming voice called out in question.

Ev groaned, slouching down in his seat. All eyes turned to him as his baritone voice replied, "Yeah. It's just Ev, sir."

"Very well, Mr. Myers. Could you tell us why the control group in Elton Mayo's Hawthorne experiment produced more than the other employees?"

Fuck, Ev cursed inwardly, scanning his notes for an answer that probably would have been there, had he been paying any attention.

Chapter 2

Nude Modeling, Day One

Ev was actually excited for his first nude modeling gig. He showed up without any hesitation or lingering embarrassment, no matter what Leo said to him. The extra cash already filled his account, in a metaphorical sense at least, and none of his personal boundaries were being challenged. He got undressed in a nearby bathroom and put on a fluffy white robe—one his mom had sent him to school with for the treks back and forth to the communal bathrooms, though Ev usually just wore a towel. In this situation, he was grateful for a little extra coverage until it was time to get going.

To kill a spare couple of minutes until it was time to head to the classroom, he checked his Facebook account. There was a new post by his cousin, James Howard. It was a photo of James standing on the sprawling green lawn in front of their neighborhood church with his arm around the shoulders of a petite, brunette, mini-Stepford-wife-in-training.

Ev knew the type—crucifix around their necks, skirts that never fell above the knee, sensible high-heeled shoes, and Momma-approved amounts of makeup and hairspray. They'd been creeping him out since his first day at the children's ministry program—making big doe eyes at him like they wanted to lure him in for trouble, or saying his name in sing-song voices, giggling and using their best manners as long as the adults were around. As soon as the kids had a moment alone, they'd come for him, flirting in brazenly dirty ways, making him generally uncomfortable.

Just because of who his parents were, Ev was always highly visible, hugely popular, and utterly unable to blend in. Those girls treated him like he was nothing but a stepladder best used to get them closer to God, marriage, kids, and a life of comfort. Ev had managed to avoid their snares but clearly James hadn't.

Frowning down at the forced smile on his cousin's face and the completely fake, carefully orchestrated nature of the picture, Ev could only be glad he was as far away from home as he was, and about to engage in an act that would absolutely horrify his entire extended family. He could sense the trickles of sweat dripping down James's back, and could almost hear the screaming held in behind his tightly clenched jaw and full, toothy grin.

That wasn't James. James was sarcastic, laid-back, with a wry wit and natural, effortless charm.

Or, at least, he had been, before they'd taken him away. One fuck-up was all it had taken. Then he'd vanished for months. James eventually came back from a sleep-away camp that was part of a special church program for troubled youth, and he was a totally different person. The program was called The Pathway to Manhood. In his head, he simply thought of them as the Pathway people. After doing a fair share of digging, Ev had discovered some intensely disturbing rumors about the Pathway camps—whispers of brainwashing, imprisonment, and even torture. It was run by a small, tight-knit group of men who were pillars of the community as well as former graduates of the same program. Ev's father had a lifelong friend on the board of directors at Pathway. Several others were from their family church. Those connections tied Ev and James to that place whether they liked it or not.

Before camp, Ev had been close to James. Afterward, they never saw each other except maybe from across the house at huge family events. Their parents had made sure of it.

That had been years ago. James drank the Kool-aid, whereas Ev had avoided it. He was glad to have gotten out, but he couldn't help looking back once in a while, if only to yearn for solutions. He didn't want to think James was a lost cause, but seeing that photo on Facebook made it feel true. James was just as demented as the people he and Ev used to secretly make fun of before it had all gone so drastically sideways on them.

He put the phone away and slowly, carefully emerged from the men's room. He followed a relatively empty hallway in the top floor of the arts building to the classroom where about fifteen painting students were waiting behind easels. They were all mostly his age, though a few older students were sprinkled into the ranks. It seemed an even split between men and women, too. The thing Ev liked most about being on the east coast, studying at a distinctly non-religious institution, was the diversity of the people he was constantly surrounded by. There wasn't a single Stepford-wife-in-training in the bunch.

The room itself was nice and spacious. The high, cathedral ceilings were spotted with several skylights letting bright shafts of light into the white-walled space. The floors were dark wood, splattered everywhere with paint.

The teacher, named Günter Ahlm, Ev would peg to about thirty-five years of age. The guy had a ridiculously stereotypical ponytail and dainty round spectacles perched on his nose. He'd been nice enough so far during their brief in-person interview and over the phone. Mr. Ahlm motioned Ev toward the center of the room and began to demonstrate a few different poses. He was going to have Ev run through each of them during the class while up on a slightly raised platform in the middle of the cavernous studio. On the platform was a large amount of carefully draped beige canvas material, a beat-up old stool and a white pedestal.

"We're ready when you are," Mr. Ahlm said with a patient, calming smile.

"Okay, cool."

Ev untied the robe and took it off without raising his gaze.

"Let's do the seated pose first."

Ev climbed up onto the platform and stool, then assumed the half-turned pose the teacher had asked for. He picked a spot on the wall that was marked with a shallow but sharp dent and didn't shift his gaze from it.

The students' focus on his now-exposed body felt like fingertips brushing his skin. The eerie sense came from all directions and gave him goosebumps following a pleasant shiver.

Right away, he enjoyed the rush and was glad he'd gone through with it. The light scratching sound of charcoal sticks on heavy paper filled the air, tickling Ev's ears. Art was being created. Unique visions, differing interpretations of the same, mundane sight were being captured in two dimensional forms to be judged and admired. Ev couldn't draw a straight line to save his life but that didn't mean he couldn't appreciate artwork of all kinds in his own ways. To him, art combated the lies of his childhood world. Politics, religion, and small-town, ingrained tradition were best battled with the truth of individuality and freedom of expression. To even be a small part of making that happen made him happy in a quiet, private way.

Sixteen sets of eyes stared hard at his spread thighs, the twist of his waist, and the lift of his strong chin. The deliciously taboo, stark reality of it was heady; a subtle thrill he wouldn't soon forget. His complete nakedness made his skin feel tight even as the attention made his heartbeat quicken and body surge with energy. Despite his father and his community, Ev was doing something forbidden. They couldn't stop him. It felt like he was triumphing in a small, safe way against all of the ministers, teachers, family members, and inane talking heads he'd left behind in Kansas.

The next few hours proceeded with only his shifting of position every twenty or thirty minutes to mark the time. No one bothered him or spoke to him, other than Mr. Ahlm.

When Mr. Ahlm announced the end of class and began to give verbal reminders to the students for their homework assignments, Ev couldn't believe it was finished already. All he'd done was stay still and let his thoughts run wild. He felt peaceful, like he'd meditated rather than worked. As he donned his robe and went to get changed, he began looking forward to the next modeling session.

The next three modeling sessions proceeded much the same way over the course of the next two weeks with two classes scheduled per week. By the second week, the shock had almost entirely worn off as he got naked and climbed onto the platform. The students rarely looked him in the eye, especially because he stayed focused on various spots on the walls, the view out the high-placed windows, or nothing at all. Sometimes he got stiff, or needed to scratch an itch he wasn't allowed to reach for, but those became his only complaints about the lucrative job. One of his favorite perks of the gig was getting to wander past the easels filled with the students' work at the end of class, if he managed to get his robe on before they'd all packed up to leave. It thrilled him to see their interpretations of his body, and to witness the magic their talent captured with only charcoal and paper. Everyone had a different view, a different story to tell. No one drawing or artist was the same.

On the sixth session, he was more than happy to follow Mr. Ahlm's direction for the first pose, in which he was reclined against a decorative pillar with one knee bent and the other leg extended, one arm bent to prop up his head and the other lying open on the platform at his side.

In the far corner of the room, a door opened and closed. The click of booted footsteps peppered among the charcoal's scratching. He wanted to look, but without breaking his pose Ev could only just make out a man's form at the back wall. The man seemed to be speaking to the teacher. They shook hands and lingered closely. Another set of eyes was added to the mix. The additional scrutiny tightened Ev's skin, making his hair stand on end from his calves to the top of his head.

When the man walked closer, toward the platform, Ev swallowed hard and told himself not to move. He walked into Ev's line of sight.

When their gazes met, a strange jolt hit Ev. Right away, he knew why.

Ahh, fuck, Ev swore internally, glancing away. His face heated and he feared a blush so powerfully, his balls drew up. Dread and discomfort twisted inside him. It was just like when he'd accidentally catch John's eye in the locker room while they were both naked and no one else was around. It was exciting but there was danger there. Ev couldn't run from it this time. There would be no fleeing the awkward moment by grabbing his bag and jogging for the exit. He was stuck in place for scrutiny.

The guy had dark auburn hair, vivid, sky blue eyes and was probably the most attractive man Ev had ever seen. He made John look like a troll. The redhead came even closer, staring up and down Ev's body.

The blush came with whispers he may or may not have imagined. The redhead circled the platform, taking in every angle. Never had Ev been more aware of his nakedness or felt more self-conscious.

With a honeyed tenor, the redhead called, "Hey, Günter, it's okay if I walk around awhile, right?"

Don't get hard, you dipshit. Don't you fucking dare.

The whole fascination with John had been a fluke, or so Ev had thought. It was an ego trip. It didn't mean he was gay. To feel similarly curious about the redhead scared Ev a little. His body temperature rose, his heart beating harder. Time slowed down, thick like syrup. He used the fear to kill the swelling arousal.

As the minutes slogged by, all of Ev's anxiousness faded to a manageable buzz. He couldn't see the redhead any longer, but felt him there like the itch he couldn't scratch on the middle of his back.

"Okay, let's switch poses."

"Oh, thank god," Ev murmured, scratching his back vigorously enough to have left red marks.

"Next will be a lying down pose," the teacher said from a few feet away. Ev lay down and let the teacher guide him to the right angle with gestures. "Bend your right leg a little more. Let your hand fall open. There. Nice."

Before long, the redhead walked into view again. He paused beside an easel where a petite Korean student with her black hair in a tight bun atop her head was deep in concentration as she worked on her sketch. Biting his thumb, tilting his head slightly to one side, the redhead stared hard enough to bore holes in Ev's skin. In response, Ev's nipples tightened and his fingers twitched. The urge to fidget into a more comfortable position was almost irresistible. The light scratching of charcoal sticks surrounded him.

"Really lay in that shadow beneath his leg. Do you see it? Here?" It was the redhead again, his voice sweet and almost lulling. He walked up to Ev, making him flinch slightly, then gestured to the air beneath Ev's right thigh, drawing through it with a hand.

Don't look at him. Don't think about him.

He wore paint-splashed jeans, heavy, black boots and a few layers of shirts, some also paint-splattered, but his neckline was low enough to show a large triangle of tan skin dusted with golden chest hair. He was maybe in his mid-twenties, possibly older. The guy wasn't scrawny or big, but somewhere in the middle, right where Ev wished he wasn't. When the redhead turned to the female student, the muscles of his back stretched his layered shirts, pulling them tightly over his body, which Ev forced himself not to imagine. His dark red hair curled a little around his ears, tickled the nape of his neck.

He turned toward Ev again and they locked eyes, for just a moment. Ev looked away first, his stomach flipping over, his balls suddenly too cold in the room's previously warm air.

Why had he agreed to this again?

It was the longest hour of his life. The redhead never left. He remained there, watching Ev as he pulled the white robe back on for the trek back to the bathrooms, his face hotter than it should have been, invisible ants crawling all over his body.

Ev took his time getting dressed, trying to wait it out, but when another guy came in to use the urinal, Ev left rather than linger at the mirror like a creep.

The redhead waited for him in the hall.

"Hey, nice work in there," the gorgeously featured guy told him. He stood a couple of inches taller than Ev and was at least as built as him. With his tongue thick and clumsy in his mouth, and his arm hanging dead at his side, at first Ev didn't move to shake with the guy or say a word. But the guy was determined enough to wait.

"Thanks. I just started doing this a couple weeks ago," Ev finally replied, shaking with him, feeling the warm, dry grip of a strong hand wrapping his own.

"Yeah, I thought you looked new. I'm Adam. Adam Buchanan. I teach here in the summers. Right now I'm working on putting together a show of my own. It's taken up most of my time. I..." He frowned, brushing the rosy swell of his lower lip with his thumb, barely biting the lip with white teeth. "I don't suppose you'd be interested in some additional work?"

"Work?" was Ev's dumb reply. He pushed his hands into his pockets and tried not to think about how naked he'd just been in front of this slightly intimidating guy.

"Yeah, modeling. My focus is really specific. I'm looking for a guy your age and your look really works for me. The pay would be good, but it would be more of a time commitment than what the school asks. I don't know if that's an issue, or..."

"So I'd model for you?"

"Yeah, my studio is just a few miles away. Not too far. Interested?"

Ev breathed out a laugh and squeezed his eyes shut as he felt his blush returning. "I mean, I could use the extra money. Would I be n-naked?"

"Mostly. Yeah." Adam's cheeks dimpled, framing a perfect smile. "My current work centers on figure studies of the male form, so nakedness is kind of the whole point."

"Right. Sorry." God, he felt stupid. "That's fine. Yeah, I guess I'm interested."

"Great. Okay, then I'll give you the heads-up about my subject matter." Adam glanced up and down the hall. A pair of painting students slipped out of the classroom, didn't pay them any attention and went right for the stairwell, leaving Adam and Ev alone again. Part of Ev wished he was leaving with them. Why had he agreed to model for this guy? Wasn't everything about that a really bad idea?

"So, my focus is on exposing the vulnerability in male sexuality," Adam said, his voice lowered. "My work is quite sexual in nature, so if that's a problem for you, I completely understand."

"Oh, uh... sexual like how, though? I mean, I'm not gay. Just... so you know. I'm not like, into guys."

Adam laughed a little, his dimples even deeper that time.

"I don't know why I said that. Sorry. Fuck," Ev groaned.

"No, it's okay," Adam assured him. "I'm not focused on any particular kind of male sexuality, just more in general. Men aren't usually allowed to be vulnerable in traditional gender roles of our society, so I try to look for that and show it in unexpected ways."

"Oh. Yeah, I guess that sounds fine. What, like, specifically do you mean, though?"

"Well, it's kind of hard to put into words. If you'd like to come by my studio, I can show you some works in progress and you can decide. No pressure. I'd never ask you to do anything you weren't totally comfortable with. It's not porn. Just art." He shifted to the other foot and frowned for a moment.

"Jeez, I just realized I haven't even gotten your name."

"Ev Myers."

"Ev," Adam repeated, like he was trying it out. "Is that short for something?"

"Yeah, Evelyn." The name had gotten him teased since he was a toddler. It had a lot of negative connotations for him, though it was also the name of his maternal grandfather, who had always been one of Ev's favorite relatives before he'd passed away.

"Wow. No shit? Oh my god. I love that. That's... that has to be one of the most beautiful names I've ever heard. Evelyn Myers. Jesus. You know, I really think this was meant to be? I think you just might be my muse. Your name alone... it just summarizes everything I'm passionate about. The traditional in the context of the modern, the changing definition of what it means to be a man in our society, the feminine in the masculine... Incredible. Sorry, I'm rambling."

Ev's eyebrows both raised. He felt so put on the spot, it was like he was shrinking. "That's the weirdest reaction to my name I've ever had, to be honest. Most people think it's a pussy name. Even if they don't say as much, I can usually tell."

Adam's brow furrowed. His bright blue eyes pinned Ev down, making him unable to move or even think. "Your name's something to be proud of, Evelyn. Don't you dare let anyone say otherwise. It's a family name, I guess?"

"Yeah."

"There you go. It has deeper meaning for you too, then. As a rule, one should never let the opinions of others define them. Remember that."

Ev didn't know what to say to that, so he didn't say anything. He didn't know why he was so struck by Adam's appearance. The colors of his features were intense, with the blue of his eyes, the dark, fiery red of his hair, the rosy color of his lips and smattering of freckles over his nose covering the warm tan hue of his skin. Like John, Adam wasn't too much of a man's man. There was something delicate about his bone structure, though his body intimidated enough to make up for it. He had nice lips. They looked soft and there was a defined crease down the middle of his bottom lip, which curled under in a slight pout.

Ev realized Adam seemed aware he was staring at his lips and quickly looked down instead.

"So, when do you want me to come by?"

"When are you available? I'm sure my schedule's more open than yours."

"I don't know. I'm around tomorrow night, around six."

"Oh, great. Yeah." Adam reached into his back pocket and pulled out a small pad of paper and pencil. Flipping the pad open, he scrawled down an address and phone number, then ripped off the page and handed it over. "This is my place. Do you think you just want this to be a look and see thing, or would you be up for sitting for me too?"

"I, um," Ev stammered, feeling more overwhelmed by the moment. There was an intensity to Adam that made Ev feel like a total idiot. "Could we play it by ear?"

"May I ask what's making you hesitate?"

Ev shrugged, licking his lips, feeling nervous. "I don't know. I guess it just might be weird to get naked in front of you when no one else is there."

"Why? Is it a security concern? If there's a way I could put you at ease, I'd—"

"No. I can take care of myself. It's uh… You're just kind of…"

"Is it because I'm gay? If it is, I can assure you I'd never presume to—"

"No. It's not," Ev blurted out. "I'm just…" he sighed. "I'm just shy, I guess."

"You didn't seem shy in there." He thumbed back to the classroom.

"They're not you. You're kind of intense."

"Yeah," Adam admitted. "I can be."

"And I guess I'm not really a sexual person, so if that's what you're looking for, I don't know if I'm your guy."

"Interesting," Adam commented, looking thoughtful. "Are you at least curious?"

Ev chewed on the inside of his cheek and nodded.

"I'd never judge you. Okay? You're giving me so many ideas right now, just looking at you. That's really rare. Protecting you is going to be really important to me if you agree to do this."

"Okay."

"See you tomorrow at six, then?"

"Yep." He took that as his cue to go and started walking, hoping Mr. Ahlm was still in the classroom so they could discuss plans for the next class.

"Thanks, Ev," Adam called. Ev smiled back at him. A rush of sensation rolled up from his feet, through his balls and up into his gut. It made him weak and helpless, but in strangely pleasant ways.

Chapter 3

Private Performance

Ev showered and did some man-scaping before he left to go to Adam's; not because he planned to get naked. He just wanted to be prepared for anything, or so he told himself. He really couldn't wrap his head around it—the thought of taking it all off in front of that guy with no one else around, especially if the poses were more sexual in nature, whatever that meant. Ev's imagination ran away with ideas as he soaped up. By the time he needed to rinse off, he was completely hard. What if that happened at Adam's? He'd be so mortified, he'd die.

"Fuck, I'm an idiot," he moaned, trying to think of something else. It didn't work, so he quickly jerked off, thinking of Adam watching him jerk off.

That didn't mean he was gay, either. He just liked attention.

Ever since he'd been born, Ev's identity had been wrapped up in completing his father's vision of the perfect family and being the ideal son of a conservative, Southern Baptist, Republican Senator. Whenever someone seemed to see Ev just for himself, outside of all of those other labels and expectations, he became enthralled.

Once he was dressed again, he began his walk. After mapping the route on his phone from the Lehigh University campus to an address located further into the city, he'd decided it was in walking distance. Hopefully he wouldn't get too sweaty on the way and make his shower completely pointless.

Once he arrived at the building, he had to triple check the address just to make sure. It was a high-rise building of luxury condos, not a hole-in-the-wall place like he imagined. But the address matched, so he went inside. A security desk blocked the way. Walking up to it, he said, "Yeah, Ev Myers to see Adam Buchanan in 16A."

"Evelyn Myers," the guard read off of a list. "Yes, I have you down. Go right ahead."

"Thanks."

An elevator took him up to the sixteenth floor, upon which there were only a few doors. He went to the first one on the left and rang the bell.

Adam opened the door a moment later. "Hey, welcome." He leaned against the door as he held it open and gestured Ev inside.

"Holy shit. This place is impressive," Ev told him. The space was massive, with an open floor plan and pristine views of the sparkling city in all directions through the floor to ceiling windows. A mix of contemporary and antique furniture on a dark-stained hardwood floor were arranged to create cozy nooks in a subdued color palette. His gaze climbed to the brilliant views. Ev found himself looking for paintings hung on the walls, but there weren't many walls to decorate. He spotted a mix of abstract, impressionist, and realistic paintings, which didn't tell him much about Adam's particular style, or whether they were done by the same artist or not. The apartment was mostly open space and windows. The centrally-located chef's kitchen was wide open and gleaming with granite countertops and stainless steel appliances. "This is not what I was expecting."

"Yeah, art is my life but it's family that makes it possible."

"Your parents?" Ev guessed.

"Mm-hmm. They left me everything when they passed."

"God, I'm sorry," Ev winced.

"No sweat, but thank you."

The air inside was cool after the long walk, which helped him feel more comfortable instead of worrying anymore about perspiring. After thinking it over, though, he realized being cold would not be ideal if he was actually going to go through with this. That was getting ahead of himself, though.

"Come on over and see what's what," Adam said, nodding to a separate room off to the right, which hadn't been in view until they'd walked deeper into the place. "Can I get you anything?"

"No thanks."

They walked through a doorway and into a more colorful section of the apartment. The floor was tiled, splattered with even more paint than the campus painting studio had been. A few pieces of furniture decorated the space—an armchair, a pair of side tables, and even a narrow bed on wheels, made up with white sheets. More floor-to-ceiling windows made up the left-side wall. The rest were bare, white, and equally speckled with wild sprays of paint. Directly ahead was a doorway and to the right an easel. After Ev's eye skimmed over all of this, it was drawn in powerfully by massive canvases painted with more realism than Ev had expected. There was so much detail and dimension interspersed with rougher, thick brushstrokes and portrayed with a rainbow's worth of color.

One showed a close-up profile of a bearded man, his eyes downcast and lips softened as if on a sigh. Each one of the curling hairs in the beard was defined, in all different colors woven together. Another showed two men embracing, the gentle touch of their fingers the focus of the piece. More paintings were tucked behind these, with only the edges peaking out. There was so much life to the subjects, they were almost hyper-real, leaping off the canvas. The effect hypnotized. It felt safer to continue watching the artwork than to turn away and possibly get surprised by a man made of paint crawling out of the frame and into the room. Following that train of thought, he realized something.

"I expected more nudity," Ev admitted.

Adam chuckled. "I cover the more risqué pieces when I'm not working on them, but I really haven't gotten much started yet. I've been looking for the right inspiration and model to capture what's in my head."

He crossed to the stack of canvases propped against the wall and eased one out from behind. It showed a seated man, legs fallen open. From behind him, a figure had an arm circled around, gently cradling the subject's penis in a hand. There was something in his expression that Ev couldn't look away from—fear or hope or a pained acceptance.

"These are amazing," he said honestly. "You're really good. I mean, I'm not an arts' buff, but I'm impressed."

"So does that mean you'll do it?" Hope lingered in the question. Led by instinct, Ev found his answer.

"I think so. Yeah. I will. But…" How to say it? "What are you going to expect here? I'm guessing it's not just posing."

"It can just be posing, if that's where your comfort level is."

Thinking of his family and church, when he wished he wasn't and was focused only on his own preferences instead, Ev fought not to get sidetracked by conditioning. What they thought about Ev posing for this man didn't matter, or so he tried to tell himself.

"I'm not a prude or anything," Ev clarified. "I was just… wondering. Like, would touching be involved?" The painting Adam had set out indicated one of his last models had been touched.

"Not without your permission."

He imagined it without wanting to—being touched like the subject of that painting had been, by another man. It made a shiver race up Ev's back. Folding his arms tighter, he squirmed.

"Would I need to be…" Ev exhaled, tripping on the next word, feeling mortified for even thinking it.

"Hard?" Adam guessed, maybe by reading into Ev's body language, his arms wrapped around himself, his fingers rubbing his lips.

"Yeah."

"You wouldn't need to be, no. But, total honesty, I would be able to work with it if you were."

Ev blew out a breath. "How old are you?"

"Twenty-five. You?"

"Almost twenty."

"Okay. No pressure, Ev. If this doesn't work for you, you can bail at any time. It's okay. You won't hurt my feelings."

"You're not gonna, like, put my name on these are you? Or tell people?"

"I'll totally honor your privacy in whatever ways you request. I swear it. My work hinges on honesty. What happens here only leaves this space through the artwork. I do take reference photos, but I keep those locked up when I'm not using them."

Ev hesitated, mostly because he really wanted to do it, and the realization scared him. It made him question his ability to make rational decisions. There were so many dangers here; he'd be crazy to stay.

Adam just waited, watching.

"I know what they pay at the school for the models," Adam said, interrupting Ev's indecision. "Twenty bucks an hour, right? Double that for your hourly rate when you sit for me, and that's just to start. If this works out, I'll increase the amount as we go."

"Adam, that's insane. I can't take that much money from you for this."

"I insist. I'm a professional, hiring you as a professional model. I'll be photographing you, as I said, in addition to simply using you as a reference for my paintings. The rate I'm paying is not astronomical."

"Really? Wow, maybe I should've just done this instead of go to school."

Adam just raised an eyebrow at him, looking profoundly patient and equally as determined. "Well, you are suited for it, in my humble opinion, but an education is invaluable. I say do both."

There was another pause, filled with tense anticipation.

Ev pulled off his jacket. Folding it over his arm, he said, "Okay."

The idea of getting forty bucks an hour was ridiculously amazing, but that wasn't what convinced him. It was the temptation —something he'd successfully resisted his whole life, and he was just plain exhausted by the effort. Maybe it was time to take a calculated risk.

"Okay," Adam agreed. "If you'd feel more comfortable changing into a robe first…"

Steeling himself, Ev took a deep breath, then pulled his shirt over his head. Bare-chested, feeling his nipples stiffen, he said, "Kind of cold."

"Right. Sorry," Adam apologized. He pulled out his phone, tapped at it a few times and said, "There. The heat'll take a moment to warm things up. I've got space heaters too." Walking away, he emerged only a second later, wheeling a small heater up to a bed. Adam shifted the bed slightly under the lights overhead, then turned on a few professional looking large soft box boom lights, shifting them closer and angled to cast light on the bed. The heater was shifted even closer. The set-up was similar to various television and photography studio sets he'd visited as the Senator's son—though without the bed and nudity—and the familiarity was comforting.

While Adam fussed with the arrangements, Ev unbuckled his jeans. It took a flare of courage before he was able to push them down, toeing off his sneakers and socks along with the pants. That left him only in snug, black, low-rise boxer briefs, the thin cotton straining to contain him even though he was completely flaccid. Needing warmth more than anything, Ev walked into the path of the space heater, rubbing his hands together, then rubbing his arms. Right away, he felt more comfortable and less tempted to run for cover.

Once Adam had things arranged to his liking, he finally turned around. His gaze swept down Ev's body, then upward to his face. Ev tried to read into the look, or the thoughts behind it, but couldn't.

"I'd like to do some sketches, maybe take some photos, just to see what's working. It'll probably take a while for me to narrow it down to one pose. Who knows, maybe I'll start a few pieces at once. Are you sure you don't want a glass of water or anything before we start?"

"Nah, I'm good. Um," he reached for his briefs, stopped himself, then went ahead and hooked his thumbs under the waistband. He felt Adam watching as Ev slid the underwear off. By the time he'd stepped out of them, briefs wadded up in his hand, he was breathing harder. His balls drew up, his skin both hot and cold in places. It felt wrong on many levels, in ways it hadn't in the classroom earlier that day.

But Adam wasn't reacting in a negative way, or telling him to cover back up; he just kept scrutinizing the view of Ev's body. "Would you rather lie down or sit to start?"

"Whatever you want."

"Okay, then come lie down here," he said, pointing to the bed. Ev shuffled over, fighting the urge to cover himself with his hands. "Are you okay with me using my hands to help position you? Be honest."

"Yeah, that's fine."

"Okay. If you change your mind, just tell me."

Ev sat on the edge of the bed, then lay back.

"Shift up the bed a little more."

He slid upward. Adam's hand touched Ev's knee. "Relax your legs. Let them fall open." Gentle pressure urged Ev's legs apart. Ev thought his breathing sounded too loud in the quiet of the room. The light touch of Adam's fingertips on the inside of Ev's left knee sent a thrill to Ev's cock. Inwardly, he groaned with dread, his tension reflecting in his expression.

"Bring your arms up so your hands are on either side of your head. Just relax them." Adam arranged Ev's hands, letting the fingers curl, the back of his hand resting by his face. "Good. Keep your head turned to the side." The curled fingers were by his eyes. His chest rose and fell, with each breath seeming to come quicker than the last.

Watching from the corner of his eye, he saw Adam draw a sheet over, letting the corner of it cover Ev's stomach, keeping his chest and genitals exposed.

"Nice," Adam murmured, his eyes everywhere, all over Ev. Ev got the sense that Adam had gone into his head, concentrating on his ideas and plans instead of judging Ev's body in any way, which helped Ev stay calm. Adam went back to the supply cabinets along the wall and brought out a large camera with a long lens. He moved close again, bringing the camera up to his eye and adjusting the focus. The soft whir of the machinery was a pleasurable little sound, acting like a tickle over Ev's cock.

He closed his eyes when his dick twitched.

"Fuck," Ev cursed softly, frowning slightly. The camera focused, then clicked. It was so damned quiet in there. The air was thick. The shutter closed again and again. Adam moved around the bed, catching Ev from many different angles. The heater blew the light fragrance of his cologne over. It was a masculine smell. Ev liked it. He liked the soft click of the shutter even more and, as he thought about how he was in this attractive man's apartment, naked on a bed, in a position he'd been ordered into, his cock continued to swell and become rigid.

At first he hoped Adam couldn't tell, but as it became more pronounced, his dick actually lifting from where it lay on his hip to jut up into the air, Ev broke the pose. He tugged the sheet down and cursed again, mortified.

He couldn't breathe, wouldn't inhale.

"Ev, it's okay," Adam told him softly. "I'm a guy, too. I know how this works."

Ev sat up, ran a hand over his hair to the back of his head, bowing it. He kept the sheet pulled over his lap.

"I'm not gay, all right?"

It came out more defensive than he intended.

"All right," Adam allowed, verbally surrendering the argument to Ev.

"I mean it. It's just… the attention."

"I get it. I do." Adam waited for him to say something. When he didn't, he added, "This works even better for the pose if you're okay with lying down again. No one else sees this. Okay?"

"You swear?"

"I swear. I'll keep your face cropped out or in shadow."

It was too quiet in there. There was only breathing, looking, the rush of the heater and the anticipated click of the shutter, though the camera hung at Adam's side, dangling by the strap.

Somehow, Ev was able to lay down again. He tried to put his hands back the way they'd been, though he may have edged his hand closer to his face in order to hide behind it.

Adam tugged at the sheet, drawing it mostly off of Ev, with just the corner lying softly against his hip. A gentle touch at his knee guided his legs apart, and Ev got even harder. Adam knelt with one knee on the bed, pointing the camera's eye down at him. Breathing more heavily than he should have needed to, Ev felt himself become completely erect. He wasn't a small guy, but when he was at full mast, he was big.

The camera's shutter clicked.

"Fuck," Ev said with barely any sound.

It went on and on.

Low and close, Adam said, "The light's not catching you as well as I'd like. Is it okay if I spray you down with some water?"

"Yeah," Ev said, avoiding eye contact.

Adam walked away, came back with a spray bottle. Ev tried not to move as the sheet was pulled off completely. The first spray made him flinch, the drops moistening the swollen muscles of his chest. Once Adam started, he didn't stop until he'd sprayed Ev from face to knee. When Adam sprayed Ev's cock, Ev's breath caught a little, then sped up as the water dripped slowly down his shaft.

Adam pulled the sheet back into place, his fingers brushing Ev's hip as he did, causing him to suck in his stomach at the tickling, unexpected touch.

The camera lifted, snapping away. Soon, Adam walked away again. He left the camera behind and grabbed a sketch pad instead. Standing over Ev, Adam frowned as he vigorously slashed at the pad of paper with a pencil, dashing off lines and curves.

Ev's interest did not wilt, and the longer it went on, the more he ached. He drew his hand even closer, his breath coming regularly against the back of it.

"If you need a break, tell me," Adam said, distracted and drawing as quickly as he had been, as if racing against the clock.

"Are you kidding?"

"No."

"You're drawing, though."

"Do you need a break?" Adam insisted.

"Yes."

His dick was so sore, he was afraid to move, but he had to move.

"Okay. Break time."

Adam didn't stop drawing. He kept at it, as vigorously as he'd been.

Ev moaned as he drew his legs up, then rolled onto his side. He didn't need to look and see if Adam was still watching. Ev could feel it like a touch.

He sat up, cupping his balls despite his self-consciousness. The drawing stopped. It was too quiet again.

"Do you have a bathroom I could use?"

The subsequent pause filled with things Ev didn't want to see or know.

"Of course. Right over there, through that door."

He stood and walked awkwardly to the indicated doorway, trying not to feel the touch of Adam's attention on his ass as he went.

Chapter 4

The Hard Part

It took forever to get there and once he did, he closed the door harder than he intended. Leaning back against it, standing in a spotless, shining, full bathroom decorated in white and grays, Ev grabbed hold of his throbbing dick and began tugging. He let out a too-loud moan and came in seconds, shooting over his fingers and onto the floor at his feet. Tingling from head to toe, shuddering with aftershocks, he slowly came down. For a long moment he stood there, shocked at himself, then sprang into action, grabbing toilet paper to wipe the floor clean, then furiously washing his hands and forearms in the trough sink. He splashed his face as well, staring into his own eyes in the mirror.

He looked shell-shocked, flushed and guilty. How in the world was he going to leave that bathroom? Adam would know what he'd done, how fucked-up he was. But there was no way out other than past Adam. He was trapped.

Glancing down at his wilted cock, Ev felt anchored to the spot. He couldn't go, wouldn't move.

Minutes passed.

There was a soft knock on the door. "Hey. Evelyn? You okay?"

He opened his mouth to call back with yes, he was fine, thanks, but the only thing that came out was a low whimper. Shutting his mouth again, Ev squeezed his eyes closed as well.

He remembered a snippet of conversation, overheard at a party back home at the end of senior year. A girl named Olivia, whose family had left the church, gossiped in the hallway of an overcrowded house. Partygoers holding plastic cups spilled out into the yard and filled every room to almost bursting. It was loud as hell but all Ev could hear was, 'You know what they do in that place, right? It's called conversion therapy. The parents pay these sickos tons of money to take their kid and lock them up for as long as they say they need to. Weeks, months, years—it doesn't matter. Every day, they make the kids do lots of manual labor and the only people they're allowed to talk to are the ones feeding them this garbage about how there's no such thing as homosexuality, how those behaviors are only a signal that something's wrong with the person doing them. My neighbor told me the men who run the program lock themselves in a room together with the kid and they strap the kid to a chair. They attach these things to their dicks and show them pictures of homosexual behavior, then fucking zap them with electricity down there so they associate what they're seeing with pain.'

In the memory, Ev held his breath, listening to each and every word, wanting to ask questions but afraid to voice them. He'd never been more scared in his life, piecing those things together with what he'd seen happen to James.

In reality, Ev wasn't breathing much either, and he felt just as scared.

"Please open the door," Adam asked. The intention behind the questions further unraveled him. Adam wasn't asking with a teacher or employer's authority, or with a friend's commiseration. There seemed to be other things hidden in there, of which Ev was both fascinated and terrified.

Maybe it was the artist's sensitivity. Or maybe it was something else entirely.

Ev tried to get out of his head, because being stuck in that room was bad enough without dredging up old terrors.

"Please?"

From the sound of it, he was right on the other side of the door, maybe leaning against it.

Why couldn't Ev move? What was he so scared of?

I'm fucked up like James. I'm damaged. Wrong. Maybe they should have taken me away too. Maybe I should have confessed so they could have fixed me. Maybe the pain would have been worth it.

But then he thought of that photo of James, publicly posted to social media, with one hundred and fifteen likes, and how big of a lie it was in so many ways.

They hadn't fixed James. They'd broken him.

He rubbed a hand over his face, ignoring the way his arm was shaking.

The handle turned. He hadn't locked the door. Wincing, turning his face away as Adam eased into the small room, Ev willed himself to stop trembling. He leaned forward, gripping the edge of the sink. He imagined the buzzing sound of a jolt of electricity, a boy's shriek of agony. The air shifted warmer as Adam got closer. Something soft was brought around his back, laid over his shoulders.

"Here. Are you okay?"

Yeah, fine, he would have said, laughing at himself. But all he did was let out a hitching breath as another man, bigger and wiser than him, gently tugged the robe around Ev's shoulders.

There had been so many people Ev couldn't trust. How could he dare begin to with this one? Whether it was desperation or confusion causing Ev to falter behind his façade, wasn't it time to stop hiding?

Ev could run, find another door to close himself behind, live in the past instead of moving on, like he'd promised himself he'd try to do.

It was just so easy to say nothing, to be quiet and still and not let on about anything. It was his default state of being.

In memory, he saw his uncle's hand squeezing James's arm, dragging him forcibly away while James's eyes reflected only terror. In his imagination, he heard screaming.

"Come on. Come sit down."

It was too much. He let Adam lead him, with a hand to Ev's back, out of the bathroom, through the art studio and into the living area. Beyond the dark apartment, lights outside began to twinkle. Adam brought Ev to a soft armchair which he sank into, pulling the robe closed around his hips.

Adam walked away, came back with a tall glass of water and passed it over. Ev wanted to apologize, to laugh, to explain, or even to not need the drink. Eyes lowered, he sipped the cold water, letting the chair's softness draw him in deeper. He tracked Adam when he went into the open kitchen area, flicking on a light. Taking things out of the cupboards and fridge, laying them out on the counter, Adam seemed to be preparing food.

At first, Ev watched from afar. Then, without knowing why, he got up and walked over. He sat on a stool, facing the range and Adam.

"You gave me such a gift today," Adam told him with a brief touch of eye contact. "I'll be painting all night, I can tell. Can't wait to get started."

His eyes were so blue in the dimness of the mostly dark apartment, only a single overhead light and some under-cabinet lights fought to ward off the night.

"I'm a good listener if you want to talk about it."

"I don't know what's wrong with me," Ev said, his voice thick and clumsy from lack of use.

"There's nothing wrong with you," Adam countered. "You're exactly who you were intended to be, even if you don't know who that is yet."

"You can't know that."

"I can, actually," Adam said with a cocky grin that made Ev grin slightly too. With his hands wrapping his now half-empty glass of water, his feet hooked behind the rungs of the stool, he felt so very confused. "Tell me about yourself, Evelyn Myers," Adam said with a teasing, lighthearted air.

"Not much to tell, really." Ev shrugged. Adam set two thick slices of breaded eggplant in a hot skillet. The sizzling scent made Ev's mouth water. "I was raised in Middleton, Kansas. My dad's a state Senator. He's been moving up the political ladder since I was a kid, so that's probably why I'm kind of quiet. It was mostly a shut up, behave, and remember your manners type of atmosphere. He's really into sports, too, so that was kind of my life until I started college. Varsity football and baseball."

"That sounds like a list of what your dad's about, not you."

Ev breathed out a laugh. "Yeah. Story of my life, right? That's why I didn't take the scholarship I got to play football with Kansas State. It was a great opportunity but..." he made a face and shook his head. "Nah. It was my one chance to finally listen to myself instead of him." Ev sat up straighter, ran his thumb over the smooth glass. "He was pissed. Still is. I'm a business major, but mainly because it seemed like the best thing to do. I'm not crazy about it or anything. College is when you're supposed to figure yourself out. That's what I'm doing."

"By nude modeling with a guy you just met?"

Ev repressed a smile. "I guess. I work in the admissions office three days a week, trying to cover my expenses. Doesn't pay much, which is why I thought I'd do the modeling too."

"Kind of a wild choice for a vanilla Kansas boy. You said something about liking the attention?" Adam said with the briefest glance, laden with so much subtext, it felt like a physical nudge.

"Yeah." He'd said that to explain away his boner. God, it was embarrassing. His face heated again.

"Maybe being stuck in your dad's shadow for so long makes you want some of the spotlight for yourself?"

"Could be."

"You don't have to try to spare my feelings," Adam said with clear sincerity, pushing the patties around with a spatula. "If modeling isn't your thing either, tell me. Sounds like you've had enough pressure to do what other people want you to do. You should listen to yourself for once. Your own instincts."

"Mm," he grunted, noncommittally. "No, I still like the attention."

"You sure?" Adam raised an eyebrow.

From you, yeah.

"Look, I'm sorry about what happened over there. I—"

"Don't. Don't apologize for that. Seriously." Adam flipped the patties, then set the spatula down and looked straight at Ev. "The whole reason I'm doing these pieces is because of how difficult it is to be vulnerable as a man, especially when it comes to sexuality. There's a whole lot of trust involved and it fucks with your head, for everyone. I'd never expect a guy barely out of his teens to be thrown into this situation and not be overwhelmed or uncomfortable. That's why it's important we be honest with each other. Okay?" Ev nodded. "If you figure out, like, hey, this is too much for me, or you realize a boundary line has been reached or crossed, tell me. Please."

"I like that this is so important to you," Ev confessed. "Makes me want to do it more."

"It is important. It affects everyone, because the struggle to be ourselves as men defines so much in our culture, subtly if not outright. It influences politicians on every scale. Police, doctors, lawyers, construction workers, women, children, dogs. You name it. But why are so many men afraid to be their true selves? What are we trying to prove?" With barely any pause, he added, "Can I ask you a question? You don't have to answer if you don't want to. What did you mean when you said you weren't a sexual person?"

"Oh fuck," Ev groaned, trying to laugh it off. "Feel free to not listen to every single thing I say."

"No, I'm curious," Adam persisted.

"Jesus. Well, um…"

"Are you a virgin?"

"No," Ev said somewhat defensively. "I, you know, had a girlfriend. She was my best friend through grade school. Mia. We dated awhile."

"Okay." Adam held his chin in a hand, the other crossed over his chest. It looked like he was studying Ev, which made him self-conscious again. "A girlfriend. Just the one?"

"Not everyone needs to go beat off to Playboys constantly."

"Have you at all?"

"Have I beaten off to Playboys?"

"Yeah."

"No."

"Huh."

"No," Ev argued. "It's not interesting. It's not. It's normal. Don't look at me like that."

"All right. Sorry. Have you gotten hard looking at Playboys?"

"No. It's fake and gross."

"Wow. Strong words."

"Can we stop talking about my boners, please?"

"Well, I'm kind of doing a painting about one," Adam said, like a smart-ass, thumbing back over his shoulder. "So it seems like a valid conversation topic to me." He flipped the patties again, then turned the burner off and slid the skillet off of it. Then he planted his hands on his hips and widened his stance. He looked ready to defend himself or his ideas, in whatever way necessary.

"God, you really drive me crazy," Ev complained, rubbing a hand over his face.

Adam laughed. "I drive you crazy. Why?"

"Because you're aggravating."

"Okay," Adam said with a nod and quirk of his lips. "It's better than fake and gross."

Ev froze. He stared at a spot on the counter, blinking too much, his jaw clenched, his hands curling into fists.

His voice low, Adam said, "I'm just going to say it, okay? Because that's how I work. I don't let these things go unacknowledged, not when it matters. But I don't want to freak you out or push you away. I just want honesty here." He paused, then called Ev's name. "Evelyn."

"It's Ev."

"Do I aggravate you because I made your dick hard? Evelyn is a beautiful name. It's classy. Don't be embarrassed by it."

"Fuck! Can you not do that, please?"

"Do what?"

"You do this thing where you ask multiple questions or merge comments on separate topics in one thought. It feels like you're trying to trick me into talking about shit. Like you knew I wasn't going to acknowledge that shit and so you added the thing about my name just to jab me."

"So it's true then?"

"Stop," Ev said, his deep voice booming.

"Stop what? Stop making you think about who you are and what you want? What you like? Why? Does it scare you that much?"

Ev got up off the stool, hurrying to his clothes and escape. He was halfway there when his arm was grabbed, just like in his memory of James, only he was pulled to a halt, then turned around. Adam stood too close, his breath, his heat, his blue eyes and soft lips right in Ev's space. Staring at Adam's lips, Ev shook off his hold.

Adam touched the side of Ev's jaw, the fingers curling around it. Ev tried to twist his face away, grabbed hold of the front of Adam's shirt meaning to do... what? Push him away? Punch him in the face? Pull him closer? He forgot once he had a handful of the silky softness of the fabric, his knuckles brushing the firm chest hidden beneath. Adam was strong, maybe stronger than Ev. It was a dumb move to pick a fight with a guy who could probably kick your ass.

The moment breathed, lengthening until it was out of control.

Finally, Ev tossed his head, throwing off Adam's hand, which reached for Ev's left hip instead. It wrapped bare skin, the robe still untied and hanging open. Adam's hand traced the hipbone, his thumb sliding just inside the ridge. Ev's breath caught. Watching Adam's mouth like it was the most dangerous thing in the room, Ev frowned, fell silent.

"There's the line. You feel it? It's right there." His thumb caressed in a longer stroke, stirring Ev's cock, fast.

Adam's lips shifted closer and Ev couldn't move. He grunted as Adam kissed him, his fist tightening in the shirt, pushing at Adam's chest as his mouth chased the kiss, his head angling to the side as Adam's tongue teased Ev's lip, just a little.

The kiss ended, their foreheads touching. Ev panted.

"Now it's gone," Adam said. "It's that easy. What are you so scared of?"

"Everything. Why are you doing this?"

"Because it's important. I'm taking this off." He grabbed the robe instead of Ev's hip. With a firm yank, he pulled it free. Then he grabbed Ev's hip again, moving him backward with determination. "Lie down."

The edge of the bed touched the back of Ev's legs. Not understanding why, he obeyed. The steady, unwavering confidence in Adam told him he should.

No sooner had Ev's back touched the bed than Adam guided Ev's legs up, bending them then pushing them apart, spreading him wide with his hand grasping Ev's inner thighs. He kept manhandling him, putting his arms back up near his face, grabbing Ev's chin to turn his face more forward.

"Look at me, Evelyn, and don't move," Adam commanded.

He moved back, grabbing the camera, taking pictures without hesitation.

"Fuck you."

"Do you want to?"

Tears pricked his eyes but he wouldn't let them gather or fall.

The camera snapped.

"What are you, angry? Hurt? Scared? Horny? Look at me!"

There was a burst of clicks as Adam moved in and out, then dropped the camera to maintain eye contact.

"This is you not leaving. This is you doing exactly what I say. Why?"

Softer, "Fuck you."

He glanced down at his erection, thick and red, the drip of clear fluid slipping down from his slit, his swollen, heavy balls.

"Look at me."

His gaze snapped up, fixed on Adam. Something burned, down in the pit of Ev's stomach. The camera flashed.

"Fucking amazing." He tossed the camera onto the bed. "Are you leaving? No? Good."

He grabbed the sketch pad, turned the page, held his pencil between his teeth and began using charcoal instead, his arm moving wildly as he sketched. His gaze darted constantly between Ev and the page.

"The food's getting cold," Ev told him.

Adam lowered the pad, his chin tilting up so that he looked down his nose at his subject. "Hungry?"

"Yeah." As if to punctuate the admission, Ev's stomach growled. He broke the pose, palming his abdomen, and felt instantly guilty about it.

"Is this you staying for dinner?"

"You're so weird."

"That's not an answer."

Ev sat up. Adam waited. Ev reached for the sheet and pulled it over his lap.

"Too late, seen it already," Adam called back as he turned to go back to the kitchen, pad in hand. "Several times."

Under his breath, Ev asked himself, "What the hell am I doing?"

Ten minutes later, he was sitting on the stool again, wearing the robe though not bothering to tie it shut. A plate with a massive eggplant parmesan sandwich sat in front of him. Over in the art studio, Adam blocked in some color on a large, previously empty canvas. On a table by his side was a matching sandwich. One-handed meals seemed to be Adam's specialty, or so he'd claimed, saying it made multitasking easier.

It was a quiet meal. Adam was too focused on his work to chat, even though being so far apart from each other would have made it challenging anyway.

Gradually, Ev's hard-on softened again, though his balls ached.

It had been a long, odd day.

Once he'd finished the food, he quietly padded over to where his clothes waited and began pulling them on.

Adam glanced briefly over at him, but didn't comment for once.

"It's late," Ev explained, buckling his belt.

"You could stay."

"I need some sleep, I think. Got an early shift at work tomorrow."

Adam pointed to where Ev had been laying. "There's a bed."

"Mm. Maybe next time."

Licking his lips to cover a smile, his eyes reflecting his amusement anyway, Adam set down his paintbrush, wet with dark blue paint, and wiped his hands on a rag. Ev quickly pulled his shirt on, because Adam was coming for him again.

Standing his ground, lowering his gaze but keeping his chin raised, Ev didn't back down. Adam widened his stance so they'd be on more of an eye to eye level and hooked a finger under Ev's chin.

"That sounded sincere."

Ev stayed silent.

"Did you drive over?"

"Walked."

"It's too late to walk back. You're likely to get mugged."

"I'll take a bus."

"I can drive you."

"I'm not a child."

"I've noticed."

He leaned in, lips parted. They brushed against Ev's mouth and he kissed them. Adam made a soft sound and kissed him back, pushing in to make it more firm and passionate. When he sucked on Ev's lower lip, Ev felt it as a light tickle over his balls.

"You kissed me back. Doesn't mean you're gay, you know. The line's gone, remember? You're free."

"That doesn't make any sense."

"Mmm." Adam caressed the side of Ev's face, beside his eye, down his cheekbone, then came in for a slow, light kiss that seemed to take hours. "Kissing a guy doesn't mean you're gay. It means you kissed a guy."

"I'm too tired to think about that right now."

Adam laughed. "See, you're being more honest. I like it." He brushed his thumb over Ev's lips. "Getting hard for me doesn't make you gay, either, for the record. It just means you're enjoying yourself, and I want you to enjoy yourself, Evelyn. Give me your phone number."

Ev sighed. Adam reached into his back pocket and pulled out his phone. After reciting the numbers, watching Adam type them into his contact list, Ev walked to the door.

"Come back tomorrow."

Ev paused at the door. His hand rested on the knob. "You could ask instead of tell."

"But I like to tell you to do things," Adam said. He was right at Ev's back. When his teeth scraped over the junction of Ev's neck and shoulder, a hard shiver raced down Ev's spine. A whisper at Ev's ear, "It does it for me."

Ev's cock twitched in traitorous delight.

The moment drew out again, too long. He wasn't leaving, wasn't pulling away, but just closed his eyes and felt the heat of Adam's breath on his ear.

"Go get some rest."

"I have classes all day tomorrow, as soon as I'm done at work."

"And Wednesday?"

The back of a finger trailed down the back of his neck.

"Okay."

"What time can you be here?"

"I'm free. Whenever."

"Nine a.m."

"Sadist."

Adam laughed, too close, the sound too alluring. Ev turned the knob and stepped forward. He only looked back when he was about to walk out of sight, and there waited Adam, watching him go.

Chapter 5

Across the Line

"Where the hell have you been?"

"Out?"

Ev tossed his keys onto the desk and headed for his stack of books. There was still time to do some reading before bed, as long as he could keep his eyes open.

Leo sat cross-legged on his own bed, a notebook in his lap. "Out where?"

"Nowhere. Helping a teacher." It wasn't a total lie. Adam taught sometimes.

"Oh yeah? Which one?"

"You don't know 'em."

He collapsed into his bed, cracking open his Financial Accounting textbook. The words swam in front of his eyes, not making sense. He closed the book and laid it on his chest. His head fell back and his eyes shut too. He considered doing as Adam had instructed and sleeping it off. Setting the book beside the bed, Ev climbed under the covers and turned off his lamp. Leo didn't ask any more questions, probably taking a cue from Ev's standoffishness.

The tiredness won out. For hours, his dreams were filled with light kisses from unseen lips and firm touches from rough hands. He kept waking, sweating and startled, only to tumble back down all over again.

Tuesday was so drawn-out, normal and boring; he was almost unprepared for what he knew waited for him on Wednesday. There had been no texts from Adam, no maddening phone calls. It had left Ev trapped in his head with his memories and self-doubt.

He showered again before heading over, then took a bus to Adam's building so he wouldn't work up too much of a sweat.

He arrived right on time. When Adam answered the door without a shirt and barefoot, Ev didn't know what to say, where to look. Uncomfortable, Ev stuck his tongue in his cheek and looked away.

"Come in," Adam said with a welcoming smile, dimples and everything. "There's breakfast on the table."

As Ev walked through the door, Adam clasped the side of Ev's face and gave him a quick peck on the lips. It made Ev feel flustered. Were they going to keep kissing? What did it mean? Where was this leading?

He took off his jacket and let Adam take it from him.

"Why did you kiss me?" he asked, voicing at least one of his questions in order to feel less overwhelmed.

"Because you let me," Adam said. "And you seem like a guy who needs to be kissed. When was the last time someone else kissed you?"

Ev shrugged. "My girlfriend, probably."

"When was that?"

Ev rolled his eyes at himself, embarrassed. "Two years ago."

"Damn." A crease formed between Adam's eyebrows, his hair tumbled forward over his forehead, giving him a just-rolled-out-of-bed look. "No dates since then?"

"I'm picky," Ev explained. "And I've been busy with school."

"No one's asked you out either? You're not a bad looking guy, you know."

"Girls have asked me out, sure."

"No guys?" Ev didn't know if it was a tease or not. "And you said no?"

"I say no if I can tell it's not going to work."

Adam walked around behind him as Ev paused at the table, laden with muffins and fruit, coffee and juice in a fancy pitcher. "Have something to eat." He tugged hard at one of Ev's belt loops. "Then take these off and get on the bed."

It was almost too much to believe. When he glanced over his shoulder at Adam, all he saw was that steady determination again.

"To model?"

"Why, you have other ideas?" Adam replied, dimpled like crazy. "I'm not rubbing off on you, am I?"

"That sounded really wrong."

"Wow, your mind is just right in the gutter today. I like it." He gave Ev's ass a smack and walked away, toward his painting studio.

Ev grabbed a plate, a muffin and a banana, then pulled out a chair and tried to keep an eye on Adam as he ate. He couldn't figure out if it was wrong to do what he was doing with Adam. Technically, Adam was a teacher, though not Ev's teacher. Their ages weren't that far apart. The fact that he was a guy was the worst part, but each time something had happened between them, it had felt like Adam had tricked him into liking it.

Was he really turning gay? Was this the polar opposite of the Pathway to Manhood camp, and he was being recruited for the queers instead? It didn't seem to just be an attention thing anymore. Or was it? Adam certainly was giving Ev a whole lot of attention.

That had to explain it. Ev had never met someone like Adam before, who owned their sexuality so openly and wasn't afraid of anything. Ev had also never been seduced the way Adam seemed to be trying to seduce him. It was flattering whether the sentiments were mutual or not.

He tried to imagine getting naked in front of a female painter, being her muse in a private setting the way he was for Adam… and it felt off. He wasn't sure he'd be comfortable doing it.

But what did that imply?

Before he knew it, he'd finished eating. Almost as if he was eager to do it, he walked over to Adam and unfastened his pants. There really was something wrong with him.

He marveled at the painting in progress. He could make out the general form of his body on the bed, in peaches, blues, and creams, along with the reddish hue of his rigid cock. By the easel and on a table, a tablet was propped up and its screen showed a photo of him from Monday. The almost-out-of-frame, anxious expression on his face, the swollen, reddened state of his genitals—it made him look away, fast.

That was the image Adam was painting. Ev's stomach flipped. How could he let people see that? See him like that?

Adam glanced his way, giving his body an up and down look. As Ev continued getting undressed, Adam said, "I'm going to play with the light a little more today, so hurry it up a little. I want to do this before the sun rises too high. It'll ruin everything."

Ev stripped his boxers off and pulled off his socks. Then, he was naked again.

Adam set down his camera and came over, reaching out to manhandle Ev right away. Sucking in his stomach and tensing in anticipation of touching, Ev braced himself.

"I want you to lie on your right side, facing this way, right in this sunbeam." He guided Ev down, then pulled him by leg and shoulder into position. Grabbing Ev's left leg, Adam bent it and said, "Here, hook your hand under your thigh to hold this up and open. I'll take photos so you don't have to stay like this too long."

Ev held his leg, lifting it.

"Good. Raise your chin into the light, turn away a little more. I'm going to block out most of your face in this one, too. The anonymity is important."

He pressed gently on Ev's chest to change his angle, then the fingers brushed downward and Ev tensed up again, his feet flexing a little.

Then, it happened. Adam gently shifted Ev's dick, moving it up to lay at a specific angle on his leg. With a soft grunt, Ev startled a little, then held his breath.

"Okay, good," Adam said, frowning in concentration. "I think that'll work. Try to stay just like that."

Ev finally exhaled, breathing hard, his gut a riot of reactions and emotions.

He should have said something, should have protested.

Adam took pictures. Ev kept feeling the ghost of Adam's fingers pulling at his dick.

"Okay, reach down and touch yourself."

"Why?" he rasped.

"Please? I need to see how it looks."

Ev complied, reaching down between his legs with his other arm and folding his slightly swollen cock into his hand. He turned his face away even more, wanting to hide from Adam and his camera.

Adam moved around the bed, snapping photo after photo.

Ev's embarrassment only grew. He let go of himself and moved to cover his genitals instead. The camera kept snapping away.

"Great." Adam looked down at his camera. "Relax. I'm going to check these on the bigger screen, then we'll probably go back to yesterday's pose for a while."

Ev curled up into a ball, hiding his face behind a hand.

It took several minutes before Adam returned. He pushed at the bed, changing the angle in relation to the sun and turned on a few directional lamps, shining them from careful angles onto Ev. When he finally got around to helping Ev find the pose again, Ev was calmer, his dick soft.

Gentle nudges from Adam's hands moved Ev over to his back, then guided his legs apart. He spent a few long moments arranging Ev's fingers where they curled near his face. After brushing the backs of his fingers against Ev's arm, Adam straightened and walked away, to his easel.

It felt like hours passed, though it may have only been one.

Ev's thoughts went to weird places, circling around on his decisions, his circumstances, and muddled desires. He thought of the wary expression his mom would have as he ran out to play in the yard with James. In his mind's eye, she wore a sundress, her blonde hair blown-out in waves that framed her face and her eyes, as dark as Ev's. He thought of the way Mia had cried out with pain the first time he'd tried to fit his whole dick into her. He remembered coming home from hours upon hours at practice, stripping down and laying motionless and sore on his childhood bed, listening to the soft noises of his house the same way he was currently listening to Adam paint.

When Adam sat down on the bed at Ev's side, he wasn't expecting it. He jolted a little, like waking from a nap.

In Adam's hand was a bottle.

"Would it be okay if I worked some oil onto your skin in places? It would help me get some shine references. I could also tell you where to put it if you'd rather do it instead of me."

"Y-yeah. That's fine."

"Yeah?" Adam asked, flipping open the cap, his eyebrows raised.

"Mm-hmm."

"Thank you."

He poured some oil into his palm, then worked his hands together. Reaching out for Ev, Adam smoothed the slick over the curve of his shoulder, down his arm and around to his forearm. Then he caressed over Ev's chest, lightly massaging the oil into his defined, firm, pectoral muscles and down the center of his abdomen. When Adam's hand didn't halt its progress and rotated around to grab tight hold of Ev's cock, Ev gasped and shuddered. He closed his eyes.

"Okay?"

"Mmm." Ev frowned, then felt himself spreading a little more, his hips pushing into the grip when Adam slid his hand downward to Ev's root.

Ev's left arm reached across to grab hold of Adam's arm. Adam paused, then. When Ev said nothing, Adam tugged up the shaft, his palm sliding with the oil. Panting a little, Ev let go of Adam's arm and grabbed hold of Adam's knee instead.

Adam slid his hand back down the shaft again, twisting around on the tug. Ev was completely hard and his hips thrust slightly again on the down-stroke. Fingers brushed the hair back from Ev's eyes, back from his forehead, too.

It kept happening. Soon Ev was dripping wet, and not just with oil.

Adam let go, brushed over the head of Ev's cock with his thumb, then down under the ridge. He rubbed down over Ev's balls, taking them in hand, rolling them there before letting go.

When he started to shift away, Ev gripped hard at Adam's leg.

"Don't," he pleaded.

"I need some pictures. I'll be quick."

He had never been so stiff, needed to come so badly, or been more ashamed of himself. All of it was pure anxiousness. He returned to the pose and let Adam take his shots, trembling every so often as he did.

The camera was set aside.

Adam climbed onto the bed below Ev, nudging his legs widely apart and kneeling between them. Leaning over him with one arm braced on the bed, Adam gripped Ev's straining erection in a hand and watched his face.

"Okay?"

Ev nodded. The tugging started fast and kept going even faster. Ev let out a hard moan, fucking Adam's fist. Cringing at the reaction, hating himself a little, he was trapped between loving every part of it and wishing he'd never met Adam at all.

Adam wrung out Ev's dick with tight, twisting strokes that never eased up or slowed down. Come shot from his slit in a wide arc. Adam shook the drops over Ev's stomach and worked him through it with an intense steadfastness that Ev was powerless to pull away from. He convulsed with orgasm, shuddered through the aftershocks, breathing heavily.

Gently, Adam laid Ev's cock down on his hip.

Ev grabbed for Adam's arm as he started to leave.

"Don't take pictures of this," he begged, his voice wavering. "Please."

"Evelyn..."

"Please?"

The infinite hardness within Adam—the hunger for honesty and answers—melted a little, just enough. He relented and settled back down onto the bed, then kept coming. He lay down on top of Ev. It was so strange, to be that close to another man. But there was comfort there that he needed. So, Ev held on to him, touching Adam's waist, grasping his arm. With one hand and light strokes, Adam caressed up and down Ev's side, from underarm to the bottom curve of his ass. The weight of him was heavy, and he seemed to realize it a moment later, shifting up onto an elbow to take some pressure off.

"I don't know what to do," Ev whispered.

"Just lie here a while. That's enough."

"Okay."

Chapter 6

Yield

The feel of him was different than Mia. Adam was larger, firmer, and packed with muscle. There was a measure of intimidation between them, just due to the size difference. Also, Adam had chest hair—a mat of reddish gold curls that covered his pecs and trailed down the center of his abs. It tickled against Ev's body, much more hairless in comparison.

Whenever Adam's light caress ventured low, over the side of Ev's ass, following the curve to the underside, Ev tensed. His whole body clenched, but especially his butt. His stomach sucked in, his chest rose as he held a breath. Then, as Adam's hand trailed upward, he'd relax again.

"I shouldn't be doing this with you."

"Why?" Adam sought his gaze, pinning Ev down that way as well.

"Just because."

"That's not a reason. Because why?"

"Because you're a guy," Ev said with some exasperation, wishing he wasn't having this discussion while there was a half-naked man on top of his fully unclothed, come-streaked body.

"Who said you can't do this with guys?"

Ev sighed with frustration. "You're a teacher," he tried, coming at it from a different way.

"No, I'm not. I'm not your teacher. Never would be, Mr. Business Major."

"Fuck. Fine, well, you're also paying me to do this."

"I'm not paying you to let me jerk you off," Adam smirked.

"I should go," Ev decided.

Adam planted his other hand beside Ev's body and declared, "I'd like to see you try."

"You can't be serious."

"I can't?"

"Jesus. You're impossible!" He tried pushing at Adam's chest and side, trying to leverage him off. In response, Adam thrust in a slow, firm drag with his hips directly against Ev's bare, oversensitive cock, applying pressure there. It trapped Ev's hips against the bed, forced him to let go and simply struggle to breathe. "Okay!"

"You're giving up already?" Adam said with clear disappointment.

It made Ev angry enough that he found a deeper reserve of energy. He bucked, trying to flip Adam off or slip out from under him. It began to work. Adam took hold of Ev's hands, brought them up over his head and, crossing the wrists, pinned them down. His right knee pushed between Ev's thighs, drawing up to push against his balls. Discomfort flared there. If that wasn't enough, with the hand not holding Ev's wrists, Adam wrapped a hand around Ev's throat, gently squeezing.

"Better," Adam said with a chuckle. He leaned down, licked with the tip of his tongue over Ev's parted, gasping lips and whispered by his ear, "Did Mia ever pin you down while she was fucking you? Because I will."

Ev grunted, struggled. The knee drew up tighter against his balls and his mouth worked with the pain.

"That's the problem when you've got nuts as big as yours. Much easier target." The knee rubbed against him there. The hand on his throat squeezed tighter. "Fight me. Come on."

Ev's muscles had been relaxed, but he rallied them for another try, straining upward, trying to escape that knee or squirm out of Adam's hold, to get his arms free.

It was useless. He couldn't breathe, couldn't think past the ache in his testicles.

Sinking back to the bed, lax, he went boneless.

"Do you yield?"

He nodded.

"Of course you do." He rubbed over Ev's throat, grinding his knee against Ev's sac. "Bottom." He leaned down, biting Ev's lip, tugging it before letting go, his eyes flashing dangerously. "Top." Ev suppressed a moan.

Adam's hand slipped between them, taking hold of Ev's dick. "You like when I'm on top?"

He did, Ev realized, though he wouldn't admit it. Their eyes locked. Ev tried to pull his response back down inside, where Adam couldn't see it.

Adam let go of Ev's cock, rubbing up to his chest. His hand cupped the large swell of muscle of his left pectoral muscle, then squeezed. "What do you do to relieve stress?"

"Lift weights."

"Mmm. Thought so. I've seen women with smaller tits."

Before Ev could reply, Adam slipped lower. Astonishingly, he licked over Ev's nipple, his tongue curling as it flicked. Then, his full lips kissed around it. His teeth scraped. Opening wider, he sealed his mouth around it and sucked.

"Ahh, fuck," Ev cursed, arching into the suction. He pushed to get his hands free, but Adam bore down. With a shiver, Ev felt him suck harder, enough to hurt. Gasping, his dick twitching, Ev was helpless. He groaned, watching Adam tug the nipple away from his body, the tip caught between his teeth. He let go to lick again, then resumed sucking it. The entire world ceased to exist. It was only Adam and that pressure, those sizzling reactions of his nerve endings.

When he pulled away, Ev's nipple was swollen, dark and bruised. Adam caught his eye and brushed the nipple with his lips.

"Fuck," Ev breathed, closing his eyes, arching his back.

Adam let go, climbed off, came back a second later with the camera. "Don't move," he said in command. The lens focused on him, a weird eye, seeing too much. The shutter closed again and again.

Ev knew what he must look like. His bruised nipple, crossed wrists, reddened throat, come-damp stomach and spread thighs. He just closed his eyes and waited.

By the time he opened them, Adam had a pad of paper in hand instead, his lip held between his teeth as he squinted thoughtfully back and forth between Ev and the page. His arm was tensed, the muscles working as he made finer movements with the charcoal.

"Why do I listen to you?" Ev wondered, under his breath.

"Hmm?" Adam let the pad fall to his side, then set it down while wearing a bored sort of curiosity.

"Why do I listen to you?" he repeated more loudly.

Still wearing that can't-be-bothered, dull interest, Adam approached the bed and ran his thumb through a drip of pre-come on Ev's cock-head. The thumb was brought up to Adam's lips and he sucked it clean. Then the bastard gave him a look like that was his answer right there. "I'm sorry, what?"

"You asshole."

"Mmm." His lips twisted in a smirk Ev didn't like at all, butterflies stirring in his belly. Adam sank to his knees at the bedside and took a lick up the underside of Ev's swollen, dripping cock. "Where's the line, Ev? You tell me. Is it here?" He kissed the tip, his lips hugging it obscenely, his pretty eyes bright and wicked. With hardly any effort at all, he manhandled Ev over onto his stomach. Pressing his legs apart, cupping his ass, Adam spread his cheeks and licked up the crease.

Ev cried out, came up off the bed with his arms planted under him. "Stop!"

"Really?" Adam said with cocky doubt. "Was that the line? Putting my tongue on your pucker instead of your prick? Are you going to leave now? Call this off? Tell me again what you are and are *not*? Are you only not a faggot when I'm licking your ass?"

"God, I hate you." He hung his head, breathing hard, viciously denying the need to rut and fuck his aching cock against the bed.

"Is this you not leaving?"

Ev growled.

Adam's fingertip brushed the rim of Ev's hole, his clenched knot, and Ev's arms shook.

"Beg me," Adam said, quiet and deadly.

"What is this?!" Ev yelled, his voice breaking.

"This is you not leaving."

"Fuck. *Fuck*!"

The finger dragged more firmly over his opening. "Beg," Adam commanded.

He wasn't going to do it. He wasn't.

"Pl-please."

"Louder."

"Please."

"Please what?"

"Please don't stop."

"That's what I thought." Fingers pulled at him from both sides and the wet, soft muscle of Adam's tongue took a slower, firmer lick up the center. Then he came back down and licked only over Ev's hole. Ev's whole body shook and an awful whimper slipped past his defenses. The lick came again and Ev thrust against the bed. "Don't fucking move."

The pad of paper was visible from the angle Ev was propped up at. He looked at it as Adam pressed the pointed end of his tongue at Ev's opening, trying to feed it inside. The sketch was beautiful, focused on the shape of Ev's mouth, his bruised neck, his swollen nipple. The rest was cropped out of frame, but the whole story was there.

That was when it changed on him. No matter what Adam did, Ev was trapped there. There was no leaving. For a moment, it only made him angrier, that what Adam was creating with Ev's inspiration was actually worth the aggravation. He wasn't just some kinky art freak. He was fucking good. He was making something worth a damn.

He began to let out a growl of frustration, but the tongue slipped into him and it broke the cry apart, into a rough, guttural sound. There was a maddening push as it went deeper still, that part of Adam which tormented Ev the most, claiming him in ways that couldn't be taken back or undone. And he held it there, let Ev really feel it.

The tongue withdrew. The hands let go.

"Don't move," Adam commanded.

Ev could only pant and tremble. The camera snapped as Adam circled around, seeing him too clearly.

It got away from him, then. And once it started to go, he couldn't get hold of it at all. His breathing became erratic. The panic rose. His arms gave out and he bowed his head, gasping for air. Then he knew he had to try to run. He had to go. Hide.

Scrambling off the bed, he felt the wheels push it out from under him as he planted one foot on the tile floor. Almost stumbling forward, he ran for the bathroom and some sort of sanctuary, some escape from the constant, torturous scrutiny.

Steady footsteps chased him. He heard their echo, felt the panic shove him forward faster.

He flew into the bathroom, spun to slam the door, but Adam was right there, pushing hard at the other side. Chest flexing, arms straining, jaw clenched, his fire was burning brightly as ever, but he had none of Ev's panic. He was calm. Focused.

Even terror wasn't enough to even the odds and tip the balance in Ev's favor. When he felt the door opening more rather than shutting, he gave up, staggering backward, screaming, "Stop! Leave me alone!"

When Adam did stop, right on the spot, right away, it somehow upset Ev even more. Adam just stood there, waiting, like he'd only needed the word. But a large part of Ev needed the fight, the crash and unfairness of Adam coming at him anyway.

Crumpling, his knees connecting with an agonizing crack against the tile floor, Ev folded in on himself, curling up in a ball as he broke down. His dark blond hair fell in his eyes. His hands smeared tears as he covered his face, the floor cold on his shins.

Adam took two steps closer. Without looking, guided by hearing and body heat, Ev slid forward. Resting his head against Adam's leg, wrapping a hand around the top of his foot, Ev stopped trying to hold it together. For a long time, he was a mess.

Chapter 7

What Real Men Do

"Hey, later on tonight we're watching the game down at Marco's on Birch. You comin'? There's gonna be beer."

"Nah, I'm kind of tied up. Next time, okay?"

"No sweat. You cool?"

"Sure."

Adam gave him a look like there was something he wanted to say, but was restraining himself. Ev had only answered the phone because he wanted to avoid the conversation he was about to have. Plus, the novelty of having his phone in reach, when it was usually across the room in his pocket, made the impulse hard to resist.

"Well, you change your mind, you know where we are."

"Thanks, Leo."

He hung up, then chose to keep his eyes on the phone cradled in his lap instead of the aggravating man sitting expectantly across from him. The breeze was nice. The terrace hugged the glass walls of the apartment, stretching almost the full length and overlooking the breathtaking view of the city below. On the table in front of them was an assortment of food, pre-made and pulled from the fridge.

"It's weird to be dressed in front of you," Ev said.

"Already? Huh. Interesting."

The jeans hugged him in places he wished they wouldn't, made him feel confined in awkward ways they usually didn't. Same with his shirt.

They hadn't said a word to each other since they'd left the bathroom, Ev following at Adam's heels like a dog.

"You drink beer?" Adam asked, running his fingers over the seam of the chair's upholstery. He was sitting back, arms wide, like he owned the place, which he did.

"No. You heard that?"

"I'm an observer. Always observing."

"I noticed."

"I wouldn't have given you one anyway. You're too young."

Ev laughed despite himself, but it was bitter, hurt. "Too young for a beer, but not too young for that?" He nodded in the direction of the bed upon which Adam had been tongue-fucking his ass.

"Funny how the rules work."

"Whose?"

"Mine. Our society's." He sat forward, clasped his hands together, gaining a more intense expression in the flash of his eyes and the part of his lips, like at any moment he might bite, kiss, or devour Ev. It was unsettling. "Talk to me."

Ev blew out a breath, laughing a little again. "Why do you do that? Are you doing it on purpose? Giving me orders like that?"

"Oh, I'm sorry, Ev," Adam replied with heavy sarcasm. "What's wrong, buddy?"

"I'm not your buddy."

"Glad you've noticed. Does your father give you orders?"

"No. He's more passive-aggressive, guilting me into doing things. Mom's the same way."

"Has anyone else given you orders before?"

"My coaches."

"And how did you respond to them?"

Ev shrugged, grabbed a grape and popped it into his mouth, chewing slowly. Eventually, he had to swallow and answer. "Played well, even though I didn't enjoy the game and my head wasn't really in it."

"Played well enough to get a scholarship, even."

"Yeah." He ate another grape, just to stall. "So you are doing it on purpose?"

"It's working well, isn't it? You respond to it. I enjoy it. Results are produced."

After a few deep breaths, Ev said, "How do I know you're not going to order me to do something I don't want to do?"

"Have I once not stopped when you've said to stop?"

Ev admitted, "No. But I didn't want you to do that." He felt mortified even saying that much, and couldn't raise his gaze from his hands.

"You didn't?" Adam sounded doubtful. "How do you know?"

Ev didn't know what to say.

"Because you're not gay?"

Gritting his teeth, bearing down on the shame, Ev wished he was out of there, that he was anywhere else.

"I felt you trying to rub off on the bed. I felt you quiver when I licked you. You didn't say stop. Not while I was doing it."

"What the hell is going on here, Adam?" Ev pleaded, pushed to beg for answers if that's what it was going to take to get them. "Is this just about the paintings? Do you do this with all of your models? Or do you just like to fuck with my head?"

He leaned forward even more, close enough to touch if he wanted to. "I'm trying to get you to think about why you do what you do, why you react the way you react, what you want, what you feel."

"Why?"

"Because it matters!"

"Matters to whom?" Ev yelled back, exasperated.

"You! Who are you, Evelyn?"

"Don't call me that!"

"Why not?"

"Real men don't have names like Evelyn! Real men don't do that shit together!"

Adam stood, came slowly closer, his eyes fixed on his target and Ev couldn't budge or stop it from happening. Adam straddled Ev's lap, wrapped a hand around his throat, stroking Ev's jaw with his thumb.

"Real men guilt their sons into doing things they don't want to do? Wasting years of their childhoods? Making it damned hard for them to understand who they are and what they want out of life? Real men make their sons behave and think the way that'll earn their father the most votes, appeal to the widest audience in homegrown, old-fashioned, Midwestern USA? Come on, Ev. I don't know you well yet, but I know you've got your head so turned around that you can't see where you're going. How do you know you're not going to walk off a cliff unless I tell you to change direction?" He wove his fingers through Ev's hair, grabbed a handful of it and tugged his head back a little more, looking down his nose at Ev. "If you want to go, go. Go watch the game you don't care about. Go pretend it doesn't matter that Playboys don't get you hard but I do."

Adam got up, stepped back, spread his arms to show that Ev was free to leave.

So, Ev stood up.

There was nothing to leave for, except peace and denial.

"I'm not..."

"Not what?" Adam said when Ev didn't finish.

"I'm not... attracted to guys." Adam rolled his eyes. "I'm attracted to *you*. And..."

"And?" One eyebrow raised, interest pursed his lips.

"And this guy John on the football team. And Shaun, for his body, not his face. That's it."

"Girls?"

"There's tons of girls I think are sexy. Just not the fake ones."

"Okay. Now we're getting somewhere." He took another step forward, into Ev's personal space. Ev reached for Adam's waist and held onto it. Adam lifted Ev's chin with a bent finger and rubbed gently over his sore nipple, through his shirt. "Staying?"

"Yeah."

"Good. Eat something. Rest awhile. We have time." He pinched down on the end of Ev's aching nipple, twisting a little, then brushed his lips over Ev's mouth, breathing in his gasp. "Stay the night."

"What are you gonna do to me?"

"Haven't decided yet."

"At least you're honest."

And Adam laughed.

Ev ate and wandered around the place while Adam painted. It was nice, being able to keep an eye on Adam from a distance while enjoying the breeze on the balcony or lounging in the overstuffed chairs in one of several sitting areas. With the last few sips of coffee swirling in the bottom of his mug, Ev went over to the art studio, sitting on the bed which had been getting him into so much trouble.

"Ready for me again?" Adam asked with a wicked twinkle in his eyes.

"Mm," Ev hummed, not wanting to answer that. He sipped his coffee. "If I'm spending the day here—"

"The night, too."

He gave Adam a look and continued. "I need to pick up some things from the dorm. I have some studying to do. And I wouldn't mind a…. toothbrush."

Adam dropped his arm to his side, tossing his hair back out of his eyes. Looking at Ev with intentions Ev couldn't read into, Adam said, "Fair point. I'll drive you. It'll be quickest."

"You don't need to drive me. I can—"

"Walk? Take the bus?" Adam breathed out a laugh. "You're not taking the bus anymore. Or walking."

"I have a car; it's just not worth using the gas to—"

"I'll drive you. End of story."

"Oh, really?"

"Mm-hmm." Adam took the mug right out of Ev's hand and drank the rest of his coffee. As he set the mug aside on a table he made a face. "Too sweet. Figures. How much sugar did you add, anyway?"

"That was my coffee."

"Oh, really?"

"Asshole," Ev sighed.

Adam came over, standing so close he was astride Ev's legs. He grabbed hold of Ev by the jaw and leaned down to give him a hard, dirty kiss.

With a soft groan, Ev pushed him away just enough to break the kiss. The word stop was right on the tip of his tongue, shaping his lips. Adam seemed to see it there, pausing, looking like he was enjoying himself quite a lot in causing Ev so much torment. They were breathing each other's air, noses brushing. Then Ev kissed Adam. It was softer, gentler, and he saw Adam frown, his eyes closing.

When they broke apart again, Adam said with impatience, "Okay, let's make this fast."

Putting on his shoes, watching Adam slip on a leather jacket, Ev said, "Since when are you the boss of me?"

Adam gave him an appraising glance, raising one eyebrow. He turned away and pulled his keys from a pocket in the jacket. "I don't know, Evelyn. You tell me."

Adam's car was a royal blue Mustang. As soon as Ev saw Adam walking up to it, pushing the fob that made the lights flash and the doors unlock, he let out a wild laugh. "Are you kidding me? Wow."

"You like it?" It was strange how when Adam wasn't smiling, there was such seriousness to him. It was intimidating, because it was an energized gravity, as if he was burning up from inside and the only way to cope was to consume others around him.

Adam pulled open the passenger door and held it for Ev while he got in. Wanting to protest the gesture, Ev decided instead to bite his tongue. He replied, "It's not bad."

After Adam had also gotten into the car, starting the engine, shifting into reverse and turning in his seat to rest a hand behind Ev's seat to reverse out of the spot, Ev asked, "What did your parents do?"

"Law. They had their own firm."

"And they were well off?"

They had swung out of the spot in the garage under the building, and Adam revved the engine as they drove out into daylight and onto the road. "Oh yeah. Penthouse in Manhattan, where they worked. Sprawling estate out in upstate New York. The estate was part of my father's inheritance."

"Do you still have it?"

"No. Too many memories."

"Mm. Sorry."

"It's okay." They got to a red light, Adam eased back in his seat, glancing sideways down at Ev's lap, then up to his mouth and eyes.

"How did they die?"

"Car accident."

"Jesus."

"A bus caused a pile-up that forced their car off a bridge and into a river."

For a second, Ev couldn't believe it. Then, nodding, jaw clenched and eyes closed, he swallowed some of his pride. No wonder Adam had said no to the bus. "Okay. And that's why you... Sorry. That's awful. When did it happen?"

"Five years ago."

"At least you weren't a kid," Ev murmured, watching the buildings blur past.

"Yeah." Adam cleared his throat. "I was, uh, working my way to my own law degree when it happened. Kind of shifted my worldview. My art minor became a major."

"Good. Life's too short for bullshit." He studied the fold of his hands, now in his lap, trying to imagine how much of Adam's life must have been shaken up, how hard it must have been. "Did all of their loose ends fall on you when they passed?"

"No, they had appointed my grandfather as the executor of their estate. He's also a lawyer," Adam said with a faint, cool smirk. "How do you know about this stuff?"

"I had an uncle pass recently. He was in the middle of getting a divorce at the time to someone who wasn't exactly on speaking terms with my side of the family, so it was really complicated and stressful. Not so cut and dry. Opened my eyes a little."

"I bet." Adam reached over and gave Ev's left leg a gentle squeeze. "I'm sorry, too."

"Happens to everyone, sooner or later."

They pulled up to the dorm. Adam took a spot on the street, in view of the main entrance. Right away, other students started to gawk at the car, for good reason. It was a lot nicer than most of the well-used heaps of junk they were all driving.

Ev turned to look right at Adam, who wore a worrisome, cocky expression. One hand rested coolly on the steering wheel. "You're not coming in, right? Because I have no way to explain you."

Adam bit his lip, taking a long look down Ev's body.

"Please," Ev added, ready to beg. If Leo came face to face with Adam, who was basically a teacher, and started collecting his toothbrush, a change of clothes, some other incriminating things, it wasn't going to go well. "My roommate's probably in there right now. He's a suspicious dude. There would be questions."

"Come on, *Ev*, this is just a business arrangement after all," Adam said with a teasing tone, stressing Ev's nickname as if to imply how much he didn't like it.

"Liar."

"Really?" Adam said, scrunching his nose. "You could tell? How am I supposed to learn more about you if I don't meet your friends?"

"I'll tell you whatever you want to know."

"Promise?" The way he asked made it clear it wasn't a vow he was going to take lightly.

"Yeah. I promise."

"I'll hold you to that."

"I can tell."

"Okay," Adam said with a sigh. "You're excused."

"Unbelievable." Ev opened the door and got out before Adam could say another word.

He kept checking over his shoulder as he walked up to the building, just to make sure Adam wasn't following. He wasn't, but he was out of the car and leaning back against it like he was in a commercial or something—the wind blowing through his hair, sunglasses sliding up the bridge of his nose, hand in his pocket.

Ev jogged up the steps instead of taking the elevator, just to burn off some nervous energy. He got to his room, dug out his key. Leo was inside, studying, as Ev expected.

"Well, well," Leo said, dropping his book to the table. "Look who it is."

"Hey, man," Ev smiled, trying to act normal. He wanted to avoid lying if possible, so he just headed to his closet. Grabbing the nearest bag, he started tossing in clothes, extra underwear, deodorant, his toothbrush, his razor... everything he could think of.

"Where you going?" Leo said from a few feet away, standing now and watching closely. "Moving out?"

"Nah, just, um..." He kept his back turned. "I've got a cousin in town, staying at a hotel, so I'm crashing there tonight."

"Oh, well, have fun."

"Thanks. Have fun at Marco's."

He hurried out of there as quickly as he could, his bag over his shoulder and his books under an arm.

Chapter 8

Facing the Reflection

"How much does the roommate know?"

"About what?"

Adam's weary gaze said it all.

"Well, he knows I'm modeling."

"Nude?"

"Yeah."

"What's his opinion?"

"He was against it."

"Hmm."

They were driving again, back the same way, only now with Ev's gear in tow. He felt strangely relieved to be going back, even while suspecting what was going to happen once they got there. The idea of spending the day with Adam was more appealing than spending it in the library, looking for quiet and slogging through his reading assignments.

"I have a request," Adam told him, his eyes on the road, his expression serious. "I just want you to think about it. You don't have to say anything right now."

"What?"

"I want you to stop modeling for the class. If your time is limited, I'm going to require what is available. And I'll cover any expenses you have. Money's not an object."

"Mm," Ev grunted. He wasn't sure what he felt about that. "So it's just a time thing?"

Adam didn't reply at first. He smiled, then buried the amusement before glancing tellingly over at Ev and saying, "I also don't like to share."

A flush of heat and nervousness was what hit him first, the butterflies stirring in his stomach and his face getting warm. Then, logic slowly returned to him. "But... wait. You're painting me. You're painting me butt naked and I'd think many people will be seeing these once you're done. Or will even buy some. Isn't that sharing?"

"Sharing art is different than sharing people, Evelyn."

"You're actually not going to stop using that, are you?" He sighed when there was no response.

Then, Adam said, "You're my muse. I intend to... protect you."

"From art students?"

"From everyone."

"Are you fucking your other models?" It came out before Ev knew it was going to, and was phrased more bluntly than he would have liked.

"Would that bother you?"

"Can you just answer?"

"You first."

"Fine. Yes."

"No." A couple of streets slipped by under the tires before he added, "The men in the other paintings from this collection are a couple. They're in a monogamous relationship."

"Have you, though?"

"Have I what? Fucked men? Fucked men who have lain naked on my bed? Yes. I'm not a priest, Evelyn."

They pulled into the garage beneath Adam's building, and soon found a spot. Once the car was parked, Adam cut the engine and turned more fully toward Ev.

"I'm intrigued by the way you phrased the question, though."

"It's not..." he stammered. "I didn't mean..."

"Maybe you did. Do you intend to let me fuck you?"

"I can't answer that."

"Can't or won't?" Adam tilted his head, scrutinizing. "Are you curious about it? How it would feel? If you'd like it?"

"Do you intend to fuck me?" he asked, afraid he knew the answer.

"If you'll let me. Answer the questions."

"I can't... be who I am *and* let that happen. I can't be both Ev and... that."

"Then don't be Ev. Who is that? Just be you. You have no one's expectations to live up to other than your own. Do what makes you happy. That's all you have to do. Life is short. Don't waste it following your family's expectations over the side of a bridge."

Ev frowned. It was there in Adam's voice—the hurt, the anger. His hand found Adam's and Adam wove their fingers together.

"Are you curious?" Adam repeated.

"Of course I am. I'm also terrified."

"Getting fucked in the ass doesn't make you gay."

Ev laughed. He had to.

"It doesn't," Adam insisted. "It's an act, not an identity."

"You are incredible, you know."

"It almost sounded like you meant that fondly."

With a squeeze of his fingers, he said, "I did."

Seated on a couch in Adam's apartment, Ev enjoyed a view of the city below and the rolling white clouds above. His Financial Accounting textbook lay open in front of him on the coffee table. Ignoring it, he stared straight ahead into the empty air in front of him.

"What do you like? What makes you happy?" Adam asked, from right by Ev's side, next to him on the couch.

Ev shrugged. "I don't know."

"Liar. Yes, you do."

"I like..." he floundered. How long had it been since anyone had asked him that question? How many years since he hadn't been surrounded by people who felt they knew exactly who he was? "To read. To enjoy a nice view. To just not have to talk sometimes. I like to look good, to feel strong and healthy. I like..."

"Go on."

"I like flowers," he said, rubbing a hand over the back of his neck, feeling embarrassed. "My friend's dad back home was a florist. I had a summer job for a few months learning how to do arrangements and I really... I really liked it."

"Are you getting the business degree to open your own shop?"

Ev sighed, now rubbing the back of one hand with the palm of another.

"What's important to you?" Adam continued.

"Honesty. Loyalty. Kindness."

Adam took hold of Ev's right hand, which had been kneading his left hard enough to make the skin red. Holding it tight, squeezing it, he said, "Good answer."

For a while, they sat in silence.

"What did you want to be when you grew up?"

"Astronaut," Ev said with a small smile. "To fly away in a powerful ship, and be up there, floating, watching the whole world spinning in the stars, enjoying the quiet."

"The view."

"Yeah. You?"

"Barista."

Ev burst out laughing, then couldn't stop.

"But... Why?"

Adam grinned at the memory, biting his lip and leaning in closer, "There was this one barista at the place my mom went for coffee on her way back from picking me up from school every day. He was really, *really* fucking hot."

"That's not a valid reason!"

"It was, though," Adam assured him. "I mean, it also smelled great in the coffee shop. Everyone wanted that barista and he made them happy every day. I don't know. It appealed to me." He nudged Ev's shoulder with his own. "What's your favorite flower?"

"What's your favorite painting?"

"Ooh. Touché." He let out a laugh. "Don't have one yet. Ask me again later this afternoon. Come on. Give me one or two."

"Okay, fine," Ev relented. "Purple ranunculus. Big gorgeous blooms and a rich deep plum color."

"Good! Another."

"So demanding," Ev chuckled. "Um… forget-me-nots."

"Aww. That's so sweet."

Ev shoved him.

"I mean it. It's really sweet." Adam got hold of him then, manhandling him sideways on the couch, pressing him back onto it to lie down, then climbed on top of him. "God, you're so adorable, I just want to tie you down and lick you for hours."

"I don't think it works that way."

"With me it does."

"So you just want me for my body and virginity?"

"It'd be easier that way, huh?" His mouth chased Ev's, Adam's body pressing into him. The kiss was intensely arousing—a tease as he brushed their lips together, getting Ev to open for him, then pulled away, feeling his gasps, encouraging them.

"No, it wouldn't. Not in the long run."

Adam's tongue licked into his mouth. Ev's hand cupped the back of Adam's head, moaning, rocking up into Adam's undulations. Goosebumps covered his arms and he held on tighter, needing Adam not to stop.

Hours slipped by in quiet. Ev read his textbooks, pausing only now and then to watch Adam paint. Standing in the room behind him, Ev enjoyed seeing Adam work and sculpt the paint without saying a word to disturb him. If Adam noticed Ev's presence there, he didn't indicate it. Maybe he was too deep in his trance of concentration. That's how it appeared, anyway, with his furrowed brow and the eager strokes of his brush.

The most difficult part was acknowledging it was him, Ev, on there, coming to life under the careful caress of Adam's every brushstroke. It seemed the more Ev started to face parts of himself he never knew existed, the more the likeness of this manifestation came clear on canvas. So, instead, Ev paid more attention to the way Adam used color, line, and blending to translate his ideas. It was magic, that sifting of idea into actuality, one nudge of his wet brush at a time.

Evening came before Ev grew restless.

Not once had Adam asked him to come and pose. He seemed too caught up in his work, maybe he had reached a point where he didn't even need Ev anymore. The thought of that twisted a knot in Ev's gut, and he didn't know why or how to make that feeling go away.

That's why, as the sun began to set, Ev went to the art studio of his own accord. He stripped down and sat on the edge of the bed, waiting.

Adam had one hand in his hair, pulling at it. There was a slight scowl of displeasure on his face, his gaze on the painting.

He dropped his arm, sighing. "Okay."

He grabbed his camera, slinging its strap behind his neck and letting it hang against his body. Then he grabbed his pad and pencil.

"Follow me. New pose."

Ev went, and Adam led him right up to the glass wall of the apartment in the living room, having Ev face the setting sun. "Lean on the glass like you're trying to push through it, like it was water."

After trying to accomplish this request, Ev let Adam adjust his arms, nudging his stance with gentle pressure to Ev's hips and shoulders, then to the tilt of his head.

"Good. The reflection's great," Adam said, almost to himself as he lifted the camera to his eye. He seemed to focus most on Ev's face and arms. After taking photos, Adam switched to the paper and pencil. He stood to Ev's left, just behind Ev's line of sight. All Ev could make out was the shape of Adam there, a smudge of red, tan, black and blue.

The feel of the camera lens eye, and Adam's, was what got Ev hard. The steady watching of him there, just out of reach, was what kept him that way.

He ignored it at first, or tried to.

When the pressure got too intense, the ache acute, Ev writhed slightly. Muttering, "Sorry," he dropped one arm to knead his aching cock, just a little.

Holding his pencil between his teeth, tucking the pad under his arm, Adam raised the camera, snapping a few shots as Ev groaned and tried to let his interest wilt. To manage this, he thought of things that scared him. The longer it went on, the more his head went to bad places.

He thought of the worst people possible—his minister, his father, his coach—coming through Adam's door, looking for Ev, seeing what he was doing. He thought of Adam getting a lot of publicity for his new paintings, and the images finding their way to Ev's hometown, his family, and the people he'd deliberately left behind when he went away to school, secretly never intending to go back.

He thought of men coming to take him away, like they'd taken James. He thought of specific men from his adolescence seeing those paintings, and knew what their reaction would be.

It wouldn't just be taunting and name calling or shunning. It would mean physical harm, pain, aggression, violence, and attacks.

Ev's knees were giving out. He couldn't catch his breath. Curling up there, by the window, his knees against his chest, his hands braced on the floor to steady him, he heard the camera's shutter once more. Then Adam came closer, crouching by him.

"Hey, where'd you go? You need a break?"

A creeping, crawling dread was a cold touch slithering into his belly, drawing up his balls, sending a chill down his spine. Sucking in air in a single heavy draw, struggling to let it back out, Ev started to tremble. He had to get out of there, away from the window and wide open spaces.

"I can't... I have to..." He glanced to the door, then felt his heart clench realizing even running wouldn't help. He'd already damned himself. The danger was inside his head, where it would never leave. If the wrong people discovered what he'd done, they'd come for him.

"Here. Come." Ev had stood. Adam took him by the arm and pulled him away. Down the length of the apartment, down a short hall, they came to a door. Beyond all was dark. Adam led him in.

Ev's breathing was too rough, too shaky. He liked how Adam's grip kept him anchored, but it wasn't enough. The fear, the knowledge that he was condemned for what he'd done, that there would be consequences—it stole his ability to be calm and rational. He took hold of Adam's shoulder, searching his face in the dark, knowing Adam could see much more than Ev wanted.

Glancing down at the grip of Ev's hand, Adam seemed to nod in understanding. He moved Ev backwards, up against the wall near the door. In the dark, Adam took hold of Ev's arms and pinned them to the wall on either side of his head. When Adam leaned in close, Ev's breath came rushing out. He turned toward the scent of Adam, the foreign scent of his musky cologne filling Ev's head with new, tempting things.

He tried to let go of the rest, things he'd buried and walked away from, or thought he had.

"I want to know what this is, what's upsetting you," Adam told him. "When you're ready."

Ev grunted, his lips finding the side of Adam's neck as he pressed in even closer. Then their bodies touched, flush from the hips upwards.

"Does this help?"

Ev nodded, grunted his assent.

"You're not alone. I won't let you be. Not if you need me to."

Ev pulled experimentally at Adam's hold. It didn't budge. In that moment, it felt like nothing in Ev's life had ever been as steady and steadfast as that grip on his arms. His nose and lips pressed more firmly against Adam's warm, soft, fragrant skin. Ev's eyes closed. His breathing began to even out. It felt like it took a long time.

Chapter 9

Overpowered

"What's going to help you?"

"I just don't want to be alone."

"Okay."

They ordered in food. Adam wrapped Ev in a robe, tying it around his waist himself and measuring Ev with his gaze. Then he made Ev tea and led him to a comfortable chair which Adam shifted nearer to his easel, planting Ev there with his steaming mug of Earl Grey.

Once the food arrived, Ev ate in the chair while Adam did the same standing up, continuing his work on the painting and his sketch pad, going back and forth between them.

The low, soothing jazz music playing from a set of speakers nearby lulled Ev. With a full stomach, a cozy chair, and a strong desire to avoid his memories and scrutiny of his circumstances, he stayed there a while, sometimes reading from his textbook just to keep his mind on other things.

Night fell. Ev dozed off.

Adam nudged him awake with a hand to Ev's cheek. "Come sleep in bed. You'll be more comfortable."

Ev didn't want to argue, or talk about it, so he went. Adam led him back to the darkened room, which he discovered was Adam's bedroom. It alone seemed to escape the expansive view from the windows, as the curtains were all heavy and drawn. The colors of the room were dark cranberries, grays and blacks. The bed was huge, centered in the room's space, away from the walls.

"Sleep here," Adam commanded, tossing back the bed's comforter and sheet on one side. "The bathroom's through there if you want to wash up first." He gestured to a door on the room's right side.

Ev hesitated, not sure how he felt about being asked to sleep in Adam's bed.

"Would you rather sleep alone?"

Ev rubbed his jaw, covered in light stubble, then gave his head a subtle shake.

"Then sleep here. I have to finish up what I'm working on, but I won't be long."

There was so much to say, things he had been sworn to silence about, things he'd never told anyone, things he'd thought didn't matter anymore.

"I thought I got away from it," he said.

"You're safe here, Evelyn," Adam promised, laying a hand on Ev's heart. "Do you know that?"

"I think so."

"Would it be easier to be back in the dorm for tonight?"

He thought it over, imagined having to face Leo and anyone else who happened by, maybe some guys Leo hung out with from the soccer team, and cringed. He'd taken deliberate steps away from who he'd been before meeting Adam, and it wasn't a great distance, but there was no backtracking. That door had cemented shut behind him. That was the scariest part.

"No. Not at all," he answered.

"Okay then. Get some rest." Adam bent to kiss his cheek, then walked away.

Ev washed up, brushed his teeth, and went to bed. For a few hours, he just lay there, staring at the ceiling, trying to doze off. Finally, he did, for a little while. When he woke and looked at the clock, it was almost three a.m.

Frowning, he looked around. The bed was empty, untouched, but a light was on behind the bathroom's closed door. He heard the water run.

When the light in there flicked off, the door opened. Ev looked for Adam, wanting to know why it had taken him so long to come to bed. And Adam was there, wearing a pair of black sleep pants, shirtless.

Rolling onto his back, Ev held Adam's gaze as he walked over and threw back the sheet on the bed's other side. Ev nudged the sheet further down, showing Adam he was naked. He drew up his right leg, starting to get hard when Adam's gaze skated over Ev's cock.

"I was trying not to disturb you," Adam explained, turning on a bedside lamp.

Ev thought about those steps he'd taken, the ones there were no taking back. At that moment, he was somewhere in the dark, in the middle of things, alone. He needed to get where he was headed, needed to see if it was somewhere he belonged. There was a big chance he wouldn't, that he was just fucked-up and doomed. It would be awful if that was true, but at least he'd know. He'd have figured out where his place was.

"Not sleepy anymore."

Adam measured him from the other side of the bed, then hooked his thumbs in his pants' waistband. "This okay?" he asked, inching them down.

Ev nodded, started breathing faster with excitement and anticipation. All of the danger was right there, in Adam's state of undress. It was everything Ev didn't understand yet. It was one thing to get off on another man. It was another entirely to get another man off.

Adam stripped down, containing more power and determination in his body language than Ev would have dreamed possible. There was nothing shy in him, or doubtful.

His cock was long, his pubic hair unsurprisingly red, trimmed neatly. His body was strong, intimidating.

Climbing onto the bed, Adam wrapped his cock in a hand, stroking it as he came closer. Ev licked his lips, letting his mouth open slightly. He was so nervous; he was soon dizzy, his heart hammering away in his chest. Adam straddled Ev's chest, his knees up under Ev's arms, which Adam guided up above Ev's head.

"May I restrain you?" Adam asked in a calm, softened tone. "Just your arms?"

Ev nodded.

A strap was slipped around both his wrists, then tightened, drawing them up to the headboard. Ev closed his eyes for a moment, trying to calm down, to breathe slower. But when he opened them, seeing Adam towering over him, his cock inches from Ev's lips, Ev's breath caught.

Adam widened his stance, easing his cock closer. Lifting his head off the pillow, glad for the deep darkness of the bedroom, only that single lamp left to light the space, Ev extended his tongue and licked at the head. A soft, breathy whimper escaped him as he did it again, his tongue taking a longer drag up from under the head and curling over it. He tasted skin mostly, but also something else—salty, bitter, but not unpleasant. When Adam eased down more, bracing an arm on the headboard and rolled his hips in a slow thrust, his cock slipped between Ev's lips.

"Mm," Ev moaned, closing his lips around the column of Adam's long, swelling dick.

A hand clasped the side of Ev's jaw. A tender, low voice told him, "You're safe. No one hurts you here. It's just you and me."

Ev frowned and sucked, his tongue hugging Adam's flesh. Adam guided Ev's head back down to the pillow, then began thrusting, moving shallowly on Ev's tongue. There was nothing scary or threatening about it. Somehow, it made Ev feel cared for, and that he was caring in return for someone who made him feel safer than he'd been since he was a child. Having Adam on his tongue, pushing and pulling between his lips, sliding back into his mouth, was a display of trust. Ever since James, all Ev had wanted was someone to be able to trust this much. He'd always been afraid it would never happen.

In his chest, something tight loosened. That didn't mean the fear was gone. But the harder he suckled Adam's cock, swallowing over and over again, the more contented Ev was. Pulling at his arms helped too. He tugged at the bonds to feel them, closed his eyes, and gave over.

When Adam came, he'd pulled back so only the end of his cock was stretching Ev's lips, which were hugged around him. Hot come coated Ev's tongue and he moaned, swallowing. He watched Adam stroke himself through it, breathing heavily, his eyes downcast and chest heaving. Ev swallowed down every drop Adam emptied into him, breathing heavily through his nose.

He opened his lips, gasping, and Adam slipped free. He thrust lightly against Ev's stubble-covered jaw, up his cheek. Ev turned his head to catch Adam's dick again with his lips and tongue, moaning as he sucked it again for just a second. Adam caressed Ev's jaw, up to his ear, his temple. Shifting backward, Adam lay his larger body down atop Ev for a moment, catching his opened mouth in a deep, probing kiss. The teasing lick of Adam's tongue searching Ev's mouth, the feel of him using his whole body to push Ev down to the bed, to pry him open and get deeper made him moan. Adam angled his head farther, sucking Ev's tongue, then pulled back to bite at his lower lip. Reaching down between their bodies, Adam grabbed hold of Ev's erection and gave it a tug.

"I'm glad you enjoyed that, too. Tired yet?"

Ev shook his head, just a little

"How far are you going to let me take this?"

Ev had no answer, but his breathing quickened. He spread his legs, letting Adam settle between them.

"I have your permission? Stop me at any time."

Ev nodded.

"Say it."

"Yes."

Adam seemed content with that. He sat back on his heels, rubbing over Ev's chest and the swollen muscles of his pecs, then rubbed downward, over his stomach. He took hold of Ev's heavy, aching balls and rolled them. Ev thrust into the touch, fucking air.

Something bright and burning flashed in Adam's gaze.

He stopped touching Ev for a moment, lunging sideways to the nightstand. From it, he pulled a bottle of lube.

"Flip over; get your knees under you. It's okay to be scared. I'm not going to hurt you."

With a desperate grunt of fear, Ev rolled over, drew his legs up under him. Adam nudged them apart, spreading his ass even more. Letting out soft moans of trepidation into the bed, Ev let his head rest there.

First, a wet hand gave a twisting squeeze from root to tip up Ev's cock. His fear was working to wilt his interest, but that firm tugging had him crying out roughly right away. No woman had ever touched Ev with that much eager resolve to wring him dry. But before he had adjusted to it at all, there was pressure at his hole. No sooner had he felt the nudge than a finger was sliding up into his ass.

Back arching, hips tilting, Ev cried out louder, the pitch climbing as the finger sheathed itself to the last knuckle. It was so far inside him, he was startled by it and pushed a little as if to force it back out. The only thing that accomplished was to get Adam to chuckle darkly and begin pumping the finger, penetrating him with it in long strokes.

Ev grunted, trembling. "Fuck. Oh fuck," he begged. The other hand kneaded his cock-head gently, making him writhe, twisting on the sheathed finger and inside that grip. Shivers of pleasure were causing pre-come to drip from his cock, and the wet squelch of Adam's hand on Ev's dick got more pronounced.

Lightening his touch, Adam rubbed out and over Ev's rim with one hand and with the other, let Ev's cock ride along Adam's opened hand, feathering it with a soft touch. When two wet fingers pushed into his ass, Ev whimpered and thrust harder against the hand. They went deep, prying him open from the inside and Ev got very still, tipping up his ass and just hoping Adam didn't hurt him.

"Lots of pressure, now. Any pain?"

"Mm," Ev hummed. "No."

The fingers pulled out again, rubbing over his rim, circling it before plunging back inside.

"No one else has you like this. No one even gets close," Adam warned. He pulled his hand away from Ev's cock to caress his ass, kneading his cheeks while his fingers pumped. The longer it went on, the easier they slid.

The feel of that—being slowly, deeply, carefully finger-fucked —pushed Ev beyond restlessness. He simply needed, but what, he wasn't sure.

"Oh, please," Ev whined. "Oh fuck, please."

"Please what? Please stop?"

The fingers stuffed him full. They twisted around, rubbing. Ev's knees were weak; his stomach fluttering with nerves, and thrills were shooting out through his body. His lower lip trembled on a gasp, his arms straining as he pulled hard at the strap.

"Or please more?"

He imagined Adam stopping, pulling out, untying the straps binding Ev's wrists and telling him to go to sleep instead. It couldn't happen. Ev wouldn't let it. If they stopped now, Ev would be more scared and miserable than ever.

But if they continued?

"Please more," Ev managed, his voice gruffer now. He was glad his face was hidden, because the shame was threatening to rip him apart from the inside.

Adam gave Ev's dick a firm, complete tug and kept doing it, faster and faster until he was jacking him. Ev cried out, his deep voice shivering the air. He quivered and came. Semen shot over his chest and legs. On the come-down, a third finger was pressed through his throbbing sphincter, stretching him out wider than he thought possible. There was so much pressure filling him up in there. His cries gained an edge, more frantic and primal.

Rubbing his forehead against his arm, feeling like he was coming apart, he let instinct pull him for the first time and he got up onto his knees instead.

"Easy now, I know it's a lot."

A strong grip on his left hip drew him back and the three fingers twisted up into him on another push. He made another soft, wild cry.

"I need you to try to relax now, Evelyn. Let's just do this awhile, okay? It's just my fingers. The more you relax, the more you'll like it."

In and out they slid. Sometimes he pushed against them on the in-stroke, sometimes to hurry them out. He tried clenching up, too, but that only moved Adam to rub at Ev's rim with the other hand, stroking the sensitive skin beside where the fingers pumped away. That forbidden, dangerous spot became the focus of his attention. It was the whole world. But it was dark there, in that bedroom, and no one could see. There were no spectators, no cameras, no one to judge. No one stopped them, or tried to.

As Ev's body relaxed, losing much of its tension, he felt himself giving into it. His breathing evened. His hands hung loosely from their bonds. He stopped frowning and breathed through parted lips. Each outward tug of the fingers fucking him caused a light shiver; his goosebumps were steady from head to toe nearly the whole time.

"How's that?" Adam asked, pushing in and holding there, the fingers spreading inside Ev.

Ev made a soft, moaning exhale and realized his dick was struggling to get hard again.

Adam caressed up Ev's spine to his neck, then scratched over his scalp. Ev pushed his head back into the touch. Adam grabbed hold of his hair, pulling lightly to force Ev's head back, and rubbed him from the inside.

"I want you. Can I take you?" It sounded hungry, full of all of the power that Ev no longer had. In those few words were so many things Ev had sought and not found in the other men in his life, other role models. There was respect, trust, honesty and raw passion. "I take things like this very fucking seriously," Adam added in warning. "This means something to me. If you give me this, I swear on my life I'll safeguard you in whatever ways you need me to. It'd be a beginning, not the end."

"I'm scared." Ev heard himself confess, and he thought of other terrifying moments in which he'd also been naked and vulnerable. They'd all ended badly.

"I know, but this is the most powerful way to not be alone, and I will take care of you, Evelyn. I swear I will. Do you want this?"

"Yes. To try. Even if they hate me for it."

"Evelyn," Adam sighed. The pain in his voice, sympathy for Ev's turmoil, moved Ev more than anything else had.

"Go on," he grunted, trying to psych himself up like he had before games he knew he was outmatched for, but which he had to play anyway. "Do it."

"This is about no one else—no one—but you and me. You hear me?"

The fingers pulled out. Something else prodded at Ev's tender, highly stimulated opening, swollen up a little now. Hands caressed along Ev's sides, his hips, and thighs. Ev's toes flexed. He closed his mouth, breathing through his nose.

"Just relax," Adam said soothing and caressing.

After a few moments, Ev did, just a little. The pressure intensified. There was pain—distinct and intimate —as he was entered, and he shouted.

"Okay. You're okay. Deep breaths. Try to stay relaxed."

He clenched on the intrusion, and it was so strange. He was so full, stretched and connected to something that felt nothing like fingers. Adam pushed gently deeper, drawing Ev back by the hips. Crying out, startled by what he was allowing to happen, Ev stayed still and let Adam work his way inside. With little in and out movements, he went farther and farther. It seemed to never stop, and when Adam was mostly sheathed, but still went deeper, Ev began whimpering, though he tried to muffle the sound of it against the bedding.

Adam sighed, sounding blissful. He caressed Ev again and his thrusts became longer. Ev made a frantic, wild noise on the first longer thrust, as he was claimed all at once, the pressure of Adam's entire cock unraveling the ties holding Ev's mind together. There was a distinct transference of power between them. Ev felt it happen, as he was fucked up the ass by a man bigger, smarter, richer and more capable than him. Adam was experiencing Ev from the inside, possessing him bodily in ways that Ev would never be able to forget or undo.

The fear of that had Ev shaking, grunting almost constantly. But Adam kept caressing as he moaned. His hand found Ev's softened cock, stroking it. The pleasure of that on top of the ache and terror of being taken was confusing, muddling the edges of everything. Ev almost didn't want to enjoy it. It would have been easier to only hurt and feel so utterly emasculated.

When he did get hard, and began to react to the tugging, despite the unceasing movement and ache in his ass, Ev broke a little, pleading, "I'm sorry. Oh fuck, I'm sorry!"

Adam leaned down, folding his body against Ev's, and kissed his neck. "Shhh… you're okay. I've got you. You feel so fucking good."

His thrusts grew shallower, harder, and Adam seemed to come with a heavy groan. He licked and teased the skin of Ev's neck as he kept stroking him closer to climax, wrapping an arm around Ev's chest as Ev came with a swallowed moan and a hard shudder.

"Oh god. Oh god, I'm fucked," Ev cried, delirious.

"Not the way I think you imply," Adam said. He pulled out, making Ev yelp. Rolling Ev to his side, Adam unfastened the restraints on his wrists and massaged the feeling back into his arms. As Ev lay there, breathing unevenly, feeling exhausted and sore, Adam worked to clean him off. He made one side of the bed with new sheets, then helped Ev roll over to do the other side. When Adam climbed back into bed, he asked, "How are you? You okay?"

Ev had no response other than to shift closer to Adam, reaching out for him. After laying a hand on Adam's arm, Ev felt Adam draw him in, folding him in an embrace.

"Sleep a while."

In seconds, Ev was unconscious.

Chapter 10

The Things We Don't Talk About

Sometime after the sun came up, Ev lay in bed, awake. He was on his left side, with Adam tucked up behind him, one arm slung around Ev's waist. It was nice to not be larger than his lover for once, to be the one taken care of instead.

There were ramifications to what he'd done, letting Adam fuck him. Ev wasn't sure how to live with them. It made him want to curl down further under the sheet and hide from the world and his choices as long as he could. The more he thought about it, the more his body tensed.

"Talk to me," Adam said sleepily against the back of Ev's neck.

"It's nothing. I'm fine. Go back to sleep. You've gotta be tired."

"*I've* gotta be tired?" He kissed beside Ev's spine, then said, "I'm listening if you're ready to talk."

Ev sighed. "Let's just... sleep a little more. Okay?"

"Is this regret for what we did last night?"

"No, of course not," Ev replied out of instinct to placate rather than truth.

"Because it's okay to feel overwhelmed, if you do. Talking through it will help."

"I don't regret it. I mean, I wouldn't undo it, I just don't know what it means."

"What it means regarding your identity? We've been through this. It doesn't have to mean anything. It can just be enjoyable."

"No, that's not..."

"Then what? Tell me. I'm listening."

"There's just... I don't know. I left things behind in Kansas. Bad things. I really wanted them to stay there. I never wanted to face..."

"Face what?"

Ev let out a breath, tried to calm down. Already, his head was spinning, his blood pumping. It made him overheated and squirmy. "You don't have to do this, Adam. It's not your problem. You don't have to fix this. I'll deal with it."

"I can't help if I don't understand what's hurting you."

Ev blew out a breath. "I don't..."

"Don't what?"

"Don't know how to talk about this. I've never talked about it. Ever. I promised I wouldn't. I—"

Adam pulled at Ev's shoulder, rolling him onto his back and staring down at him. "Who told you not to talk about it?"

Ev closed his eyes.

"Come on. There's no one else here. You're an adult now. Whoever pressured you as a kid to keep quiet does not have the leverage they once did."

"I don't know what to say."

"Start at the beginning. Or tell me the basics."

"The basics." Ev echoed. He tried to stop thinking about it, and focus on Adam instead. The scent and feel of his skin against Ev's was comforting, stoking Ev's desire to touch and get close, despite his fear. He rolled his thumb over Adam's nipple, feeling its softness. "My cousin. His parents. Chaos. Nightmare."

Adam watched him, waiting.

"I was... twelve." Adam frowned severely. Ev added, "He was thirteen. We were..."

"Come on. Keep going."

Ev paused, wondering if he was really going to say it out loud for once. His heart pounded. Adam caressed Ev's chest. "We were getting changed into bathing suits to go in the sprinkler in his back yard. He..."

The words wouldn't come. There had been so much effort put into not talking about it, to overcome, that it felt impossible. Adam folded his hand over Ev's where it laid on his chest.

"Did he hurt you?" Adam asked, sounding angry.

"No," Ev blurted. "It wasn't his fault. No matter what his parents say. It was just... touching. He touched me. Pulled on my dick. Laughed about it, then did it again. I knocked his hand away, told him to knock it off, mainly because it was making me hard. But he gave me a funny look and said, 'Did you like it?' and touched my balls with his fingertips, really lightly. We were right next to his bed, and my knees felt shaky, so I sat down. He sat next to me and pulled on my dick again, slowly. He told me to lie down, so I did and he just... kept doing it."

"Let me guess. They found you. His parents."

"Yeah," Ev brushed the curls of Adam's chest hair. "His mom, my aunt, walked in on us and screamed. She yanked him off of me and hit him across the face really hard. She handed him off to his dad. My uncle dragged him away by the arm and James looked so terrified. My aunt wrapped me in a blanket and called my parents to come get me. It was..."

"Did they punish you?"

"No," Ev said, feeling old hurt at the memory. "But James... he was sent to this religious camp called The Pathway to Manhood. It was conversion therapy, run through our church. They called it a sleep-away camp for troubled youth who've stepped off of the path to manhood. They help you find where you've strayed off of the path so you can get back on it again."

"Brainwashing," Adam groaned. "I've heard of those places but never... Fuck."

"I was terrified. I didn't want them to take me too, so I said I was sorry, that I didn't want him to do it, which was a lie. It worked. They didn't send me with him. They thought it was all his fault. By the time he got back, and I saw how different he was, it was too late to change my story and take the pressure off of him. They thought I was just saying it for James' sake, not because it was the truth."

"How was he different?"

"Stick thin, blank stare, creepy fake smile, always talking about scripture all the time. He looked miserable, like he was dying inside but wouldn't accept it or see it. And nothing I said made any difference, but it was up to me to act like I never liked boys or liked the way James had touched me, or else the same thing would probably happen to me. People in our school would talk about that place and the ways they'd hurt the kids there. They'd torture them with blocks of ice or heated coils or electricity, teaching them to associate gay sex with pain and fear. I don't know if they really did that stuff, or if it was just rumor, but still... Just the thought of that was convincing enough. I just... did what they expected me to. I was a coward."

"No, that's survival, not cowardice," Adam assured him. "Seeing adults you'd believed you could trust betray James that way? Criminalizing natural behavior? Of course you had to protect yourself. I'm just glad you did. But Evelyn, what you must have gone through, growing up like that, being so scared all of the time just to be yourself."

"I got so good at denying that stuff that as soon as I felt any attraction to someone I'd push the feeling down, deny it, and go work out instead. I got really good at lying to myself. Soon, I never believed my own feelings were real. At least things made some sort of sense again, for a while. But once I got to senior year..."

"What? What happened?"

A sinking feeling drew him down, away from the confession.

"I never told anyone this. I mean, people knew about James, after, but... No one... No one knew about this."

"What didn't they know?"

"I was doing okay. I'd figured out how to cope. It was fine. It could have just gone on that way. I was turning into exactly the sort of obedient robot my dad tried to make me into." Ev ran a hand over his face, hiding his eyes. He stopped talking. His jaw felt welded shut. His pulse throbbed in his temples."I don't know how to explain it so it doesn't sound bad."

"I would never judge you for being hurt. Just tell me what happened. Someone else was involved, right? Who was it?"

"My coach. Football coach."

"Oh Jesus, seriously? What did he do to you?"

"No, it..." he shifted out from under Adam, sat up instead and drew the sheet over his lap.

"What did he do to you? Did he touch you?" Adam demanded.

For a few minutes, Ev breathed through the burning in his chest, hating himself.

"Adam, I..."

"Did he touch you, Evelyn?"

"It's not just about that, okay?"

"Then please tell me. Help me understand. Start at the beginning. How did it happen?"

"I, um... I had this tendency to get dressed really slowly because I noticed one of the other guys on the team liked to look at my dick when I got dressed in the locker room. I didn't really think about it, I just did it. I lingered. Put on a show. The others would clear out, except for us and we wouldn't say anything. It would just... happen. He'd look. I'd stand there, straightening my stuff, maybe touching myself a little. Coach. He, uh... he noticed." Adam had a look on his face like he was ready to tear someone's head off. Ev struggled to believe Adam cared enough to get that upset on his behalf.

"What did he do to you?" Adam demanded furiously.

Ev rubbed both hands over his face, groaning. He didn't want to say it. Saying it was bound to make it even more impossible to pretend it away. But maybe that was the whole point.

"Did he rape you?"

"No."

"But he did touch you?"

"It didn't... it didn't start like that. He would tell John to get lost, get out of the locker room, so of course John would be out of there in a second, afraid Coach noticed what he'd been looking at. Once it was just the two of us, if it was an after school practice..." Ev felt like he was going to puke.

"Keep going. You're doing great. Just get it out. If it was after school, he'd..."

"Get really angry, shout at me to do thirty push-ups while I was still standing there naked. So I'd drop to the floor and start doing 'em. But he'd walk around me, watching. He'd kick my feet apart, more and more, with the toe of his sneaker as I was doing the push-ups. Once I finished and stood up again, he'd shout for me to do thirty jumping jacks and—"

83

He started having trouble breathing. Panting, he felt Adam squeeze his hand and hold on.

"And he'd look down at my crotch with this smile on his face the whole time, and it would hurt. My dick would slap against my leg, my pelvis. He'd shout for me to go faster, and laugh. I'd finish and cup myself, but he'd yell at me to do it again. Thirty more jumping jacks. I mean, it happened a bunch of times. I could have tried to get out of there faster, to avoid him, but it was the only thing I had to make me feel like that part of me existed, being in there with John like that."

"When did that fucker touch you, Evelyn?"

"It only happened once. I pulled a muscle in my groin, tried to hide it, but he got me to admit it. He took me in this room, had me lay down on a table, and told me to pull my shorts down. I was scared of him, of what he could do to me if he told my dad anything about what I was. He belonged to my church. He knew people who could make my life hell. So I did it. I pulled down my shorts. Then he told me to pull my underwear down too. I got 'em down a little, but he pulled them down farther, to my knees. He started to massage my pulled muscle, the inside of my thigh and that whole area. The weird thing was, it helped. It made the muscle cramp ease."

The more he explained, the faster the words came out. He let them flow, wanting to be rid of them. "But with his left hand, he cupped my... genitals... and was squeezing them in little pulses, my balls and my dick. He rubbed my shaft with his thumb. It, uh... made me hard. So he pulled my shorts and boxers off completely and spread my legs. He went back to massaging the inside of my thigh while he stroked my dick. I was freaking out, making... noises. Shaking. The closer I got to coming, the more he rubbed into my ass crack. And he... stuck his thumb into me. I was shocked. Frozen. He kept stroking until I came, then licked the come off of me. It was disgusting. *I* felt disgusting. I just wanted him to stop. But before he took his thumb out, he made me promise not to tell anyone if I didn't want my parents and my minister to find out I was a faggot. Once I promised, he stopped, and I was glad, and it was over. I wanted it to be over."

Adam was breathing hard. He pulled Ev into a firm hug, didn't let go. He stroked Ev's hair and sounded like he was trying to calm down. Feeling Adam's upset helped Ev stop shaking and breathe more normally.

"I didn't want them to know. I didn't want to be taken away like James."

"God, I'm sorry, Evelyn. I'm so sorry you went through that. What a damn nightmare. You were already isolated, afraid. Your coach was supposed to protect you, be a confidant, not blackmail you into silence after...." He blew out a breath. "No wonder you're having a difficult time with all of this, and feel so confused. Thank you for telling me and for deciding to trust me. I know it wasn't easy. Please know that you deserve much better than you've gotten."

"I've turned into exactly what they warned me not to be. I can't go back there now."

"Why would you want to?" Adam lamented. He released Ev from the hug. Ev sat back and ran his fingers through some of the red-gold hair on Adam's leg.

"They're my family. They didn't always hurt me. They just didn't know me. That's why I needed to get away, why I came here for school. For so long I wondered if I was... gay, or bi, whatever... because I liked parts of what happened. But it wasn't until I got here and got some perspective on it that I realized maybe I wasn't at all. Like you've been trying to tell me, just because you let someone touch you or jerk you off doesn't make you gay."

"Is that the conclusion you're coming to?"

"Adam, I'm sitting here naked with the guy I just had sex with. I don't know. It's different with you."

Adam's phone began buzzing on the far nightstand.

"I'm sorry, just give me one moment. We're not finished with this."

Ev nodded.

Adam got up, and went to see what it was. Phone in hand, tapping at the screen, he gave nothing away.

"Damn." He set the phone back down.

"What?"

Adam ran the side of his finger over his lip in a thoughtful gesture. "Take a quick shower, then put on some underwear and the robe."

"Why?" he laughed it off, though an uneasy tickle of warning squirmed in his belly.

"Because no one sees you nude but me. Someone's on their way up here."

"Who?"

"My grandfather."

"Oh. Crap." Ev stood, looking around the room and down at himself. "Shouldn't I just get dressed completely?"

"I'll tell him you're my model, which you are. The robe would make the most sense in that context."

"Adam, I..." he floundered a little. "I have classes today. And work. I don't want to go, but I have to."

"What time do you have to be there?"

"Ten."

"All right." Adam strode to the bathroom. Ev followed. Inside, Adam turned on the water in the massive walk-in shower and began washing himself off, running a bar of soap all over his tan body. Ev both needed to watch that and couldn't watch because of how much it made him want to go to Adam, or crawl back in bed with him. "We'll figure it out," Adam called from under the water's spray. "It's still early." He rinsed himself off, blew out a spray of water and stood there, glistening and gorgeous. Walking out of the shower, he grabbed a towel and dried his face. "All yours."

"Yeah, seems so," Ev said under his breath with awe.

Chapter 11

When Care is Taken

When Ev emerged from the bedroom, freshly showered, in his robe and boxers, he heard voices before he saw anyone. The place was so damned big, the echoes off all of the glass and wood carried far. He rounded a corner and saw Adam speaking to a short, elderly man with a full head of white hair and a beard, dressed in a woolen gray suit. A younger man in a black suit stood by the apartment door, his hands folded in front of him like he was awaiting orders.

"Ah, here he is. Granda, this is Evelyn. Evelyn, this is Damhan Ciar."

"Nice to meet you, sir," Ev said. He extended a hand and it was shaken right away with a strong grip. Damhan looked him over warily for a moment before letting go.

"He's wearing your robe," Damhan noticed with a sideways glance to his grandson.

"Yes, he's a friend who's modeling for me."

"It's seven in the morning."

"We, uh, had a late night," Ev explained. "Adam was nice enough to let me stay over."

"It's not like I don't have the space. Granda, I was about to make some food to get the day started. Are you hungry?"

"No, boy, I ate hours ago, but thank you."

Ev could see the resemblance between them, in the shape of their noses, the quirk of their mouths. All of Damhan's hair was white, but Ev could imagine it had once been red as well.

Damhan held out a folder to Adam that had been tucked under his arm. "Here. Take these. Get them back to me when you can and I'll get them over to the estate lawyers."

"I can drop them off myself if it's easier," Adam offered.

Damhan flapped a hand. "You hate those bastards. Let me do it. Gives me something to do."

"If you say so." With a glance to Ev, Adam asked, "What do you say? Omelet? Coffee?"

"Sure. Thanks."

"After we eat, I'll drive you back to school."

"I can take the bus. It's fine. You're busy."

"No. I'll drive you."

Damhan laughed a little, leaning against the kitchen counter.

"Doesna' like the bus," Damhan commented.

"Neither should you," Adam frowned.

"Evelyn, has my grandson been nice to you?" Damhan asked with what sounded like genuine interest, walking a few steps closer as Ev sat on one of the stools. "He takes after his father, more often than not. Thinks he knows better than everyone else."

"He's been nice," Ev admitted, choosing his words with care.

"Good. I hope so."

"Were you also a lawyer, sir?"

"Me?" he laughed. "Oh no. My wife was."

"Granda was a surgeon."

"For too many years. Retired now, even from the board of directors."

Damhan took the stool next to Ev, folding his hands on the granite counter.

"So, boy, he must be a special one to know you come from lawyers. You didn't even tell Italo that much, and you dated him for nigh on two years."

"Fuck," Ev breathed with barely any sound, running a hand over his mouth.

"He is," Adam grinned, pouring a bowl full of whipped eggs into the skillet. "And he's not Italo."

"Oh, I can see that. He's got more than two brain cells to rub together, doesn't he? And manners."

"I was going through a phase," Adam sighed, chopping vegetables on the cutting board. "Can you tell me you didn't date a few girls in your younger days for stupid reasons?"

"Oh yes," Damhan agreed.

"Plus, some people are worth being honest with." Adam glanced up at Ev, who felt some of his panic lessen.

"And what does your family do, Evelyn?"

"Politics," Adam said.

"Oh, I'm sorry to hear that. And I did ask him, by the way. Not you," he scolded Adam. "Let him answer his own questions, for Christ's sake. Ya bully."

Ev laughed.

"So, Evelyn," Damhan said with heavy emphasis on the name, turning to address Ev directly and ignoring Adam's smirk. "Do you plan to also go into politics?"

"God, no," Ev answered, then tried to backpedal, some of his old instincts kicking in from when reporters would lob questions at him. "Sorry. I mean to say that my interests lie in other areas. I'm studying for my degree in business. I'm going to, um," he chewed his lip, bowed his head. "Try to open my own flower shop or landscaping company or something."

"Ahh. I see." Ev felt a blush rising and wished he could get out of there. "A romantic then, are you? No wonder my grandson likes you. Dreams *and* ambition. Oh, but this bashfulness will never do. He'll eat you alive."

"What are you trying to do to me, here?" Adam complained, though Ev was amused.

"Nothing, nothing. I'll leave you two some peace before you start your day." Damhan edged off the stool with a groan. Adam turned off the burner and set the skillet with the eggs aside. Wiping off his hands, he went to show Damhan out.

"Stay," Adam told him. "You just got here."

"I'll make up my own mind, thank you." He gave Adam's shoulder an affectionate squeeze. "Come out to the house sometime. Bring Evelyn."

"I'll think about it," Adam said. "Can I just ask… don't mention Evelyn to anyone. He's still finding his way and his privacy is important."

"Is that because of the politicians?"

"Mm. Partly."

Damhan nodded. "Good to meet you, son," he told Evelyn.

"You too, sir."

"And you," he pointed a finger at Adam. "Be nice."

"I'm always nice," Adam replied.

"Ha!" Damhan turned to the elegantly attired and patient man waiting by the door. "Shall we, Craig?"

"Yes, sir. Ready when you are."

Craig opened the door and held it. Damhan gave Adam a kiss on the cheek and stepped out into the hall. Once they'd gone, Adam went back to cooking, sliding the first omelet onto a plate and handing it to Ev. The coffee had been brewing, so Ev walked around to fill a mug.

"I'm sorry about that," Adam said, looking concerned as he drew Ev in by a hand wrapped around his waist. "I know you didn't want anyone involved in this. He just knows me too well. He is discreet, though. He won't tell a soul. I'll make it up to you, and we'll be more careful."

"No, it's okay. It went well. In a weird way it feels more real now, with someone else knowing. He's very kind."

"He is," Adam nodded. He caught Ev's mouth in a kiss that turned heated but stayed slow.

"Eggs'll burn," Ev murmured.

"Fuck," Adam groaned, letting Ev go after another moment and turning back to the stove.

Smiling despite himself, Ev poured coffee into a mug. "What house did he mean?"

Adam added vegetables to the eggs in the skillet. "His estate. It's an hour or so out of town, up north. He never really forgave me for selling my parents' properties off, so he's assured me I'm going to inherit his home, but with a stipulation that I can't sell it off."

"Wow. Sounds pretty generous to me," Ev said, dreaming of being handed a whole estate for nothing but a promise.

Adam gave him a steady look. "I'd refuse the estate entirely if it wouldn't go to my cousin instead if I did. She'd trash the place and not give a shit." He pushed his omelet onto a plate. "I'd much rather have money to live comfortably on than the responsibility of maintaining a sprawling piece of real estate I have absolutely no use for. How would you feel if your parents willed you their home in Kansas?"

"Mm. Good point." Ev sat with his coffee and dug into his eggs. Adam stood in front of him, eating while standing. "Sit with me. You always eat on your feet. Relax a little."

"But I have a nicer view this way."

Ev turned to look behind him at the sparkling morning vista of the waking city.

"Not that. I don't give a shit about the windows right now."

Ev didn't know what to say, so he just ate. "I feel bad you keep cooking for me and buying me food. I need to cook for you later or something."

"So does that mean you'll stay here again tonight?"

Catching Adam's gaze over the edge of his mug as he drank some of his own freshly poured coffee, Ev shrugged. "Yeah."

"I haven't scared you off?"

Shaking his head, Ev thought of the weekly phone call he owed his mother, the explanation he'd have to give Leo, and every other way Adam didn't fit into his life.

"They're not going to understand this. I don't even understand this," Ev admitted.

"Don't freak yourself out with the big picture. Do you want to stay here tonight?"

"Yeah."

"Decisiveness. I like it. Do you need pocket money? Have any bills that are due?"

There was a credit card payment he needed to make, to begin to pay off his books. But he couldn't take Adam's money. The more Ev stalled in answering, the fiercer Adam seemed to get. He braced both hands on the counter and leaned forward. "I owe you for the modeling work."

"It's not work."

"It is. You work for me instead of the art department, because I require your time."

"I can't work for you and sleep with you."

"Look at me." His omelet mostly eaten and his coffee halfway drank, Ev set down his fork and mug and sat back. Raising his gaze to Adam's face, he braced himself. Blue eyes blazing, Adam said, "This isn't a request. I need you in order to complete my work. I need your time and your body, here. I am compensating you for that, so bring me your bills and I will pay them."

"You can't do that."

"You also need to provide me, today, with your schedule; listing all of the time you will need to spend at the school, so I can anticipate when you'll need rides and when I will have you for myself."

Swallowing hard, setting his jaw, body tensed, Ev had no concept of how to argue with such directness. He felt he needed to, somehow.

Adam asked, "Do you remember a few hours back when I was inside you in various ways? That was you agreeing to let me take care of you. I *will* take care of you, Evelyn. I'm fucking serious about this."

Ev surrendered with a meek, "Okay."

"Now would be a good time for those manners of yours. Say, 'Yes, sir. Thank you.'"

"Yes, sir. Thank you," Evelyn managed, breathing harder than he should have needed to.

"Bring me your bills and your schedule. Have them ready when I pick you up. What time should I be there?"

"Six."

Adam glanced at the clock on the wall, then began to come around the kitchen island and right for Ev. He turned Ev's stool around, hooked a hand under his jaw to tilt his face up and yanked open the robe with his free hand.

"You're flushed. Either that means you're angry, or..." His hand folded around Ev's dick through his boxers. It was completely hard. Another yank pulled Ev's cock out of his underwear. Adam grabbed a bottle of cooking oil from behind the counter's edge and drizzled some on his palm. "Clasp your hands tightly behind your back."

"Please..."

"Do it."

Ev clasped his hands behind his lower back. Adam nudged Ev's knees apart and wrapped his dick in the oil-slicked hand. Then he began jacking him hard and fast, the squelching of the oil obscenely loud as it eased the slide of Adam's fist.

Ev gave a hard shudder, gasping wildly. Adam tugged his chin even more upright. "Good. Let me hear you."

With a desperate cry, Ev helplessly undulated into the rapid, squeezing tugs.

"No, be still."

Gritting his teeth, eyes rolling up, Ev tried to not thrust.

"Open. Now."

Adam's hand lingered on the head of Ev's cock, squeezing, rubbing. Obeying, Ev opened his lips, unclenched his jaw. Adam's thumb stroked Ev's lower lip. An aching whimper broke free.

"Better," Adam coaxed. But Ev couldn't stay still, and felt he should push down his need to yell. He tried, though, to do as Adam commanded. Adam's fist slid down Ev's shaft to his root, caressed over his balls, twisted back up the shaft and squeezed over his head. The sounds Ev made grew more primal. The thumb at his lip was too tempting, so Ev licked it. Adam caressed over Ev's tongue, trapping it momentarily. Ev whimpering again, pleading. Adam let go to rub up Ev's stomach to his chest, twisting a nipple, then reaching once again for his dick after he'd grunted in reaction.

Slower, stroking, he asked, "Are you mine?"

"Oh fuck. Yes."

"Mine to care for? You'll obey me?"

"Yes. Fuck. Please." With an embarrassing, soft whimper, he came, shooting over Adam's fist. The hand slipped through the hot fluid, stroking him through it. Ev suckled Adam's thumb, rocking subtly into his hand.

The thumb pulled out, his chin was forced up.

"Say thank you. Manners."

He panted, still shaking, the grip of one hand on the other the only thing keeping him together. Adam's touch feathered over Ev's softening cock. "Thank you, sir," Ev had barely uttered when Adam's mouth was on him and tongue in him. Ev opened wide, moaning, kissing Adam back with more need than he knew how to process or express in any other way.

Chapter 12

The Managing of Secrets

The encounter with Adam's grandfather acted as an awakening of sorts for Ev. There had been no judgment or pressure in it, and Damhan's attempts to defend Ev from Adam's more forceful personality quirks warmed Ev even further to new possibilities.

Everything up to that point in Ev's experience, tied to affection or sexual physical interactions with other men, had been tainted with layers of pressure to feel ashamed or fearful of his natural reactions. But he'd tried to leave all of that behind by moving away and working toward his future, hadn't he? What good would it do to keep following those same trails and keep giving in to impulses he knew came from hateful people? Just because members of his family or community wouldn't approve of what he was doing, it didn't mean everyone would feel that way. If they did, maybe it would just help him see who was worth his time and who wasn't.

When Adam pulled the Mustang up to the side of the road close to the administration building where he was due for a short shift of work, Ev hesitated before getting out. The engine idled; people on the sidewalks stared at the vibrant, impressive vehicle—as well as the people inside it. Someone from the school office waved when they noticed Ev. He waved back.

"Where should I pick you up at six?" Adam asked.

Ev pointed to a tall brick building across the open school square, on a road perpendicular to the one they were on. "I'll be over there. Call me if you don't see me and I'll track you down."

"Okay. I'll be thinking about you."

"Me too."

Adam wasn't leaning in or touching Ev at all. Part of Ev appreciated the courtesy of not letting on to the true nature of their relationship—if you could call it that yet. But part of him felt like that denial of reality was only allowing his oppressors to win all over again. His aunt and uncle, his own parents, his coach and so many others were there in spirit, gloating. Maybe he could cross lines in private, but he'd never do so in public.

Or so they thought.

Ev reached for Adam's hand and folded his own hand into it. Adam waited, wearing his curiosity clearly on his face.

"I don't understand all of this, but I do know this is better for me than where I've been."

Adam didn't reply, he just watched, hearing every word and translating every subtle cue of body language as Ev knew he could.

With a sigh and a slight frown, Ev leaned over the center console in the car. Adam met him halfway, after a pause, but it was Ev that made contact, giving Adam a light, chaste kiss.

"Thank you," he murmured against Adam's lips. "See you later."

"I'll be here. Call if you need anything." Adam told him with a brief caress of Ev's jaw.

Then he was able to move and let go. He opened the door and got out with a wave back at Adam.

Adam stayed parked by the curb until Ev walked out of sight. Though Ev could tell people had seen what he'd done, he didn't mind one bit.

It wasn't until after his Marketing Management class that Ev finally ran into Leo, whom he sometimes crossed paths with on the way to the cafeteria for dinner on Thursdays. Of course on that Thursday, Ev wasn't headed to the dorm's eatery, but to meet Adam.

Messages had accumulated on Ev's phone. He'd skimmed but not replied to them, since he was trying to deal with priorities first and let everything else slide. Once he made eye contact with Leo, he knew he couldn't avoid him, but he had no idea what to say.

"What the hell, man? Where you been? Just because you're staying with your cousin, you can't answer a text?" Leo said with irritation, hiking his bag higher on his shoulder.

Ev scanned his memory of Leo's messages, only recalling something about a toothpaste emergency. Ev had borrowed Leo's and Leo couldn't find where Ev had left the tube.

"Sorry. I've had my hands full," Ev told him, running a hand through the back of his hair. They stood near the building's exit, with the sidewalks, street, and campus square beyond in purplish twilight.

"You're coming back to the room now, though, aren't you?"

"I, uh..."

Adam had arrived. Ev spotted the blue car first, the redhead in sunglasses standing beside it second.

"I can't," Ev finished.

"What do you mean, you can't? It's your room! You can't avoid it forever. What's going on with you this week anyway?"

"I've just gotten wrapped up in this thing, and with work and school on top of it to balance out, I just don't have time to—"

"To what? What thing?"

"It doesn't matter," Ev sighed, wanting to be out the doors and away from Leo's prying.

"Obviously it does, or you wouldn't be bailing on everyone like this. You also forgot you'd asked Marina over to study for Thornton's class. She showed up at the room last night and was pissed you ditched her."

"Ah, shit. I forgot."

"No shit you forgot. When are you coming back to the room?"

"I don't know." Ev kept sneaking glances at Adam through the glass doors, feeling pulled in two directions.

"But you're coming to the game tomorrow. You have to."

"Dude, just... lay off. You're worse than my ex-girlfriend. I made a commitment to someone. A teacher. I have to follow through. It's fucking up my schedule, so when I have things figured out, I'll let you know. Okay?" The more he said, the angrier he felt.

It was too similar to the ways his parents always pestered him to show up at rallies and fundraising events, no matter what else Ev had going on. Something about the way they'd remind him about his commitments always implied how much he'd be disappointing them if he didn't do exactly what they wanted. But they wouldn't just come out and tell him to be there or else A, B, or C would happen to him. They'd just nag him and emotionally blackmail him into complicity. It wasn't, "Ev, we really need you to be at town hall by eight p.m. for the press conference." It was, "The town hall press conference is at eight. You know what your father would think if you were late. It's your job to be there too."

Pulling out of the memory, he took his annoyance with him.

"It's really fucking stressful and you're not helping me right now," he yelled. Conversations stopped around them as they drew attention.

"Whoa. Chill out," Leo told him, raising his hands.

"No. What do you expect me to do, Leo? I can't be everywhere and do everything."

"If you're so stressed out, then bail," Leo said quietly, like he was trying to bait Ev into lowering his voice too, and lessen their mutual embarrassment. They were drawing a small crowd.

"I'm not bailing on this. It's important to me."

He hadn't realized that was true until the words were out of his mouth. Once they were, he stopped short and let it sink in. He'd heard Adam insist what was happening between them was important, but Ev hadn't really believed it until he said it himself to someone who wasn't involved.

"Okay," Leo agreed. "I get it. Whatever this project is means a lot. I'll lay off. You want to talk about it?" He took Ev by the arm and led him out of the middle of the entryway and over into a nook leading to a couple of classrooms' doors. The crowd began to disperse.

"Maybe. But he's waiting for me. I have to go."

"Who's waiting for you? The teacher?"

"Yes."

"Does he have something over you? Are you failing a class or something? Why are you so on edge about this?"

Ev shifted his weight from foot to foot and took a moment to readjust his bag's strap on his shoulder.

"Because it's fucking with my head and making me deal with the shit that made me get the hell out of Kansas in the first place. I guess you can't always run away from your problems."

"I hear that."

There was a pause then—a lull in the conversation where Ev could have told Leo what was going on, or at least part of it. He let it slip by and said instead, "I'll be stopping by the room tomorrow morning. We can get into this more then, okay? I've really gotta go."

"All right. Take it easy, Ev."

"You too."

Leo clasped Ev's hand and bumped shoulders with him, then gave him a pat on the back to send him on his way.

Pushing out through the building's glass doors, Ev was glad for the blast of cool, fresh air. He was smiling even before he'd made it down the steps, hurrying over to Adam at a slow jog.

"Hey," Ev said in greeting, biting at his lip to lessen his huge grin. Adam touched Ev's arm, as if to lead him toward the passenger door. Following instinct, Ev leaned in and kissed Adam on the cheek.

"Been a long fucking day without you, brown eyes," Adam said, his cheeks dimpling though he wasn't overtly smiling.

Ev let Adam guide him into the Mustang and said, "Let's get out of here."

"My pleasure."

As they drove away, Ev glimpsed Leo out on the sidewalk, watching the Mustang with a blank, shocked face.

Chapter 13

Picture of Vulnerability

"Call me crazy, but you actually seem eager to do this."

"You're crazy," Ev said without any ability to stop grinning like an idiot. There was a lot he'd have to deal with eventually, but for the rest of the night, it would just be him and Adam. Ev felt strangely high just thinking about it.

"So convincing."

"Thanks."

Ev slipped his boxers down, the last bit of clothing left on him. They were in the art studio. Several paintings in progress—all of them of Ev—were lined up on one wall. Daylight was fading fast but Adam hadn't turned on any lights in the room. When he picked up the camera, fiddling with the lens, Ev was ready.

"How do you want me?"

"Ooh, loaded question. Should I answer honestly?" Adam glanced up briefly, with the filthiest smile Ev had ever seen on a human being.

His curiosity piqued, Ev replied with a slow, "Maybe."

"Wet, hard, panting, fucked-loose, spreading yourself and begging me for more. Maybe with a thin trickle of come leaking from your pretty ass?"

"Holy fuck." Ev laughed, trying to play off his shock and sudden bashfulness.

"How do you want me?" Adam countered.

"Here. With me."

Adam's expression shifted, filling with a sweeter emotion. When he walked quickly up to Ev and caught his mouth in a slow kiss, Ev had to drop his gaze, then shut his eyes completely.

"I like your honesty," Ev told him.

"I like you."

"I guess you do, or else you wouldn't want to keep painting me."

"It's not about that."

"I know," Ev confessed, his voice barely loud enough to hear. "You take care of me."

"Damn fucking right, I do," Adam said just as softly, though the words were fierce. He kissed Ev's top lip and took tighter hold of Ev's jaw. Tilting his face up, Adam held it there, though Ev kept his eyes closed. Adam's thumb caressed along Ev's cheek. "Are you very sore?"

Ev shook his head.

"Good. After we take care of this, I'm going to take you again. You'll enjoy it more the second time. I'll let you decide whether it happens before or after dinner. I usually eat late, but if you're starving, tell me." Ev swallowed. Adam's finger trailed down the line of Ev's throat, following his bobbing Adam's apple. "I can't wait to be back inside you."

As Ev let out a shaky breath, Adam reached down between their bodies and wrapped his hand around Ev's swelling erection. Massaging it, Adam said, "Easy. Control your breathing. Try to slow it down. Did you bring what I asked for?"

Ev nodded, stammering, "It's... in my... my b-bag. My credit card bill and t-the... fuck... schedule."

"Good. Thank you. Get on the bed."

With relief, Ev moved forward, past Adam to the staging area with a tripod set up for the camera. The last fading light of day shone upon it with colors ranging from violet to burnt orange.

"I've something specific in mind. Get on your knees on the bed, here, then lean forward until your shoulders and face are flush with the bed. You'll need to arch your back quite a lot. Keep your hands spread on the bed, down by your shoulders. I want your expression to be soft. Imagine I'm inside you already. There's no pain, just a slow push and pull. You need more, don't want it to end."

Ev kept his eyes shut and imagined it. Softening his lips, slowing his breathing, he let everything fall away but the feel of Adam nearby. No one could hurt him or even get close to him there. He was safe.

The camera's shutter clicked near enough that he suspected Adam was doing close, cropped-in shots from up by Ev's head, which made it even easier to relax.

Minutes passed.

"I'd like to try something. I need a specific expression on your face. Something vulnerable."

"Okay. Like what?"

"You trust me?"

"Yeah. Of course."

He heard a snap of a plastic bottle cap, the squirt of liquid. A moment later, a finger twisted up into his ass. Brow creasing, lip quivering, Ev gasped. The camera's shutter clicked over and over again.

The finger pulled out with torturous slowness, then was replaced with something else—cool, firm, and narrow. It pushed a few inches into him and was left there.

Through barely opened eyes, Ev saw Adam walk around the bed, release and raise the camera from the tripod and continue photographing him. Goosebumps rose over Ev's skin. He clenched, then relaxed.

"Feels nice?" Adam asked from behind the lens.

"Yeah."

"I'm focusing on your mouth and your back. That's all. Tense the fingers of your left hand. Good."

"I shouldn't like this."

"Says who? Whatever voice in your head is telling you to feel bad, tell it to fuck off. It's not allowed in here."

Ev ached from being so hard, his cock dripping wet, his balls throbbing. Adam set the camera down and walked around behind Ev again. The object inside his ass moved a little, beginning to pump in and out shallowly. His arousal swelled more as he was stimulated in a wonderful new way.

"Can I sketch you? I won't be long. Tell me when you need some relief."

"I need some relief."

Adam laughed. "Nice try."

The object pulled out. Adam rubbed over Ev's hole. Moaning, Ev fought not to break the pose as Adam's finger slipped into him, pushing in deeply.

"Do you like that?"

Ev nodded, breathing harder.

"No pain?"

"No."

The finger withdrew. It was replaced again with the object.

Adam fetched his pad and pencil, then came to stand near Ev's head as he got to work.

"You know," he said with a conversational tone, the scratching of the pencil's lead over paper a tickle in Ev's ear. "If you were anyone else, I'd bring another guy in here to tongue your hole while I drew your mouth. The results would be gorgeous."

Ev opened his eyes, looked at Adam. The question must have been in his eyes, because Adam said, pointing his pencil at Ev, "No one fucking touches you, that's why."

"And because you don't share."

"That's right. You're learning."

For a long while, the only things that existed were the scratching of Adam's pencil and the wind whistling against the windows. Ev's erection had softened slightly thanks to deep breaths and attempts at relaxation, but the thing up his ass kept him from completely losing interest. When it felt like he'd been half-hard for an hour, he complained, "My balls are killing me."

"Would you like me to suck on them for you?" Adam asked as if he was asking what toppings Ev liked on his pizza.

Ev let out a heavy, shaky breath and swallowed back a pleading moan.

Setting down the pad of paper and pencil, Adam circled the bed.

Right away, Ev's heartbeat sped up. He heard the snap of plastic again, the squirt of fluid, the soft rustle of fabric. Then the object inside him tugged out of him inch by inch, rubbed up his crack, then pushed back inside even deeper.

"Roll onto your back. Lay lengthwise on the bed but keep your legs spread."

Nearly desperate, Ev obeyed. Once he was on his back, Adam climbed onto the bed as well, between Ev's legs.

"Draw your legs up. Grab under your knees and pull them back."

Ev groaned and did it. He could see the object poking out of his ass, couldn't look away.

Perhaps noticing the focus of Ev's interest, Adam took hold of the thing. He slowly pulled it out again. It was a small sex toy of some sort, slightly tapered with a handle on the end and light blue in color. It was shiny wet with lube. After it had been set on the bed, Adam reached for him, his hand pivoting at the wrist. His index and middle fingers touched Ev's opening. The fingertips parted his rim gently. Ev's cock twitched.

"How's that?"

Ev exhaled loudly, grunted and tilted his head back. He closed his eyes, focusing on the sensations.

"Answer."

"Good. It's good."

"And this?"

The fingers pushed past his tight outer ring, and were fed completely into him. A brief downward look showed Ev Adam's hand hugged up tightly to his ass. He clenched on the fingers and rocked his hips in a purely instinctive movement.

"Good." Ev rocked again, more intentionally, liking the way it made the fingers move inside him.

Adam leaned forward sharply, opening his mouth.

When he saw what he was about to do, Ev begged, "Adam, please…"

Steadying Ev's sac with his free hand, Adam took one of Ev's balls into his mouth and tongued it before sucking. With a rough cry, Ev felt fluid drip from his cock and he rocked steadily against the fingers.

Adam let Ev's sac slip from his lips, then opened wide, changed his angle and took Ev's entire cock into his mouth instead.

"No, fuck," Ev growled, grinding on the fingers, then whimpered as they nudged something incredibly sensitive inside him. He realized it hadn't been accidental as Adam did it again. While Ev writhed at the bombardment, Adam sucked him hard and fingered that spot inside at a steady pace. "A-adam. Adam, fuck..."

Ev's orgasm hit him hard, his head spinning and his body convulsing. The fingers prodded that sensitive spot and Adam sucked him through it. He'd barely caught his breath or felt steady enough to make the room stop spinning when he saw Adam was now kneeling closely to Ev's body, his cock in hand and angled down to enter him.

Panting, Ev stared at the sight of Adam stretching Ev's hole with his spread fingers, and sliding his flushed red cock-head between them right before removing them. He felt his rim hugging the blunt, rounded head, saw the way it stretched him out, the pink of his hole against the darker tint of Adam's wet, stiff dick.

With low, gruff little grunts, his lip quivering, Ev watched Adam feed his cock into that little hole. The pressure was less intense than the night before, the pain almost non-existent. Ev almost wanted it to hurt more and found himself trying to push down onto Adam to make it happen. So Adam grabbed hold of Ev under his thighs, holding him down as he was entered.

"Oh god. Oh god," Ev moaned. He bit down hard on his lip, wincing as Adam stuffed him full.

As soon as Ev had a second to savor the strange and wonderful fullness, Adam tugged back, pushing in and riding him at a gentle pace. A glance up at Adam's face showed he was glowing with a slight sheen of sweat, his red hair fallen into his dangerous, keenly intelligent eyes, his rosy, plump-lipped mouth shaped around eager gasps. Seeming blissful, Adam held Ev down harder, rode him even slower. Ev trembled on each withdrawal, grunted on each inward push.

When Adam gave Ev his whole length and held there a moment, Ev grabbed hold of Adam's ass, pulling him in and trying to keep him there.

"Who's in charge here?" Adam teased. "Raise your arms above your head."

Ev raised them. Adam spread him wider, pulled out almost completely, then sank back in. Ev let out a wild cry, his back arching up off the bed. Adam's hands slid up Ev's legs to his knees, then his ankles. Gripping them and keeping Ev spread in a wide V, Adam resumed riding him at an easy pace.

Letting his head fall to the side, his chest rising and falling with heavy breaths, his whole body surging with energy and sizzling reactions to every touch and push, Ev soon relaxed completely.

Adam brought Ev's legs together, knees bent, both pressed back to his chest, then twisted to one side. Adam turned Ev's body without withdrawing, still thrusting. With Ev's legs drawn up as far as they'd go, twisted to the right, Adam leaned in and took him faster, pounding his hole. It drove the air from Ev's chest and he gulped for air, gasping softly with each rut.

Adam growled, grinding hard into him and holding there. His mouth worked, his movements more shallow.

"Fuck," Adam breathed, then chuckled, panting. He pulled out and Ev's breath hitched to feel it, the pop of Adam's crown passing through his rim. Two fingers pushed into Ev's throbbing opening, swiped around, then pulled out. A trickle of fluid dripped down Ev's butt cheek. When Adam lifted his fingers, Ev saw they were soaked with pearly come. Adam painted Ev's hole with it, concentrating as he made Ev his canvas instead of just his subject.

"Good. Stay just like that. Beautiful."

Adam climbed off the bed, went to get a bottle of water and took a swig. His eyes never left Ev's body, even when he toweled himself off and took another drink. Come continued to drip from him and his hole felt a little swollen, puckered up.

Coming back to the bed, Adam leaned in, kneeling on the edge to give Ev's ear a light nip. "Let me order dinner."

"I was going to cook."

"I realize that. Let me order in food instead tonight."

Ev mentally surrendered, then gave a nod. Adam shifted to lay behind Ev, wrapping an arm around his waist and palming his stomach. It was cozy, comfortable. Closing his eyes, Ev sighed and shifted back into the embrace. A kiss pressed to the back of his neck. A hand caressed over his thigh, drew up and rubbed in light circles over his wet hole. The kiss to his neck came again. Ev reached behind himself for a handful of Adam's red hair, soft as silk between his fingers.

Chapter 14

Puppydogs and Pushovers

"Who's Italo?"

"Hmm." Adam smiled fondly; his gaze lowered, then rose again. "He's hopeless. And my ex, but you know that."

"Tell me about him. Why didn't you tell him about your parents?"

Ev had a grilled chicken and apple salad, which he ate from the comfort of the chair beside Adam's easel. He'd showered and put on the robe. Adam painted while picking at his own salad now and then, but mostly ignoring it.

"Because I met him right after I lost them. He was my distraction. My escape. The last thing I wanted was to open myself up to him like that." Adam dipped his brush in a purplish red splotch of paint, then dragged off the excess. "Besides, Italo wouldn't have cared anyway. He was a musician. The only thing that mattered to him was his music, and getting regularly, viciously fucked."

Ev breathed out a laugh of disbelief.

"What?" Adam shrugged. "It was simple. Physical. I'd paint. He'd play. We'd screw, sleep, wake up and do it all again. For a long, long time."

Ev popped a big bite of salad and apple into his mouth. After he'd swallowed he said, "Weren't you... lonely?"

"He barely left my side," Adam said with a raised eyebrow. "Like a puppy."

"Yeah, but if you could never tell him anything important..."

Adam shrugged again. "It was all I could handle at the time. Eventually I got too frustrated to deal with him anymore and told him to get out. It never... progressed. Grew. It was always exactly what it had been. Nothing more. But it helped me deal with the loss. I'm grateful to him for that." He slid the paintbrush over the canvas, blocking in shapes. "What about you? With Mia? How much did she know?"

"Well, she probably knew about my cousin, at least in part. Almost everyone around me did. It was part of the 'recovery process' to admit to sins or crimes, so he told everyone his parents asked him to tell, and they told others. I was the victim in the scenario, so it was mostly awkward. She hinted that she knew, but we never really got into it."

"So she didn't have any idea you were not exactly like the other boys?"

"No. She didn't know about the locker room or my coach either."

"And were you lonely?"

"Maybe not lonely, but... not completely content. All of that was always between us, those secrets. It kept us apart."

"So, is it nice to have someone to talk to about it all now?"

"Yeah. I feel... lighter."

"Lighter with a tender ass."

Ev laughed. "Yeah, that too." He remembered, then, how Leo had gaped at the Mustang, pulling away earlier, and his laugher died. "Does everyone know you're gay?"

"Yes," Adam said with confidence. "My parents' money and liberal, progressive philosophies protected me. I came out when I was sixteen."

"And you never regretted it?"

"No. It's who I am. When people react negatively, I just avoid them in the future."

"I think Leo might have seen me kiss you. And drive off with you."

Adam's expression told Ev exactly what he thought about that. "So? A kiss doesn't mean anything. Especially one on the cheek."

"I kind of want to tell him."

"Tell him what?"

"That I'm with you."

"And that you submit to me in every conceivable way?"

"Well," Ev hesitated. "Maybe not tell him *that* much. But, I mean, is this more than a fling to you, or…?"

"Evelyn…" Adam let out a breath, licked his lip and hesitated." Maybe I'm crazy, but I've been trying to figure out the best way to ask you to move in with me, and not just because you're my muse. It's not bullshit when I say I intend to take care of you. Maybe I do enjoy the chance to save someone, not from a bus, but from leading a life that's not genuine or fulfilling. That's all I've been trying to do since they died. We don't have much time here, in these lives of ours, and what little time we do have shouldn't be spent in courtrooms defending the guilty or arguing over inane laws that have no major impact on the world. Nor should it be spent living the life someone else wants you to. We should live, create, express our souls and love one another, completely and dangerously. So, no, it's not a fling. I know we've only been together a few days, but can you really see me letting you walk out that door and not look back without some solid fucking proof that you don't want this? When you kiss me the way you do and smile at me like only you can?"

There was so much wrapped up in those words, so much of everything Ev craved—honesty, respect, and loyalty. It demanded an equally brave response. "I do care about you, Adam. That's why I feel like I want to tell Leo. To have something like this that means something to me… I can't hide it. I can't taint it like everything with James and Coach was tainted. If I hide this, it becomes something dirty, and sinful. Shameful. And maybe I need to prove to myself that it's not."

Adam came over, crouched by Ev's knees. He wrapped a hand behind Ev's calf and kissed his inner thigh. Ev ran a hand through Adam's hair.

"I'm not stupid to trust you like this, am I?" Ev wondered. He'd always been a pushover when it came to sex and emotion. Was this just more of the same, only on a much grander scale?

"No." Blue eyes flashed. "And I'll prove it to you."

Ev nodded, hoping it was true.

Soon, as most of Ev's salad was consumed, Adam said, "Time for some studying and class work, I think. You're welcome to do it wherever is most comfortable."

Ev stood and wandered to the door of the studio, gazing into the darkened open living area, with only the city's twinkling beyond to light it. It was a little eerie, all of that space with no one to fill it.

Adam seemed to notice the direction of Ev's stare and reached for his tablet. With a few taps of his fingers, he turned on most of the lamps and mood lighting in the apartment. The place glowed with warm light and looked much more welcoming. Another tap of Adam's finger brought up the stereo system, playing through speakers throughout the place. It was light jazz, nothing intrusive.

"Better?"

"Yeah. But, how do you live here all alone? Doesn't it drive you crazy?"

Adam's lips pressed together in a frown. "No. I was always an only child. My parents worked constantly. I never liked having servants, so I'd avoid them. But it's rarely empty here."

"What do you mean?"

"My friends like to spend time here while I work. I have the room and enjoy the company. But since I've had you here, I've asked them not to come."

"Who are they, if you don't mind my asking?"

"Glen's a friend from college. She'll stay here a few days at a time while visiting town. She has relatives here, but usually spends more time in the apartment than with them. And there's Oliver." Adam set down the tablet and wandered closer. "He's probably my closest friend. He's also a Dominant, like me, but he has a couple of submissives who are devoted to him. One is Jackson. He's a cardiologist with a wife and two young kids, as well as an understanding with the wife that he can submit to Oliver whenever he feels the need. The other is Rune, who used to be part of a motorcycle gang. Covered in tattoos, really bad-ass looking young guy. He was in an accident about a year and a half ago and lost his hearing. Oliver's really good with him. Rune says their time together is a big stress reliever. They'll come over and get into a big, wild scene. Oliver gets pretty hardcore with them. He's into some extreme kinks. Gives me some inspiration, though. Sometimes, Oliver likes to bring back others to play with his subs. He's got a knack for finding gay curious guys at the clubs or online. He'll have Rune and Jackson take their time with them while he watches and directs things. He'd love you, by the way, which is why I'm hesitant to have him over."

Adam fingered through Ev's hair. "Blond, brown eyes, hard body, muscular chest, large, dark nipples, huge, heavy cock and an irresistibly big set of balls." Adam palmed them, rolling them in a hand. "Your lips, the roundness of your ass. You're a very sexual creature, Evelyn. Powerful, vulnerable, and tempting all at once. It's why you inspire me so much."

It challenged Ev to just stand there, letting Adam play idly with his sac.

"If Olly saw you, his mind would go to filthy places instantly. He's headstrong, doesn't ever stop trying to get something he wants. In his mind, he'd have you strung up in chains with Rune alternately flogging and fucking you. He'd slide a sounding rod into here..." Adam caressed the slit in Ev's cock-head. "And have Jackson lick you until you screamed for release. But he's also into medical kinks. Maybe he'd just want to play doctor for a few hours... spread your ass open wide, take a look in all of your holes."

"Yeah, okay. Don't have him over," Ev said with a tense shiver in his deep voice.

Adam grinned, chuckled, and gave Ev a kiss. "No one touches you. Even with their eyes, if I don't think it's right or safe for you. Okay?"

"Okay. How did you meet him anyway?"

"We grew up together. Olly and his brother Neil were my best friends. Neil moved to New York City, working as an investigative journalist. Olly used to work in journalism also, but lately he's taken to day trading. Professionally, he's a real shark, no matter what he's doing. But he's very devoted and does have a softer side. Rune sees it more than most. Olly became an expert at sign language for him."

Ev couldn't imagine it, those men in Adam's space, doing those things while he painted. "And they really do all of that stuff here? In front of you?"

"They do like to show off. And they know I'm discreet."

"Do you ever participate?"

Adam exhaled, a restrained little smile curving his lips.

"It's okay. I know you're not a monk."

"I have. Yes. Rarely. I use protection. When there's a gorgeous man trussed and fucked loose and begging for it, it can be difficult to resist when my lovers are as few and far between as they've been."

"That's what I am?"

Adam nodded, giving Ev a lingering kiss that was all gentle brushes of lips and hot breath. Still, Adam rolled Ev's balls in his hand, making him hard.

"Go study," Adam whispered in command.

Ev groaned.

Chapter 15

Asking For It

Adam's apartment was much more conducive to studying than anywhere else Ev had been. In the dorm, Ev and Leo's friends constantly streamed in and out of the room. Wearing headphones only did so much. Unfortunately, it seemed most of the guys' priorities went in the order of beer, sports, then women. The only use for classwork was to keep them in school and near the parties. But Ev was determined to use college as a boost to get him away from his family and hometown. In order to do that, he needed to be successful and find a job right out of school—not an easy task with the way the job market had been.

When Ev wasn't trying to study in the dorm, he went to the library, but people were always present. They wandered around, whispering, acting as constant distractions when the textbook failed to hold his interest and people-watching seemed much more entertaining.

In Adam's home, there were no other people. There was only the quiet, the jazz, and the spectacular views.

He finished the majority of his workload over the span of four hours. Near midnight, he called it quits and set the books and notebooks aside.

Adam hadn't emerged once. When Ev went to check on him, Adam still painted, though much farther along. The form on the canvas came alive. Once again, Adam's talent struck Ev. As if with magic, he transformed the ordinary with only brushes and color.

"I'm gonna head to bed, I think."

Adam peered back over his shoulder without really turning. "Okay. Goodnight."

"Oh. Uh, goodnight. I thought you might be coming, but…"

"Do you need me to?"

"No," Ev blurted to cover his doubt. "You're working. I don't want to interrupt you, I just wasn't sure how long you were going to be. I have a really early class tomorrow, and—"

"Eight thirty on the east side of campus."

"Yeah. And it's getting late, so I just wanted to let you know I'm gonna hit it. If you're staying up later to get stuff done, that's totally fine."

"Evelyn," Adam said with patience. "Are you asking me to come to bed now?"

Ev rolled his eyes and folded his arms. "I would like that, but you don't have to if you don't want to. I mean, you don't have to stop just because of me. You're already taking care of a lot, and I get that. I do. I don't want to overstep, or…"

Adam wiped off the brush he'd been using. "I need to wash off some of my supplies and I'll be in."

"You can take your time. I just—"

"I'll be in."

"Okay."

Ev edged out of the doorway, then hurried down the hall, hissing under his breath, "I'm so fucking stupid. Whiny, nagging little bitch."

He went to the bedroom, used the toilet, and brushed his teeth. For good measure, since he felt overheated and crazy, he splashed some water over his face. Then he stared at himself in the mirror over the sink for a good couple of minutes wondering why he had to be such a moron. Then he headed to the bed. It was bad enough he was in some kind of relationship with a guy, but he didn't know how to act, how to do normal things like go to bed at the end of the day without it being awkward and strange. Nothing made sense.

He pushed off his boxers, hung the robe on a hook on the wall, and slid under the covers. Seconds later, Adam appeared, just as Ev was lying down and pulling the sheet back up. Unfastening his watch, emptying his pockets, then pulling off his shirt, Adam stayed quiet at first.

Then, he asked, "Do you always sleep naked?"

"No. Not usually."

"There are many health benefits, I'm told, if you do. Don't feel you need to on my account if it makes you uncomfortable."

"Okay."

"Are you sure? You sound tense."

"Yeah."

Adam went in the bathroom and closed the door. Ev groaned and tried to calm down while staring up at the ceiling.

When he came back out wearing pajama pants, Ev panicked a little, feeling unable to express himself in ways that didn't seem demanding, pathetic, or impolite.

"So, you're going to sleep?" he asked Adam, who pulled back the covers on his side of the bed.

"I was going to, yes. Why? Do you need something?"

"Fuck," Ev breathed, barely audible. Louder, he stammered, "It's just… if you wanted to do something together first, I'd be cool with that."

Adam's cheeks dimpled with amusement. Ev's gut rioted with insecurity, his body too awkward, his words pitiful. "Play a quick game of poker, you mean?"

Grabbing a pillow and sticking it over his face to hide behind, Ev grumbled, "Fuck you. No."

"You're blushing." Adam tugged the pillow out of Ev's hands and tossed it aside.

"Yep." Ev chewed at the inside of his cheek, stayed motionless and kept his gaze locked to the ceiling as Adam slid off his pants and got into bed.

"Are you hard up? Need some relief? Permission to masturbate? …Sex?"

Ev's mouth worked, but no sound came out. He closed his eyes, frowning, then rubbed a hand over his face like that might help snap him out of it.

"Evelyn, I can't read your mind. I try to read your cues when you're somewhat obviously in the mood, but if this is going to continue, you're going to need to be honest with me about your needs."

"Do you know how weird and difficult it is for me to say this stuff out loud? I'm still new at this. Really new. And it's still a head trip to do it at all let alone come out and ask you to do it to me."

"Do what? Have sex with you?"

"Yes."

"That's what you need?"

He bit down hard on his tongue, then grunted. "Mm-hmm."

Adam shifted to lay on top of Ev, looking down at him, his arms propped on either side of his body. "So you enjoy getting fucked in the ass?"

"Please don't make me say it."

"You can just nod."

So, he did. Right away, something inside him loosened. It became much easier to breathe and lie there, naked and horny. Adam leaned to his left for the lube, and rubbed some over his dick. Ev watched him doing it, the way his fingers slid over his shaft, playing with it, getting it wet. He felt impatient to be able to feel it pushing into him, claiming him, marking him as Adam's alone. Already half hard, Ev spread his legs to give Adam more room. When Adam hooked his arms under Ev's legs and bent them sharply back, effectively tipping Ev's ass up for fucking, he wasn't really ready for it. He'd expected there to be some touching and stuff before getting to that point.

Adam bent down momentarily and sucked hard on Ev's right nipple, pulling the skin away from his body. Ev had his hands on his thighs and moaned forcefully, his chest arching up into the suction. Adam let go, licked up and over the thick, stiff dark circle, then sucked it again with a pleasure-filled hum.

Then, without any pause at all, he shifted upward, his dick aligned with Ev's hole, and Adam pushed to enter him.

"Ahh," Ev cried, wincing as the head passed through his rim. Once it was through, the small ache and pressure eased. Adam thrust inward, sliding fairly easily to stuff Ev full. In fact, he sheathed his cock so painlessly in Ev that a hard shudder of arousal shook Ev as Adam bottomed out. Moaning pleadingly, he leaned forward, wanting to catch Adam's mouth in a kiss. Everything about him

116

looked hard and hungry. Tucking his hair over one ear, he caught Ev's lips, biting at them as his hips nudged Ev's ass, grinding there.

"Say please."

"Please," Ev begged, his voice breaking.

Adam tugged hard on Ev's cock, didn't ease up and pulled slowly back. Ev cried out, then grunted as Adam re-entered him immediately.

"Feels almost like I belong here," Adam smirked. "Arms over your head. I want you relaxed and open, because you want this, right? You like the way my cock fills you up?" He rubbed around Ev's rim, then over the patch of skin behind his balls, triggering nerves there in an explosion of sensation. Further up, to Ev's root, Adam rubbed, following the line of his erection to the dripping head.

"Yeah," Ev gasped. He let his head fall back, his eyes closing, muscles relaxing as Adam built a rhythm of shallow thrusts and gave Ev's dick another hard tug. "*Ahh, fuck.*"

"Nice?"

"Mm-hmm." He bit his lip, pushing down into the thrusts.

"You want it sweet or hard?"

"Hard," Ev rasped.

"Good boy," Adam grinned.

He gripped Ev's thighs, pinning him down, and started to give it to him hard and quick, slamming into him. Adam's pelvis spanked Ev's ass on each push, his balls nudging Ev more gently. With one hand, Adam gave Ev's dick yet another hard yank, pulling it upward by the head and Ev came with a hoarse yell. Semen flowed over Adam's hand and he gave a dark chuckle.

"I like this side of you," Adam said, giving Ev's left cheek a hard squeeze, then rubbed again over the place their bodies joined as Ev came down. Adam stroked down Ev's cock only to pull on it, doing that over and over as he emptied his load, making desperate little cries. When Adam finally let go of Ev's dick and gave one of his stiffened nipples a hard twist instead, Ev moaned again, panting.

He leaned in for a teasing, light kiss, as if only to feel Ev's roughened breaths against his lips, and said, "I'm not nearly done with you, sweetheart. With practice comes staying power."

In a swift movement, Adam pulled out, brought Ev's legs together, then rolled him onto his right side. He pulled Ev's curled legs up against his chest. "Hold these here," he instructed, then lay down behind Ev. With one slow, never-ending push, he was reclaiming Ev's throbbing asshole, stuffing it once more.

Ev gave a breathless moan, nuzzling his pillow and unable to deny how wonderful it felt to have Adam inside him. The position enhanced the way Ev liked the display of Adam's power over him, and his tender care. Adam, fully seated, wrapped his free arm around Ev's chest, holding him so their bodies were flush and Ev's back was tight to Adam's hairy chest.

"Lift your top leg, just a little."

Adam tugged back out once Ev had done it, and the slow withdrawal, the tugging against his inner walls, was indescribably good. When Adam's crown caught on Ev's rim, he pushed back in again.

A kiss came to the back of Ev's neck. There was so much affection in it, that light, silky brush. Ev trembled, anticipating everything, struggling to breathe, but it was the sweetness of Adam that hurt the most, cut the deepest through a lifetime of layers of protective denial.

The ragged sob broke loose, but he clamped his mouth shut fast and turned his face toward the pillow in shame.

Adam wouldn't have it, it seemed, because then he was pulling Ev's chin to the left, catching his mouth over his shoulder in a passionate kiss. He never stopped moving, slow like the tide, crashing into Ev and breaking him apart.

As they kissed and Adam had him, Ev reached down between his legs, caressing the junction of flesh moving inside flesh with fascination and reverence. After he'd begun to touch there, Adam growled and kissed him harder, licking him open.

His hand palmed Ev's chest as he slammed in deeply, holding there. His face was awash with profound relief as he unloaded inside Ev, pumping shallowly.

Settling back down on the bed, hugging Ev to him, Adam stayed like that for a while. Ev kept clenching on the thickness impaling him, like his mind couldn't believe it was real, though his body knew the truth well enough.

Something nudged the back of Ev's neck, like the tip of Adam's nose. Adam's hair tickled Ev's ear.

"I adore you," Adam said.

Ev overlaid Adam's hand on his chest with his own, weaving their fingers together.

"Me too." Ev whispered. "But... I'm scared out of my fucking mind. I've tried for so long not to be this and I can't... I can't keep telling myself it doesn't mean anything. I don't know how to be proud of what I am."

"You're Evelyn, and you're mine. So what if you're, like, thirty percent gay. Maybe. You're breathtakingly vulnerable when you let your guard down. I know what it means that you're trusting me this much."

"Every guy I've interacted with has hurt me."

"I know. That's why I'm trying to be so careful with you." He hummed, then sighed. "I love being able to feel you from the inside when we talk." He gently kneaded Ev's pectoral muscle. Pulling the nipple, he asked, "So, you like the rough stuff?"

"Guess so."

"Mm, I'll keep that in mind." The bed shifted. Ev saw Adam propped up on one arm and looking down at him with more than a little pride.

"So if you're a Dominant, then I'm what?"

"Submissive. Mine."

Ev smiled at that. "You're confident about that, huh?"

"Yes. All right my sexy, submissive Evelyn, come to the shower. I'll wash you up."

Ev didn't argue, biting at his lip as he felt Adam withdraw at last, though doing it while studying Ev's expression.

Adam took his hand to pull him out of bed, then walked behind him to the bathroom, guiding him with a hand to his shoulder and lower back. The bathroom tile was cool on Ev's feet. In moments, Adam had the water on full blast. They got inside together. Adam moved Ev up to the wall under the spray from the rainfall shower-head above them, nudged his feet apart and eased him forward so his hands were planted on the wall in front of him. He took the handheld shower-head off the wall and angled it up between Ev's legs, directing the spray at his cheeks. Two fingers

119

twisted up into him. Arching his back, bowing his head, he felt Adam wash him out, probing deeply.

"You don't really know a man until you've washed out his ass for him," Adam teased.

Ev laughed, shaking his head. The fingers jabbed into him.

"You get tighter when you chuckle."

"Fuck," Ev sighed.

Adam pulled out, retrieved a sponge and started to lather Ev up.

"You've had a hell of a week, kiddo. I'm giving you tomorrow off. It's your longest day, as far as your schedule goes. Focus on school. Get some sleep in your own bed. Go to the game or hang out with your friends."

"You're kicking me out? I thought you wanted me to move in?"

Adam manhandled him around so they were face to face. Pushing a hand through Ev's hair, Adam leaned into him, nothing but hard muscle and heat.

"Are you saying you will?"

Ev nodded.

"You can think it over if you need to."

"I want to be here. Things make more sense when I'm here. I feel like I might be able to figure out who I am. I don't want to lose that."

"Good. But I still think you should take tomorrow off. Breathe a little. Have some fun."

"I thought that's what we were just doing."

Adam bit his lip, then tilted his head to give Ev a kiss that went deeper than initially expected. But when Adam's tongue was in his mouth, Ev grabbed a fistful of red hair and savored it.

"I adore you," Ev sighed.

"Too late. I said it first. Doesn't mean as much now."

Ev nipped at Adam's chin. "Ass."

Chapter 16

Making Fun

The next morning, Adam and Ev picked up a breakfast of some farm fresh egg and biscuit sandwiches along with some coffee from a small farmer's market on the way in to campus. As they walked in the crisp morning air, anything seemed possible. Surmounting a bout of nerves, Ev found the courage to slip his hand into Adam's for a few minutes until they had too much food to carry to manage it anymore.

As Adam took their coffees from a barista and handed one over to Ev, he said, "That was a big deal for you, wasn't it? Holding my hand?"

Ev shrugged, trying to play it off, though he knew he was probably blushing again. "I guess so."

Adam gave him a knowing look, as Ev now knew him to do, and nudged him. "How does a Senator's son grow up to be so lacking in confidence? I thought the whole political game was learning how to present yourself with some bravado and intimidating the competition with your charisma?"

"Well, it's sometimes like that," Ev allowed. He set the coffee on the counter in order to unwrap his sandwich and start eating it one-handed. "But the spotlight was on my dad, not me. I was always told to shut up and look good, make a good impression and always smile, no matter what. It was all about appearances and responding in exactly the right way or not at all. My cousin and I argued in public at an event once when we were younger. I didn't stop paying for that one for almost a full year."

"What do you mean, 'paying for it'?"

"They didn't hit me or anything. It was just a lot of dirty looks, grounding, and speeches about what a disappointment I was. They just never let it go, always held it over my head. I apologized over and over but it didn't help."

"Hmm. Well," Adam glanced over at him as they began the walk back to the car. "You're in a different world now. Time to be your own man. Make your own rules."

"Maybe. Doesn't really feel like they've let me go yet. Now they hold over my head the fact that they're paying for my tuition. I try not to worry about it."

Adam gave this a frown.

Too soon, they were driving into school grounds and the pressure descended again.

Adam found a parking spot near Ev's morning class. Ev finished the last few sips of his coffee and Adam told him, "I have a lot of errands to do today. Bank, meeting with a colleague, meeting with my lawyers and then scouting out possible galleries for the show. Some of those are going to take me out of town. Call if you need anything, but I don't expect to be back until late. Let's plan on me picking you up by the dorm when you're awake and ready. Just call and I'll come by."

He pushed his red curls behind an ear. Ev liked what Adam was wearing—a slim green button-down shirt with a tailored grey vest, a brown jacket over that and dark, well-fitting jeans with boots. Imagining having to go twenty-four hours without any contact with him made the air thicker, harder to breathe. A strange fear manifested, whispering to him that if they parted too long, Adam would stop caring and might forget about Ev completely. He knew it was dumb, but he couldn't deny the feeling.

"I'll miss you. Don't make fun."

"Why would I ever tease you for being sweet when that's the part of you that makes me hard?"

"Yeah? *That's* the part that makes you hard?" Ev grinned.

"Well..." Adam caressed up Ev's thigh and gave him a light, unhurried kiss. It didn't matter that there were students hurrying to classes all around them. Ev's priority was saying a proper goodbye to the only person who really saw him.

"I've gotta go," Ev said, spying the clock.

"Be safe." Turned sideways with one arm slung over the steering wheel and the other over the back of the seat, Adam watched him go. Ev closed the door and waved.

Right after Ev turned to jog up the steps he heard the beep of a horn and saw Adam had rolled down the window. "Hey! I'll miss you too, brown eyes."

Smiling so wide his cheeks hurt, Ev could only stand there a moment until Adam pulled away. Only then was the spell broken and Ev was able to run to class.

It was almost ten when Ev headed back to the dorm to switch out his books and notebooks before his next class. There wasn't a rush; he had a good hour between the end of one and the start of the next, so he slowed to a stroll, trying to let his mind settle and his head clear.

He passed a few people he knew, and smiled hello to each, but mostly his thoughts were on where he was —the gorgeous fall landscape of the campus, where he'd be for the next two and a half years—and where he wanted to go. His dream of having his own flower shop always seemed just that—a fantasy. What was more likely was that he'd be sucked back into the ever-turning wheel of the election cycle and public appearances, doing the family thing for a while until he got his feet under him and enough money saved to break out on his own.

But, being with Adam helped show Ev that maybe things didn't always have to follow the path his family had laid out for him. The thought of staying out on his own was scary, though. Where would he go? How would he live?

The prospect of moving in with Adam was also intimidating. He suspected it would just be like crashing there over and over again with all of his things readily accessible, too, but Ev also knew there were only so many paintings Adam could do of him before he'd need to move on to a different subject matter. But where did that leave Ev? How would he make money? What would he be to Adam when the business aspect of their relationship ended? Ev also wondered if Adam would continue to insist to have as much control over things as he'd done so far. Physically, sexually, financially, and practically, Adam liked to call the shots. The large part of Ev that enjoyed it was tempted to feel ashamed for failing to man up like his parents always warned him he needed to. They would have been heartbroken to see him playing the woman in their relationship. Not only was Ev betraying their beliefs by committing homosexual acts, he was doing so in the way that would cause his parents the most grief. Guilt crept in again, making him doubt everything.

"Hey! There you are," a female voice exclaimed. Ev stopped short, his train of thought screeching to a halt too. It was Marina from his Marketing Management class.

"Oh hey. What's up?"

"Oh, nothing, just you bailing on me the other night. What was that about? I came by your place like you asked me to but you weren't there, no message or anything."

Ev deflated a little. "Yeah, I'm really sorry about that. It was one of those days. Shit just kept happening and I had to deal. I hope I didn't waste too much of your time."

Marina was cute, with short black hair, a heart-shaped face and pretty eyes. There was definitely an attraction there, he was a little surprised to realize, just a different sort than the kind he had with Adam. Marina was all soft curves and delicacy. Even just standing next to her made Ev want to cuddle her close to see what kind of perfume she wore and how she'd feel against him.

That was all reaction, though. Base impulses. Marina drew Ev in the way Ev drew Adam in. While Marina would be the yielding softness and comfort for Ev in that pairing, it was the other way around with his male counterpart. The difference made an entirely new viewpoint open up for him, seeing himself from new angles.

Marina hummed and tossed her hair back, then gave him a hint of a smile to show she wasn't upset. "Nah, it's okay. How about you make it up to me over dinner tonight? Your treat?"

Biting at his lip, Ev squirmed a little. "Jeez, I'm sorry, I can't. I actually just started seeing someone and I wouldn't feel right about it. But if you're coming to the game tonight, I'll probably be there with some friends. Soda and pizza is totally on me if you want to join."

Then it was her turn to look deflated. Her bow of a mouth quirked to the side. "Maybe. Who's the lucky girl? Anyone I know? I guess you're bringing her to the game?"

"It's not, uh… you wouldn't… It's not someone you'd probably know. They're out of town tonight. That's why I was headed out with the guys."

"Maybe I'll see you there, Ev," Marina winked, walking past.

"Cool. Later."

He blew out a sigh of relief and hurried on his way to the dorm. Keeping his head down, avoiding eye contact, all he wanted was to be in his room for a moment's peace and quiet.

The lobby was fairly deserted, though there were the few typical weirdos sleeping on the couches like they were homeless or nocturnal or something.

He took the elevator, pushing the door close button repeatedly to hurry things along. When it opened at his floor, he strode down the hall to his door, which was slightly ajar.

His heart sank. No peace and quiet was going to be had.

Ev pushed open the door and stepped inside. Luckily, it was just Leo in there, and not a crowd of people.

"Hey. How's it going?" Ev asked, closing the door to keep any wanderers out.

Leo's response from his perch, sitting on the couch, was quick and defensive. Leaning back and throwing his arms wide, he asked, "How long have we been friends? Almost a year and a half, right? Do you really think so little of me, man? Do you even consider me a friend at all?"

"Whoa." Ev dropped his things and folded his arms, widening his stance just in case this was headed in the direction of a fight, which is what it felt like. "What the fuck, man? Where is this coming from?"

"Just answer me," Leo snapped.

"Yes! Yes, you're my best friend here. You know that."

"No, obviously I don't know anything."

"Would you please just tell me why you're so pissed?"

Leo jutted out his jaw and folded his arms too. At least he wasn't coming at Ev, arms swinging.

"I just don't understand why you wouldn't tell me anything. Anything! Clearly it's not that big of a deal to you. If you were in the closet, you wouldn't be kissing some guy out on the damn sidewalk."

"Oh my god," Ev groaned, rubbing his hands over his face. "Oh my god, dude. It didn't... It wasn't..."

"You think I'm a homophobe or something? That I'm a hateful person?" Leo ranted, angrier than Ev had ever seen him. He was even angrier than when Mike Thomas dumped the contents of an entire can of beer on Leo's bed.

"Jesus! No! It just... happened, okay? I just met him a week ago! That's why I haven't been here. It's been... a lot to deal with. My priority wasn't exactly to send out an announcement to everyone. I'm not out. I'm not... gay. I'm just... figuring things out right now."

Leo took a few breaths, slipped off his hat and put it back on again. "What about that shit about your cousin?"

"I have no cousins out here. It was a lie. I just told you that because I didn't want to tell you I was sleeping at a male teacher's place."

"He's a fucking teacher? Are you shitting me?" Leo had leaned forward, elbows on his knees, eyes wide, eyebrows raised, mouth agape.

"No! He's just... an adjunct professor in the art department. He's not my teacher. I was just helping him with a project. Modeling. Then it kind of... changed."

"And you're actually sleeping with this guy? Like sleeping, sleeping? You're boning a man just out of nowhere?"

"It's not boning." Ev let his head fall back, wishing he'd gone anywhere else but back to the room. "He's nice. Funny. Smart. He... asked me to move in with him."

"Ev, man, you are gay."

"I'm not," Ev laughed. "I'm not gay! I dig girls. I've had sex with them and I would again if I wasn't with Adam. I'm... I don't know. I like both."

"There's a word for that, you stupid shit."

"*You're* a stupid shit."

"Good comeback."

"Fuck you. Just give me a break." Ev walked over to a chair and flopped down in it, slouching down low and covering his face again.

"You can't move in with this Adam guy."

"Oh, are you the boss of me now?"

"Why did you have sex with him after only meeting him a few days ago?"

"Because I wanted to?"

Leo rolled his eyes, shook his head. "So how did this work? You said you'd model for an adjunct professor, went to his place alone, got naked and let him fuck you? And you don't think there's anything alarming about that?"

"Who said I let him fuck me?"

Come on, said the weary look Leo gave him. "I have known you for a year and a half. You're not exactly the type to make someone bigger and older than you your bitch."

"I'm not his bitch," Ev said, sagging with exhaustion.

"Well, we have a difference in opinion on that."

Ev rolled his head on his shoulders and chewed on his lip for a minute. "So, you're okay with this?"

"No, I'm not. I think you're being incredibly dumb."

"I mean the fact that I'm less than one hundred percent straight. Maybe."

"Dude, give it up. Because you already did. You gave it up. You gave up your ass to a dude. Stop trying to argue for straightness because it doesn't fucking matter. No one cares."

"Liar."

"Okay. Some people care."

"Wait." Ev gave him a sharp look. "No one else knows about this, right?"

"Ev, you fucking kissed this guy in public. At the school, on the street. Multiple times, it seems, because Greg told the whole fucking football team he saw you kissing a guy outside the dorms."

"Holy fucking Christ," Ev winced. "That's it. I need to drop out."

Leo made an exasperated noise and stood up. "Ev, if you kiss dudes where people can see you, you can't be upset that they notice. And who cares if they know? Doug's boyfriend goes to all his games and the after parties. You're not the first gay ever. It's only news because you never told anyone you're into guys."

"So…" it was all scrambled in his head, crazy alarm bells blaring, making it hard to think at all. "You know gay people?"

"I can't even deal with you, man," Leo lamented, gazing up at the ceiling. "Do I know gay people? Yes, I know gay people. My uncle's gay. This know-it-all guy from high school who shared my bus is gay. My brother's best friend is gay. Meghan, that hot Asian chick from my psych class, is gay. Can I stop now? Do *you* know gay people?"

"No, not really." He was blushing. He felt it and hated it. "But I guess my football coach was gay, because he kind of molested me my senior year. And my cousin was gay before they found him touching me and sent him away to learn how to be straight instead."

Leo looked like Ev had punched him in the gut. He rubbed a hand over his mouth and Ev could see him breathing harder. Unable to see that any longer, Ev curled forward, bowing his head, feeling shaky and nauseous.

"Ev…" Leo had moved closer. Ev flinched a little. "Have you told anyone?"

Ev shook his head. "Just Adam."

"Have you had counseling or anything?"

"No. I haven't told anyone else. I didn't have words for it before. But since I told Adam, I guess I do now, since I said it all out loud and had to think about it again. But I don't… I don't talk about it. We don't talk about it."

"Who's we?"

"My family."

"Ev, you need to seriously talk to someone about this. Get some help, or guidance. Something. You need me to call someone? Get someone over here or make an appointment or some shit?"

"I don't know. I…"

He could feel the lump of his phone in his pocket. He dug it out and dialed, then put it to his ear.

"Hey, is this a bad time?"

Leo was sitting right there, waiting, listening. Ev was kind of glad.

"No, I was just getting into the car," Adam replied. "Is everything okay?"

"Maybe. No. Not really. I… Leo saw us, so I just told him stuff. That I'm… with you. And that stuff about what happened to me before. And he says there's rumors going around about me being gay, that the whole football team knows and… Leo thinks I should talk to someone. Get some help."

"Are you ready for that? The school counselor is great at her job. I've heard wonderful things. I agree with Leo that talking through this would be good for you, if you can open up to someone else that much."

Feeling tense, uneasy, Ev rubbed his neck. His eyes prickled so he squeezed them shut.

"Give her a call, Ev. Make an appointment."

"Yeah. Maybe." He was so close to crying, but he wouldn't do it in front of Leo, or while talking to Adam on the phone, like some kind of needy crybaby.

"Do you need me to do it for you?"

"No, I can do it."

He rubbed his eyes dry.

"Are you sure? Do you need me to come over there?"

"I'm okay."

"I can be there in an hour if you need me to come, but you need to tell me either way."

Ev let out a deep breath, getting it together a little. He could feel Leo watching him.

"Evelyn?"

"I'm here." He exhaled deeply again. "I'm okay. I'll see you in the morning."

"If you change your mind, call."

"Okay."

"Can I talk to Leo for a moment?"

"Seriously?"

"Yes."

Ev sighed and held out the phone to Leo, who looked confused for a moment, then took the phone.

"Hello?"

Ev could only hear one side of the conversation, no matter how hard he tried to eavesdrop.

"Yeah, it's 985-555-4323," Leo said, reciting his own phone number. "Yeah, no problem. Yes, sir. I will. Okay. Yep."

He handed the phone back to Ev, who put it right back to his ear. "It's me."

"Promise me you'll take it easy and get some rest," Adam told him. "Nothing stressful today."

"Okay. I promise."

"Are you okay?"

"Yeah. I am."

"It'll be all right, sweetheart. I swear it will. I know it's a lot right now."

Just like that, Ev choked up and silently wiped a tear away as soon as it fell.

Leo got up, grabbed a tissue box and came back with it, passing Ev a tissue.

"Okay," Ev said, his voice thick. "Thanks."

"I'll see you in the morning. Call if you need to."

"Okay. Bye."

He hung up and pressed the heels of his hands into his eye sockets.

"He made me promise to keep an eye on you," Leo said. "He definitely sounds like a teacher."

"Yeah, he does. Sometimes. He's bossy but in a good way."

"Ev, you've gotta tell someone back home about your coach, man. What if he's doing that to other kids?"

"I don't know. I don't have proof. Or a support system."

"Like hell you don't. My momma and all her sisters will be on the next bus if I said the word. Where I come from, they don't stand for no kiddie touchers."

"I was eighteen," Ev murmured. "He waited until the end of the year to do it. Before that he'd just... humiliate me."

"Don't make excuses for that piece of shit."

"I don't want to talk about it anymore."

"Okay. That's fine."

Ev glimpsed the time on the alarm clock. "Shit, I've gotta get to class."

"Lemme walk with you."

"I don't need a babysitter."

"Maybe not, but you do need a friend."

Ev stood, gathered his books, and didn't argue. When Leo followed him out, Ev felt a painful twinge of gratitude that he didn't know how to express or process.

When they were in the elevator, Ev's emotions kept trying to chase up on him, so he kept his head and his eyes down.

"It's gonna be okay, Ev," Leo told him just before they got to the ground floor.

Ev gave him a tense smile and nodded. As the door opened and Ev stepped out, Leo clapped him on the back and stayed right at his side.

Chapter 17

Appearances

A few guys gave Ev weird looks on the way to class, but Leo stayed on top of it, heading off any comments or uncomfortable stares by saying things to the gawkers like, "Hey, what's up," to shift the attention to himself.

At the classroom, Leo left him with another clap to his back and said to give him a call if Ev needed anything on the way to work.

Ev took a seat at the side of the room by people he didn't know and tried to just focus on the lesson, not his swirling thoughts.

It worked. By the time class was over, he was more able to hold his head up and use at least the appearance of confidence to deflect any glances. He had barely enough time to grab a burrito at a food truck before it was time to report for a shift at work in the admissions office. As he was happy to discover, it seemed no one had heard the rumor about him there, because his shift remained as pleasantly boring and uneventful as usual.

After work, as soon as Ev walked through the door to his dorm room and saw Leo geared up in school colors for the game that night, he knew he didn't have the energy to go. The whole week had caught up with him, lying across his shoulders like a thousand pounds of dead weight.

"You're not going, are you?" Leo guessed, sounding like he already knew the answer.

"Sorry, man. Don't have it in me. I might go down to the gym, sweat it out a little, then watch TV."

"I totally get it. I'll stay and hang with you."

"You really don't have to. Go to the game. You dig 'em. Everyone'll be there, so go have a good time."

"There's always gonna be more games, Ev. What kind of friend would I be if I just bailed on you when you're dealing with so much? Plus, your dude kind of scares me and I promised to watch out for you."

Ev smiled despite himself, trying to stop and failing. "He's not my dude," he laughed.

"Whatever. I was pretty far away when I saw him, but I did see how much bigger than you he is, and you're not a small guy. Plus, he sounds like he could kill me with only his mind and force of will."

Ev laughed again. "You're crazy."

"I'm not crazy. This guy talked you into doing butt-sex when you weren't even gay a week ago. *That's* crazy."

"Can you stop talking about that? My god, man."

"Sorry, it's just a little alarming."

"Adam isn't coming to get you."

"He might if I drop the ball on this." Leo took off his hat and tossed it into a pile of his stuff in the corner. "So we're doing the gym? I'll put on my stuff."

Ev let the weight drag his shoulders lower and pull his head to fall backward. "I don't have the energy to talk you out of doing this just because you feel bad for me."

"Ev, shut the fuck up and go get ready. Or are we skipping right to watching TV? You look dead on your feet."

"No, I need to move a little first. Let's do this."

A morning breeze swayed the oak tree soaring up into the clear blue sky, tousling its green and gold leaves. As sunlight filtered through the dancing branches, sunspots and shadow were tossed around, restless. Ev, though, remained still. He sipped some water and leaned on the windowsill, watching the world wake up.

Leo was still asleep. Ev had woken early. For at least an hour, he had lain in bed, turning things over and over in his mind. He got up to shower and dress, then came to stand by the window instead.

By the door were two bags, ready to go. He'd packed them the night before, right after making two incredibly important phone calls. Now that it was morning, everything felt different.

He couldn't really believe how much Leo now knew. It took some of that heaviness from Ev, so for that he was grateful. But now, instead of the worry of secretiveness, he had the challenge of guarding exposed vulnerabilities.

It was nice up there, watching the campus slowly come to life. At the same time, he felt crowded in. Too many people filled too confined a space. You could never really get away, had to always be aware that people could see you, speak to you, or come at you. There were shared bathrooms, shared eating spaces, even shared sleeping spaces.

It was too much like being at home, when eyes were always on the family. Escaping the need to present a carefully sculpted image hadn't happened here, and wouldn't. Ev knew it. Now, the pressure grew. Some people knew Ev had been hiding his attraction to men. Some didn't. He didn't know how to be both the man his family and community expected him to be, and be the man who was Adam's lover. Logically, he knew they were the same person at heart. It didn't feel that way in practice.

But the funny thing was, the person he'd thought he needed to be was less happy than the new Ev he'd discovered in such a short period of time.

It was too soon to move in with Adam. Ev hadn't known him long enough to make the decision to take such a drastic step, not when it took him in a deliberate direction down a path away from everything that was familiar and comfortable.

Yet, his bags sat by the door. It wasn't everything, but it was something.

A blue Mustang pulled up to the curb across the street.

Ev broke into a big smile and turned from the window. He slipped his phone into his pocket after it bleeped with a text message alert and went to get the bags.

"Hey, man," Leo said, sounding groggy and shifting to sit up. "You leavin'?"

"Yeah. Adam's here."

"I'll walk you out. I feel like I need to see this guy face to face."

Ev shifted the bags into his grip. It only took Leo a moment to slip on some shoes and a hat. Then, he held the door for Ev and closed it behind them as they went.

The ride down in the elevator was quiet.

Going to college where he was, so far from home, and choosing the major he had were Ev's first attempts at independence. They wouldn't be his last. Sure, he'd make mistakes, but hopefully he'd learn from them, too, and they wouldn't be for nothing.

This was where Ev stood emotionally and psychologically as he walked out of the dorm and into the morning light, joining with it instead of just watching from above. He had a friend in Leo at his side, and possibility before him in the form of Adam, waiting with a smirk on the sidewalk just ahead. The only things dragging along behind were all of the ties of his past he hadn't found the skill to unravel.

"You have bags," Adam said happily once Ev got closer.

"I do," Ev smiled, going in for a brief, chaste kiss as Adam wrapped him in a one-armed embrace, then slipped the bags from Ev's shoulder, shifting them onto his own. "I can get those," he protested.

"I know," was the entirety of Adam's stubborn yet chivalrous response. "And you must be Leo. So good to meet you officially," Adam said, extending a hand.

Leo leaned in to shake with him. "Same here, Mr. Buchanan."

"Jesus, just call him Adam," Ev laughed. "He's not that much older than us."

"Adam's fine," he told Leo with good humor. "I really appreciate you stepping up and being there for Evelyn yesterday. Says a lot about the strength of your character."

"Ev's my boy. He's a good guy. I wish he wasn't going through as much as he is."

It was hard to hear them talking about him like that, but Ev kept his eyes focused downward and his mouth shut.

"We have a busy day ahead today, but I think we'd both really like it if you came by for brunch tomorrow and saw the place.

I'd like Evelyn to feel completely comfortable there, and that means bringing his world and the people who matter to him into it."

"Yeah, of course. I'll be there."

"Thanks," Ev said to Leo, finally speaking up. "I'll text you directions. It's in walking distance if you don't mind a little exercise."

"Ready?" Adam asked Ev.

"Yeah." To Leo, Ev said, "We'll talk later. Thanks again for being so cool about everything."

With a wave, they crossed the road and loaded Ev's bags into the back of the car before taking off.

Chapter 18

Given Over

"How are you?" Adam asked once they were underway.

"Don't know. Glad to be spending the weekend with you and getting away from here until Monday."

"You do seem overwhelmed. What usually helps you deal with stress? I know you mentioned exercise before. Is there anything else?"

Ev thought back to ways he'd coped in the past when the pressure got too intense. "It depends, I guess. Sometimes hiding away from everyone and being in my own head for a while. Sometimes… jerking off to things."

"Things like what?"

Ev shrugged.

"I'm only trying to figure out how to help," Adam said.

"You are, just by being who you are, and being here. I've never really had someone to run to when I needed to get away before. Even with Mia, I never told her some of the things that were stressing me out or the things that brought me comfort, so there was distance there instead of… you know, reassurance that everything was okay. And you… you know what it's like, having to be someone who gets judged for your family and your… behaviors."

"Do you need to take it easy today? Should I give you a pass?"

"No, I want to help. I'm doing this with you. It's important to me too. You're really talented. You have a vision that deserves to be shared. It means something more than shit like hollow campaign promises or winning football games."

Adam nodded, turning the wheel as they pulled into the garage of his building. "Okay."

They found a spot near the elevator. Adam pulled Ev's bags from the car. Meanwhile, Ev felt restless in a way he wasn't sure how to settle. The clash of the straight son of the Republican Kansas Senator against the quiet, submissive, bisexual painter's muse and hopeful future flower shop owner created chaos inside him. The new incarnation was so much more vulnerable than the previous. It seemed difficult to fight that battle when everything in him just wanted to surrender.

But he liked how much privacy they had at Adam's place. It cocooned Ev safely inside.

Up the elevator, into the apartment, then back toward the bedroom they walked. The deeper they went, the more Ev tried to let go and leave things behind to be dealt with another day.

Adam opened up a door leading to a dressing room off the bedroom. The walls there were lined with cabinets, drawers, and racks for hanging things. Part of it seemed empty. There, he set down Ev's bags. He told Ev, who lingered in the doorway, "Store your things here. If you'd like to unpack now, I can make you something to eat, brew some coffee."

The restlessness intensified to a buzzing, like insects swarming under his skin, in his head. If he opened his mouth to speak, they'd sting his tongue, swell his throat. His fingers moved in a jittering way over the wood of the doorframe as Ev tried to be still, to find calm. It eluded him. Everything felt wrong, dangerous. Nothing was safe.

"C'mere," Adam said, pulling Ev back into the bedroom. He rubbed Ev's upper arms, the side of his neck. "You're so tense," he lamented. One of his hands kneaded a knot at the junction of Ev's neck and shoulder. Closing his eyes, Ev felt the size, strength, and heat of Adam in front of him. Somehow, Adam had found his way through the storm already. He had emerged on the other side, in the clear. Maybe all Ev had to do was follow and trust in those footsteps.

He pulled closer to Adam, inhaled deeply of the scent of his cologne and aftershave.

Those things were good, but they were false—a pleasant chemistry instead of a natural perfume, like burying your nose in a bottle instead of a flower. The bottle could sting or even repel, while the flower was only soft and yielding, the fragrance elusive but perfect—an artwork all on its own.

Instinct weakened Ev's legs, causing him to bend and kneel at Adam's feet, touching his chest, stomach, then his hip as he went. Adam's fingers caressed over Ev's head, through his hair, probably not understanding, but waiting to see if he would. Ev knew the feeling.

As soon as he settled on his knees, Ev knew it was right. His hand found Adam's bulge. Burying his nose between it and Adam's hip, Ev found the true scent of his lover. It was better, more real and honest, speaking of all of Adam's masculinity and strength. It emanated sweat, skin, and life.

Ev's fingers found Adam's fly, his fingertips hooking inside Adam's waistband, wishing for permission to act, knowing he couldn't ask for it in words without humiliating himself.

His lips worked over the bulge, mapping it, and feeling out the flesh beneath as he drew more of Adam's musk into his nose. It chased back the buzzing fast.

"Go on," Adam urged, seeming to understand how much Ev needed it.

With unsteady fingers, he somewhat impatiently worked open the jeans, popping the button fly, pulling down the zipper. Parting the denim, Ev took hold of Adam's boxer briefs as well and slid everything downward. His lips parted, Ev didn't contain the trembling gasp of need, twisted around an aching primal sound. His thumb brushed the soft curling red hair at Adam's groin and the end of Ev's nose plunged into the curls, then lower, nudging Adam's shaft, then the base of his sac. The skin was velvet warmth and pulsing life against Ev's frazzled nerves. With a shuddering, gruff exhale of pure bliss, he felt goosebumps break out all over his skin. He stayed there, breathing deeply, giving over to what he'd found with complete abandon and worship.

He didn't worry about what Adam saw, or what he thought. All that mattered was savoring that core of his being, and the gentle press of Adam's fingertips against Ev's scalp, following it back from forehead all the way around to the nape of his neck.

Quietly, but with the force of command, Adam said, "Take off your shirt. Drop your pants. Show me."

Ev did it hastily, ripping the shirt over his head, yanking open his own fly and pushing the fabric down to his knees along with his boxers, before reaching to caress that downy hair once more.

"Hands clasped behind your lower back."

It took some effort to relinquish the tactile pleasure, but Ev managed it. As soon as he had, he felt how even more grounded. His cock strained. Showing Adam his hardness was part of giving himself over, falling into the comfort of scent and limited touch. When Adam stepped closer, letting Ev nudge at his balls with lips, nose and chin, Ev's goosebumps tightened again. He let out a heavy, desperate moan that he would have been ashamed of in any other circumstance.

For a few, long, decadent moments, there was only breathing and Ev got lost there, his worries slowly tumbling away. Adam's cock had begun swelling as soon as Ev had first touched him. Now erect, its heat and hardness was something else to pull close to, breathing it into his lungs, head, and spirit.

The thumb of Adam's right hand pressed at Ev's full lower lip, his fingers hooking under his jaw. "Open wide. Stay open. Don't close your lips. Just breathe."

Ev let his mouth fall open. The sounds he was making grew rougher, louder, his breathing quickening as Adam used his left hand to lower his cock, slipping the head between the O of Ev's lips and onto his tongue.

"Breathe," Adam hushed, stroking Ev's jaw and quivering lower lip, then down the column of his throat. He pushed his cock a few inches deeper, until the head was near the back of Ev's mouth. There was so much of Adam filling that inner space, lying on his tongue. He inhaled around it, drawing air past flesh and down his throat. He exhaled with unrestrained, whimpered moans. If Adam pushed any deeper, he'd be in Ev's throat, possibly cutting off his air, but Ev loved having him so far inside.

"Really deep breaths, now. Relax your body. You're safe."

Ev obeyed, and his nerves calmed completely. The buzzing had gone, the restlessness faded away. Fingers caressed through his hair, down the side of his opened jaw.

"Close your lips. Don't suck. Just breathe deeply through your nose."

He let his lips hug Adam's shaft, holding him snugly in place. With grunts and groans, he shivered in delight as Adam's praising caresses intensified Ev's calm. Ev's cock was achingly stiff, his balls hanging heavy and full. He felt that he was wet, the thrill of his position making pre-ejaculate drip down his dick.

"Good," Adam said, with a smile in his voice, and something like pride. The weight of his cock, and the taste of it as well, was making Ev's mouth water. He swallowed around it once and shifted his position with a slight grimace as the ache of his erection became difficult to bear. "Be still," Adam told him. "I know you can." He brushed Ev's stretched lips where they wrapped Adam's shaft. "Focus only on this and your breathing. Nothing else matters."

He knew it was true. After a keening whine of discomfort, Ev pushed past it, back into the calm. With little motions, he petted Adam's shaft with his tongue. A fresh shiver raced down his back as Adam gave Ev's hair a gentle tug.

"Just beautiful, sweetheart," Adam sighed.

Ev didn't know how much time had passed, but then Adam said, "Okay, when you're ready, you can go ahead and suck."

It took him a few additional moments to break the spell. Adam's touches hypnotized, and he didn't want to have to leave the peace he'd found there, on his knees. But Ev's cock ached, feeling like it would snap right off if he touched it. He became cognizant of how he'd begun whimpering with the pain.

So, he began to suckle Adam. Once he'd drawn the taste of him down his throat, felt the way his saliva slicked the slide of cock on tongue and between lips, he wanted more. The rhythm of that was another kind of trance, another place of calm. With soft, hungry moans, Ev bobbed on Adam's cock, liking the steady, wet pump of it in and out of his mouth. Ev's tongue chased it on withdrawal, licking at the head and the drip of tangy fluid there. He shuddered as Adam stiffened and held Ev's head in his hands, thrusting faster as he got closer.

"Open wide," Adam said breathless and gasping. Ev opened up, extended his tongue and watched Adam stroke himself to completion, coming over Ev's tongue, into his mouth, over his lips. Some dripped down his chin. Ev made little gasps. "Stay. Stay open."

Adam was watching him, panting, stroking himself through it. Some come began to drip down Ev's tongue and into his throat and he struggled not to close his lips and swallow it all down, especially as it threatened to trigger his gag reflex.

"Okay, swallow," Adam allowed, catching his breath.

Ev moaned and happily obeyed.

"On your feet now, gorgeous," Adam said, gripping Ev's arm to help him up.

Ev got his feet under him and got one glimpse of his deeply reddish-purple, shiny wet cock. He closed his eyes as Adam rubbed with his thumb from the tip of Ev's cock, down, pinching the ridge between the side of his index finger and the pad of his thumb.

Ev's knees gave out.

Adam caught him, using his body to keep Ev propped up, holding him in a hug. "Easy... easy. Let's have you lie down."

"Sorry. Just got dizzy." He was moved back to the bed, eased down onto it. Adam removed Ev's shoes, socks, pants and underwear, then rubbed up his thigh as he crawled onto the bed beside him. Gazing through his eyelashes at Adam barely skimming the underside of Ev's aching erection with his palm, Ev shivered and begged wordlessly, his fingers splayed and pressed down hard against the bed at his sides.

"This?" Adam said, brushing the ridge of Ev's crown with a fingertip, "is incredible."

He shifted lower and licked just over the wet tip of Ev's cock, cleaning away some of the clear fluid there and swallowing it with a hungry moan. Ev pleaded again, whimpering like an animal, not trusting his voice with words. When Adam made a circle around Ev's crown with his fingers and thumb, then squeezed, Ev's mouth fell open again as he shouted, and kept shouting, his whole body convulsing, bucking into the pressure. But Adam didn't stroke or tug, he just maintained that ring of pressure on the head and Ev couldn't shut up. The edge of Adam's fingernails raked across the very tip of Ev's purplish head, as he teased it with his other hand without letting go. More pre-come dripped from him and his hips snapped into the constant grip. Then Adam grabbed hold of Ev's balls, pulled down hard on them, and gave him one impossibly tight, complete stroke.

Awareness fell into blackness.

A hand clasped to his cheek. Blue eyes looked down into his.

"There you are." Adam smiled, then kissed Ev's forehead. He rubbed over Ev's chest as he caught his breath and got his bearings. "You passed out for a minute there. Just relax. I'll be right back."

Adam shifted off the bed and went into the bathroom. He came back with a wet washcloth. He brought it to Ev and used it to cool his face and forehead.

"How do you feel?"

"Good." Ev glanced down at himself, saw his softened cock and the come splattered all over his stomach and some up onto his chest as well.

Adam saw where he was looking and said with decisiveness, "Don't touch it. I want to let it dry, so I can see it on you while I work." He left the washcloth across Ev's forehead and took his hand. Ev wove their fingers together and lowered his gaze. "Better now?"

Ev nodded. "Much."

"Evelyn, what you just gave me?" He nodded to the area where Ev had knelt, then gazed into Ev's eyes. "The honesty of that act? It was an incredible gift. You know that, don't you? I realize it wasn't easy for you to do that. It means quite a lot to me to be trusted that much."

He kissed Ev, smoothed back his sweat-damp hair.

"I have something very specific in mind to work on today. All you need to do is lie still, so you'll have plenty of time to rest, but first I do need to ask you to wear a few things for me. Would you do that? I promise if you do, I'll make it up to you after I finish tonight."

"Okay," Ev said in a rasping voice.

"Great," Adam grinned. He got up and walked into the dressing room. When he came back, he carried a lump of white with some other things on top. He set them above Ev's head, where he couldn't see them clearly. "Okay, so, the first thing I need is for you to stay soft while I work. To accomplish that, I'm going to put a chastity device onto you." He picked something up and held it for Ev to see. It looked like a small metal cage with narrow bars. Biting at his lip in concentration, Adam began to fit it onto Ev, sliding his balls through the ring at the base, then sliding his dick into the cage before closing and locking it. "What do you think? Love it? Hate it? I know self-control isn't everyone's thing."

"I don't hate it," Ev said, feeling shy. He appreciated having a way to keep from embarrassing himself with his arousal, but he was scared of what it would feel like to begin to stiffen while wearing the cage. "But won't it hurt?"

"Try to breathe through it if you start to feel pressure. If it becomes intolerable, I'll take it off."

"Okay."

"Good. Now, the second thing is crucial for this painting's concept to work. This is a representation of the stereotypically feminine on an undeniably male body. It's another way to express your vulnerability in the piece."

"What is it?"

Adam picked up the white cloth, holding it between two hands.

"That's a cheerleader's skirt."

"It is," Adam said with a mischievous twinkle in his eyes. He glanced from the skirt to Ev's come-stained, sweaty body and groaned.

"What?"

Adam tried to laugh it off but it seemed something was really bothering him. "This is going to be really difficult for me."

"What is?"

"Here, slide it on. I got it in a larger size. I can just pin it in back to make it fit your hips. It can ride low; I just need it to cover your genitals."

Ev was too weary to argue, though he didn't love the idea of wearing girls' clothes, even for Adam's artwork. Once Adam had pulled the skirt into place, he rolled Ev onto his side to pin it in back after the buttons weren't enough to keep it snug. Then he smoothed down the pleats of the skirt to check the length.

"Fuck," Adam groaned.

"What?"

Adam rolled his eyes and clenched his jaw. The smile he gave Ev was a strained one.

"Would you just tell me what's wrong? Do I look like a freak? What?"

Adam cleared his throat and sat up straighter. "I, uh, really need to get this done today. It's the largest block of time we'll have this week to do it, so I don't have a choice."

"Okay…?"

His lips puckered a little.

Ev laughed, "Adam, what?"

"You look really good," he said with a heavy sigh.

"Good? Thanks?"

Adam shot him a look of warning.

"Oh my god. I'm the one with a cage on his dick."

Adam stood, hands on his hips. "I have work to do here," he said with exasperation."And it involves looking at *this* all day. All fucking day, Evelyn."

"Well, you know… use some self-control or something," Ev said with a rising blush.

"Yeah, we'll see," Adam said ominously. "Stop blushing, it doesn't help."

"I can't control that," Ev laughed.

Adam picked up something else from the bed and pushed Ev farther onto his side, then pulled Ev's legs up so his knees were curled to his chest. A wet finger popped through his rim and twisted up his ass. He started breathing hard and tried to turn his face away to mask his expression. The finger pulled out and in its place something cold and slick pressed at Ev's asshole.

"Don't clench," Adam said, sounding stern.

"Adam…"

It was slowly pushed through his rim and Ev cried out. It got wider, then stayed wide, stretching him out, only to taper off to nothing. But Adam's finger pushed at it, and whatever it was, was quickly buried in Ev's ass.

He wanted to ask, but the words wouldn't come. He could feel it in there, filling him up. And it started to make him hard. As the bars of the cage bit into his swelling flesh, he cringed and grimaced.

"That's an anal egg. That's to help keep you in a vulnerable mindset. It's important for the piece."

"I'm already wearing a skirt and a cage on my dick. I already felt vulnerable."

"Who's in charge here?"

Ev rolled his eyes.

"Are you saying you need me to take it out?"

Ev bit his tongue.

"Hmm?"

"No."

"Good. Come on."

Adam took Ev's hand and began to pull him up.

"I can't walk around like this," Ev protested.

"You can and you will. No one else is here."

"There's an egg in my ass!"

"Yeah, well soon you might have something a lot bigger in there instead. Stop blushing."

"I can't not blush."

"Clearly." Adam pointed a finger at him. "Don't fuck with me right now. I'm skating a very thin edge." There was one telltale glance downward, and the ferocious lust behind it pushed Ev hard into a meeker mindset.

"Yes, sir," he said in soft surrender.

Chapter 19

Hard Work

Ev poured a small cup of coffee and ate a cheese Danish while Adam set up his work station in the art studio. The way Adam kept obviously not looking at him didn't ease Ev's nervous flutter of butterflies.

After getting something in his stomach, Ev felt steadier and headed over to Adam.

He'd gotten his well-used wooden palette full of a rainbow of colors, his brushes ready with a cup of water and rags. A fairly large canvas rested on the easel.

Adam handed him something without turning. "Here. Put these on too."

"What are these, stockings?"

"Yes."

"I don't know how to put on stockings."

Adam growled softly, then took the stockings back. "Lie on the fucking bed."

Ev went without a word. Adam rolled one of the white stockings, gathering it in his hand in almost a donut shape, then pushed Ev's foot through the hole and rolled the rest up his leg. At the end was an elastic garter which Adam tugged high up Ev's thigh. Then he did the same with the other leg.

His fingers lingered, following the hug of the sheer white stocking over Ev's hairy, muscular leg. His hand pivoted at the wrist, pushing up to palm Ev's butt cheek. Adam's thumb pressed through Ev's hole, nestling there with the cord dangling from the egg. Letting his legs fall open, giving Adam a view up the skirt, Ev tried to control his breathing.

"What position did you play in high school?"

"Wide receiver," Ev said, realizing the irony.

He thumb pumped shallowly, making Ev shiver and grunt. "Tell me you don't like it, that you don't want it."

"I can't."

There was a firm tug at the cord. Ev yelled in surprise, then grunted with gritted teeth as the egg slid out, passing slowly through his rim again.

Adam pulled him up, turned him around and bent him over sharply at the waist, flipping the skirt out of the way. Ev braced an arm on the bed. Adam grabbed lube, twisted two fingers up into Ev, then spread them apart as he undid his fly and pulled out his cock with the other hand.

It happened so fast, Adam's movements hurried and rough. Only a second later, the fingers pried him open, spreading his hole and Adam's cock touched him there. Hands gripped his hips tightly. Adam thrust hard.

Ev yelped in surprise.

He breached Ev, panting, and pulled Ev back onto the dick impaling him. He kept Ev sharply bent at the waist and sheathed himself with rough little ruts. Ev's cock was wet and the egg had helped stretch him a little, but the roughness of the sex shocked him. Once Adam had burrowed completely into Ev, his dick fully claiming its prize, Adam gave Ev's right cheek a hard slap, then spread him and rubbed his rim. Ev's dick strained against the cage and he moaned in pain from it, wishing it was off.

Then, after only a moment to breathe, Adam fucked him, taking him hard and fast. His hips beat Ev's ass, slapping against it as his stiffened cock drove into him.

"Oh fuck," Ev gasped wildly.

"Beg me," Adam growled.

"Please. Fuck. *Ahhh...*"

Ev palmed the cage enclosing his aching cock while Adam kept fucking him at a dizzying pace. Adam's dick pounded him; Ev couldn't catch his breath or stop yelling, pleading nonsensically.

Adam pulled out completely, thrust up through Ev's crack, slapped his hole with the head, then pushed in with one impossibly long thrust that had Ev gasping.

"Please take this fucking cage off."

"No."

After two slightly slower thrusts, Adam was pounding him again, until Ev throbbed everywhere. Adam came with a hard moan, staying in Ev as he unloaded, gripping his hips in a bruising hold.

"Okay, I feel better now," Adam sighed.

Ev growled back at him, trying breathing exercises to begin to will his arousal away. The speed and roughness of the sex had helped stave off a full erection, but there was still plenty of discomfort, now in both his ass and his genitals.

Adam withdrew his dick, then shoved the egg back up into Ev instead, getting a whimper for his troubles. Adam pulled Ev up straight to rest back against Adam's chest. The skirt was flipped up in front, the cage examined. "You'll be fine," Adam decided.

"You owe me."

"Oh, I realize that." Adam kissed Ev's neck, then helped him lay down. Adam arranged him in the desired pose, his legs together, the right knee twisted demurely over the left leg to help block the view up the skirt and also show plenty of thigh. It was a feminine pose, but easy enough to maintain. "It's just a matter of finding out what you really want."

"Mm," Ev hummed, gazing warily at his tormentor.

"What kind of sex did you enjoy most before we met?" Adam asked. He had a drawing pad in hand and sketched away, studying Ev's body as he worked.

"I don't think that applies."

"Just answer the question."

"There was a girl right after I ended things with Mia who rode me once. I liked it. She was on top, held me down. Mia had trouble taking my entire dick without it hurting her, so I always had to be really careful. It was nice to lay there and have someone else do all the work without the worry." Ev tried to get a read on Adam's expression and intentions, but he seemed lost in the work of sketching, his mind elsewhere... or maybe not. "But you're not actually thinking about..." he laughed.

Adam glanced up at Ev's eyes, then away.

"No way. I can't imagine you ever letting a guy fuck you up the ass."

"I'm not a virgin. It's just been awhile. I don't let anyone do that to me unless I trust them and really care about them."

"How long is a while?"

"I was nineteen. So, six years ago."

"And you're actually thinking about letting me..."

"You have a huge, delicious cock, Evelyn. Yes, it's true I've not ruled that out as something I'd like to get fucked by."

"Wow. That's... hot."

Blue, dangerous eyes flashed at him again.

"Change of topic to spare your discomfort," Adam said abruptly. "When's your appointment?"

"Monday," Ev said, reluctant to talk about something else.

He'd called the school counselor's office the night before to schedule a time to talk with her. Then, he'd let Adam know via text what he'd done.

"Good. Hopefully it'll be helpful to you and can be a regular thing. You said you also called your mother?"

"Adam, I don't want to talk about my mom right now."

One red eyebrow raised in what seemed a judgmental expression.

"Stop thinking about sex."

"How? You said I might get to fuck you later. I can't exactly ignore that."

"We're working. Let's try some civilized conversation."

He set the sketch pad down and shifted over to the easel instead. Ev guessed that meant he was happy with the way things looked, though the throbbing in Ev's rectum told him as much.

"What did Mom say?"

"Same old, same old. She asked about my health. If I was dating any nice Republican girls." Adam snorted at that. Ev shook his head and continued. "She said I had to come back for the holidays to do some campaign stops with Dad since it's an election year and it's important to the family that we all make a united front in order to help Dad get the win. You know, the usual bullshit. Oh, and my cousin, James, who had such a great time yanking my dick is getting married in a couple of weeks. I was also told my appearance at the ceremony was mandatory, even if it means missing classes. They're all just so proud of him for committing to such a nice girl. They were set up by their parents through the church. What a nightmare."

Adam caught his eye, and Ev liked the steadiness he saw there. "You're not going."

"Yeah, I had the same reaction, though it didn't pass my lips. But if I don't go, they might cut me off. They pay for my dorm expenses and all. My meal plan. My tuition comes from my college fund, but my parents pay for everything else."

"Mm, dorm expenses and meal plan. Very crucial."

"Don't be a smartass. What if this doesn't work between us? What if you decide you don't like me in a few days?"

Adam's cheeks dimpled a little as he pursed his lips. His red-gold eyelashes lay briefly against his face as he lowered his eyes. "That's not going to happen."

"You can't know that."

"I do. Haven't I told you I take this all very fucking seriously? I care about you, Evelyn."

Ev bit down on his back teeth, feeling like the bed—hell, the whole floor—had been pulled out from beneath him. There was too much sincerity in Adam's tone to ignore, but what he said was a big deal, to say the least.

"If I don't go to this wedding, it'll fuck up my whole life. They won't let it go. This is tied to all of that shit in my past."

"I see that. But you know what's also fucking up your whole life? Pretending you're straight. Ignoring the pain they caused you in criminalizing your moment of innocent experimentation with your cousin. Let's bypass this for now. What about the holiday request? The campaign stops?"

"Not gonna happen," Ev said. "I promised myself I was done with all of that when I came back to school for this term. I spent my whole summer lying through my teeth for them about everything that matters to me and I can't do it anymore. I need to be done. I need to be on my own now."

"Good," Adam said. "Then we're decided."

"Oh, are we?"

"I know what it's like to be left without a parental support system when you're barely an adult. And your circumstances are much worse than mine were. I had a convenient cushion of money and property to fall back on. You don't have that, but is it worse to take the chance on having to provide your own future, than to be force-fed one you know you'll hate?"

"I can't stand it when you make sense," Ev groaned, squeezing his eyes shut.

"I'm not trying to trap you here. I'm just trying to get you off that hook you're dangling from. The great part about being free is that you can do anything you want."

"Like wear some girly shit and a cage on my dick and let a stranger paint me like that?"

"After what we've shared, you're really going to call me that?"

"Sorry," Ev relented. "That was unfair."

"Straightforward question. You ready?"

"Sure."

Adam gestured between them with his paintbrush. "Is this working for you?"

"What part?"

"All of it. You, former football star, wearing a cheerleading skirt and stockings, while sporting a well-fucked ass and dealing with a fair share of sexual denial thanks to a toy that makes you more aware of when you get turned on and by what. Me, standing here with a serious need to have even more hot, sweaty sex with you, talking to you about things no one else will. Living with me. Submitting to me. Letting me assume responsibility for your care, even if what that translates to doesn't make any sense at all to anyone else. *This*, Evelyn. Is this working for you?"

He didn't even stop painting. He just dipped the brush in a cream puddle and frowned angrily at the canvas. Sometimes it was really difficult to be on the other side of that canvas, to have no way to see what it showed, and how much dangerous truth it claimed as its own.

"I wish it didn't."

"Yeah, that'd be easier, wouldn't it?" He seemed so riled, like he might punch a hole in that canvas instead of touching it with his brush. With a frenzied little laugh, he shook his head and concentrated on mixing cream with brown. For what purpose, Ev might never know. "That was a shitty way to answer, but I appreciate the honesty of it."

"Am I supposed to be proud of this, Adam?" Ev asked, with more emotion creeping into the words than he wanted. "Is there any part of this I shouldn't feel terrified by or ashamed of?"

"Yes. Yes, Evelyn. You should. Things that make you happy shouldn't also make you hate yourself. When I ask if it's working for you, I mean exactly that. Is it working for you? You, with that mop of blond hair I'd bet you've only had since you moved away from home. You, who looks at me sometimes like you wish I'd hit you instead of kiss you. You, who knelt at my feet in my bedroom and gave over so much of yourself like you needed me to have it, like you trusted me with the truth more than you trust yourself with it. I'm not asking if you're giddy with excitement, or bursting with impatience to call Mommy and tell her about your new beau. I'm asking if this is working for you. Work, as in effort and change and pursuing a goal."

"*Stop*. Yes. It is. You're right, okay? Just like you always are. Is that what you want me to say?"

"No, I don't need to be right. I need you to stop tearing yourself in half by trying to go two directions at the same time. If this is who you are, be this. Be this you, not their version. Yours. I love this version of you. I…"

He quickly looked down, clenched his jaw. Ev stopped breathing, then resumed, too fast.

"It's okay, I know you didn't mean it," Ev said to cover up the awkward moment.

But Adam got slowly pink in the face. Ev hadn't seen him blush before. For a long time, neither of them said anything, but somehow, it was suddenly easier to lay there as he was, dressed as he was, with the aches he had. And each time Adam glanced over to compare the living with the creation, a small thrill twisted around in Ev's stomach.

Chapter 20

Payback

They took a break for lunch, or rather, Ev did. Adam kept painting. Lingering in the doorway behind him, watching him work without wanting to intrude too much, Ev ate a sandwich.

A call came in over Adam's tablet. Ev wasn't sure if he should walk away and give Adam his privacy when he moved to answer.

He tapped on the button to answer and set down the brush in his hand. With a glance behind him, he twisted the screen slightly counterclockwise. The shift put a blank wall at Adam's back, instead of the doorway where Ev stood.

The video call took over the screen.

A young guy with buzzed short black hair, light eyes, and black-and-grey ink tattoos all down both arms and up his neck was there, signing something. It had to be Rune, Ev realized with fascination.

"No, it's not a bad time," Adam said while signing back, his hands forming shapes with more than a little bit of ease. It occurred to Ev that he hadn't asked if Adam knew how to sign to Rune also, but he guessed he had his answer. He wondered also how cozy their relationship was, some of his defenses rising. "I'm with a model, but he's taking a break."

Ev resented being referred to as a model, but then thought of all of his privacy concerns, and Adam's self-professed dislike of sharing, and understood.

Adam gave a frustrated sort of expression, his lips getting tight. "I'm not avoiding him. I have something going on in my personal life and I need space." The soft responses, almost too quiet for the tablet to pick up, continued to be mirrored with what Ev had to assume were the sign language counterparts."Yes, I know he's my friend, but he's not always good at respecting my boundaries." Adam waited a moment for the reply, then said, "It's different with subs. I'm not his sub. I don't have a contract with him."

There was a longer pause. Adam looked away from the screen, hands resting on his hips. A knocking sound came from the mic as Rune hit his knuckles on the table in front of him, and Adam looked back down at the screen. "Sorry," he apologized. "I can't answer that. I promise I'll explain once I'm able." Rune tilted his head to the side and signed something. "I know what it sounds like. You're still not getting an answer out of me."

Rune was fairly good looking, Ev decided, but it didn't turn him on. Instead, it made him angry. All he could do was imagine all of the kinky things he and Adam must have gotten up to together.

"Maybe," Adam said, sounding a little tired. Then, "Yeah. I've gotta go. Bye."

He tapped the screen and ran a hand over his mouth, keeping his back turned to Ev.

"What was that?" Ev blurted, wincing a little at the bite in his voice.

"A call from a friend."

"Rune?"

Adam finally looked back at Ev, his expression masked, which only riled Ev's defenses more.

"Yeah, actually. It was."

"What did he want?"

"To check up on me." It was a much shorter answer than Ev had wanted.

"I've been really fucking honest with you, here," Ev said angrily, his voice trembling. "I expect the same back."

"Good. You should."

"Adam," Ev said in warning when there was no elaboration.

A subtle smile, barely there, showed on Adam's rosy lips. "You're jealous."

"Fuck you."

"Have you ever been jealous of a guy like that before?"

"What was he calling you for? What was that all about?"

"He wanted to know why I've told Olly to stay away and why I won't take his calls. He wanted to know if something was wrong."

Ev thought back to how Adam had kept deflecting with his answers.

"You haven't told them about me," he guessed.

"No. Not at all. But Rune guessed it was because of something like that, that I'd taken a sub of my own and didn't want to include them in it."

"Why did you say maybe?"

Adam's smile sharpened, staying hard and cool. There was something about how he did that that kept Ev alert and on his toes, bracing for anything.

"He asked to meet you on his own, without the others."

"I thought you didn't tell them about me."

"I also just told you he guessed anyway."

"You've been with him."

"Yeah. I told you that."

"No, you said you'd participated, but didn't say how or with whom. Are you going to be off fucking this guy when I'm at class?"

"We never said anything about being monogamous."

"Until now."

"Is that what you want? For me to only be with you?"

"Don't you want the same thing from me?"

"Oh, no one touches you," Adam grinned.

"You've decided that."

"Yeah."

"Don't I get the same respect?"

"You want that?"

"Yes."

"Okay."

"Okay?"

"Yeah. Okay." Adam walked over in a quick stride, palming Ev's pectoral muscle, twisting the nipple and catching his mouth in a brief, heated kiss. "Jealousy's sexy on you. I like it. I've never had anyone get that possessive of me before."

"Well, maybe I don't like to share either."

"Then that'll work out well for us, I think. We're agreed."

"I guess so."

The tweaking of his nipple stirred his cock. With a grimace, Ev asked, "Please stop."

"Mm," Adam hummed, running the pad of his thumb over Ev's stiff nipple. "We need a safeword."

"I thought you were painting."

The reminder did the trick. Adam's hunger faded as he surrendered to the nudge, though he was slow to stop playing with Ev's chest.

"Why didn't you tell me you know sign language?"

"I know sign language," Adam said levelly.

"Ass." Ev yelped as Adam grabbed exactly that, reaching under the skirt and squeezing. "Paint. Go paint."

After giving Ev a nerve-wracking measuring up and down glance, Adam turned to do just that.

"And you learned just for Rune?"

"It's kind of important to be able to communicate with friends and submissives."

"You drive me crazy."

"Likewise," Adam smiled back sweetly.

"You look nervous."

"Well, that might be because I'm nervous," Ev said in what he thought was a perfect imitation of the smart-ass tone Adam sometimes got with him. As Adam stepped closer to where Ev was sitting on the edge of the bed, he caressed Ev's neck and tilted his chin up. Ev asked, "Why am I always naked around you?"

"Because you're prettier without clothes." He said it fondly, ogling everything Ev had to show. "Art demands nudity."

"Or cheerleader skirts, apparently."

He'd taken that off as soon as he'd been given permission. He was, however, still wearing the stockings, at Adam's insistence, as well as the cock cage.

"I would love," Ev said earnestly, "to be able to take these off and be even more naked for you."

"Mm." Adam's lips quirked to the side. "No, I really want to do this while you're wearing the stockings."

"If I'm going to have sex with you, I need access to my own dick. Can you at least take the cage off?"

"Say please," Adam smirked.

"God, that expression of yours is really unnerving sometimes. Please. Pretty please."

They'd already had a weird dinner together, where Ev had felt more objectified than he'd ever experienced before. But the contrast of the physical chemistry between them and the mental play of their conversation was the weirdest part. It kept Ev stimulated in many different kinds of ways, which in turn only left him feeling more helpless.

And at the back of his mind, behind everything else that was going on, was the memory of what Adam had said, and how he'd actually used the L word. That alone was quicksand beneath Ev's feet, drawing him in, making it impossible to move an inch, even to save himself.

"So, how is this happening? You're still dressed, by the way."

"Can I tie you up?"

"Seriously?"

"Yes. Seriously."

"Okay?"

"Can you give me a more definitive answer? Yes or no."

"Yes. I'm just confused."

"You trust me?"

"I do."

"Good. That's all I need. Oh, and a safeword from you, just to be… well, safe. If you need me to stop abruptly and untie you, this word will let me know your needs, without question."

"Yeah, I get the concept. Just because I'm from Kansas doesn't mean I'm completely vanilla."

He looked around, searched for an idea. His gaze caught on Adam's red hair, and with his thorny personality… "How about 'rose'. Does that work?"

"Yes. It does."

Reaching into his pants pocket, he fished out the key to the chastity device. Ev let out a sigh of relief as Adam crouched down to unlock and remove the cage. As Adam fiddled with it, Ev closed his eyes and enjoyed the scent of Adam's hair. It helped soothe his frazzled nerves a little.

He felt a tug and, a moment later, the metal was off of him. He opened his eyes to look and saw Adam lean down, taking Ev's cock into his mouth and sucking on it.

Ev growled and bit his lip, one of his hands going right for that red hair, getting a handful of it as Adam pulled back, giving him incredible suction, before pushing back down again. The feel of it, the sight of Adam doing it, the sounds—everything only intensified Ev's profound gladness of where he was, no matter how or why he got there.

Adam pulled off with a soft slurp. Ev breathed hard and Adam looked up at him, blue eyes wide and watchful.

"Slide back and lie down on the pillows."

"You're going to let me touch you a little, right?"

"You want to help stretch me out?"

"Yeah." Ev felt a wave of heat as the admission passed his lips, his skin pebbling.

"You're big, so we'll need to be thorough."

"I can do that," Ev said, feeling unabashedly horny now.

Adam stood, beginning to undress as Ev got harder in anticipation.

"You really are driven by your senses, aren't you? It's incredible. You're the perfect audience for an artist, soaking everything in through your pores, cherishing all of the subtleties."

He pulled off his shirts, then unbuckled his pants, working them down before pulling away his grey boxer briefs. Ev couldn't quite believe he was going to get to top another man. Just imagining being sheathed in Adam took Ev's breath away.

Naked, Adam climbed up onto the bed. Power emanated from him like the strongest musk. Like a magic potion, the sight of Adam's muscular body affected Ev in many different ways—roughening his breath, making him want to spread, or beg, or just lose himself in Adam's warmth and vigor.

Adam climbed up until he was the one lying on the pillows. Right away, instinctively, Ev plunged his nose and mouth into the soft red curls of Adam's groin. He smelled clean, fresh, so Ev had to nudge the skin and inhale more deeply to get the true scent of him.

With a heavy sigh, Adam palmed Ev's head, undulating. "Love how you do that," he breathed.

Lips parted, breathing in Adam, Ev felt at peace. "Don't shower next time," he said.

Adam chuckled. "I was trying to get ready for you."

"I like being able to smell you."

"I can tell."

Ev pushed lower, positioning himself between Adam's legs. Drawing them up, letting them fall open, Adam was peering down at Ev while biting his lip, looking restless. Palming the underside of Adam's thighs, Ev moaned and mouthed over his groin. He ran his lips and tongue around the base of Adam's cock, over the soft skin of his balls, then behind them. Adam tilted his hips, drawing his legs up even more.

"Please, can I?" Ev begged, the tip of his nose brushing Adam's crease.

"Fuck, yes," Adam moaned. He reached for a small bottle on the nightstand and tossed it to Ev. "It's flavored. Peach."

Popping open the cap, Ev made a sour face as he got hit with the fake peachy smell.

"I'd rather smell you than the lube."

Adam laughed again. "Noted."

Ev worked some onto his fingers, then closed his eyes and let himself savor what he was being allowed to do. It felt safe, private. He could indulge fantasies long kept strictly to himself without worry or hesitation. He sucked lightly on Adam's balls and fingered through his crease, teasing his opening which felt so tight, feeling sure he'd never get it open enough to put his dick there.

"Go on," Adam encouraged when Ev hesitated. "You won't break me. I'm fairly sturdy."

Ev gave him a doubtful glance, then drew back into himself as he prepared to take the first lick. His tongue ran firmly over the clenched pucker of wrinkled skin. He pointed the muscle and pushed at the middle of the opening, working his tongue through the gap. With a heady groan, letting the scent of Adam fill his head, Ev let go. Adam's fingers scratched over his scalp and he pushed deeper, with a shiver working outward from his spine and down his limbs. He reached for his cock, which was fully erect and aching.

"Don't fucking touch it," Adam panted. "That's mine."

"Fuck… please…"

"No."

Ev ran his tongue over Adam's hole once more, then pushed a finger through his rim instead. Ev's dick dripped at the sight of it, and Adam moaned.

"I'm feeling really gay right now. This is amazing," Ev said with a lust-roughened tone.

Adam shook his head, smiling and running a hand over his face with a groan, "Just finger me. I'm glad you're finally into being gay."

"I really am," Ev said with a sigh.

He watched his finger pump inside Adam's hole. Invigorated, he wanted to fuck and conquer and never let the moment end. "Thank you for this," Ev said without raising his gaze.

"You're welcome," Adam replied with what sounded like affection.

The finger soon slid easily, coated with the peach lube. Ev gave it a taste, licking Adam's rim, then tried to push his tongue in along with his finger. As he accomplished it, he moaned. Adam gripped his legs, drawing them back.

"Add another finger, you big-dicked fucker."

Ev laughed and complied. When the second finger pushed in, he watched Adam wince and react with discomfort.

"You okay?"

"Yeah," Adam frowned.

Ev buried his two fingers and twisted them around. Adam's ass gripped them so tightly. He couldn't believe how warm and soft Adam was in there, holding on to the fingers as if he didn't want to let them go now that they were inside him. Ev mouthed over the place his hand plunged into Adam, breathing him in, peppering kisses.

After only a few pumps of his fingers, Ev was told, "Add a third."

"It's too soon."

"I'm impatient. And I'm in charge."

Ev reluctantly added a third finger, pushing most of his right hand into Adam's hole. He went back to sucking on Adam's balls, which seemed to make Adam crazy—grabbing at Ev's head, moaning loudly and arching off the bed.

Ev worked his hand gently in and out, nuzzling Adam's groin. The grip of the hand in his hair kept him there.

"Okay. Time to tie you down," Adam declared.

"Just a little longer? Please?" Ev's nose nudged the soft red curls. Adam's rigid cock slid against Ev's cheek.

"No way. C'mere."

Ev sighed with regret and pulled his fingers out. He crawled up and rolled onto his back as Adam sat up and got on top.

The leather cuffs were already attached to the bed. Adam fastened them around Ev's wrists first, attaching each one to a bedpost by a short chain.

Once his arms were secured and pulled tightly into place, Adam moved to bind Ev's legs next. Each ankle was pulled toward a corner of the bed, then similarly shackled. The whole process was so sexy, Ev was dripping again, his dick like an obscene, wet, reddened exclamation for more.

"Can I gag you?" Adam asked with wicked twinkle in his eye.

"Yes," Ev answered, too horny to care.

Adam grabbed the gag from the drawer in the nightstand and fit it between Ev's jaws. It was plastic and firm, something he could bite down on. He liked it right away and lifted his head to assist Adam in getting the strap fastened around the back of his head.

"If you need me to take it off, just shake your head, 'no'," Adam told him.

Ev nodded. His body was nearly immobilized by the cuffs. He could barely lift his hips from the bed, and other than his head, fingers, and toes, that was the only thing he could move. Realizing he was completely at Adam's mercy and about to have Adam take him for a ride, Ev knew he had never wanted anything more in his life. While making soft, pleading sounds, Ev watched Adam straddle his hips. Adam reached behind himself and steadied Ev's dick. It was against Adam's ass, his cheeks hugging the head. Slowly, Adam's wet, stretched rim pushed down, swallowing Ev's dick.

Ev shouted, quivering, as Adam gradually sank down onto him. Ev had no way to stop or hurry it, and he loved it. Panting, sweating, he was slowly engulfed. The squeeze of Adam's ass on

Ev's cock felt unbearable. The head and a couple of inches were inside him. Ev couldn't stop trying to thrust farther, even when he attempted to force himself not to, not wanting to hurt Adam like he had some previous partners. Luckily, the bonds held him down. Adam remained in charge.

Ev felt grateful for it.

But, as Adam sat there, breathing, scratching lightly over Ev's chest, Ev's desperation climbed. The squeezing tightness didn't ease. He needed to thrust, but couldn't.

Adam's fingers found each of Ev's nipples, pinching and twisting them in opposite directions. Ev cried out around the gag, straining in the bonds. Sensation pulsed from those spots on his chest, the junction of his legs.

It began so gradually, Ev didn't notice it at first, but Adam began riding him. He rose up, sank down in gentle movements. A shuddering moan shook Ev and he tensed from head to toe, needing all of it, a helpless bystander to Adam's diligent methods of taking him completely apart. Those three connections were everything. Adam had him.

Time spun outward. Ev felt hypnotized by the rise and fall of Adam's gorgeous body, the sight of his faint, triumphant amusement, the flash of his red hair and blue eyes, the strength of his body, the rigid line of his cock and soft weight of his sac. Kneading Ev's chest, closing his eyes now with a blissful expression, Adam took his pleasure. Ev submitted to it, pleading with small whimpers. His climax approached and Adam sped up the pace. Ev cried out, pleading, convulsing and biting down hard on the gag as he came. His rasping shouts were fevered, gruff, and his body spasmed as Adam rode him slowly through it.

It felt like all of his worries and tension had expelled through his dick and into Adam. It left nothing but a pleasant tingling over the surface of his skin.

Boneless, spent and quite happy, Ev stayed lax as Adam unfastened the ankle cuffs and folded Ev's legs back toward the headboard instead. Adam attached each ankle to a new chain, clipped to the ends of the headboard along with his wrists. Once both were tightened, the position had Ev's ass pulled wide open.

He'd been taken earlier, of course, so Adam didn't bother with prep. He only slicked lube onto his stiffened cock and lined up. Ev grunted, wanting it, watching as Adam fed his dick through Ev's opening. The stretch and pressure filled him in the most glorious way. It was the only way this could have ended, Ev knew. It wouldn't have felt right without giving Adam this part of him. Ev relaxed as he hadn't been able to when it was his cock inside his lover. He welcomed each thrust, bearing down onto them, wanting to take Adam in.

When he'd bottomed out, Adam caressed over Ev's rim, asking, "Better?"

Ev nodded.

Eyes closing, Adam began to move, riding Ev in long, lazy pushes.

"I think," he panted, "I'm a better fit. Don't you?"

Ev nodded, grunting, letting his head fall back, loving the way Adam's thrusts nudged him. Since he was able to use his full length and he wasn't too big, like Ev, it was easier on both of them. It woke Ev up to how much he'd begun enjoying being the receiver during sex. There was no pressure to perform or having to worry about hurting his partner. He could just give over to it and enjoy the feelings.

Adam came before Ev wanted him to, growling and pushing in deep as he unloaded. Ev whimpered in complaint as he withdrew. When Adam fed three fingers into Ev instead, Ev relaxed again.

"Mm, I have an idea," Adam said with a devious grin.

He shifted around, twisting so that he was straddling Ev's chest, then sank down, letting his balls tickle Ev's gagged mouth and chin. A hard shiver chased down Ev's spine. Adam kept fingering Ev, keeping him stretched wide and stuffed. It began to make Ev hard again, his body struggling to make it happen.

Adam reached back and unhooked the gag, then pulled it from Ev's mouth. Opening up, Ev mouthed over Adam's balls. Adam sat back and let them sink into Ev's mouth, stroking Ev's cock with his free hand.

Ev gave a hard moan, his body trying to push onto the fingers, into the tugs, but the pose he was in kept him still. Adam sat back more, letting some of his weight fall onto Ev's mouth. Breathing became difficult and Adam stroked faster. Ev shuddered, his orgasm close. Ev pushed his face up into Adam, the scent of him, the warmth, and Adam took the cue, sitting back even more, smothering Ev with his groin. The scent, mingled now with sweat and come, swirled in Ev's head, his nose, and his lungs. He needed it more than oxygen. His chest heaved, seeking air he didn't want. Adam stroked harder, his fingers massaging Ev's sweet spot.

Ev came, convulsing.

It wasn't as strong as the first orgasm, but it went on forever.

The air rushed back into his lungs and he gasped for it. The cuffs came loose. Before he'd caught his breath, Adam lay in his arms, looking him over, pulling him close. Ev just burrowed down into his embrace, laying his head upon Adam's chest, winding his arms behind his back. Ev's hair was petted, his temple kissed. He felt raw, exposed, unable to account for what he'd done or why he'd loved it so much.

Maybe Adam sensed Ev's unease, because he said, tenderly, "It's okay. I've got you," as he caressed Ev's worries away.

Chapter 21

Punishment

Another benefit to staying at Adam's place was his home gym. It was located in the same hall as the master bedroom, though farther back in the distant recesses of the apartment. This worked well for Ev. While Adam worked on painting, Ev headed for the gym to expend some energy.

Lying in bed or studying wasn't working for him. He tried for several hours before giving up. Evening had arrived, but too much flew around in his head. Conflicting thoughts bumped into one another and set off explosions. He kept thinking of James, of the way he'd been taken away completely against his will because his parents had paid people to essentially abduct him, and how he'd come back so drastically changed. He also thought about everything that had been said between himself and Adam, not to mention their deeds.

It was still too much—a reality he had sunk waist-deep into, but the waters around him were too dense for movement. Trapped, Ev waited for the wrong person to come along and catch him doing things he'd sworn he never would.

In the gym, a treadmill, free weights, a leg press and a boxing bag awaited him. After going for a half-hour run on the treadmill, Ev switched to the boxing bag. He envisioned many different faces upon it—from his own to his family members', his old friends and crushes, his coach, his minister and so many others.

He'd taped up his hands and slipped on Adam's gloves, so his knuckles were spared, but soon his whole torso ached as he whaled on the bag, the impact reverberating up his arms into his shoulders, tensing his chest and back muscles. But he bore down and poured everything he had into hitting back.

Sweating and grunting, for a while nothing else existed but breathing and thrumming with the beat of his pulse. Warm drips ran into his eyes, so he'd swipe his arm across his brow, maybe break for a drink of water, then steady the bag, and keep going.

His first clue that Adam had been watching was a touch to the back of his neck. After the first initial graze, a hand grabbed tight hold of him there. It startled him a little, making his heart jump. Lips brushed his ear, saying, "Hold the bag."

Ev steadied the swinging bag with both hands, his eyes closing as more of his focus centered on the hand gripping the back of his neck.

"Touch your forehead to it."

Trying to catch his breath, Ev obeyed, liking the way the heavy bag steadied him too.

A hand grasped his left hip, drawing it back. His feet were nudged apart. The other hand on his neck let go, rubbing down his sweaty back, along his spine, all the way down.

It happened so fast, it left him grunting roughly with surprise. After his shorts were pulled down in back, two sweat-damp fingers twisted up into his ass, sheathing there completely. Clenching on them as a hard shiver raced down his body, Ev's mouth worked as he swallowed air.

He'd barely adjusted to the claiming feel of the way the fingers had been pressed up into him when they were withdrawn, replaced instantly with something thicker. Adam held Ev by both hips as he drove slowly into him, entering him with a barely audible sigh.

There was no pain, only pleasure, and Ev made a desperate sort of whimper. Hating the weak sound of it, he punched the bag and clenched up. Adam only pushed harder to bury his cock in Ev's ass. Another violent shiver shook Ev as Adam kept moving, fucking him with steady, slow movements. Goosebumps pebbled Ev's skin. He beat his fist against the heavy bag once more, rolling his forehead against the canvas. He arched his back as the next withdrawal of Adam's dick brought a begging sort of mewl to Ev's lips.

"How does that feel?" Adam asked, caressing around in front of Ev's hips, down to palm his balls through the shorts, his thumb hooking around the root of Ev's swollen cock.

Ev couldn't speak. He panted out a few syllables, rocking back into the next thrust, trying and failing to hump Adam's hand. He felt wanton, high on the sensations and the way he felt he could let go of everything but Adam's orders. Nothing else mattered when Adam took over like this.

The hand cupping his sac squeezed, making Ev groan and quiver.

"Answer, boy. How does this feel?" He was given a long, unending thrust, and Adam's dick just kept sliding into him, rubbing right over Ev's sweet spot.

"Good," Ev panted. "Feels good."

"Sir."

"Feels good, sir."

Adam pulled out, spread Ev's cheeks. Ev shivered as the moment drew out. When a fingertip stroked over his rim, he quivered and gasped.

"How good?" Adam asked with dark undertones.

The finger rubbed in and out of his rim and Ev gasped again. "Please."

"Sore?"

"No. Please. Don't stop."

"Sir."

"Please, don't stop, sir."

"Don't stop what?"

The finger circled his entrance with a light touch.

"I want it," Ev rasped.

"Want what?"

The finger dipped into him, bringing him momentarily up on his toes.

"Your dick. Fuck me."

"Sir."

"Fuck me, sir," Ev begged.

"Who are you angry with, Evelyn?"

There was pressure at his rim, then it eased as he was entered and claimed again. Adam held there inside him, their bodies joined.

He pushed down the front of Ev's shorts so that the elastic pulled up from just under Ev's balls, lifting them to press against his hard cock.

"And don't even think about lying to me," Adam warned, giving Ev's right nipple a hard twist that shot straight down to Ev's dick, making it drip. "Are you angry with those people who hurt you?"

"No one hurt me."

Adam gave a bitter laugh and resumed fucking him. Each thrust took Ev a little more apart, unraveling his ability to do anything other than stand there, bent over and spread, taking every inch with pure pleasure.

"Who are you angry with?"

"Me."

"So you come and pound on the bag, hmm?" The word pound was punctuated with a firm slap of Adam's hips to the curve of Ev's bare ass, his dick bottoming out. Adam rubbed the skin of Ev's sac between two fingers, causing Ev's breath to catch. "You want to be punished, boy?" Adam growled by Ev's ear.

Ev nodded, rolling his forehead against the bag, pushing back into each inward slide of his lover's cock.

"Because you've done dirty things?" Adam whispered. The tip of his tongue licked lightly along the shell of Ev's ear and more pre-come dripped down his cock at the feel of it, especially when Adam caught Ev's earlobe between his teeth and bit down. He shifted his angle and the next push rubbed hard against Ev's gland. Frowning against the surge, crying out after trying to hold the sound in, Ev felt his knees tremble, his legs weak. "I told you…" *thrust.* "I would never…" *thrust.* "Hurt you, Evelyn." *Thrust.*

Adam moaned, stilling as he came, giving Ev every drop of his seed.

With barely a pause to recover, he pulled out and gave Ev's ass a firm slap.

"Get in the art studio. Jog. Go. Now."

"But…"

"Go!"

Adam stayed right at Ev's back, slapping his butt as he grabbed hold of his shorts and jogged, his dick bouncing with each step. It felt unbearably hot in all the right ways, taking Ev back to familiar places.

When Ev got to the studio, his face red with embarrassment, cock aching from the bouncing, his ass dripping come, Adam pushed him toward the bed.

"Lie down on your back. Stretch out your arms and legs to the edges of the bed."

He lay down. Adam pulled off Ev's shoes, socks, then his shorts. Quickly, he cuffed Ev's ankles to either side of the bottom of the bed, then did the same with his wrists at the top of the bed. After reaching for his supplies near the easel, Adam found a clean, dry, long, narrow-handled paintbrush. Turning it around in his hand, he used the end to tickle Ev's hole, watching his face as he fed it up his ass, just a few inches.

Ev's whole body tensed on it. His dick was red and fully erect.

Leaving the brush where it was, Adam leaned down over Ev, with one arm braced on the bed at his side.

"This is your punishment—getting to feel just how much you want this. I won't hurt you. Not for the reasons you want me to. You haven't done anything wrong." Adam caressed Ev's tip with feather light touches. "This is not something to be sorry for. But if you want to feel your truth, then lie here while I work."

Adam went to find another brush, selecting one from his collection of unused ones. With the soft bristles, he petted Ev's wet tip, painting with the fluid of his desperate need to orgasm. The beautiful torture of each lick of the brush's hairs caused Ev to hump every stroke, his thighs quaking and cries unfiltered but rough.

It wasn't enough to get him off. Adam took the damp brush and went to his painting with it, touching it to the canvas in careful strokes. He considered his work, stepping back and biting at his lip, then returned to the bed to gather more fluid on his brush, petting Ev's tip, collecting each drop from his slit.

"I won't tell if you won't." Adam used the fluid again to add to his creation. He gave the painting a scrutinizing squint. "It really does add something. The perfect touch, I think."

It went on. Every so often, Adam would return to the bed, taking what he needed for his painting. Whenever Ev's erection began to wilt between Adam's visits, he would simply fuck Ev a little with the brush up his ass, teasing his puckered rim with the tip before breaching him with it, sliding the wood as far as it would go.

The concentration reflected in Adam's expression aroused as much as each touch. Once Ev had been breathing hard, sweating and aching for a while, skating the edge with clear desperation, Adam set down his brush. He returned to the bed, stood by Ev's feet, then climbed slowly up onto it and on top of Ev.

With audible little gasps and grunts, Ev's anticipation skyrocketed. Moving painfully slow, Adam prowled into place, then leaned down so that his mouth hovered by Ev's straining, reddened cock. At first, Adam simply gave him a subtle smile. Then, his rosy lips parted. The end of his tongue pushed forward as he opened. Ev moaned, a begging sound. His hips rocked upward, trying to make contact, so Adam gripped them and pinned him down instead.

"Please," Ev panted, broken. "Fuck, please…"

In no hurry, Adam's smile widened. His tongue got so close, Ev felt himself pushing as hard as he could to try to meet it. His dick jumped. His balls, swollen and heavy, drew up. Staring, Ev grunted, his chest heaving as Adam finally gave the gentlest lick, his tongue dragging up through the divot in Ev's cock-head. Adam's talented hands bore down, gripping Ev's hipbones hard enough to bruise. The pain, the need, the sight of Adam like that, so wicked and teasing Ev right where he most desperately needed him to, the focus of so much fear and doubt—it struck him. The wave of sensation rippled outward from between his legs. Hard shivers forced a raw cry from Ev that rose in pitch when he was slammed by his third orgasm that day. He was mostly shooting blanks by that point, but the dizzying pleasure was strong.

Humming, Adam closed his lips around the head, sucking on it with force. Ev threw his head back, panting, dying, trying to undulate. The sensations were overwhelming and bordering on painful. Adam sucked him to the root, then pulled off and pulled the paintbrush out of Ev. He rubbed Ev's hole with two fingers as he came down.

This is who I am now, Ev realized. *How does he know me so well when I barely know myself? It is my truth. He sees it in ways no one else might, not in the whole span of my lifetime. I need this. I need him.*

It was terrifying but undeniable.

"Please don't share this," Ev asked quietly, with exhausted terror and the whole of his heart.

Adam's smirk had fled. In its place, the counterpart to Ev's yearning to be consumed. Ravenous, Adam growled and came at him. He slid upward, his hand wrapping behind Ev's head, their mouths crashing together. With a moan, Adam kissed Ev's sense away, his lithe, strong body rocking gently against Ev's hip, his hardness undeniable.

"No more fear. Let it go," Adam said, his eyebrows tilting in a plea as their gazes locked. Kissing below Ev's ear, he whispered, "You're beautiful. This is the real you. Don't hide it anymore. Don't."

Ev let out a sigh and relaxed, letting Adam press him down.

Standing out on the terrace, Ev gripped his steaming mug of coffee and squinted into the brilliant morning daylight. The city sprawled outward from where he stood sixteen stories up in the air. It rolled toward the horizon in gentle hills, the denseness of the trees and foliage increasing in the distance. Birds soared through the near-cloudless air. Other than the constant whoosh of wind, it was quiet.

His hand tucked into his empty pocket. A conscious decision had been made to leave his phone turned off. Once it drew closer to the time Leo was due to arrive, Ev would check it, but until then, it was a symbol of many connections he was happy to be parted from, at least temporarily.

The image of James and his fiancé rose in Ev's mind. Soon, his entire extended family would be gathering to celebrate that union, and Ev would be absent. It would be one of the first clear signals of his departure from the flock.

It was time to go. If nothing else, his time with Adam had proven to Ev that the wider world held more for him than he'd thought. The reasons to go outweighed the need to stay.

The door behind him opened and shut. A glimmer of red being tossed by the wind teased in his peripheral vision, but he didn't give into the temptation to look.

"It's cold. Come inside. You're shivering."

"How do I do this, Adam?" Ev asked. He shook his head at himself. "I'm not self-sufficient. I'm not an adult. Not really. I'd be homeless. They'd *want* me to be homeless, if I admitted to this. I don't... I don't know. I do love them. I know they love me too. But they... they'd say I'm sick. That I need treatment, so I can get better. They'd want me to get better."

"Are you sick?"

"Of course not," Ev admitted. "But maybe... maybe they'd be different than the others. Once the shock wore off, maybe they'd accept it."

Adam sighed heavily. Walking forward, he faced Ev, then wrapped him in a hug and pressed his lips to Ev's temple. Returning the embrace, Ev inhaled deeply and enjoyed the sense of added steadiness.

"You can't control the reactions or opinions of other people."

"I know. It's just that I can't expect you to be my only support. It's too much to ask."

"You don't have to ask."

Ev could feel Adam's heartbeat against his chest, and the tickle of Adam's hair against his ear. He was warm, sturdy, and a shield against the wind.

"What have you decided?"

Ev let go. He let Adam guide him back toward the door and into the apartment again.

Once the gusts were closed out, things became much quieter.

"I'm not going back. I'll need to tell them I'm taking a break from the family obligations in order to find myself. They don't need details."

"You'll live with me?"

Ev bit his lip and nodded. With a shy bow of his head and a brief upward glance, he said, "Yes, sir."

Adam gave a breath of what sounded like relief. He cupped Ev's jaw in a hand and kissed his other cheek. "Good boy. I'll take such good care of you."

"I'd love that," Ev answered, choosing the words with intention. He found Adam's hand, weaving their fingers together. Keeping his head bowed, he said, "I don't know how to thank you for everything you've done for me."

"You don't need to thank me. I already have everything I could want, right here."

He lifted Ev's chin with a finger. Eyes downcast, Ev leaned into the kiss, brushing his lips against Adam's and holding his hand tightly.

Chapter 22

Impressions

An hour before Leo was due to arrive, Ev offered to run to the market down the road to pick up some food. After letting Adam take care of the cooking for days on end, Ev felt determined to help host the brunch, since Adam was already providing the setting. It had taken some persuasion in the form of kisses and promises to obey Adam's every command later on when they were alone again. In the end, Adam's state of distraction as he worked on one of the larger paintings in his studio allowed Ev to get his way.

As Ev strolled out of Adam's building and headed down the city sidewalk, he turned on his phone. It took a minute or two to start up and begin to gather any messages he might have missed while it was shut off. While it worked, he made it all the way down one block and halfway down the next. He expected to have a text message or two from Leo waiting. What he didn't expect was to have notifications popping up one after another after another.

"What the hell?"

There were emails, texts, and social media alerts. Nervously, he clicked to investigate. A comment posted on Facebook led him to a photo he'd been tagged in.

"Oh fuck. Oh no," he breathed, tensing up with alarm. He stopped walking and stepped aside, closer to the curb in order to get out of the way of other pedestrians hurrying this way and that.

Ev stared at the picture showing him and Adam standing together outside the dorms. Adam's hand wrapped around behind Ev's back in a noticeable, intimate way. The caption read, 'Teacher's pet. Gee, Ev, what would Daddy say?'

It had been posted by an obviously fake account with the name of Major Boring. The profile picture was of a piece of graffiti that defaced one of the bronze statues on campus. The person was friends with a good majority of the school. The photo had gathered several hundred likes and countless comments. Once he saw some comments speculating about what Adam liked to do to his pet, Ev stopped reading.

He dropped the phone to his side, his hand covering his mouth, his eyes wide with shock.

This seemed destined to get back to his father. He felt it. It might have already happened. Someone could have easily emailed the photo to his father's public campaign address. Clearly they knew who Ev's dad was and how his politics clashed with Ev's coziness with Adam.

They knew way too much.

"What the fuck do I do?" he asked no one.

He could un-tag himself, but to what effect? The post had gone viral. Too many people had seen it.

A few months ago, Ev had been standing on a stage with his parents, listening to speeches about how the ruling to make gay marriage legal nationwide was tearing the country apart, sending its morals in a downward spiral that only the most steadfast leaders could correct through a hard-line stance for the sake of the American family. Now, he was on social media with his male lover.

He'd done it. He'd put himself there.

He just hadn't expected to be forced to face the consequences so quickly.

His phone rang. Dread was a cold, hard pit in his stomach. Reluctantly, he glanced at the screen. The caller ID told him it was Julia Myers, his mother.

"Oh fuck me," he groaned. He clicked the ignore button, then stood there, frozen.

His calls with his mother were a perfectly scheduled, weekly occurrence. He'd just talked to her two days ago. There was no reason for her to call unless it was an emergency.

The phone had fallen silent.

It began ringing again.

"Oh my god, leave me alone," he yelled. Various pedestrians around him gave him strange looks.

But the caller wasn't his mom. It was Leo. For a second, Ev hesitated in answering anyway, just out of sheer paranoia.

He gave in and answered, saying, "I'm freaking out, man."

"Why? What happened?" Leo said with instant concern.

"Someone tagged me on Facebook in a photo with Adam. Like they saw me with him on the sidewalk on campus and took a picture of it. It's been seen by hundreds of fucking people."

"Ev, calm down, dude. You haven't been hiding. You kissed him in public. We've been over this."

"I know, but they mentioned my dad in the caption, as in they know who my dad is. They could have sent him the picture. And my mom just tried to call my phone when there's no reason for her to call right now."

"Ev. Calm the fuck down. I'm on my way over right now. We'll talk it through, okay? Where's Adam? Isn't he with you?"

"I went out to get food for us." Ev glanced all around where he'd been standing, scanning the crowd. He wondered if there were any Southern Baptist churches nearby with a connection to the Pathway to Manhood program. He'd read that they were a nationwide organization, present in all fifty states. "What if they come after me?"

"Who? The nosy fuckers on campus?"

"No! Never mind. Just come over. I'll meet you there."

After hanging up the phone, Ev continued on to the market rather than turn around. Adam was counting on him to get the food, and Leo was going to get there expecting to eat soon, but there were other reasons for the decision, too. All of his life, Ev had been trained to bury feelings and present a calm, composed demeanor when in the public eye. If something upset him, his job was to think around the problem privately, rather than ranting and raving to his parents. This expectation had actually taught him to be fairly self-sufficient in most aspects of daily life. Whether it was a rough day at school, bullies, not doing well at a game, being criticized by his coach or teammates, or simply struggling with the clash of his wants versus the severely limited options being presented to him, Ev was mostly on his own.

His parents' passive aggressive style only added to the dynamic. If he opened up about being disappointed in a bad grade, the response would be that he obviously didn't work hard enough. It was the same thing with any sports-related heartache. Bullying events were never reported to the school to avoid making it public record that Ev was a snitch. His father also firmly believed that if you tattled, you were only asking for more punishment. And, always, when in doubt, they simply told him to pray.

Ev had been fairly young when he'd realized praying wasn't going to solve his problems, though he hadn't told his family as much.

Ev's emotional outburst at Leo was simply the product of timing. Had Leo called a few minutes later, Ev might have calmed down.

Walking through the market, gathering ready-made food in his basket, selecting some fruit, tea, and small bags of flavored coffee, Ev let time settle his restless mind.

There were two distinct problems at hand. The first was the photo and the reality that not only had many more people been informed of his relationship with Adam—a teacher at their school and a man—but going forward, Ev would either need to deny the relationship and hide it from view, or do the opposite.

The second problem was his family, and whether they'd seen the photo and the consequences of that if they had.

Ev thought around the problems from all angles, seeing them from his point of view as well as that of his peers, family, and the current political landscape in which their lives were being staged.

By the time he'd walked back to the apartment, rode up in the elevator, and knocked on the door to be let in, Ev had mostly made up his mind.

Adam answered the door with a paint-splattered rag in his hand, wiping up stray drips on his arms with it. He leaned in to give Ev a quick kiss on the lips. "Hey, how'd it go? I was just about to clean up and start getting things ready."

"There's a problem. We should talk," Ev told him.

Folding his arms, Adam widened his stance and lifted his chin, gazing down his nose at Ev. "What problem?"

Ev walked past Adam. He headed for the kitchen and set the bags down on the counter.

"Someone got a picture of us together and posted it on Facebook. Many people have seen it. My parents were mentioned in the commentary, so I've been connected publicly now not only with you, an employee of the school, but with my father as a public figure. I also had a call come in from my mother. I didn't answer it. I need to decide on how to approach this first, because I'm guessing they were emailed the picture."

"Okay, first of all," Adam began, holding out an opened hand. "Are you okay?"

"At first I wasn't. But this isn't the first time the media has picked up a story about me or my parents that I wish they hadn't. I'm better now, but this is a big fucking deal."

Dropping his gaze, Ev turned to the bags and began unpacking them.

"I can do that," Adam said, striding over to intervene.

"Just let me? Please?" Ev asked. "Doing things helps."

"Okay," Adam relented.

Ev set out plastic containers filled with freshly made sandwiches and pastries. He grabbed one of the bags of coffee, then went to brew it.

"Are you going to get in trouble because of this?" Ev asked.

"With the school?"

"Yeah."

"I shouldn't, no. But even if they did make a stand on this, I don't need the job. Being with you is the priority over that."

"Okay," Ev nodded. Adam was searching Ev's face, maybe trying to read into the eerily composed, serious nature of his expression.

"There are only two options, here," Ev continued. He scooped coffee grounds into the filter, then went to add water from the tap. "Either we completely deny and avoid public appearances together, hoping the gossip will blow over quickly, or we carry on as we've been doing and don't let them see they've touched a nerve."

"No gray area?"

"No." The water added, Ev started the coffee maker with a touch of a button and turned to face Adam again. "The first option only hurts us. The second option hurts my family, which would create direct consequences for me."

"I've never seen you like this," Adam commented with fascination, holding his chin in his hand while studying Ev. "It's the wide receiver in you coming out, mixed with the Senator's son. Very interesting. I like it. Incredibly ballsy and kind of hot."

A smile threatened for a moment, but Ev plowed ahead. Adam saw it anyway and smirked a little.

"So what's our play here?" Adam asked with a slight narrowing of his eyes.

"Second option, no question. I'm not hiding myself away anymore, especially for stupid reasons. You drive me to school. They'll see us together. I'm not going to avoid being out in public with you just because I'm afraid of being seen. If I'd wanted to live that way, I'd have stayed in Kansas."

"*Really* fucking hot, actually," Adam said mostly to himself. Ev's smile broke free again before he reined it back in. "So what about the consequences?"

"Well," Ev let out a heavy breath and planted his hands on the counter, leaning slightly over it. Adam edged closer. "I have a confession to make."

"To your parents?"

"To you."

"Oh. Interesting."

The doorbell rang.

"Fuck," Adam murmured.

"No, it's okay. Leo can hear this. He already knows the rest of this."

"All right," Adam said, sounding doubtful. He turned and went to get the door. Ev returned his focus to setting out the food.

Opening the apartment door, Ev heard Adam say, "Welcome, welcome. Come on in."

"Is he losing his shit?"

"Surprisingly, no. So you know about this?"

Eavesdropping, Ev kept glancing up as he brought the food out to the table.

"The picture?" Leo asked, strolling in at Adam's side. "Yeah. God damn, Mr. Buchanan, this place is insane."

"It's just Adam. But thanks."

Leo was gaping, craning his neck to look in every direction possible. It made Ev crack a smile.

"Hey, man," he called. "Come on over. Have a seat. Dig in."

Ev ran his hands through his hair and went to kick his shoes off in the bedroom while Adam and Leo headed to the table. Walking at a quick pace, he retreated to the dimness of the place where he'd been sleeping more often than his dorm. He toed off his shoes near the doorway and let out a heavy exhale. Taking a second for himself, he leaned back against the wall, pushing his hands into his pants pockets.

"Evelyn?" Adam called from down the hallway.

"I'm…" his voice came out weaker than expected, so he cleared his throat and tried again. "I'm fine! Coming!" Softly, to himself, he groaned, "Fuck."

He felt cold, shivery, and nauseous. In the dark of the bedroom, it was safe to let it out. He needed to get it together in order to go back out there.

The sound of boot heels coming down the hall made Ev groan.

"I said I'm fine," he called, but by the time he got to the last word, Adam was there. There was a look on his face of his typical scrutiny and willingness to call bullshit to Ev's lies and subterfuge.

"I know what you're doing. I'm not your fucking constituent and neither is Leo. You don't need to perform for us. If you can't talk about this yet, I'll show Leo out. We'll reschedule."

"No." Ev knew all of his inner conflict and terror was showing. "I said it's fine and it is. This is what I do, Adam. I close a door, fall apart, pull it back together and plaster on a happy face."

"That's a fucking awful way to live, and I think you know it." Adam scolded, his blue eyes ablaze. "Stop trying to impress us. Why on earth would you think you need to?"

"Habit. Worry."

"Worry about what? Leo? Me?" Something must have moved behind Ev's eyes at that, because Adam seized it. "Why are you worried about me? Of all things?"

"I'm a…" his breath failed him, his chest tight. "I'm a fucking pansy when I get scared, and of course I want to impress you."

"With lies? Acting? What have we been doing in that goddamned studio, huh? How have I not convinced you that I want you bare, honest, and vulnerable in every sense? This isn't about what I like in my sexual partners, you know. This is about me and you. Me and you. Look at me."

Ev tried, but he couldn't raise his gaze. Tears burned. He bit down on his tongue, blinking his eyes to clear them. Adam forced Ev's chin up, holding it in a hand.

With barely any sound, Ev said, "I don't want you to think less of me."

"Trust me to understand that it takes much more bravery to be truthful. Please. Think about who I am. Hmm?" He took fierce hold of Ev's gaze, wouldn't let it go. "A lawyer, first. Right?"

"You'd have been a fucking terrifying lawyer," Ev admitted softly.

"What does a good lawyer want to get?"

"His way. The truth. To be convincing."

"Right." He moved more fully in front of Ev, came closer, pinned him to the wall by pressing against his body. "Would you like to know what I want, Evelyn Myers? Tell me if I'm convincing enough or not."

Ev swallowed hard, watching Adam's mouth.

"I want you to tell me every single one of your dirty little secrets. Things you never dreamed of being able to share. I want you to let me in... here." His index finger prodded Ev's chest, right over his heart. "All the fucking way in. No one else is invited. Not even Leo. I want you to make yourself completely, maddeningly weak, in every way you can conceive of. Physically, emotionally, logically, whatever. It is my job—my job—to take care of you when you're weak, whatever that means. Whether it's telling your best friend you need some time to yourself, or giving a fairly fucking large piece of my mind to your lovely parents, or holding you when you're scared, or pushing inside you—as far as I can get—so you don't feel alone anymore. That's what I fucking want. So tell me, are you convinced?"

"I love you," Ev said, nearly swallowing the words, he was so afraid to let them go.

The ferocious energy in Adam melted and he crashed into Ev, kissing him while frowning and holding him by a firm grip that wrapped the side of his neck.

When they broke, Adam breathed, "Fuck." His lips brushed against the other side of Ev's neck, his breath heating the skin. "Fuck." Adam's teeth scraped the spot, and a pleasant shiver raced up Ev's spine, his hands gripping Adam's hips. "You knew I meant it, didn't you?"

Ev stayed silent, his eyes closed, his body tense.

"I haven't said I loved someone since they died."

Ev combed his fingers through Adam's red curls.

"It doesn't... come easily to me."

"You don't have to say it."

Adam was still frowning; Ev saw when Adam pulled slightly back. He gave Ev a light kiss, lingering, and mouthed against Ev's lips, "Love you, Evelyn."

It felt like falling, flying. Breathing harder, Ev held on tighter and kissed Adam back.

Chapter 23

Confession

The three of them sat around the giant mahogany table, carved with delicate scrollwork and clawed feet, sitting in high-backed, richly upholstered chairs in violets and reds, beside floor to ceiling windows letting in the mid-day sun and spectacular views for miles.

"He said he has a confession to make," Adam told Leo, who had a sandwich paired with a mug of coffee and a wide-eyed stare that tried to capture all of their surroundings. Adam sat on the other side of the table from Leo, turned sideways to face Ev, who was perched on a chair by the end of the long table. Fingers tented, eyes sharp, leaned forward, Adam was a captive audience. Leo, not so much—which was fine with Ev, who wanted as little attention as he could get.

"What kind?" Leo asked before taking a large bite.

"The kind I've never admitted to anyone before," Ev said with a surge of self-consciousness. He sat back in his chair, ran both hands over his mouth, then sat forward again, resting his elbows on his knees.

"Take your time," Adam said.

"I know," Ev sighed. "I…" He stopped, ran a hand over the back of his head and looked down at the floor as he began to speak. "My cousin, James, was taken away against his will to a conversion camp. Adam knows this already. You don't, Leo. They kept James against his will for months until he declared to the church and his family that he was no longer gay."

"Brainwashing, kidnapping, torture," Adam interjected.

"Fucking hell, man," Leo said, dropping the food and frowning with worry at Ev.

"I was just a kid. So was he, but... It scared me, obviously. He was sent away because they found us together, but they thought it was just him touching me, that it wasn't consensual. But after James left, I tried to find out more about the place they took him.

"After he came back, James wouldn't talk about any of it, not that he wanted to talk to me at all, about anything. But others would talk, and there were accounts posted online, anonymously. I spent years learning as much as I could about this place.

"The Pathway to Manhood, is what it's called. They're all over the country, everywhere, in every state. They work through the church and are backed by other anti-gay organizations. You have to pay in order to attend, and it's a lucrative business. But they have licensed psychiatrists working with them, who really believe the therapy works, that if you want to be cured, they can cure you."

"James didn't want to be cured," Adam said, sounding angry.

"Maybe not at first, but did he change his mind? He had to have. He came out completely different. He never said a bad word about the place."

"What did you hear? What did you find?"

"The locations are usually remote. They cover all windows with black tarps, so you can't see inside. They're staffed by people who went through the program and were cured. They all wear these... pouches... around their necks. Magic beans, symbolizing the potential in each man to return to his path and achieve his goals.

"Depending on how you get there, your treatment varies. Some people go right to therapy, group sessions. They're assigned chores and do hard manual labor in order to cleanse their spirits. They aren't allowed contact with the outside world. But people who are brought there, like James, by their family... they're locked up. Confined. Sometimes, if they're young and naïve, they're told they have AIDS, that they're the last gay man on Earth and if the government finds out, they'll be executed. They condition them to see homosexual acts as something distasteful and negative, so they aren't tempted by them anymore."

"How?" Leo said with disgust.

"Lots of different ways. Usually by showing images or video or sounds of gay men together, then introducing negative stimulation. They might go the fire and ice route. That involves setting blocks of ice on the subject's hands or genitals. Fire is coils of heat wrapped around the flesh. They turn on the heat when the images appear, and turn it off when the images go away. They also might apply electricity to the genitals, or give the subject nausea-inducing drugs, then surround them with glasses of urine while playing sounds of gay sex. I mean, you get the idea."

"They did this shit to your cousin? When he was how old?" Leo gaped.

"Thirteen."

"God damn. God damn, Ev," Leo groaned.

"But as soon as you tell them you're not gay anymore, they stop all of that, immediately. They accept you and let you begin to help others."

"You're telling us all of this for a reason. What is it? What are you saying, Evelyn?" Adam demanded. He wasn't rising to the bait at all. He stayed locked on, honed in, and peering right between Ev's lines.

"I'm saying…"

He couldn't finish.

"It's all right. We're listening. We care about you," Adam promised.

Ev couldn't speak. His throat had closed up. He got out of his chair, pacing. Leo was glancing between Ev and Adam, looking tense.

Ev reached for a glass of water he'd brought to the table, drinking from it.

Finally, he tried again. "I'm saying… I… I wanted them to take me. I prayed for it. I even saved up my allowance money to cover the fee and I tried to find a way to go without my parents finding out. I'm saying I—" His voice broke. He turned his back to them, holding the back of his head. Footsteps approached. A solid, warm presence at his back smelled beautifully familiar. Closing his eyes, Ev said, "I wanted them to hurt me for being this way. I wanted them to fix what's *wrong* with me."

Wiping his eyes, Ev felt Adam's strong hands grip his shoulders. A kiss was pressed to his cheek.

"Please tell me you didn't go," Adam begged.

Ev shook his head. "I was too scared. I fantasized about it. I even tried to duplicate the treatments I'd read about on my own. I'd look at gay porn and stuff my underwear with ice cubes. I'd bite on a belt to keep from screaming."

Glancing back over his shoulder, Ev saw Leo with his hands tented in front of his mouth, his eyes wide.

Adam wrapped an arm around Ev and held him. It helped Ev take a deep breath and feel a little better.

"My point," Ev said, "is that I realize now, after everything at home, everything with you, Adam... there is no fixing this. I tried. I really did. And I could see through the acts of the people they counted as success stories. They're all haunted. Damned. They're not cured. So, I can't undo this, or correct it. I have to live with it. My parents might still think they can fix me, but I know better. Whatever the fallout is from them finding that picture of us... there's nothing I can do for them. I can only hope they'll still love me. But I have to be ready to have them let me go."

"Screw them," Leo shouted. "No fucking way. Who could do that to their kid? That's not right. Ev, you've gotta get away from them. *Away.*"

"That's what I'm trying to do. That's why I'm here instead of Kansas. That's why I'm with Adam."

"We're here for you," Adam told him, turning him around to be face to face, clasping the side of Ev's cheek. "I swear it."

"Absolutely, Ev. Whatever it takes," Leo chimed in.

"Thanks," Ev said, still feeling powerless against the obstacle facing him. "Really. Thank you, both. I appreciate the support. I'm sure as hell not used to it."

"What are you gonna do about school?"

Adam let Ev go as he began to pace a little, thinking it over. "Face it head on. Let them see I'm proud of being with Adam and that I don't care if they know about it. If they see us, the photo's a non-starter anyway."

"You can handle that?" Adam asked.

"I'd like to think so. I guess we'll see, right?"

—▭—▭—▭—

Monday morning was the true test. Ev had his Behavioral Theory in Management class. Adam planned to give him a ride in.

One thing Ev held on to, which had gotten him and his family through other scandals, was the knowledge that people are much less likely to comment on something to your face as freely as they would when hidden behind an alias on a computer. Standing up to them with bravery, not letting them see your fear, meant being able to handle just about anything.

"In a weird way, they did prepare me for this exact situation," Ev said as they reached the outskirts of the campus. "Though they'd never see it that way. All of those years, forcing me out into the spotlight whether I wanted it or not, for reasons that had nothing to do with me or what I wanted... You can't let it intimidate you. They're just people. People will always have opinions, but if you show them what you want them to think, a lot of times they'll follow your lead."

"Possibly, but there is real danger here. Don't forget that. Be careful," Adam told him with a warning look, his blue eyes darting sideways before focusing back on the road before them. "Don't let anyone get you alone. Watch your back. If anything happens or if you have any doubt, call me or find campus security, right away."

"All right."

They pulled up to the building in which Ev's class was held. Not many people were around, and the ones who were seemed half asleep.

"Call me if you need a ride earlier than when we agreed," Adam said. "Good luck with your appointment with the counselor."

"Thanks." He glanced over at Adam, unsure whether he'd want to say goodbye in the car or not. A second later, Ev's question was answered when Adam opened the driver's side door and got out, then came around the car. Ev took a deep breath before stepping out after Adam had opened his door for him, holding it open like a true gentleman.

On guard, Adam's expression seemed defensive, watchful, almost angry. Ev slipped his hand inside Adam's, stepping up into his personal space. With a plaintive expression, Ev said, "I'll be fine."

Jaw clenched, eyes hard, Adam didn't seem convinced. "If your parents try to call you again…"

"I can't avoid them forever."

"It might be best not to give them fodder for their fucked-up cause, and leave them in the dark as long as possible. Let's tackle one hurdle at a time. If we can get through the next few days, I have somewhere I'd like to take you on Wednesday."

"A surprise?" Ev smiled.

Adam smiled back, not letting on. Then, hand hooked around the side of Ev's jaw, he pulled Ev in for a very public but tender kiss. Wrapping his arms around Adam, Ev returned the kiss and opened up to it, even if it did make his heart pound against Adam's broad chest to do it.

"Please be careful," Adam asked in a whisper.

"I will."

As nervous as he was about what they'd just done, it felt just as scary to step back from Adam and head into the building. Ev noticed each person who stared, though no comments were made. When he waved to Adam and hurried inside, Ev kept his head high but didn't make eye contact with anyone. He saw a few people he knew casually, and said hello to them first, before they could notice he was there. They all said hi back. Reaching his classroom, Ev found a desk, opened his bag and pulled out his notebook and pencil. He looked right at everyone who came into the room, and everyone who glanced back at him as they all sat there, waiting on the professor.

The more time that passed, the less it felt like a big deal. The morning proceeded in a normal way.

A few hours later, once the class was over, he checked his phone on the way out and over to his shift at the admin office. He'd had it on silent and saw he had missed a call from his father. A voicemail message awaited him.

Stepping into the shade under a large oak tree, Ev pushed down on the queasy flutter in his stomach and listened to the message.

"Ev, this is your father. Your mother and I have been trying to reach you. Call me back as soon as you can. There's something we need to talk about right away."

Ev groaned and deleted the message.

"Hey, Ev!" someone called. He looked around, seeing Mark from the track and field team. Ev waved and yelled hello.

Part of him just wanted to know, to face it. He didn't want to hide; even from a lecture or whatever it was his parents had in store for him. It seemed better to know than to guess and let his panic make the call for him. He knew he'd told Adam he'd leave it alone for now, but instinct told Ev to man up. If meeting and falling for Adam had taught him anything, it was that worrying about something was never going to help a situation. The only way to know the truth was to stand in its path and let it reveal itself.

He pushed the button to call his father's number.

"Ev?" his father asked after picking up.

"Yeah. It's me. What's up?"

"Someone emailed a very disturbing pair of photos of you to my public email address. Do you have anything to say about this?"

"How can I have anything to say if I haven't seen the photos?"

"They show you and a male teacher at the school. Together."

"Okay."

"Ev, if you have a problem, you should have come to us first so we could find help for you. If this is what I think it is, it's something better handled in private. Discreetly. Especially now, when so much attention is focused on me and the family. You know that. You know better."

"Dad, all I'm focused on right now is school. Trying to do well in my classes and establish my own life. I can't help you with your image anymore. Who I spend time with is really none of your business."

For a moment, there was silence on the other end. Then, Brandon Myers said, "I see. That's all you have to say for yourself?"

"Yeah, pretty much."

"Fine then. If it's not me you want help from, I'll put some people in touch with you who can help you get a handle on your illness."

"Dad, I'm not sick! I don't need help. I need you to realize I'm an adult now and you don't have a say over my choices anymore."

"I was afraid this was going to happen. You should have stayed close to home, gone to one of the schools I initially presented to you. But now it's too late. We'll just have to deal with the consequences. It's for your own good, son. You know how much we care about you."

"Dad, don't send those people here! I don't need—"

The line cut out. The call ended.

Chapter 24

Fighting for Freedom

Ev had trouble paying attention at work that afternoon. Staring wide-eyed and un-seeing at the paperwork waiting to be filed, he debated calling Adam, and what exactly to say when he did. Instead, he let time slip by. At the end of his shift, he stepped outside, the cool breeze blowing the hair back from his face. He scanned the sidewalk, the road, and the grass where people lingered under trees or on blankets.

He needed to make his way over to the counselor's office, but telling Adam had to come first.

With dread, Ev pulled up Adam's name in his phone and pushed the button to call him.

"Evelyn? What's wrong?"

Ev rubbed his forehead, the sprawling campus around him full of too many watchful strangers. As long as they could see him, he wasn't safe. "I, um… I don't know what to say."

"About what? What's going on?"

He looked around for unmarked vans or large SUVs with tinted windows. Every person who caught his eye was a suspect, a potential danger.

"I'm a little… overwhelmed."

"Why?"

"I don't…"

Even if he hid, they would find him. They were going to find a way.

"Is someone giving you a hard time?"

"You're going to be mad."

192

Adam got quiet. Ev was really glad Adam wasn't there in front of him. The distance helped lessen Ev's panicked dread of Adam's reaction. "Why am I going to be mad?"

"I promised you that I wouldn't call them."

"Your parents?"

"Yeah. And I…"

"You called them."

"My dad."

"What did he say?"

He didn't want to say the words out loud, making them real. If he didn't say it, it might just stay a nightmare, not a fact.

"He, uh… said he's going to put me in touch with people who can help me with my illness. He's gonna… he's going to send them for me, Adam. And I don't… I don't know what to—"

Adam cut in, asking, "Where are you right now?"

"On my way to the counselor."

"I'll meet you there. I'm on my way. Go get inside. Go wait in her office. I'll be there soon."

The call ended. Ev started to walk, but with each step he took, he felt urged to move faster. Soon, he was jogging, sprinting, running as fast as he could, arms pumping, lungs burning.

An hour later, Ev found himself sitting with Adam, the counselor, Victoria Amstberg, and a couple of police officers. The situation had been explained. He felt cold, drained, and tense.

"What would you advise we do to ensure he's safe from these people?" Adam asked the officers.

"Make sure someone is with you at all times," the officer said. "You can enable the GPS feature on your phone, which can help us find you in an emergency. Just be smart about this. Don't go out on your own. Don't let anyone you don't recognize corner you. We'll take a look into this organization, see what we find. If they really do intend to abduct you, Mr. Myers, then at least we know who to watch out for. If they do try anything, they'll be charged for it. There will be consequences."

"Good," Ev murmured.

"Let me make sure again that we have all of your information. You live in the dorm on campus?"

"I was, but now I'm going to be living with Adam."

"My building has impeccable security," Adam told them.

"Good to hear."

They took down all of his contact information and both addresses. Then they gave him phone numbers to call if anyone suspicious contacted him. Soon, the officers left and only Ev, Adam, and Victoria remained.

"Talk to me, Evelyn," she encouraged. "What are you thinking right now?"

"I can't believe this is all really happening. The anticipation for it has been with me my whole life, so in a way, I'm relieved? But it's scarier than I'd thought it would be. I mean, I know my parents love me. They still do. They just truly think these people are doing good work. That they're helping the people they take. It just leaves me feeling... lost. Overwhelmed."

"And how does Adam fit into all of this for you?"

Ev glanced over at Adam, who reached out and clasped Ev's knee. He was sitting forward, tense, ready to spring up and attack anyone who made a move for Ev.

"Adam... he represents the future. He's where I'm going. Everything with my parents and the church is the past. He's what I'm fighting for. They're what I'm fighting against."

"Do you feel safe with Adam?"

"Yes," Ev replied, right away. "He's the only one who makes me feel safe right now. I know he wants to protect me. Help me."

They talked a little longer, then Adam ushered Ev out and over to where the car was parked.

"Can you just promise," Ev asked, keeping his voice low, scanning the darkness of the evening for threatening shapes, "that if something happens, you'll find me and get me out of there? No matter what it takes?"

"That's *not* going to happen," Adam said forcefully. "They're not taking you."

"But if they do..."

"Then they will fucking *pay.*"

Everything was still quiet on Wednesday morning. Ev drew into himself. Not speaking much, focusing on studying or posing for Adam in his downtime, he'd had a couple of days to relax as much as was possible.

Now, after picking up breakfast on the go, they drove out of the city and towards the northern countryside. Ev was content with not knowing the destination, as long as it got him out of range of the church and his parents' people. The tension had both Ev and Adam ready for any change in environment.

They listened to music for the fairly long trek, with the wind blowing through the windows. Ev dozed a little. When he woke, they were rolling slowly up a long, tree-lined drive to a stone mansion on a hill, surrounded by lush, carefully landscaped vegetation.

"What is this place?" he asked drowsily, rubbing at his eyes.

"Damhan's home. He's just left for a trip for a few days, so he let me know we could use it if we wanted. He likes to lend me the keys as a way to tempt me to keep it once I inherit it."

"It's really nice," Ev said, sitting up straighter and peering at the impressive, old-fashioned home.

They parked in front and got out of the car. Adam went around to the trunk to unload a large knapsack and supply case. Eying the plentiful supplies, Ev began to guess the reason for the trip.

"So there's no one here?" he asked.

"Not a soul."

There weren't any neighbors, either. Turning in a circle, Ev saw not a single other building or sign of humanity nearby.

"Mm. So… what are you up to?"

With such a pleasantly overcast day, the lack of bright, direct sunlight made it that much more tempting to go wandering around the flowering grounds. The temperature was in the low sixties. It was perfect, mild, fall weather.

"Follow me," Adam said with a tilt of his head.

Around the back of the sprawling home there had been an impressive attempt to landscape with low maintenance plants and plentiful thickets of trees that stretched to the sides of the property in both directions as far as the eye could see. Beyond the tree line waited an open rolling meadow, thick with wildflowers in violet, crimson, gold and fuchsia interspersed with tall, waving grasses that reached almost to chest height and was relatively clear of trees.

Rubbing at the back of his neck with one hand, Ev said to Adam, "I'm gonna take a wild guess and say this is planned for a background in a new painting of yours."

"Well, now you've just gone and ruined the surprise," Adam said in his smart-ass way, but with an adorable smirk. He set down his supplies and unzipped the knapsack. It was full of small-to-medium sized blank canvases, as well as some other odds and ends.

Taking a deep breath, Ev filled his lungs with the fresh scent of the billions of flowers being tossed in the breeze before him. Birds sang in the treetops by the house, which cast a wide, but faint, shadow over where they stood, right on the edge of an opening between copses of trees. The clouds above were laced together and thick, creating layers piled one on the other reaching up to the heavens.

"It's nice out here. Quiet." Insects buzzed or chirped. The wind whistled. There was no road noise, no engines roaring or other signs of anyone around. "Reminds me of home, only with more hills."

"Is that good or bad?"

Ev shrugged. "I never had an issue with the geography of where I'm from. Only the people I had to deal with. When you're so much different than everyone around you.... It just makes it hard to feel like you belong. It's like the whole of your life is trying to push you out. But... where do you go? How do you know somewhere else will be any better?"

"Is that still how you feel? Like you don't fit in?"

"Hmm." Ev smiled faintly at him, watching him unpack and get everything spread out around him. He even unfolded a tall, narrow easel with a tray. There was something soothing about the methodical way Adam carefully arranged everything, organizing his well-used, splattered and half-empty tubes of paint, his variety of brushes and rags. Ev felt he could just stand back and watch him for hours, quite happily. "You make me feel like I fit," he admitted, feeling self-conscious and dropping his gaze. "Everywhere else... I'm still waiting to see what happens."

Raising an eyebrow and looking like he was trying not to seem too proud of himself, Adam said, "Well, that's something, at least. Can I ask you something?"

"Shoot."

Adam lifted a medium-sized canvas from his stack and set it on the easel. Without turning to face Ev or even looking up from what he was doing, he asked, "Did everything with your cousin give you any trust issues with partners?"

"Male partners?"

"Whatever," he shrugged.

Ev took a moment to think about it. Adam ran one of his favorite thick brushes through his hands, watching the meadow like he was seeing things from his imagination projected there.

"Not the way you mean," Ev answered. "Or how I think you mean, anyway. The whole larger situation did more to make me afraid to trust people rather than James in particular. He never told anyone the truth about us."

Adam stopped at that and turned to look Ev in the eye.

"Think about that," Ev told him. "He was essentially kidnapped, brainwashed, tortured... and not once did he tell them I wanted it as much as he'd wanted to do it."

"How can you be sure he didn't if you never spoke with him about it?"

"They would have come after me. They would have alerted my parents or the ministers that I had issues that needed correcting. James knew I'd wanted it. So, why didn't he rat me out?"

"Did he know? Are you sure he knew?"

"He..." the air ran out of Ev's lungs and he scanned his memories. There had been attentive eagerness in James's blue eyes, and the way he'd leaned over Ev, pulling for more in very real ways. There had been the way Ev made soft cries, feeling overwhelmed but good—amazingly so. "Yeah, he did," Ev decided, nodding.

"So he chose to keep that information from them."

"Yeah."

"You still trust him?"

Ev flapped his hands in something like defeat, or maybe the refusal to worry. "I don't know. But things aren't as cut and dried as everyone's pretending they are. So, to answer your question, no. I don't have trust issues with partners because of him. It's kind of crazy, I guess, but what happened in that bedroom with him still feels private, like it's still only ours. They don't know what it really was. They don't get to take that from us."

Adam held Ev's gaze, and Ev remembered everything they'd done together—as well as everything Ev still wanted to do.

"When you think of James, what's the biggest thing in your heart and head?"

"That I wish I could save him. I wish there was a way to help him be free."

"Maybe the best way to help that happen is to set yourself free first."

Adam walked over to Ev, setting a hand on the swell of Ev's chest and leaning in to lightly kiss his lips.

"What if it all goes wrong?" Ev asked.

"What if it doesn't?"

"Trust me."

Ev was tempted to smile. They'd shifted a little closer to the meadow. The blindfold tied around his head was made of a length of white, soft, cotton fabric. Some light filtered though, but he couldn't make things out other than the large patches of shadow created by the trees and building towering before him. Adam slowly undressed Ev. His shirt tugged up over his head, drawing his arms upward with it. His jeans were unfastened, the zipper tugged down.

The scent of the flowers was so strong, and it made Ev feel like he was home, even if he was actually somewhere he'd never been in his life, doing things he couldn't anticipate.

Maybe he should have been nervous, or shy, or uncertain. But he was calm and comfortable as Adam peeled down Ev's pants and underwear, leaving him to stand there completely nude against the natural blanket of nature at his back. The movements of Adam's hands against Ev's body, first in removing his clothes, then positioning him, were so confident and demanding, it helped Ev feel even more at ease. He was pushed, pulled, pressed and caressed.

"Imagine you're in the gym, alone. You're angry, charged up, ready to go. There's a boxing bag in front of you."

Ev tried to put himself there. He widened his stance, setting his right foot in front of his left by a good margin, then raising his fists. His shoulders were lowered, his core strong.

"Perfect. Stay just like that."

Adam walked away, then came back. Ev tracked him by the soft crunch of his booted footsteps over the thick grass. Something barely heavier than air landed on Ev's shoulder, then the upper edge of his left cheekbone, then his arms and the top of his curled fist. Those feathery touches remained.

"Try not to shake them off."

Ev realized what they must have been—flower petals.

He imagined how he must look, ready to fight, a symbol of masculine strength and power, sprinkled with something undeniably feminine and fragile, full of color and a more subdued, simple kind of life. Smiling a little, he couldn't help but love the concept. Not only was it a great idea for a painting, but Ev felt it spoke to a deeper part of who he was in ways no one but Adam understood. Ev had been fighting his whole life, but those flowers were something he yearned for. They were one of the few things that could melt the cold, hard pretense he'd so carefully armored himself with.

"You're good, you know," he told Adam.

"I'm glad you think so," Adam replied. "But don't you dare move. No smiling. Look angry." And a moment later, "I said no smiling."

Laughing between the words, Ev said, "Don't you have an imagination? I can't scowl for hours at a time."

There was more crunching of soft footsteps, then a wave of heat against him and the faintest brush of lips against his. "I like when you stand up for yourself," Adam whispered. "Keep doing it."

"Yes, sir." Heat and touch faded away. He tracked Adam's footsteps back to the easel. It was hard to tell if he was actually painting or sketching or just standing there watching. After a little while in which nothing was said and Ev focused only on maintaining the pose, he commented, "I just thought you might be more the unquestioned obedience type of guy."

"Why, because I like to be in charge? What's the fun of that if there isn't some banter and a little tête-à-tête to keep things interesting? In the short time we've been together, haven't I challenged you at every turn, Evelyn? I'm not interested in a lover who's a pushover with no opinion of his own or the ability to defend himself. That doesn't mean I want you to openly defy my orders, but I welcome any chance to press at you harder to see if you'll yield."

Ev wanted to reply, but wasn't sure how. So, instead, he let Adam's questions float around inside his mind as he held the pose and slowly grew more and more sore from the strain.

When Ev was finally allowed a break, he groaned and stretched, extending his arms to the sides as widely as he could, flexing his feet and bending his legs. Then, he sat in the grass and leaned back, propping himself up, his arms braced behind him. "I've gotta say, you've been very well-behaved so far today."

Ev couldn't quite tell where Adam was until he spoke up in answer from a few feet away. "What's rule number one?"

"Hmm... You don't share?"

"Exactly."

"But there's no one else here."

"How can we be sure?"

"Great, now you're making me paranoid."

"That's not my intent. We are essentially alone here, but I haven't searched the house, or ruled out the possibility of neighbors stalking through the brush."

A chill raced up Ev's spine.

He strained his ears, hearing only low, mostly indistinguishable sounds from all directions—the rustle of grass against tall wildflowers, the whoosh of the breeze in his ears, the snap and tap of one thing against another. Something brushed against his ear and he jerked his head away, his heart beating faster. Then something small and hard was pressed to the side of his head.

He thought about what his dad had said, the threat he'd made.

"Adam, I'm gonna take the blindfold off," he said shortly, his chest feeling compressed, like some great weight was crushing it.

There was no answer.

"A-adam? Adam?!"

Ev reached for the blindfold, but his arm was grabbed, then twisted up behind his back. He yelled and something was jammed into his mouth and against his nose. It was fabric, smelling strongly of some kind of chemical that made him instantly try to recoil and fight. He bucked as his other arm was twisted behind him as well, and in his ear, an unfamiliar male voice hushed, "Shhh... Time for a little nap."

Suddenly lightheaded, Ev felt his grip on wakefulness slipping fast—too fast. He cried out, yelling Adam's name. His body was too heavy, the grip of several hands on him too strong. Like a curtain coming down, all went black.

Chapter 25

Rescue

"He's waking up, sir."

"Good. Mr. Myers? Are you with us? Almost."

Ev wrestled his eyelids opened. They seemed to be three times as heavy as usual.

The strong, undeniable need to vomit surged up from deep in his gut. Retching, he recognized something that looked like a bucket next to him. The full contents of his stomach ejected into it. Between heaves, he gasped for air, his head pounding with a massive headache.

"Keep him turned until we're sure he's done. Another minute will do it."

His surroundings swam, making no sense. It was dark, the space he was in confined. There was a sense of movement and jostling, which only added to his disorientation and nausea.

He tried to speak, but all that came out was a mumble.

Ev tried to move and realized he was bound in place. He was also still completely naked.

"Okay, flatten him out. Secure the base. Fit that back in his mouth. Make sure it's tight."

The world tipped over and he squeezed his eyes shut until it stopped. Whatever he was bound to clattered into place. Something soft, like fabric, was forced between his teeth. It stayed there, prying his jaws apart, his teeth sinking into the yielding texture, his saliva wetting it. He felt it being tied around behind the back of his head, which someone lifted momentarily until the job was done.

Somehow, struggling, he managed to get his eyes opened. He was flat on his back.

"There you are," a chipper but masculine voice said. It carried weight with it, as if the speaker was used to speaking often and confidently to a captive audience. Ev tried to fix his eyes on who was talking, his gaze sweeping his field of vision. A man who looked like an overly-styled news anchor or local politician sat at Ev's left side. He had brown hair, brown eyes, a square jaw, cleft chin and a bleached, toothy grin. Wearing a tan suit with a blue button-down shirt underneath, he leaned forward, his hands clasped between his knees.

Ev mumbled again. The gag made speaking impossible.

"Yeah, sorry about that," the guy frowned, sounding like he wasn't actually sorry, but felt he should suggest he was. "That's mainly so I can ensure you have a chance to really hear what I have to say. Once I'm done, I'll take that out. Sound good?"

Since Ev couldn't respond, he grumbled at the nameless dickhead through the damp cloth, biting down on it as his anger grew as big as his fear.

"How close are we?" the guy asked, but not of Ev. He was looking up past the back of where Ev lay tied down.

"Thirty minutes, sir."

"That'll work. Keep that handy just in case." He nodded to something Ev couldn't see, but the way he'd said it made Ev's stomach churn uneasily, his balls trying to draw up into his body.

"So. Mr. Myers, maybe you're wondering how it is we found you. I'm assuming you know who we are? But maybe not. Well," he laid a hand on his own chest. "I represent an organization that's great friends with your family—your parents as well as your church family. I've been placed in charge of welcoming you to our treatment facility, which is where we're headed to now. Is any of this ringing a bell?"

Ev narrowed his eyes, breathing harder out of anger instead of fear.

"It does!" the guy said happily. "That's wonderful. Check that off the list, right?" He chuckled good-naturedly, his body rocking slightly with the movement of whatever they were inside. The more

Ev looked around, he saw it was the inside of a van, the walls and ceiling painted black.

He thought suddenly of Adam, and got scared, worried. He tried to sit up, fighting the bindings. There was one across his chest, and one across each of his wrists and ankles.

"Sir?" the man behind Ev asked.

"No, not yet. He'll settle down, won't you, Mr. Myers? Aren't you curious about what I have to say? You aren't going anywhere other than where we're taking you. If you don't see that yet, you will soon."

The dickhead was right. Ev couldn't budge. He told himself to save his energy and be smart about this. The best way to help himself was to keep his wits together.

When Ev stopped fighting the tough, thick straps, collapsing back to the surface beneath him, the man said, "That's better. Now, where was I?"

Visions of torture, interrogation, and attempts at brainwashing swam through Ev's mind. He remembered all of the frightening scenes from his vivid imaginings, elaborately detailed over many years of mental toil. Was that what was about to happen?

Somehow, he grew even more still, his body feeling colder.

"Oh, right. Well, it wasn't difficult to determine where you've been staying. Darn that social media, right? Invasions of privacy and all of that." There was a merry chuckle, a shared joke with another man deeper in the shadows by Ev's feet. The man showed his teeth when he laughed, parting them slightly and looking like a humanized but unhinged ventriloquist dummy. "But you realize *everyone* knows about Adam Buchanan, right? I mean, you're a smart kid. And news spreads as fast as wildfire these days. No secret is safe." Another hearty chuckle. The man sat back, seeming quite comfortable and calm. "So, we were keeping a close eye on his building. Saw right away when you two took off together this morning, and figured we had our shot!" A brighter laugh. "To turn a phrase."

Someone else laughed, then a third.

Ev realized what the laughing was about and began to panic, his heart pounding, eyes shooting open wide, and breath squeezing out of his lungs, suddenly leaden.

They'd shot Adam.

Ev felt like he was falling through the bottom of the van, through the earth itself, the voices around him coming from far away.

He envisioned Adam, collapsed and bleeding out in the grass beside his painting supplies, and no one else around for miles. Adam turning gray, all alone, his heartbeat slowing to a stop. No help was coming.

Ev tried to snap out of it, to think rationally.

These were devout, religious people. They wouldn't commit murder, even for this, even of a known, professed homosexual. Would they?

"Mr. Myers? Mr. Myers?"

He tried not to listen, to just go away somewhere else, alone, to change some dial in his head where he could turn the world off and pretend nothing had happened, that he was still on the edge of the meadow, posing for Adam.

It wasn't working very well. He couldn't stop trembling. A feeling of deep upset and a need to cry was nearly overpowering. The thought of losing Adam, that it might have already happened, was dizzying. It was too big and painful to begin to comprehend.

"I apologize for the measures we had to take. Your very *soul* was in danger, don't you see? That man you've been spending so much time with, he's dangerous. *Incredibly* dangerous."

Ev latched onto the present tense description, taking it as a desperately needed sign that Adam was still alive. He forced himself to breathe more slowly, to calm back down.

"We're not the enemy, Mr. Myers," the man at his side professed with seeming earnestness. "I'm sorry we had to meet under these circumstances, but your family is very concerned about the disturbing choices you've been making. Maybe you feel like our methods are extreme right now, but it was a priority to us to get you away from the influence of that man, so that you can finally see what it is you've been doing to yourself."

Ev didn't believe or trust a word the guy said, but it was hard to stay fixed on those instincts when he sounded so invested in what he was saying, without a hint of doubt in himself or his words. He had plenty of charm—the kind people like Ev's father used to help themselves rise up the political ladder, into places of influence and power.

Knowing the tactics didn't completely help Ev tune out the promises and persuasion.

In a strange vehicle, with unknown people, drugged and held against his will, he sped along to a remote mystery location to possibly be tortured or worse. To be confronted with someone saying they had his best interests at heart was hard to ignore.

"Now, we've already apologized for the measures taken today, and we can assure you they're for your own good." The man raised his eyebrows, giving Ev a leading look, his lips pressed tightly together. "Adam Buchanan is dangerous. That's a fact. We've already had a doctor do a brief medical evaluation and there are signs you've been... taken sexually... against your will. Signs that you have been bound and that a man has anally penetrated you."

His breath catching, Ev felt the squirming of ants over his skin at the thought of these men examining him while he was unconscious—spreading his cheeks and poking at his asshole to see how tender it was. He'd had sex with Adam that morning, upon waking. Some bruises marked his body from bondage and rough, consensual sex.

A jittery, shaky feeling swept over Ev.

Lowering his voice and imbuing it with regret, the man said, "I'm deeply sorry you were forced to endure that. It must have been painful, humiliating, and quite scary, huh? When a man has been raped in that way, it has severe consequences, mentally speaking. The shock is so great; some are even able to convince themselves that they wanted it to happen. Has that happened with you, Mr. Myers? I hope not. I hope you are able to see the trauma and evil that has been committed upon your body, sacredly created by our Lord and Savior."

He took a closer look at Ev's eyes, leaning down over him, filling more of Ev's vision. "Was it that man, Adam, who raped you? He's a proven sex offender. The history is there, so I wouldn't be surprised. However, we've learned that he also associates with cruel and depraved individuals, so I have to ask... did other men rape you? Did Adam instruct others to force themselves upon you, Mr.

Myers? If you could nod your head yes for me, I'll remove the gag now so you can give us their names."

"But, sir—"

"No," the man cut in, eyeing his companion. "No, Mr. Myers has earned that much. You're safe now, son. It's our sworn duty to protect you from these evils, and we will do everything in our power to set things right. So please, nod your head for me?"

Ev stayed still, trying to keep it all straight in his head, to not listen to the lies. If Ev let them believe Adam raped him, they might not torture him in the hopes of 'curing' his homosexuality, but Ev couldn't let them think Adam was a rapist, even if it spared Ev suffering. It felt like James all over again.

The swaying movement of the van and disorienting feeling left behind by whatever they'd drugged him with made it hard to keep hold of his resolve or certainty.

"No?" The man sat back again, sighing. "Okay. We'll give you more time to get adjusted. We realize it's hard to admit to such despicable, disgusting acts, even when you've been forced to participate against your will. But the Lord will give you the courage you need. The good news is that your family and your church family are prepared to protect you from such predators. You're in good, safe hands. Truly. Can you feel God welcoming you back into his open arms? God forgives you, Ev. Can I call you Ev? If you repent in your heart, that's the biggest, best first step. Move past the shame and back into the strength and conviction of righteousness."

Chapter 26

Breaking Point

It wasn't comforting, he told himself. It didn't make sense. They were just trying to get him to stop being gay, and there wasn't anything wrong with being gay.

But the boy in him still wanted to believe, wanted to take the path that would lead him out of the confusion and scorn. He'd tried to find it for years. Now, it was right under his feet. Confident, convincing men waited at his side, pointing the way. Either he could take the first step, which would be easier than he'd ever dreamed, or he could fight them.

Fighting them would only lead to suffering. Going with them would spare him that. Those were the only options.

Someone blindfolded him again. They told him it was to protect the identities of the people caring for him, that as soon as he willingly accepted their help, consenting to go along with their requests, they would take the blindfold and the gag off. All it would take, they'd said, was for him to nod. Then, once the gag was removed, say, "I'm ready."

It would be so easy.

They'd moved him from the van and onto a gurney, wheeling him outside, then into a closed space. He was cool, then too warm, then freezing while being moved from one space to another. Still naked and completely uncovered, the shame overwhelmed him at being so exposed to an unknown quantity of people.

The gurney stopped.

A hand clasped his arm, above the elbow.

"Now, Ev, I'm leaving you for a little while in the care of our staff physician. He's going to take care of you while I'm gone. Unfortunately, he's forbidden to speak to you until you've accepted our help, to protect his identity. If you need me to come back and help you, all you need to do is nod your head, all right? That's all you have to do."

A cold hand touched Ev's thigh, making him squirm and grunt with discomfort.

"That's just the doctor."

Another set of hands touched Ev's arm. There was the feeling of liquid being swabbed onto the inside of his elbow, then the pinch of something tight around his arm. He knew what came next, but still grunted in shock as the needle was fed into him. Once it embedded in the inside of his elbow, cold pressure grew as fluid rushed into his body through it. He began to shiver and shake from head to toe, the cold now inside as well as out.

He wanted to ask that they raise the temperature of the room, knew they had to see him shaking, but was mute, unable to do anything but either lay there or to go along with what they wanted of him—and that would mean betraying everything he was, and Adam too.

"The nurse has inserted an IV so we can get some much-needed medicine into you. You don't look well, Ev. That's something we need to fix, fast."

He needed to tell them he didn't require any medicine, that he was fine. He struggled against the binding on his wrist, but couldn't even jostle the needle, which was now taped in place.

A dizzy feeling washed over him then. A weary, heavy feeling took him and the room started spinning.

They'd drugged him. He knew it, but could do nothing about it.

Adam will find me, he told himself.

Adam's been shot, he remembered.

There was no more explanation. Only some heavy footsteps, clip-clapping over a hard floor, then the opening and closing of a door. The man at Ev's side had vanished.

He was moved again, his body soon too heavy to shift as they dragged him sideways off of the gurney and onto something else, all of the bindings released. As soon as he lay in place, new straps wound around his wrists. His legs were set in stirrups like he'd seen pictures of for use in gynecological offices, spreading him out. Then, his ankles were bound in place on the stirrups.

Fluid—cold, strongly smelling of alcohol, and stinging—was spread with large swabs over his body from chin to ankle. When they coated his penis and sphincter with it, the stinging bloomed into full, inescapable pain, clawing up into his body from the outside. When he began to shout through the gag and buck, they only swabbed on more. He told himself he was imagining it, that they weren't really adding extra fluid to those sensitive areas to deliberately cause him pain. That's what it felt like, though. He shuddered, fought back a sob, and felt the soaking swab circling the tip of his penis, forcing the fluid into his urethra, dripping down into it. Liquid fire burned away at him. Straining every muscle in his body, pushing off the table, he felt a hand gently steadying his penis and continuing to apply the stinking, scorching solution to his most sensitive spot.

The burning intensified and deepened, making him tremble uncontrollably.

Nod your head. Do it. All of this will stop. Give them what they want. You don't have to really mean it.

But if he cooperated with them in any way, there would be no going back. He'd have sold out Adam and himself.

But no one is coming. You're trapped here forever unless you do something to make them stop. You know they will do anything to get their way.

They let go of his penis, but it was too late, he was already in agony and there was no making it end.

There was the snap of a glove, or so his imagination suggested. Then, pressure against his sphincter. Something warm pushed into him and he grunted, shuddering again. The pressure filled him, going inches deep. Whatever was penetrating him moved around, feeling him out. It poked at him from the inside, testing his elasticity, silently measuring every reaction.

How many were watching this? How many people were in the room, taking notes, evaluating his progress or lack thereof? Trying to find homosexual qualities to his reactions to the invasive touches?

The panic grew in size and strength. The clawing need to get out overwhelmed everything else. He began crying out. His shivering became violent, all of the warmth in his body draining away.

The thing up his ass pulled out. A cuff wound around his upper arm, then began to squeeze, like they were taking his blood pressure. Something round and cool touched chest. Something hard, cold and metal pressed against his sphincter, then was forced through it and he cried out louder. It kept pushing into him, going farther than the first object, feeling more wrong in many ways. It hurt and the pressure from it increased. It was spreading him, he realized, opening up inside his anus to pry him apart. Once it had widened inside him, it didn't decrease in size or shift at all. The ache from it was a throbbing constant, though the shame was much bigger.

The blood pressure cuff eased slowly. Something stuck into his ear. Then poked up his nostril while the end of his nose was lifted by an unknown person's finger.

How many people were there? Were they laughing silently to themselves? Noting how pathetic he was? Enjoying his discomfort and humiliation?

They began to stick other things into his ass, between the jaws of the contraption locked into place, forcing his hole to spread as much as they wanted it to, stretched beyond his personal limits. The ache throughout that area of his body grew, but the sharp poking of swabs or sticks or whatever they were, scraping at him from within, made him scream.

Someone began to manipulate his penis, touching every inch of its surface, then did the same to his testicles. They were pulled on, lifted and twisted.

He wanted to nod. He really did. He knew they would stop, if he did.

Something touched the hole of his urethra in the tip of his penis. He shook his head from side to side, begging without words.

His protest weren't heeded. A thin, hard object was forced into him there, through his slit, and he quivered with shock, gasping through his nose. The pain was of a new, viciously intimate sort as his penis was slowly impaled.

Behind him, a door opened and shut. Footsteps clip-clapped over a hard floor, coming right up to him.

He didn't want them to. Fighting the bindings with his waning strength, grunting thickly between his muffled shouts, he tried to deny what was happening.

Frozen, drugged, impaled in two kinds of ways, bound and petrified, Ev had barely enough awareness left in him to realize how he must look, and the disgrace was very real. It made him feel incredibly small, stupid, and utterly helpless.

The man from the van said, from right by Ev's ear, his breath warm there, "You know, it's very dangerous to have sexual relations without using protection. We'd never forgive ourselves if we didn't do every possible test to rule out disease or infection, no matter how deeply inside your body we need to check, especially since you've been repeatedly raped by a known sex offender."

The stick pulled slightly out of his cock, scraping against it from inside with intolerable friction that had Ev screaming again. The stick lingered, the last inch of it still inside for a moment, then pulled completely out. He throbbed and wished he could cover himself somehow.

The jaws wrenching open his ass spread farther still and Ev's breath caught, his fingers splayed, his desperation strong as a bright scream bubbled up, erupting while barely dampened by the wet gag.

"Do the tests again to make sure. All of them. This is too important to not take every measure we can."

Ev wept. The sharp scraping at the inside of his ass resumed. The stick jabbed back into his penis, stuffing it and going even deeper.

By his ear, that suave masculine voice said, "All you've gotta do is nod, Ev. Show me you're ready to be free. Are you ready? I've got a nice, warm bed waiting for you. You can call your parents, get some rest. Come on. I believe in you. You can do it."

Cold, pain, and shame. That's all he knew.

"How does that feel? Does that feel good?"

He shook his head.

"Do you want it to stop?"

He nodded. It took him a full second to realize what he'd done.

With a startled yelp he tried to think of a way to take it back, to undo it.

"Well, you heard him," the man said more loudly. "Okay, everyone. He's had enough."

Everything that hurt withdrew, went away. The comfort of just not being touched between his legs felt tremendous. They laid a blanket over him. It all just kept getting better. The rewards were immediate and intoxicating, but all he could think was, *What have I done?*

The bindings were released. The needle was removed from his arm. The blindfold and gag stayed on, but they helped him sit up, then stand, then sit down in a wheelchair waiting there for him. Once he was seated, they wheeled him out into a warmer space.

Drawing the blanket closely around him, still shivering uncontrollably, Ev couldn't figure out if he'd just made a huge mistake or not. He wouldn't wish to be back there on the table for anything.

He wanted to hope that someone was going to come rescue him, but there didn't seem to be any way. It was just a fantasy. He wondered if James had those fantasies when he had been held in a similar place. Had he hoped the whole time that Ev would come rescue him somehow? The thought made Ev nauseous with the crushing pressure of guilt.

He didn't want to be glad he'd nodded, but he was.

They went down a few hallways, turned sharply once or twice. The chair stopped. The gag was finally untied. He groaned, stretching his jaw as it came off, his mouth and tongue dry and cottony. Then, the blindfold came off too.

He was in a very small room, with a cot, no windows, and a tiny table. There was a wooden cross on the wall directly in front of him, and a Bible on the table. The man from the van stood at Ev's side, and he held a full cup of water, the glass damp with condensation, telling Ev the water was cold. Trying to lick his lips with his dry tongue, his gaze fixed on the water, he heard the man ask, "Who else hurt you, Ev?"

"No one else."

You mean no one. Why did you say it that way? Adam didn't hurt you. Right?

He remembered running to the bathroom in Adam's studio, hiding behind the door, begging to be left alone.

"Okay. Is there anything else you'd like to tell me?"

Ev shook his head, but didn't say anything more.

The man handed over the water.

Ev sighed with huge relief, grasping the cool glass with trembling hands, cradling it between both as he tried to bring the rim to his lips without spilling any.

"We'll have the results from those exams soon, so we'll be able to tell you whether or not you've contracted anything. Did Adam Buchanan use protection when he raped you? I bet he didn't, did he?"

Ev tried not to react, but the questions caused him to tense up. They'd never used condoms. Not once.

"Yes, unfortunately that's very common. Well, there's nothing to be done about it now. If you have contracted a disease, we'll figure out the best course of treatment for you, okay? Nothing to worry about. We're here to help. You want us to help, don't you, Ev?"

He nodded again, hunching down in the blanket, clutching the frigid glass.

Ev's voice was rough, dry, as he tentatively asked, "C-can I... some clothes? Please?"

"Of course. I'll see what I can do about that, all right?"

"Thanks."

The man left, shutting the heavy door behind him. A bolt turned and, trembling, Ev stared at the cross, unsure what to think, or do.

Chapter 27

Off the Path

Hours passed, and Ev slept through some of them, worn out and slipping into unconsciousness on the cot, the blanket wrapped around him. The drugs must have had something to do with it. They muddled his thoughts, though he felt clearer upon waking.

Without a clock or a window, he couldn't tell how much time had passed. Without a glimpse of daylight, he didn't even know whether the sun was up or down.

No clothes had been delivered to his room, which left him drawing into himself, equal parts scared and confused. He hated that some of what the man had said made sense, and how sincere he'd sounded when saying they were only acting on behalf of Ev's family. He could even see things from their point of view. If they thought Adam was dangerous and preying upon Ev, it made sense that they would try to get him away through whatever means necessary. They would anticipate his instinct to fight back, to stop them from taking him. They'd want him to listen to what they had to say, instead of letting him rant and rave. The blindfold, even the physical exam were not things he could logically say were uncalled for.

Questioning himself and the decisions he'd made, Ev's thoughts circled back around again to James. He had already gone through all of this because of Ev. He'd had his life shaken up, and endured therapy for years. Ev had done that to him. Maybe everything that was happening now, to Ev, was warranted. He was hurting others, as well as himself.

Still, he knew he couldn't undo the feelings he had for Adam. Adam, who'd been shot because of Ev.

What did that mean? Where had he been shot? Was he okay? Was he dead? What was happening to Adam out there? It must have been serious; there was no sign Adam had been able to even make an attempt to stop the Pathways people from taking him, and for Adam to not even try wasn't like him at all.

He couldn't keep from imagining it. Thoughts of Adam bleeding, Adam dying, were horrific. It all only made Ev feel like more of a lost cause.

He *wanted* them to hurt him. He wanted them to tell him how sick he was. He wanted to pay for what he had done to James and Adam.

The room and the unknown space beyond it were quiet. He didn't hear any voices, or the rustle of distant movement. He didn't detect a hum of electricity coursing through the wires in the walls, or the whoosh of air through vents. All was still and silent.

Maybe they'd left him there to stew for the night, locking him in, walking away.

It could be many hours until anyone showed up again.

After what could have been minutes or days, he heard noise. The strange, worrisome sound reminded him of playing football, and the sight of the other team, running as one, directly towards him—screaming, riled and ready to slam into his team as hard as they could.

He pictured huge, wall-sized men padded with gear, running right at his little room. The louder the sound got, the tenser Ev became. He shifted into a crouch, drawing back into the corner of the room, the far edge of the bed, his knees pulled up to his chest.

Footsteps ran up the hall beyond his room, coming right for him.

The door burst open. Ev cringed, cried out. Three large men wearing business casual attire poured into the room, their expressions frantic and angry.

"Grab him! Go, go, go!"

"Hey! Hey, stop! *Leave me alone*," Ev yelled, trying to fight them off through his own lethargy.

One of them hit him, hard, in a solid punch across the face. The world spun, tilting, fading.

They dragged him along, a strong arm looped under each of his arms.

The blanket pulled off, left behind. Beyond the room, cold air hit him again. Even that wasn't enough to completely rouse him. His head throbbed, his senses muted. Had the punch done it? Or were the drugs still in his system?

"You got sedative?" one of them asked.

"At the van. They keep the supplies in there. Come on, move! The cops are almost here. We've gotta get him and the others clear."

They hauled Ev down a hallway and through a set of double exit doors. It looked like the community centers back home where his father gave speeches in the lead-up to his campaigns. The walls were painted in hues of beige, the structures minimal and generic, without any identifying features.

Outside, full night had fallen. The darkness closed around them, swallowing them up. Other black shapes in the night crowded around a pair of vans. The brake lights glowed red. The men on both sides of Ev manhandled him toward the closest van. Near the back of the opened doors, someone waited with a syringe and a vial.

"Shoot him up."

"No, please," he tried to cry out, his voice cracked and weak. "Don't! I'll cooperate!"

In the distance, sirens could be heard, growing louder by the second.

But the man on Ev's right sneered, "We don't have time for this. I'll handle it. Hold him steady."

The man on Ev's left hooked his arms around Ev's, locking them behind his back. The other stood facing Ev, a small leather club pulled from a clip on his belt. Liquid terror flooded Ev's weakened body, but he didn't even have time to react or fight. The first brutal blow across the side of his head didn't knock him out—merely drawing stars to fill his vision, his ear ringing, the pain sudden and huge—but the second one did.

When Ev woke, he realized before even opening his eyes that he was strapped down again. It felt like a metal spike had been driven through his skull and that something like a bowling ball had been lobbed at the side of his jaw. Anticipating more pain in other parts of his body, already helpless to a bright wash of pure fear, he fought as hard as he could, trying to sit up, to free his arms, screaming roughly and thrashing.

"Hold him! He's gonna hurt himself!"

"Kid! Hey, kid! Knock it off!"

Ev's eyes cracked open. He panted, wheezing. Again, he had a sense of movement, even while lying down. The familiarity told him he rode in another vehicle, another van. Medical equipment and several unknown people surrounded him. It occurred to him, dimly at first, that he did recognize the person seated closest to him, but he couldn't place the face.

That confused him enough to get him to stop struggling.

"Who...?"

The young man was covered in tattoos and piercings and he began to move his hands in specific, strange ways.

He was signing.

"Oh. Oh fuck, you're... you're that guy. Adam's other sub. Rune. That's your name. But..."

Rune pointed at Ev, then made the OK sign, looking curious, his eyebrow raised.

"I don't know," Ev replied, lying back, trying to catch his breath and think through the fog of the world's worst headache. "I don't know if I'm okay. Where... where am I? What happened? Why are you here? What's going on?"

He looked around a little, his panic fading enough for rational thought to take over, and saw for himself where he was just as the other man, at Rune's side, explained.

"You're in an ambulance. On the way to the hospital to make sure you're okay and those fuckers didn't do any weird shit to ya."

The guy was big, scarred and scary, with a salt and pepper beard, matching long hair, wearing an old leather jacket with patches on it and jeans. Rune also wore a patched leather vest and jeans. A female EMT watched a heart monitor attached to Ev.

"Who the hell are you?" Ev asked. "How did I get here? I don't... I don't understand..."

"I'm Max. Rode with junior, here, for a while, before he took off on us. Heard you were in trouble, so we went to get you out. Cops got there first, of course, but the creeps snuck you all out the back, tried to slip away to another fuckin' hidey hole. But we know this area just as well as they do. Cut 'em off and pulled you out."

"You pulled me out?"

"Yeah."

"Of the van?"

"The Pathway van, yeah. They tried to shoot us with fuckin' tranq guns, but luckily we've got some target practice under the ol' belt. Put an end to that shit."

"You shot them?" Ev rasped in shock.

"Shot the tranq guns, not the guys. Do I look stupid to you? There were cops everywhere."

"Where are the cops now?"

"Still back there. Back behind us too." He thumbed at the rear doors, and Ev realized he could see flashing lights through the glass.

"But why... why are you here?"

"You're Adam's kid. He's still fucked up, so it's on us to make sure you stay safe until he can get here."

Fear swelled, a balloon growing inside Ev's chest, pushing at everything enough to hurt. "Why is he fucked up?"

"I think you should let him rest," the nurse interjected.

"No!" Ev cried. "I need to know. Is he okay?"

"Sir, please—"

She guided the gurney to lay flat. The beeping of the heart monitor was frantic and fast.

Max gave her the side-eye, then said to Ev, "Adam was injected with a heavy dose of sedatives. He overdosed and things got hairy for a minute there, but he's at the hospital and he's okay."

"Oh my god. Oh fuck..." Ev fought to breathe, to think around it. "How'd you find me?"

"License plate on the van. Heard the report go over the radio, met the cops at the compound, circled around to the back, just in case."

"License plate? What are you talking about? Who got the license plate? Adam was the only one there, and if he was unconscious..."

"Who says he was the only one there?" Max asked. "The 9-1-1 call had to come from someplace."

The EMT interjected again, sounding really pissed off, "Okay, that's enough. Sir, please try to rest. We'll be at the hospital in four minutes and get you evaluated. Are you experiencing any pain?"

"No, I don't... my head hurts, I guess. And I'm sore... I... I don't know. Dizzy. My head..."

"Okay. There's nothing to worry about. You're in safe hands."

"That's what they said, too," Ev murmured.

Rune signed something to Max, who signed back to him, but Ev had no way to tell what they'd said. He stopped trying to keep track and closed his eyes.

Many questions swirled inside Ev's aching head, but they wouldn't come out. Once they'd processed him and done their own evaluation of his condition, deciding to put him on IV fluids and to monitor him over the next twenty-four hours, Ev closed down. He knew they were worried about the head trauma and the unknown cocktail of drugs he'd been injected with. His penis and anus were still a little sore from the first round of tests, so it hadn't helped when they'd been poked and prodded a second time. They'd told him they hadn't trusted the doctor at the compound to have been licensed and skilled at the procedures they'd performed on him and, fearing internal damage, had gone ahead with a too-thorough exam, but at least he hadn't been restrained, blindfolded and gagged during it.

Ev didn't want to talk to anyone, so it was probably fortunate that it was Rune who'd been appointed his babysitter, since Ev didn't know how to communicate with him anyway.

He even feared asking about Adam, not wanting to hear more bad news that would only make him feel guiltier about the damage he'd caused.

From his seat at the side of the room, facing the door, Rune took several video calls on his phone. With his phone propped up on a table in front of him, his conversations were gestures only, no sound. Pretending to sleep to avoid having to interact with anyone, Ev found himself watching Rune's hands shape the air, his facial expressions mirroring the intent of his messages.

A little later, someone besides a nurse, doctor, or police officer came into his room. Wary, Ev glanced up at the handsome, tall man with dark hair and intelligent, hazel eyes. Dressed in a full, seemingly expensive gray-colored suit, he looked like he'd just left a board meeting or court room. He pushed a wheelchair closer to Ev, and in the chair was Adam.

Ev didn't know what to do, what to say, how to act.

A nurse accompanied them. Adam seemed drowsy, weak, and wholly unlike himself. Only a hint of the usual fire remained in his eyes, though as his gaze locked right onto Ev, it flared a little.

Adam's wheelchair stopped by the side of Ev's bed.

For a moment, there was only tense silence, filled with Adam's building rage. He wasn't even blinking.

Meanwhile, Ev's heart pounded. His throat felt squeezed, his reaction complicated by layers and layers of fear and exhaustion.

"Are you all right?" Adam finally asked. He reached for Ev's hand, laid on the bed, an IV line taped onto the back of it. Ev flinched away, the fear still too fresh to fight, but Adam was determined. He took the hand, keeping it in a firm hold.

Ev couldn't speak, or begin to convey what he was going through. He didn't want to get upset there, in front of all of those people. He wasn't okay. Not at all.

Undaunted by Ev's quiet, Adam told him, "Evelyn, this is my dear friend, Oliver, who I've told you about. He's been here, watching out for you, but was giving you some space until official introductions could be made."

Ev nodded, his bruised and swollen jaw clenched and his eyes lowered.

In a softer tone, Adam asked, "Are you in pain?"

Raising his eyes, staring out the window to his left and the first signs of dawn, Ev felt tears gathering, but he didn't let them fall.

"Please. I've been so goddamned worried," Adam begged.

"They told me they'd shot you," Ev said, his voice thick with repressed emotion.

"Hey, I'm fine. *I'm fine*," Adam said, leaning forward, covering their linked hands with his other one.

"And I knew there was no one around to help, or... Stop the bleeding, or..."

"Look at me, Evelyn," Adam said firmly. When Ev struggled to manage it, blinking too much, his throat burning, Adam added, "Please."

Tuning out the others, the room, and the world beyond, Ev met Adam's gaze. Everything sat right on the surface—all of Ev's anxiety and exhaustion and confusion. How he'd thought Adam was dying because of him. How he'd begun to think he belonged at that place, and deserved to be hurt. He let Adam see all of it.

"I'm fine. Did they tell you I was shot with a sedative?"

Many layers of upset and truth stood in the way of his answers. From Ev's left, he heard snapping fingers. They looked to Rune, who began to sign while directing his message at Adam. Ev felt all of the history there, between the others. It drew them together in ways that excluded him.

"Max," Oliver said. "He left once Ev was checked in and secure."

"Good," Adam said. Of Evelyn, he inquired, "But... I need to know if they hurt you."

"Clearly they did," Oliver said somewhat defensively.

"I need to hear it from him," Adam retorted with the kind of sharpness that came out in tense moments between people who were as close as family—instantly forgiven, expressed to vent inner turmoil. He'd heard his parents talk to each other like that in private all the time.

"He's not ready to talk about it. Look at him. Let him rest."

"I don't need you protecting him from me."

"Stop," Ev said, feeling tired.

Adam ran a hand over his face. Rune began signing again. Ev wished he knew what it all meant. No wonder Adam had chosen to learn the language.

"Okay," Adam relented. "For now, you rest. But when you're ready, we'll tell you what happened. I don't even have the whole story, but between Olly and Rune, we can fill in the blanks."

Rune signed something, somewhat frantically, his gestures sharp and his frown severe.

Oliver explained for him, saying to Ev, "He wants you to know the police have all of the Pathway people in custody. No one got away."

"Okay. Thank you," Ev replied to Rune.

"They're discharging me," Adam explained. "I'll go take care of that, get my things, and come back here to wait while you rest. Rune will stay for my own peace of mind."

Rune signed something else. Adam added, "And his, as well."

Ev nodded, completely aware of how that simple gesture had more significance for him now. It unsettled him. Commiseration had its consequences.

"Don't let anyone who looks suspicious near him," Oliver told Rune, signing the counterparts to the instructions.

Adam leaned in to press a kiss to the back of Ev's hand, then reluctantly let go. A moment later, Oliver wheeled Adam from the room and Ev closed his eyes, too drained to keep them open.

Chapter 28

Process and Release

A veritable feast of hospital cafeteria food had been laid out in front of Ev on a tray. Jackson, Oliver's other submissive, was due to arrive soon with clothes for Ev to change into, fetched from Adam's apartment.

Explanations and confessions alike remained locked inside of Ev, down past where he could reach them, but he felt a little better. He dug into some roast beef and potatoes with plastic cutlery, surrounded by Adam, Oliver and Rune. They'd shut the room's door for privacy. Oliver idly kneaded Rune's shoulders, massaging him in a way that was clearly appreciated, if the satisfied hint of a grin on Rune's face was any clue.

"Tell me how you are," Adam began. The words burst from his rosy lips, their importance mirrored in his straight posture and worried gaze.

"You really aren't good at *asking* for things, are you, dear?" Oliver teased.

"Don't interrupt."

"How can I if you're the only one talking?"

Both of them signed as they spoke. It seemed strange at first, that visual reminder that Rune—still a stranger to Ev—listened in to every word they shared.

After a pause where Adam seemed to be waiting for Oliver to stop talking, he then repeated himself with, "Tell me how you are."

Oliver rolled his eyes and signed something.

"Don't do that," Adam scolded. To Ev, he said, "Do you need them to leave?"

"No," Ev replied. He was too tired to care. He could tell Adam trusted these guys implicitly. Plus, Ev had no sense of privacy anymore, or whether he had any way to control whether he had it or not.

"Those Pathway fuckers… they tried to get into your head. I can see as much."

Ev nodded, then cringed. Inwardly, he resolved to stop nodding entirely if he could help it.

"What?"

How to explain it? How to even start?

"They…" he stammered. "They blindfolded and gagged me. I was… naked. They took me while I was naked. Adam was painting me," he explained to the others. Oliver translated everything Ev said into sign language. "And they… used that to make me uncomfortable. There was one man. I don't know his name. He was the only one that spoke to me. The whole time, they said if I nodded, they'd… stop."

"Stop what?" Adam demanded when an explanation was slow to come.

"I don't want to talk about this," Ev murmured.

"Please try. You'll feel better to get it out, and you'll help me to stop losing my fucking mind with worry about what you've gone through. Please, Evelyn."

Ev shifted uncomfortably, rubbing the back of his neck. "I don't know… It was… cold. Confusing. The way they explained things… it kind of made sense, but…" Clenching his jaw, even though doing so hurt, he felt the need to push the rest down, to let it live inside rather than expose it, or what he'd done. At the same time, he knew the reaction was exactly what the Pathway people wanted. They wanted him to keep quiet. That's how they were able to do what they did, without consequences. They scared people into silence, making them doubt themselves.

"Don't let them make you feel ashamed of what they did to you. Don't you dare."

"Maybe you should give him a break," Oliver cut in.

"This doesn't concern you, Olly!"

"He's been traumatized!"

"I know that!" Adam yelled.

"Stop," Ev rasped, feeling exasperated. "Just stop arguing. They tried to scare me, okay? They injected me with drugs and let some guy who was supposed to be a doctor do tests on me, because they said you were a known sex offender and they could tell you'd raped me."

The room fell quiet. Their collective attention focused on him. He kept going to fill the tense silence. "They tied me down. They were... touching me. Inside. Used instruments I could feel but not see. And it... it hurt. It *all* hurt, but knowing it was them doing it made it worse. It made me feel... disgusting. But... the whole time I knew they'd stop if I nodded and... I didn't for a long time."

"But you did eventually, didn't you," Adam guessed.

"I didn't mean it. I swear. But they asked if it hurt. If I wanted it to stop. And I did." He realized how it sounded, so he added, "It meant more than that, though. It meant I was agreeing with them, about all of it, and saying they were right, and admitting you hurt me and that you were bad, but I know you're not, okay? I know that."

"Hey." Adam gripped Ev's arm, his face painted in concern.

"It was just a lot. I didn't like that some of it made sense. It wasn't just the drugs, or the pain, or being so tired."

"Do not feel guilty about that," Adam told him urgently. "You were protecting yourself. You had to."

Ev had set down his cutlery and folded his arms across his chest, sinking back into the bed and wanting to vanish. He felt small, and soiled. "But I'm... I'm okay. I'm fine. Nothing they did left a... you know. Mark."

"Like hell it didn't," Oliver seethed.

Now that he'd said all of that out loud, it helped him move past it and into realizations of the predicament he was in. The self-conscious worry lessened, making way for a greater ability to see clearly how things needed to go.

"I don't have any choices here, Adam," Ev explained, feeling exasperated. "I don't like telling you this stuff, but what else am I supposed to do? Keep it from you? Keep it from everyone? What good does that do? The way I feel right now, questioning everything, but especially myself—that was their goal. I'm not stupid. I see that. They want me to feel ashamed. They want me to stay quiet. Crawl into my hole and pretend I don't exist, so my family doesn't have to face what I am. That's what they want."

"But you're going to do what, instead?" It was a push, guiding Ev forward.

"The opposite, probably. Which means I have to admit to this. I have to do the opposite of what they want, or else they win."

"Admit it to whom?"

"Everyone." He looked into each of their eyes, one by one. "Not just you or the people who helped me. It has to be bigger than that. For so long—my whole life—they've tried to keep this sacred, a secret passed only to those involved or at risk. But the rest of the world outside of it sees it the way it really is. They'd see it's fucked up, or they would, if they knew. I feel that. Being away, it's helped me get more perspective, but..." He took a deep breath, glimpsing the next steps, even as he dreaded taking them.

"I need to go to the media with this. Tell them who I am, who my father is, and everything about the Pathway. It'll be a scandal. They'll eat it up. The more people that know about the Pathway, the safer we'll all be. They had others there, Adam. Other victims. I wasn't the only prisoner. The more that people know about that place, the less they'll be able to creep around and abduct their targets."

"It feels like doing that would be moving incredibly fast. Maybe you should focus on taking care of yourself, and worry about the rest later."

"How would that help me, Adam? News stories are strongest when they're fresh. I'm in the hospital. My face is bruised all to hell. The cops are here. They can investigate everything going on now. If it waits, it would have less impact."

"How are you going to tell them about this when you can barely tell us?"

Ev let out a breath, his head spinning. The more he let it breathe, the more things slowly fell into place, the way they had at the market after he'd found out about the Facebook post. It helped calm him down. He felt stronger, clearer, like things might be making sense again.

"I have no choice. I'll find a way." Something occurred to him, and he sat up straighter, lighting up a little. "This is what we've been working toward together, isn't it? Male vulnerability? Being honest, and weak, and all of that? That's what you and I are about. It's why we're together, and it feels like the most sincere way to face this problem."

"Evelyn, you know what this will do to your father, though, don't you? It would likely sabotage his ability to get re-elected. Are you okay with that?"

"Yeah, I get it. Conservative, religious Republican has his gay son kidnapped, tortured, and brainwashed in order to turn him straight. Gay son escapes with his lover and turns to the press for support, pointing fingers at his whole family. There's only one way that plays out. They've pushed me to this. It's all or nothing now. That's the only way we stay safe. What if it was a gun instead of a needle? What if the overdose had killed you? If no one knows they did this, they could do it again. There are other branches of that place. We need to scare them off. Public attention is the only way to do it. I won't live in fear of them. Driving them out is the only strategy that makes sense."

Oliver smiled. Ev caught his eye, and Oliver said to Adam, "Your sub's kind of badass."

That made Ev smile a little too.

"You think this could work?" Adam asked Oliver.

"Is this you asking for my professional opinion?"

"Yes."

"I do. With this kind of predator, you've gotta come right back at them. No fucking around. No hesitancy."

Adam seemed unsure. Taking his hand and giving it a squeeze, Ev asked, "What are you thinking?"

"I don't want to risk your life over a cause, even a good one."

"We won't. We'll be safe. Careful."

"So if I impose conditions, you'll agree to them?"

"I will."

The moment drew out. Ev imagined the others following the threads of the plan, seeing where each offshoot led. Ev took another bite of food and tried not to acknowledge that he knew what the look on Adam's face meant.

"Go on, say it," Ev invited.

Oliver laughed soundlessly, like he knew what the look meant, too.

"How can you have forgiven them for this? I can see that you have. And it pisses me off."

"They only wanted the best for me. I believe that," Ev replied. "They just have a different definition of what that means than we do."

Adam shook his head, covering his mouth with a hand, and murmured, "Fuck."

Oliver stood over Rune's chair, both of them holding steaming paper cups of coffee. Ev finished eating and drank some tea, hoping it would settle his nerves. They'd gotten the warm drinks from a vending machine down the hall, so the tea was weak, and the coffee sour, if the faint puckers of distaste on the others faces were any clue. Still, it was nice to sip something that heated him up from inside. The chill was still hard to shake.

"Are you ready to hear this?" Adam asked, signing the words.

"Yeah. Go on."

"I'll tell you what I know, then Oliver can fill in the rest," Adam began. His coffee was set on Ev's bedside tray, half-drank and left to cool. "I saw them come out of the trees. Several men had guns pointed at you. You had the blindfold on and had no idea. The one in charge held my eye, finger raised in front of his lips as if to warn me and I knew if I made a sound to warn you, they'd shoot. They came right up behind you very quickly, and one of them held a gun to the side of your head as another one grabbed you and held the rag in front of your mouth to knock you out. It happened so fast, like they'd had a lot of practice at this type of thing, which I guess they did. I kept staring at that gun and I knew I had to help you somehow. I had no clue how. I thought maybe they'd shift their focus for a minute, and I could do... something. But then a pair of them came up to me after they'd began dragging you away. One had a gun pointed at me. The other had a syringe. They kept the barrel leveled right against the center of my forehead while injecting me in the neck with whatever the fuck was in the syringe. It happened faster than I expected. They backed off. I stumbled toward the house, away from them. That's all I remember. They told me I fell in the grass a few feet away from the easel."

Oliver set down his coffee to use his hands to sign with them instead. "They used a dose that was too large for his body size. I don't think they cared whether it killed him or not, just that he was out of the way."

Ev frowned at him, trying to understand, to guess how Oliver had gotten involved, how the rescue had even happened.

"Mrs. Santiago was your hero yesterday," Oliver told Ev, the steady seriousness of his gaze conveying how much had rested on one turn of fate.

"Who's that?"

Adam said, "Damhan's housekeeper. She's his companion, runs the house, and keeps him on his toes. I should have guessed. She's usually out on Wednesdays, doing errands, but if Damhan was out, maybe she was using the quiet time to catch up on laundry or something. Sometimes she travels with him. Usually if she sees me arrive, even if I don't ring the bell, she'll come out to talk. Since she didn't come out, I thought the house was empty."

Adam sounded exhausted. Was it a side-effect of the sedative? The overdose? Or just the combined effect of it all weighing down on him? Ev would have asked him to lie down with him if they'd been alone.

"She told the police she saw Adam painting you," Oliver said. "And she was embarrassed by the nudity."

Imagining it, Ev felt self-conscious and guilt-stricken. His gaze dropped to his hands.

Adam clasped Ev's arm.

"She's a seventy year old woman, raised in Spain, living a private, quiet life with an old man," Adam explained. "She's not a prude, but she'd have drawn the curtains to give us privacy and vowed to not disturb us."

"But she didn't do that," Oliver interjected. Adam gave him a questioning look. "She went to the front of the house, watching for other visitors. She was trying to ensure no one would come upon you—solicitors or gardeners or what have you. Not because she was ashamed of having a naked man in the gardens, but to protect you.

She planted herself in a chair by one of the large front windows, watching the road while she folded laundry. She saw the van pull up, and the men pour out of it with guns. When they skirted the house and headed into the trees, she called 9-1-1 right away. She knew going out there to stop them herself was not an option."

"How is she doing?" Adam asked Oliver, seeming worried.

"Better. They sedated her as well initially, due to the shock."

"Damhan's with her," Adam explained to Ev. "Back at the house. Her family is on the way to pick her up and once they do, Damhan's eager to see how you're doing. I've been keeping him informed."

"When the van left with you inside of it, she came out to check on Adam. She turned him on his side, tried to keep him breathing and stayed with him where he'd fallen on the lawn, unconscious, until the police and ambulance arrived. But she fainted when the EMTs began to take Adam away, and after explaining how they dragged Evelyn into the van. It was a lot for her."

"She got the make, model and license plate of the van," Adam said with a little more vigor. "That's how they tracked you down."

Now, Rune began to explain his part of the tale. Oliver watched him closely, not taking his eyes off him once, but saying everything Rune could not. "My old club's home base isn't far from the Pathway complex. At the club, they routinely listen to the police radio chatter, so they can give a heads-up to any friends of theirs that might be targeted, but also to help out where they can. They heard the reports going over about an abduction, and that all units were directed to go to the complex."

Here, Oliver looked over at Ev for a moment, speaking for himself rather than Rune. "I'm Adam's emergency contact. Mrs. Santiago knows this, and has my number. She called me after speaking with 9-1-1. I headed over to Adam, but I let Rune and Jackson know what was going on."

Adam spoke up then, and with an apologetic sort of tone admitted, "I'd texted Rune some basic information about what was happening with you, Evelyn, over the past few days. Once we knew the Pathway organization might have been alerted and be a threat, I reached out to Rune knowing he might be able to help us figure out where their organization was located locally. He'd been gathering those addresses already. It helped speed up the reaction time, though I hope you'll forgive me in speaking about you without your permission. I did it only due to safety concerns."

"That's okay," Ev said, giving Adam a tight smile. "It was a lot to react to without any notice, so I don't blame you for just trying to do what you could."

"I was going to tell you," Adam promised. "I was going to mention it after we were finished at Damhan's. First, I wanted to give you a break from all of it, and maybe have a chance to relax, but look how that turned out. I'm sorry."

"It's okay." Ev gave Adam's hand a squeeze.

Rune resumed his explanation, so Oliver began relaying his messages once more. "I'd asked the guys at the club to watch for any odd or police activity at the complex. They told me as soon as the report went out. I told them we needed to get you out of there. The police wouldn't let us move in before them. They had the area surrounded, but were working on strategies. It's a massive place to have to sweep and they were afraid they'd hold you hostage. Max had a feeling those assholes would try to slip away, rather than make a stand, so we moved to intercept."

Ev remembered, with effort, those moments as he was led to the van, the man with the syringe, the man with the club, how scared he was and how much the blows to the head had hurt.

"We saw Pathway members carrying tranq guns," Oliver relayed for Rune. "They don't seem to care much about their targets possibly dying from something meant to take down animals. We were carrying regular guns. One of their guys got tagged in the arm when Max shot a tranq gun out of his hands. When they realized we were prepared to shoot, the rest dropped the weapons. We restrained them and kept them pinned down until the police could come take them away. And you know Max and I insisted on going with you to the hospital. We wanted to make sure no one else suspicious got close to you."

"What's the sign for thank you?" Ev asked Adam. Adam placed the fingertips of his right hand, flattened out, to his lips, then moved the hand outward and down.

"Thank you," Ev said to Rune with heartfelt emotion, mirroring Adam's gesture. "All of you. I owe you so much. Without your help, I'd still be there, and I can't even imagine what they'd be doing to me."

Adam translated Ev's words to Rune.

"Then don't imagine it," Adam said. "Don't give them the satisfaction."

Rune gave Adam and Oliver a dark look, his hands still.

Seeming to understand the silent message, Adam sighed, "Go on. Say it."

Rune signed back to him. Oliver hesitated in speaking what it meant.

"What?" Ev pressed.

"He said, 'They're not going to stop coming for him, are they?'"

"Not unless I give them reasons not to," Ev replied. "There's a reason they're successful, why people decide to stay there and let themselves be brainwashed like that. Their message is really convincing. Even someone like me—I knew going in what it would be like. I've known for years, but it didn't matter and it didn't help. In less than a few hours I was tempted to see the truth through the lies and give into the persuasion, just to make the pain stop. At the same time, when I was in that room, stuck with my thoughts and memories, high on whatever the fuck they doped me with… I was horrified at the idea of my cousin being kept in a place like that, because of me. I can't let this happen to anyone else. No one should be made to doubt themselves like that, and especially not young people who are already second-guessing themselves over their sexuality. There's so much pressure to stay in the closet and not admit the truth. So much depression and suicide. The last thing kids need is places like Pathway adding to the nightmare.

"It's not about saving myself anymore. I need to stop them from hurting other gay kids. Someone needs to speak up and warn people about what's happening. If it has to be me, then I'll do it. I have to."

He waited until Adam was done signing the words to Rune. Rune replied. Adam smiled, and so did Oliver.

"We're in," Oliver said. "Anything we can do to help."

Chapter 29

Newsworthy

Oliver made it happen. As a former journalist, and with his brother's help, he had contacts in the right places. He paced the hall beyond Ev's room while Adam and Ev rested and Rune watched over them. Adam reclined in his chair, his feet propped up on the side of Ev's bed, a pillow under his head. Oliver had his phone in hand and a ferocious expression on his face. Ev watched him speaking with great emotion and wild gestures, though he was unable to hear him through the closed door.

Jackson and his wife arrived with Ev's clothes, just in time. Jackson was a tall, broad-shouldered and barrel-chested man with caramel skin and light brown eyes. He wore a light gray business suit and a haunted expression as he eagerly shook Ev's hand, whispering his regret for everything that was going on. Jackson's wife, Josefina, was a natural, curvy beauty in a flowing, flowered dress. Josefina had a noticeable, comforting, motherly air in the way she held Ev's gaze and quickly got introductions out of the way so she could ask how he was doing. She had long, soft brown hair, dark brown eyes and a warm touch as she took Ev's hand and quietly—because Adam dozed nearby—echoed her husband's regret and offered to help however they could. Some of Rune and Oliver's fire reflected in Jackson's gaze and posture. Ev felt glad to see it there. With how worn out Ev felt, and Adam's continued need to recover as well, it was nice to be surrounded by strong, capable, caring people who could watch their backs until they were back on their feet.

Ev went into the bathroom to change into the pair of boxers, jeans, and the blue shirt brought by Jackson. When he emerged, a camera crew and reporter waited in the doorway.

"Hello," the boisterous, overly-made-up and carefully styled female reporter said upon spying Ev, extending her hand to him. "I'm Nancy Birmingham with CNN News. You must be Evelyn Myers. I noticed the resemblance to your father."

"I am, yes. Thanks for coming."

"We'd love to hear what you have to say about the ordeal you've experienced."

The camera over her shoulder pointed at him, the soft whir of its inner mechanisms and the bright light mounted above the lens letting him know he was already being filmed.

He shook with her and glanced behind him for a place to sit. "Yeah, I don't know where would be a good spot…"

"If you're more comfortable lying in bed," she told him eagerly, "That would help to visually convey your situation to our viewers."

"Okay. Sure."

Adam had awakened. Oliver stood by Adam's side, giving off a protective air. They both closely watched the exchange. Adam nodded to Ev encouragingly.

So, Ev got back into the hospital bed. A nurse came in then to check his blood pressure and temperature. The camera crew filmed from a few feet away. The watchful eye of the lens made Ev self-conscious, but he just told himself to lay himself bare. The more truth that came through that camera, the better off many people would be.

The nurse left. The reporter settled into a chair by Ev's side. The cameraman stood where he could get a clear shot of Ev. Opening her notepad, Nancy looked right at Ev and jumped right in.

"Okay, Mr. Myers, your father is Kansas State Senator, Brandon Myers, is that correct?"

"Yes, it is."

"And what has your father done to you? Why have you been hospitalized?"

Old, ingrained alarm bells sounded within him then. As much as he wished it were possible to avoid holding his father directly responsible, the truth had to come out. This wasn't a family issue any longer, and no one back home was going to stand up for him. He had to do it himself.

Ev took a deep breath and focused on nothing but what he needed to say. Bruised, sore, vulnerable, worn-down, Ev didn't try to hide how he felt, but let it all come to the surface. "I wish this wasn't true, but... my father, Brandon Myers, asked an organization called the Pathway to Manhood, which operates in conjunction with our church, to kidnap me and use whatever means necessary to try to convert me to no longer be gay. He just found out that I'm dating a man, and warned me he was going to contact people to help me with my problem."

"What kind of means are we talking about here?"

"Brainwashing, scare tactics, torture, isolation, humiliation."

"Can you tell us how you were kidnapped yesterday, Mr. Myers?"

Ev reached for Adam's hand. Looking into his bright blue eyes, Ev drew strength there. He felt the camera capturing the moment.

"Go on," Adam said."I believe in you. I'm here for you."

"I know," Ev told him.

Ev turned toward the camera, and began to speak.

"My parents always pored over the news. They ingested it like they needed it to live, just as much as air. It was on constantly, and they'd become hypnotized by monitoring the reveal of each new story."

"You're worrying about how they'll react once they see this," Adam guessed."You're using the strongest weapon at your disposal. This is the right thing to do to protect yourself. They've been shaping the truth for their own purposes your whole life. All you're doing is speaking about something that actually happened. People have a right to know."

Ev met Adam's gaze for only a moment, then went back to letting his vision fill only with the beautiful bouquet that had been set in front of Ev on the coffee table. It was one of several, but this one was possibly Ev's favorite. It had a good mix of exotic, bold flowers with delicate, subtle choices. The delicate scent filled his head, chasing out everything bad. The texture of a velvet leaf skimmed between his index finger and thumb.

They were seated on either side of the table. Ev sat on the couch, while Adam had taken a chair. Oliver and Rune were both still around, but had gone out on the terrace to allow some privacy inside. Adam's apartment did feel safe to Ev, but he couldn't put his finger on why. The security downstairs helped, ensuring only the residents or invited guests got clearance to proceed inside the building. Maybe it wasn't that at all.

"Actually," Ev countered, "I'm just kind of fascinated by how much I don't want to see or hear the news right now. Before, I never had a choice. It was always in my face. Now... Without it, I can actually hear myself. I can see things clearer without that filter telling me what to think."

"Good. Keep listening," Adam encouraged. There was so much passion in him. It lingered in his gaze, his posture, the strength of his body and the energy it contained. Adam's inner fire burned into Ev, warming him up in other ways. The prolonged cold from when he'd been held captive was quite slow to fade. "What else do you hear?"

The heat from Adam touched Ev only on the surface. He tried to let it in deeper, but it was like it wouldn't go until he said the magic words.

Taking a moment to consider, weighing his muddled emotions, he let his lips shape over the beginning of the word before letting it out. "Thank you for your support with all of this. Letting me stay here, keeping me safe. I just..." He shook his head. "What I did? That severed a lot of things."

"You're scared, but not of the Pathway people."

Ev's mouth twisted up in a wordless assent, his gaze lowered with embarrassment.

"Your parents can't hurt you, Evelyn," Adam promised. His tone was strangely both comforting and angry.

Ev let out all of the air in his lungs, but the pressure remained. It filled his chest, pressed down on his shoulders, and tightened his throat. "What..." he stammered, choking up. "What I did to them was cruel."

"*Don't.* Don't do their job for them," Adam said, his voice loud and full. "They did this to you. You did nothing wrong, except try to simply be your whole self for once. The consequences of what they did to you are on them."

Blinking his eyes clear, clearing his throat, Ev tried to focus on the flowers. It wasn't working.

"Say it," Adam invited. "If it'll make you feel better, then fucking say it."

"You're already mad."

Adam stood, coming around the table.

Ev flinched involuntarily when Adam sat beside him, reaching for his arm. Stopping short, Adam raised his hands, backing off an inch or two.

With downy softness, Adam spoke, saying, "I am mad at so many people and so many things right now. You're right. Evelyn," Adam palmed his chest, over his heart. "You can't imagine what it felt like when I woke up and was told what had happened, and what they did to you. I swore to myself, years ago, that I was done losing people I cared about. And they... they..."

Ev saw it then, how Adam must have felt the echo, hearing the news that a twist of fate had interceded again, despite so many efforts to safeguard him, that Ev had been taken and Adam had slept through the whole ordeal.

Adam couldn't finish his explanation. The words were stuck behind the anger and pain. Hating that he'd caused those, Ev gradually moved to hug Adam, turning to the side and bringing his arms around Adam's side and shoulder. With a frown, Adam clasped Ev's back and the nape of his neck, holding him close. His lips pressed to Ev's neck.

"It's hard to not be jumpy," Ev confessed in a whisper by Adam's ear. "I know what I did was only telling the truth, but... they worked really hard to get where they are, and they had good intentions. I just dropped a bomb into the center of their lives. All of the wreckage that happens because of that is my fault, in some way at least. Please try to see it from my point of view, too."

"Do you know why you feel bad for them right now?" Adam pulled back slightly, so close the tip of his nose brushed Ev's. His fingers brushed the hair off of Ev's brow, then skimmed around the back of his ear. "Because you're a good man with a beautiful heart. This is why you inspire me so much." Adam's eyes danced with all of the energy he constantly conjured. It swirled in him, heating his sweet breath, making his eyes come alight with mirth and devotion to everything that mattered most. "You don't hide your conflicts, or wish them away. You show them, and the complexity of that, combined with the undeniable innocence of you... I wouldn't have you any other way. If you need to carry some regret for your family, I can't stop you. All I can do is ask you to set some of it down, when it feels right. Please."

"I love you, Adam," Ev said, feeling the tears sting his eyes, the drops gathering, ready to spill. "It would be easier if I didn't."

"Who said life was easy?"

His thumb brushed beside Ev's lips. With ache and weariness, Ev let Adam's energy pull him in. It felt as easy as falling. All it took was to let go. Then, he was kissing Adam's warm lips and Adam drew him in more tightly, keeping Ev's kiss and making it his own.

As they broke, Ev stayed turned toward Adam. Wrapped, held and cocooned in him, Ev felt even safer. The danger was there, of course; not in the form of family or enemies, but in the quality of the spark between them. It was something lasting, bright and unique. It would always draw scorn and ugliness from some, but the risk was worth the fear.

"Just rest," Adam asked, caressing the back of Ev's neck and down his spine. "I don't want you doing anything else. No worrying about anything. The world can wait."

Feeling the steady strength of Adam's body beneath his hands, Ev believed him. He let out a breath and felt easier.

"What do you want, right now?"

"Hmm." He nuzzled Adam's skin, breathing him in. A pleasant shiver raced outward over Ev's body. A faint, unseen smile curled his lips. "Maybe get something to eat, curl up in a chair and watch you paint a while."

"You sure?" A kiss was pressed to his cheek, a firmer hug given.

"Yeah. Is that all right?"

"It's perfect."

Chapter 30

The New Normal

Being in Adam's studio provided a comfortable illusion. Nothing else could get in. They had peace. Quiet. Oliver and Rune stayed out, probably at Adam's previously voiced command, going along with his dislike of sharing. There were no ringing phones, or blaring televisions. Adam simply played some soft jazz off of his tablet and all was as it should be.

Hours passed, smooth and easy. Ev dozed off on the bed, or sat where he could watch Adam paint. Now and then, Adam would venture out for food or drinks, bringing them back with him like supplies for some weird survival game they'd been caught in the middle of, where brushstrokes measured time and everything beyond the studio was deadly.

Evening fell, before full, complete night.

"Bedtime. Come on," he urged Ev, holding out a hand to pull him out of the chair. There was patience in the way he hesitated to force eye contact, like he knew it was comforting to get lost in the layers built on the canvas instead.

Ev let Adam lead him from the room. Oliver and Rune were still there, watching a movie with the closed captioning turned on, lying on a sofa together.

"Goodnight," Adam said, and signed.

"Goodnight," Oliver replied. "Sleep well. Don't worry about anything."

Once they were in the bedroom, the door closed, Ev struggled to relax again. Even the short walk from the studio had left him tense. Running a hand over the back of his neck, he lingered in the middle of the room, uncertain.

Adam looked down at his phone, frowning. He tapped repeatedly at the screen. He wasn't saying anything.

"What?" Ev asked.

"Nothing to worry about. I'm checking my messages."

"Is something wrong?"

"No."

He kept tapping. Then he put the phone to his ear, listening.

"A lot of messages, I guess." For Ev, the thought of looking at his own messages made his stomach churn, so he pushed it away.

It took a few minutes more before Adam finished. Then, he just stood there, thinking, staring at the phone which he'd set on the dresser.

"I'm going to... take a shower," Adam decided. "Get in bed, try to sleep."

"Adam, just tell me."

"Your rest is more important."

"Than what?"

"Evelyn, I'm trying to spare you all of this shit. Go to bed. We'll talk in the morning."

"No. Doesn't work like that, sorry. I did this to you. I dragged you into this mess. I put your life in danger when you OD'd. I—"

Adam came at him, kissing him quiet, then hugging him tenderly. "Stop," he whispered.

"Who was it?"

"The messages?"

"Yeah."

"Everyone. Damhan. My lawyers. The police. The school. Leo. Reporters from local and national news organizations. Fucking Good Morning America."

"Wow. Really? What did... What did they want?"

"Good Morning America? To have you on tomorrow. Well, both of us."

"Whoa."

"You don't have to do anything you don't want to do."

"I guess going on there together would be a pretty big coming out moment for me."

Adam laughed, but there was tenseness in it.

"What?"

Adam glanced down at his watch, then grabbed the TV remote from the nightstand. The screen flickered to life. It was just after eleven. The news was on most major channels. Adam surfed through them, staying only in one place for a handful of seconds.

"—local college student and son of Kansas State Senator, Brandon Myers, has spoken out about—"

"—Pathway to Manhood, which Myers claims to have—"

"—was abducted from private property yesterday in a supposed brainwashing scheme, and behind it all none other than —"

"—Adam Buchanan, adjunct professor at Lehigh University and local artist, son of Darian and Ceit—"

Adam turned the TV off. Ev's eyes felt so big, opened so widely, he wouldn't have been surprised if they fell right out of his head. He was barely breathing.

"Holy... Why... I didn't..."

"They ran with the story, dear. Great news!" Adam said with forced enthusiasm. Stepping closer, softening his expression, he said, "I mean it. This was the goal. The more they're talking about this, the safer you and I are. People like the Pathway members work best in secret. Once you shine a spotlight on them, they scurry like cockroaches."

"E-everyone knows?" Ev managed, his breathing stilted, struggling to normalize.

"Yes. Everyone knows. Did you really think CNN would bury the lead on this?"

"I... I don't know. Maybe? It's political gossip from a sophomore out of Kansas, I mean, come on."

"This has nothing to do with where you're from. This is about the church's repeated brutal and personal attacks on the LGBT community. This is about a fucking United States Senator hiring thugs to kidnap, brainwash and torture his only child. This is about proof that not only was that not the first time it's happened, but that it's happening all over the country, everywhere, right under our noses, constantly, and has been for a long, long time."

Ev needed to sit down. He shifted backwards, staggering a little until the backs of his knees found the bed's edge. Sinking down, staring at nothing, he felt Adam come near, sitting beside him, and putting an arm around Ev's back.

There was still some slight tensing when contact was made. Ev hated it, that his trust in Adam wasn't what it should be, because of those men.

"Talk to me. Please," Adam said quietly.

Ev just felt dirty. Soiled. He wanted to shower for days and not have to talk to anyone for a year, until this whole situation faded away to nothing and no one cared anymore.

Memories of being naked, being touched, being restrained, of wanting to beg and plead, but unable to because of the gag—they overwhelmed him.

"I shouldn't have talked about it," Ev whispered. "They all know now that I... that we..."

Rubbing his arms as a chill made his skin pebble, Ev shivered. Adam pulled a blanket from the foot of the bed and wrapped it around Ev's shoulders.

It felt just like when he was younger, after everyone found out about what happened with James. Parents, teachers, ministers, friends, neighbors—they all knew James had touched Ev. Ev had been forced to see it in their faces, the ways they imagined it happening, every time he left his room. Now everyone knew about him and Adam, only it wasn't just his hometown in Kansas. It was the whole world.

"This was always going to happen."

"I know. Or, I thought I did. I guess I didn't. I didn't know it would feel like this. I can't take it back, can I?"

"No. We can only move on from here. But this is a good thing. I promise. There is no secrecy anymore. Your father can't come at you. Neither can the agents of the Pathway to Manhood. The entire world will be watching, expecting them to, and it would condemn them even further if they tried. Your father will deny this until his dying breath, most likely. He'll need to distance himself from everything connected to Pathway at all costs. Their end-goal is bigger than one boy. Giving up on you means they'll be more able to survive and go after easier targets."

"But that's awful."

"Yes, it is. Think of your cousin. He was an easier target. Think of all of the other gay kids and scared gay adults out there, unable to protect themselves from this. You beat them, Evelyn."

"Did I?" Ev asked doubtfully. "This doesn't feel like victory. I can't even have you touch me without jumping and I can't—"

"You need to keep fighting back. This doubt you're feeling? That's them fighting back against your victory in here." He tapped Ev's temple with a finger. "Why are you ashamed to have people know we're together?"

He had no good answer to that. Ev bowed his head, biting his tongue. His hands twisted together in his lap.

"You kissed me at school without any bad feelings, but this is bigger, isn't it?"

Quietly, Ev said, "Yes," because nodding still gave him the creeps.

"Come on, Evelyn. Let's show them we're stronger together than individually. Let's show the good we've found, here." He laid a hand on Ev's heart, beating away with lingering fear. "In love, and honesty, and art."

There was another certainty Ev felt then, from way down deep. He took Adam's hand, weaving their fingers together, and confessed, "I can't do this without you."

Adam kissed Ev's temple. "You don't have to."

They took the offer and hired a car to drive them to the New York City offices of the Good Morning America studio the next morning. The bustle and traffic of the city was mirrored by the chaos and noise of the studio, where they had hair and makeup people flocking around them, dusting them with brushes and powder. The lights were too bright, the talent surreally beautiful, their smiles fierce. All of it had Ev drawing closer to Adam. He never once let go of Adam's hand.

During the brief interview, seated on a couch adjacent to the reporter, Ev glimpsed a monitor showing them the live feed, and the label under Adam when they focused in on him for a moment.

'Evelyn's boyfriend', is what they called him, in smaller print beneath his name. That felt like the most momentous part of the whole thing —that little label, broadcast for billions of people to read, if they cared to look.

The questions were easier to answer this time.

"Were you surprised your father was behind this?"

"Is Adam your first boyfriend?"

"Is that why they abducted you?"

"Are you afraid they'll come back for you?"

The responses waited right on the tip of the tongue. All he had to do was let them go. Once they'd been released, Ev felt so much lighter. Walking back out to the hired car, he smiled honestly, with real hope, for the first time in days.

There had been a few interviews he and Adam had done over the phone, but they limited in-person appearances. Some media gathered down at lobby level of the building, but security wouldn't let them inside, and Ev had no plans to leave for a while if he could help it. Adam had gone out one morning to stop by the lawyer's office and had taken Oliver with him. A woman had stuck a microphone in Adam's face as soon as he stepped out of the elevator and into the parking garage, a cameraman poised behind her, ready and recording. Oliver had quickly gotten them out of the way and Adam into the car.

The next day, Leo brought by more of Ev's things from their dorm room. At the time, Ev had been once more in Adam's studio. He'd spent a solid hour in the gym earlier in the morning, so he felt he'd earned the chance to laze around. There was a textbook opened on his lap. He'd been trying to make arrangements with his professors to continue the classes online or remotely, due to the extreme circumstances, and most of them had been accommodating.

Ev heard the thunk of a box hitting the ground, then the softer thud of a bag.

"They're right through there, in the studio. I'll see if Evelyn can come out," Oliver explained.

It had been amazing how much time Oliver and Rune had been spending there. They slept over, and worked from the apartment too, most days. Oliver had claimed Adam's office as his own, though he only went in there to take calls. Otherwise he stationed himself near the door with his laptop.

Ev listened to the footsteps getting louder, approaching the studio. The door was ajar, allowing him to eavesdrop.

Oliver inched the door open a bit more and, without looking inside, said, "Leo's here with Evelyn's things."

"Do you need me to handle this?" Adam asked Ev.

The layers of protection soothed some of the sting of strangeness away. Damhan had been by often for short visits, as if just seeing Evelyn sitting there in one piece was enough reassurance to get him through the next day or so. He didn't press Ev to talk, but only kept offering to help.

Leo would be different, though. He would be expecting something from Ev, but Ev didn't know if he had anything in him to give.

Ev looked down at himself. He wore a worn, old pair of jeans and one of Adam's charcoal grey robes. He'd been too overheated from exercise for a shirt, then too reluctant to leave the studio in order to get one. Without having to look, he guessed that the shell-shocked expression was still on his face. It had been there since he'd been taken from Damhan's property in the Pathway van, several days ago. He'd been eating less, his appetite close to nil, and had been losing weight.

A strong urge rose in Ev to let Adam make some excuse and send Leo away. Ev knew he had to fight it, if for no other reason than to try to reclaim some of his normal self.

Getting up out of his comfortable seat, setting the textbook aside, Ev stretched the stiffness out of his back and said, "Nah, I've got it."

Adam waited with a wary tilt to his eyebrows, like he didn't believe Ev was truly up for greeting company. Paintbrush in hand, a light periwinkle color wetting the tip, Adam stood aside and watched Ev leave the room.

Oliver hung back, silently, acting like Ev's bodyguard.

Ev's gaze found Leo, hands shoved in his pockets, glancing around the vast apartment's space. Back in the sitting area, Ev saw Rune, who signed something to Oliver as they emerged from the hall. Oliver signed back and Rune nodded, going back to his seat.

"Hey," Ev said, feeling awkward and trying on a weak smile.

"Hey, Ev. How you been?" Leo asked, brightening upon seeing him.

Ev shrugged, his bare feet cool on the gleaming floor. "I guess I don't know how to deal yet. Nothing's normal. I was studying." He thumbed back toward the studio.

"Not modeling?"

Unsure whether it was a joke or not, Ev realized that in the robe, he did kind of look like that's what he had been up to. "Oh, no. Not really. I mean, Adam is painting right now, and sometimes he looks over at me for reference or whatever, but that's it. I was just hanging out." He glanced over at the box and bag. There was a lot there. He tried not to think of Leo going through his stuff, like piles of underwear and old socks, deciding what was important enough to bring. It only added to the awkwardness of it all.

"I've been worried about you," Leo said more quietly, but with plenty of sincerity. "We all have."

"Who's we?"

"Everyone, Ev. I've been like your spokesman on campus, or some shit. It's gotten around that we room together, or we did anyway, so everyone who's ever heard of you's been coming up to me with questions, trying to see if you're okay. I mean, like kids from your classes, guys from the soccer and football teams, teachers, janitors, the registrar… you name it."

"I guess they've seen that stuff on the news."

"Kid, you're all over TV. You realize that, right? I mean, some of it is you being interviewed, so you have to realize it's out there."

"I don't pay attention. I don't watch TV or listen to the radio or anything."

"But are you… okay? I mean, you don't look good. I think that's part of why you're getting so much play in the coverage. One look at your face or one word out of your mouth and it's like you can feel what they did to you, how it fucked you up. It's not right, man."

"Of course I'm not okay."

"Can we do anything, or…"

"I don't know. I'll let you know, okay?"Ev felt as if a dam had been constructed in his throat, only letting a few words spill out.

"Are you coming back to school?"

"I'm still in school; I've just been working from here. I don't feel safe going out. Yet."

Leo gazed past Ev's shoulder. Following his line of sight, Ev saw he was spying Oliver.

"Who's scary dude number two?"

Ev smiled at that.

"Oliver. He's Adam's friend. He's been watching out for me. Same with Rune. He actually was one of the guys who got me out of there." Leo still had a strange look on his face, so Ev glanced behind himself again. He saw Oliver and Rune deep in silent conversation.

"You were rescued by a deaf guy? How is that not in the news story?"

"I don't know. Rune likes his privacy, I guess."

"So what's the plan here? What happens now?"

"Just taking it a day at a time, really. Trying to catch up with classes, do my work. I quit the job at the registration office, obviously. We heard the other day that the FBI is looking into Pathway now, the other branches. And, um…" he shrugged again. "Adam's show is in a few weeks. You should come."

"I'll be there. What about your family? Have you heard from them?"

"I don't know. I haven't checked my messages since this started. I'm not ready for… that. How about you? I hope all of this shit hasn't made your life harder. Has anyone been giving you a hard time?"

"Are you kidding?" Leo chuckled. "This is the most popular I've been in my life. I'm riding high. No worries."

"Good," Ev smiled. "Glad to hear it."

Chapter 31

Choosing Trust

Over two weeks had passed since the infamous day at Damhan's estate. The painting which had been born there, of Ev in a fighting stance, covered in flower petals, was almost finished. It was to be the centerpiece of the show.

In the darkened bedroom, Adam had showered, then joined Ev in bed. Somewhere, several rooms away, were Oliver and Rune, possibly doing things Ev's imagination couldn't even suggest. Luckily, Adam's place had excellent soundproofing.

Curling up on his side of the bed, facing Ev, who usually slept on his back, Adam gave every sign of intending to go right to sleep, as they'd been doing every night since the day that had changed everything.

Ev hadn't been flinching as much, but tension still flared in him whenever he was touched suddenly from behind. There hadn't been any intimate contact beyond kissing happening between them. And Ev knew he still wasn't ready for a lot, but... he needed something. He'd finally become frustrated enough by the state of things to take action in fixing it himself.

Ev wore pajama pants and a t-shirt. Adam only wore pants. Shifting closer to him in the bed, Ev placed himself in Adam's arms, which wrapped behind him as soon as he was near. Burying his nose and mouth in the heat at the junction of Adam's shoulder and neck, Ev inhaled deeply and tried to relax. He was Adam's boyfriend. The whole world knew it. He wanted to start acting like it.

Caressing down the front of Adam's body, Ev let his hand push inside Adam's pants to palm his cock. It felt warm and smooth in his hand. Everything inside Ev cried out to play with it, to crouch down low and breathe in the scent of it as his lips traced its shape, heat against heat.

"Don't push yourself," Adam warned in a whisper. "We have time."

"I'm not," Ev argued just as softly, his lips moving against Adam's neck. "Can you just let me try? Please?"

"You want to be in charge for a while?"

"Yeah."

"Okay."

He didn't want to talk. He just wanted to be there, where the feel of his body against Adam's was everything. There was no bedroom, no apartment, and no world. They floated, drifting in a place where secrets were kept sacred.

He pushed Adam to his back, then pulled his own shirt over his head. Sliding down, he began kissing a trail down from Adam's neck to his chest and the soft nest of curls there. Ev ran his lips over the tickling hair, cushioning soft, silky skin. He found Adam's areola and ran the tip of his tongue around it, breathing harder. Catching the stiffened nipple between his teeth, he tugged, then wrapped his lips there to suck. Adam's hand petted Ev's hair, his fingers clutching the back of Ev's head. Each rise and fall of Adam's chest moved Ev slightly, his breathing quickening.

Sliding lower, Ev kept kissing along the center of Adam's firm abdomen, pressing his lips to Adam's navel, then just below it. His fingers hooked inside the waistband of the pajama pants. Sliding them down, Ev sat up in order to draw them completely off, tossing them aside. Then, he pressed between Adam's thighs, spreading them in order to lie there. With a hungry, unfiltered groan, he placed one hand against the underside of Adam's thigh and buried his face in the tight, red curls of Adam's pubic hair. Panting with want, Ev let his focus narrow, his cares left far behind. Fondling Adam's sac, the soft skin slipping between his fingers, Ev ran his lips over the taut surface of Adam's pelvis. Hearing a hiss of complain and feeling a slight twist from Adam, Ev realized he'd discovered a ticklish spot and chuckled.

"Don't you dare," Adam warned in a rough, breathless voice when Ev's gaze flicked up, mischievously, to catch his eye.

So, instead, Ev licked up along the crease where Adam's thigh met his body, still fondling, breathing as deeply as he could. He moaned, relaxed, knowing he was right where he most wanted to be. His heartbeat slowed. For a minute or two, he just lay there, peaceful. Adam's fingers combed through Ev's hair, stimulating his scalp. The end of Ev's nose nudged Adam's cock.

"Love you," Adam whispered.

"Love you too," Ev answered, trying not to get choked up. Still, the emotion rose, filling him. It moved him, swelling his need and shifting it.

Bracing a hand on the bed by Adam's hip, Ev caught Adam's cock between his lips, opened widely. Pushing forward, Ev let it fill his mouth, breathing around the hot, hard column. A soft, aching moan slipped from him, but he held there. Adam kept fingering through Ev's hair, making shivers race down Ev's spine. His mouth wet, his tongue eager, Ev felt a drip of saliva slide down Adam's shaft, so he closed his lips and swallowed.

"Fuck," Adam moaned, his body tense under Ev. Wanting to taste more of him, Ev began to suck, drawing the fluid from Adam's tip back over his tongue and down his throat. He felt his focus narrow even more. Nothing else mattered. He had everything he needed right there, sitting on his tongue, and in the sound of Adam's roughened breaths. He had someone who cared deeply for him, and would do anything to keep him safe, and gave back love and attention. The balance felt just right.

Ev moved, bobbing shallowly as he worked to draw more of that tangy fluid from Adam, who began to tremble the harder and longer Ev sucked, humming his pleasure.

He wanted it to last for hours—at least half the night—so when he felt Adam thrust sharply, his thighs clenched, and then again, Ev knew why. Caressing Adam's sac, Ev swallowed around Adam's cock, which got even stiffer just before he came. Hot, thick semen hit the back of Ev's throat, and he drank it down, pushing to take even more of it deeper into his throat as Adam shuddered with orgasm, clutching Ev's head in both hands. The struggle to take the whole load only added to Ev's enjoyment, his breathing heavier.

When Adam was almost through it, Ev pulled back to lick in long strokes up the underside of his cock, pressing it to Adam's pelvis. His lips wrapped the crown and the point of his tongue sought the slit, playing with it to clean away the last bit of flavor.

Adam panted, recovering.

"Anything you want," he rasped.

There was no question. Ev knew. "Roll over."

Adam paused, then complied, saying, "There's lube in the—"

"Just roll over."

"Okay."

As soon as Adam settled on his stomach, his arms drawn up by his head, Ev spread him once more. Palming Adam's cheeks with one in each hand, Ev spread him and moaned as he leaned in.

"Fuck," Adam groaned again, anticipating it. Ev smiled.

His tongue touched behind Adam's balls, then licked in a straight line up through his crease, all the way to the top. Then he paused to nuzzle between Adam's cheeks, breathing against the junction of his legs.

"This was supposed to be about what *you* want."

"This is what I want."

He licked over Adam's knot, doing it over and over again, until he'd learned the texture and shape, following each small wrinkle. Then he spread him wider and did it again, pressing harder at the center. The effect it had on Adam was delicious. He'd pushed his ass up to receive, curving his back in a graceful, sexy arc. He breathed hard with soft moans at each touch of Ev's tongue.

"This is what I want," Ev sighed, owning his happiness as greedily as he could.

He pressed his tongue through Adam's hole and reached down to tug his own cock, his hand pushed down into his pants. Staying there, playing with himself, he let his tongue pump shallowly, loving how it provoked desperate sounds from Adam.

Soon, though, it became too good. He stopped and pushed out of his pajama pants. Shifting upward, Ev lay down on top of Adam, fitting his thick, long cock in the wet crease between Adam's cheeks. Then, finding Adam's hand, weaving their fingers together and holding on tightly, Ev pressed kisses to the back of Adam's neck and thrust. The effort of each push shook Ev. Shivering, rutting, he rode that tight crease, rocking against the plump curve of Adam's cheeks. Pushing Adam down into the bed as hard as he needed to,

Ev moved against him without pain, or worry, or reservation. Nothing was held back.

When release came, his come shot over Adam's lower back and Ev moaned heavily, quivering. He worked himself through it, then held still.

Adam, however, kept going.

Ev chuckled against the back of Adam's neck, then kissed him there.

"Finger me, damn it."

"Yes, sir," Ev said happily. Gathering up some of his spend, he rubbed it over his fingers, then fed one into Adam. It slid deep and Adam let out a grateful, primal sound as he kept fucking the bed. "Let me do that."

Adam shifted his ass upward, getting his legs under him.

"Mmm," Ev hummed, finding Adam's wet cock, already filling again. It slid easily in his fist as he pumped it, seeking out Adam's gland with his finger. He knew he'd found it when Adam let out a gruff cry, tensing up. Ev rubbed the spot and tugged faster.

In moments, Adam came a second time, sweaty and hot enough to feel feverish against Ev's body.

"Okay," Adam panted. "Tomorrow you're going to have to fuck me."

Ev chuckled, biting his lip with a swell of pride. He slipped his finger out and leaned in to kiss Adam's cheek. "I just don't want to hurt you."

"Yes, well, you're not in charge of that," Adam replied.

"Okay."

"Are you sure you enjoyed yourself?"

His voice sounded shattered, rough. Ev wrapped him in an embrace and rolled them onto their sides to curl up together. "Exactly what I needed. Thank you."

"I missed this," Adam told him, caressing Ev's arm.

"Me too."

"You know, when you said 'tomorrow', I didn't realize you meant 'as soon as you wake up'." Ev had three fingers inside Adam, and he took them easily enough, but Ev still hesitated. The last thing he ever wanted during sex was to cause his partner pain.

Adam straddled Ev with one hand planted on his chest, riding the fingers with steady rocking motions, his lip caught between his teeth and a hungry expression on his face.

"I've been awake for quite a while actually," Adam replied somewhat breathlessly.

"Yeah, can you stop taking showers right before we have sex? I want to smell you, not soap."

Adam chuckled and Ev felt it as a gentle but firm squeeze around his fingers. He drew Adam down closer with his free hand hooked behind his neck.

With daylight peeking around the edges of the curtains, Ev had been awakened about twenty minutes ago by Adam climbing on top of him, naked and horny. It was a good way to wake up.

Adam leaned in even closer, and right before he gave Ev a heated, lingering kiss, he growled, "I want your cock."

"Mmm," Ev moaned, the sound pushing into Adam's mouth the way Ev's hand pushed into Adam's ass. With a firm, wet grip from plenty of lube, Adam gave Ev's dick a tug.

"I'm taking it. It's mine."

"Okay," Ev said deliriously between kisses.

"Take your fingers out of me already."

Barely fighting a smile, Ev obeyed. Adam shifted forward. With Ev's cock in his hand, he aligned their bodies and carefully pressed down to take Ev into him.

"Oh no," Ev cried out, then groaned through gritted teeth. He stopped breathing until his crown had squeezed through Adam's too tight outer rim. Blowing out air, Ev struggled to bear it. His face scrunched up and he held tightly to Adam's hips, growling as he was swallowed up. "I forgot how good this feels," he complained roughly. "Oh fuck. This is going to be embarrassing."

"Don't you dare come," Adam warned. He pressed down harder, almost entirely claiming Ev's dick.

With panting exclamations, his whole body tensed from head to toe, Ev could do nothing but lay there and fight not to orgasm.

"No, I can't do it. Your ass is too tight."

"Too late. You're mine now."

Ev groaned heavily.

Adam began moving again, riding Ev, and that made it so much worse.

"I can't watch this. It's really not fair."

"I'm the one with a massive dick up his ass, you know," Adam said, sounding out of breath, but with a chipper tone that told Ev he was having quite a lot of fun.

He looked so good, moving like that, his hips swiveling a little, the muscles of his stomach and thighs flexing. Ev caressed around to Adam's cheeks, palming them, his fingertips sliding over to rub the stretched-smooth rim hugging his shaft. Adam's eyes closed over with what looked like pleasure. He leaned down, his hands planted by Ev's head, their mouths nearly touching. Ev couldn't help noticing the difference in their expressions. He grimaced, while Adam had a fantastic time, evidenced by his smirk and soft chuckle.

It drove Ev to try moving too. Gradually, he thrust counter to Adam's rocking swivels.

Right away, it made it impossibly better. Moaning enthusiastically, Ev kept doing it, squeezing Adam's cheeks while fucking him as hard as he dared.

"I can't... God... dammit..."Ev collapsed, breathing like he'd just sprinted a mile, but didn't dare let go of Adam, who rode him through the aftershocks. Tilting his head back, Ev gave Adam an apologetic smile.

"Mmm, we'll have to work on that," Adam teased.

"Your ass is killing me. I have to take my dick out of it."

Adam chuckled again.

"No, don't do that," Ev complained. "The laughing is awful."

"But I kind of want to..." Adam reached down, wrapping a hand around his dick.

Glancing down at that, Ev felt a clear, sudden urge. He took hold of Adam's wrist to stop his tug. "Don't. I want you too."

Adam looked worried now, his good humor vanishing. "It's too soon."

"You don't get to decide that. No one gets to decide when and how we're together but us. I want to be with you."

"You are," Adam challenged.

"You know what I mean."

"Evelyn..." Adam sighed, like he was revving up for an argument.

"I'm in charge of my decisions," Ev said before Adam could unleash valid excuses on him. "Me. No one else. Not even you. And I'm choosing to trust you like this. Completely."

"Why do you want this?" Adam asked, his eyes searching, the blue of them swirling like twin whirlpools Ev could sink into and fall forever.

"It feels right." He said it in a soft, private tone. "And I'm tired of feeling wrong. Or scared. Or hesitant."

"Okay." His lips shaped the word, a watchful look on his face as if he was trying to capture Ev as he appeared in that moment to reflect in a painting later on.

Ev pulled out and rolled over, shoving a fluffy pillow down under his hips to angle them.

As Adam's weight settled on him after reaching for the discarded lube, Ev glanced back over his shoulder, liking the red cascade obscuring Adam's handsome face. He was an arrangement all on his own—soft and hard, bright and pale, cold and hot. The balance of it all kept Ev entranced and waiting, hoping for more, and that it would never have to stop.

The wet slip of Adam's fingers into Ev made him grunt and settle more completely on the bed. With effort, he made his muscles relax. He didn't think about the pressure inside or the nervous tickle in his stomach. All that mattered was Adam's warmth against him, the faint sizzle of energy between them where they connected, the richness of his scent and the comfort of his proven devotion.

Adam managed to avoid causing any real ache as he worked Ev open, yet it didn't take a very long time either.

There were no more jokes. No conversation. Ev recognized the echo of shame in the physical reactions he was having. Accepting them and moving past them, he hoped he had finally found the healthiest, most honest path. Part of him suspected he would never be one hundred percent sure—not until hindsight kicked in, long past when it was useful.

A fervent kiss came to the edge of Ev's jaw and Adam wrapped him with an arm circled under his chest, caressing it. They savored a moment of adjustment, each of them owning their places —top and bottom, giver and taker, Dom and sub.

Gradually, with a sweet tremble of effort, Adam's heated breath slid against Ev's cheek as he pushed through.

Ev made a soft sound, letting it happen. He arched slightly as the inward push made him want to spread. Adam clasped Ev's chest more firmly, holding him as he was completely entered with small, patient thrusts.

Breathing hard, flushed suddenly and aware of his voluntary helplessness, he knew this, precisely, was what they were all trying to save him from. It was an act of giving over, of being utterly weak, but Ev focused on the way Adam's cock filled him up, the way it made Adam's breath catch with aching want, his hands grasping, his lips brushing, just barely touching Ev's skin in constant kisses. He couldn't find anything in that to feel badly about.

Adam rocked, pulling back, pressing in, and Ev moaned. The edges of teeth scratched the shell of his ear, drawing goosebumps. Ev reached back to caress the silk of Adam's hair and moved slightly counter to the thrusts, meeting them eagerly.

"More," Ev begged.

With a growl, Adam's teeth sank into Ev's earlobe. The hand on his chest pulled Ev back into the next thrust and Adam leaned into it, trying to go deeper, his body straining.

"More, sir."

Another rough sound and Adam's pace quickened.

Remembering, from far away, accusations of Adam forcing himself on Ev, of Adam causing pain and mental harm, Ev only surrendered more completely, letting Adam all the way in, and Ev would never need to let him go.

A few rapid, short thrusts and Adam gasped, holding deeply sheathed, giving Ev everything he had.

"Fucking breathtaking," he moaned.

Ev couldn't help but smile.

Chapter 32

Breaking the Bubble

"You asked them to give me space, didn't you?" Ev asked, lingering in the doorway to the art studio. Oliver and Rune were out on the terrace, out of earshot. "You asked way back when I was in the hospital."

Adam set down his brush and wiped his hands, turning to look his lover in the eye. He contained no guilt or regret, but only boldness, confidence, and certainty. Ev loved that about him.

"I did," Adam agreed. "You were forced to meet them because you were abducted and assaulted. They understand. What's most important is getting you through this and keeping you safe. If you'd like to get better acquainted with Oliver, Rune, and Jackson, there is plenty of time for that later. But right now they can help make sure things are all right here. They don't need to worry about if we're okay or pester me. And we can have more peace of mind."

"They're good guys. I can tell."

"They are."

"It's nice to understand why you trust them."

Ev's gaze swept the room. The paintings were accumulating. Many were finished, and a few needed more work before also being counted in the completed category. The show drew nearer, only less than a week away.

"I never intended to go to the show," Ev admitted. "To be standing there, while people see me like this? It's going to be daunting."

"You don't need to go," Adam said.

"No, I do. You've been doing everything to support me. I need to repay the favor."

"Support me in spirit."

Ev gave him a doubtful look.

"Be easier on yourself."

"Mmm."

"I mean it. You push too much."

"Wonder where I learned that?"

Flashing a charming grin, Adam turned back to his painting.

Ev wandered farther into the room and over to the window, gazing out at the city below in twilight.

Behind him, a figure filled the doorway. He saw its reflection.

"Evelyn, your mother is in the lobby," Oliver said with heavy implication.

Adam dropped his brush again, instantly livid.

"What?" Ev asked, sure that he must have misheard.

"Jackson is on his way up. I knew he was stopping by and he identified her from all of the news coverage. He talked to the guard and found out she's been sitting there for hours. Never asked to come up. She's just sitting there."

"That's so…"

"Bizarre," Adam finished. "What's the motive?" he wondered.

"Could be anything, really," Oliver suggested. "Biding her time to intercept you? Make a scene? Waiting for more people to get here and confront you somehow? Building security is waiting to hear back as to whether they should forcibly remove her or contact the police."

Ev rubbed a hand over his face, groaning.

"What?"

"She's doing it on purpose," Ev told them, feeling certain about it." She's trying to get me to come out or talk to her or something. She flew all the way here from fucking Kansas, and I can almost hear her saying, 'Ev, dear, you're not really going to let me sit in this lobby all day and night, are you? What kind of a son does something like that?'"

Adam laughed viciously, "You are not going down there. No fucking way."

"I know that," Ev said, "But—"

"No, Evelyn," Adam commanded.

"But—"

"No buts. You know she's trying to manipulate you into doing what she wants. Don't let her. Be smarter than that."

Ev exhaled. "She will sit there all night if she has to. She will."

"Let her!"

Oliver was following all of this, glancing back and forth between them.

Then Ev's phone began to ring. Maybe he'd picked the wrong day to turn it back on. So far he'd ignored all of the message alerts, of every variety, but the phone itself still functioned.

"Don't even fucking think about it," Adam told him when they saw the caller I.D. indicate it was his mother calling.

"I should just see what she has to say."

"No."

"Adam—"

"No!"

"I'm trying to be the bigger person here," Ev argued, feeling pathetic and unable to sound equally as determined. "Being petty doesn't help anyone."

Adam opened his mouth to say something, but Ev grabbed the phone and pressed the answer button.

"Jesus fucking Christ, Evelyn."

"Hello?"

From the other end, at first there was nothing.

Adam and Oliver were silent, watching, and tense.

Ev heard breathing.

"Mom?"

"I never thought you'd answer," she said in a whisper of a voice, a hollow imitation of herself. "I've been calling for weeks. I…"

Ev's mouth felt glued shut. He realized he had nothing to say.

"I-I…" she stammered. "I just needed to say… I'm sorry, honey. I just want you to be happy. What we've done to you… I just… I didn't understand. I still don't. Not really, but the thought of losing you is something I just can't… I love you. I'm sorry."

Ev ended the call. He had been waiting for those words since the day he had been caught with James. The hand holding the phone dropped to his side, his eyes wide and unfocused. With his back to the window, Ev slowly sank to the floor, his knees drawing up to his chest.

He began to cry silently, tears spilling over but not making a sound.

Adam came quickly over and crouched beside him, wiping Ev's face dry.

Oliver walked through the studio, into the bathroom, and came back with tissues.

"She, uh…" Ev tried, but his voice failed, breaking. He shook his head, cleared his throat. More tears slipped down his cheeks.

"Breathe. You're fine."

"She… she apologized, and…"

Adam drew Ev forward, into a slightly awkward hug which Ev returned, clasping Adam tightly, his breath hitching.

"She said she loves me."

Burying his face against Adam's chest, Ev pushed down on the pain and confusion. It squeezed right out through the moisture flooding his eyes.

"Of course she does," Adam whispered, kissing Ev's head.

Ev's mother had left by the time he'd recovered himself and thought to have Oliver ask security for an update. After the call, she had walked out of the lobby and flagged down a taxi.

Staring out the window of Adam's studio, Ev tried to imagine what it meant, and how it affected what was going on—if it did at all.

He decided after a while that he had to just keep moving forward and concentrate on his own decisions. He couldn't worry about his family any longer. The relationship hadn't been completely cut off or shattered. He sensed if he wanted to talk to his mother, she would make it happen. His father of course remained a whole other story, but that was okay too.

In the reflection of the glass, Ev could see behind him many of the paintings Adam had done, mostly of him. Each one told a different story, exclaiming in vibrant colors pieces of his identity he'd always hidden away. There were portraits of pain, desperation, courage, anguish, love's aftermath and so much more. To be surrounded by such visions helped his new life take shape in tangible ways. He couldn't deny any of it. Truth had been captured as art, challenging perceptions.

The paintings helped to charge his resolve, but being with Adam, who loved him, transformed Ev even further. The pull of connection and emotion felt as real as anything Ev had experienced, but unlike the love that had kept him tied to his father's hopes and dreams, what Ev had with Adam only made him feel free to be whatever was in his heart. There were no limits. And he had Oliver and Rune too, people who had saved Ev from things he diligently did not let himself imagine.

Ev had school to keep him anchored, a place to live, and food to eat. Maybe his life had progressed in a way that was wildly different than he would have ever guessed, if asked only a couple of months ago, but it belonged to him.

Maybe his father and mother were letting him go, but Ev had a safe place to land. Knowing that, all he had to decide was who to be now that he was the only one in charge of what that meant.

"I'd like to talk to Oliver."

They sat on the terrace, finishing their morning coffee. Adam was going to be leaving—heading over to the gallery space to get a better idea of layout as he decided which pieces would hang where and why. Oliver had already arrived. He'd been using a dedicated office space within the apartment—a room Adam hardly ever used. Oliver had made the space his satellite office over the past couple of weeks. That was where they could find him if he wasn't actively keeping an eye on Ev or the door.

Adam peered at Ev over the rim of his mug, one red eyebrow cocked, his lips pressed together.

Feeling a need to explain, Ev continued. "I realized you made a rule that they weren't allowed to talk to me or whatever. I mean, I wasn't there when you set the rule, and it doesn't apply to me, so I get it. Kind of. And I've wanted to respect that, because I trust you to know what's best for..." he gestured all around them. Adam's expression hadn't changed, so Ev plowed on, talking more rapidly. "And I acknowledge that we haven't really talked about the whole Master/slave thing since everything happened, though we've each been acting like it's all still in play."

"It is until you say otherwise," Adam interjected.

"Okay."

"How do you feel about that, now that you've brought it up?"

That prickly feeling came over Ev then, like fingertips tapping over his bare skin, as Adam really began scrutinizing him. It felt so intense; Ev was pretty sure if cats and dogs began to rain from the sky, Adam wouldn't even notice.

Squirming a little in his chair, Ev cleared his throat and tried to verbalize what he felt. "Well, I like it."

"Why?"

Ev sighed. "It's hard to say. I guess because I always had rules growing up, but my dad and mom didn't always lay them out really clearly. They were more learned along the way. If I did something wrong, they'd let me know with guilt trips and anger and things that would kind of scare me into going in the other direction. But knowing those rules helped me survive. It was how I got through each day, no matter how confused I felt. So now..." he shrugged. "I like that you're more direct. Everything is easier to understand and none of it makes me doubt myself or makes me feel like I did something wrong. And I still like having rules, but... you know. These are a lot better ones."

"And what does this have to do with you wanting to talk to Oliver?"

"Well, you have that look on your face like you know already."

"I want to hear you say it."

Ev sipped his coffee. It went down warm and heated him up from inside. In the cold air, his sweater and jacket kept him from shivering. The bright morning sunlight on his face was well worth the occasional chilly gust.

Ev thought about the wording of the request before he voiced it. "May I have a conversation with Master Oliver? Obviously you trust him, and me, but I wanted to officially ask for that. He's been here, helping, for so long and I think it's overdue."

"If I allow this, I want you to remember how he sees you. You're my submissive. He will respect that, but he will always see you as submissive, first, before anything else. It's just how his life is defined. If anything that's said between you makes you uncomfortable, I order you to tell me right away. I've also told him he's not to touch you for any reason, other than to protect you from immediate danger, and that rule stands firm."

"Okay." He stammered, "I-I mean, yes, sir."

"Then, whenever you're ready, go ahead. Permission granted."

"Thank you, Master," Ev smiled, liking how ferociously Adam guarded him even from his protectors.

"I would like you to trust him, and know him just a little bit better, since he is my best friend and you're... well. You're sticking around a while."

"Just a little while," Ev teased, his smile growing into soft laughter.

Adam tilted his head in the direction of the doorway leading back into the apartment. "Go on."

"You'll let me know when you're leaving?"

"Of course. Jackson and Max are coming along with me, so don't worry."

"Good." Ev stood from his seat, then leaned down to kiss Adam's cheek. Adam briefly caught his hand, their fingers just touching as Ev walked away, heading inside.

He crossed the wide-open space of the main living area, then passed by the adjoining kitchen space with the morning sun at his back, brightening the floor tiles. Pausing to remove his jacket and drape it over a counter, Ev took his coffee mug back up and continued down the hall.

Finding the doorway to the office, one of the places in the sprawling home he rarely visited, Ev peered inside. The door stood halfway opened, the windowless room dark enough that it took a minute for his eyes to adjust. A few lit lamps cast a warm but intimate glow on the wood floors, painted dark walls, and gleaming furniture.

Ev knocked on the doorframe, feeling as hesitant as he'd used to feel when facing reporters on behalf of his father. Seated at the desk, Oliver leaned back in the chair, wearing a dark grey suit with a plum colored silk tie that caught the fairly dim light. Right away, his dark eyes rose to catch Ev, pinning him down in a similar way to how Adam's gaze made him feel sometimes. Oliver had been talking on the landline phone. Into it he said, "Hey, can I call you back? Great. Thanks, Tom." He promptly hung up.

"Sorry to interrupt." Ev became aware of just how intimidated Oliver made him feel. "I asked Adam if maybe we could talk, but I didn't want to interrupt if you were—"

"Oh, no, it's fine, Evelyn. Come on in. Have a seat."

Ev eased the door open the rest of the way, then went to sit in one of the pair of chairs opposite the desk. An electric fireplace burned away on the other side of the room, lending some cozy ambiance.

Ev's instinctive reactions to Oliver fascinated him. Oliver gave off a distinct sexual air and seemed capable and intimidating, both physically and mentally. The combined effect made him wholly unlike everyone else in Ev's life, even Adam, because of the utter unfamiliarity between them. Adam's rules had been effective— creating a wide chasm between Ev and the others. It worked for maintaining calm and safety, but Ev preferred to know the people he was expected to trust, hence the talk he intended to try to have.

Settling into the leather armchair, Ev hesitated to make eye contact, though Oliver measured him in an entirely unhesitant way, leaning forward over the desk with one elbow braced on it, pen in hand as he repeatedly clicked the end.

"I guess I know why he picked this room for the office—no windows or views. Dark and imposing."

"Yeah, he never uses this place. He set it up, just in case he wanted to handle business in a private space, but he's always just wandered around with the phone to his ear instead."

A lengthy pause stretched between them, in which Ev felt Oliver waiting for him to explain. He felt other things too, like how the glimpse of Adam's erotic paintings of Ev had altered Oliver's perceptions of him, adding a noticeable sexual power dynamic between them. It was so overt; Ev had to fight back a blush and force himself to assume a normal tone of voice. Luckily, he'd had some practice with this over the many years of acting as a stage prop for his father's political schemes.

"So."He wrung his hands, then forced himself to stop and sit calmly. "I'm here because it's been weird for me to be around you every day, when Adam always said he was going to keep me away from you." Here, Oliver chuckled, setting his pen down and swiveling slightly in the desk chair.

"Can't image why," Oliver smirked, his gaze drifting suggestively down Ev's body, fixing on his crotch like he was looking for a hint of the outline of Ev's sizable cock through his jeans.

"I get it. I do," Ev said, plowing forward and trying to not let his reactions show. "The rules and all. But if I'm going to be here, and you're going to be here, we should have a little more of an understanding between us. And I'm also just curious about your take on Adam, since you know him so well."

"I don't think I should be telling you things about your Dom that he hasn't already chosen to confide in you," Oliver replied with a slight edge to his tone.

"That's not what I mean. Just things like what you said about this room, and how he uses it. I mean," Ev scrambled to get his thoughts back in order. "What's your take on all of this? Me and him together? Everything that's happened with Pathway?"

"Loaded question." His dark eyes roamed everywhere Ev had assumed they'd travel to—his lips, his groin, his chest, undressing Ev with his eyes, maybe mentally placing him on his knees, naked and shackled, or imagining how Ev acted when he got fucked. Oliver had seen Adam perform so often, from what Ev had heard, Oliver could probably fill in the blanks pretty accurately.

"Well, you're here for a reason. What is it?"

Oliver smiled, letting his head fall back slightly as he watched Ev from a different angle. "I'm here for Adam. He needs support and assistance keeping things in order, since he's preoccupied with preparing for the show in addition to dealing with all of the fallout. That's what I do. I support him. He's more than earned it."

Ev nodded. The lewdness of the way Oliver's gaze swept up Ev's thighs told him he might as well be naked. It would make no difference. In Oliver's mind, Ev had a place, and it was the job of men like himself to remind Ev of it. Strangely, though, he sensed no condescension in it.

Swallowing thickly, Ev asked, eyes lowered, "And what about me?"

"What about you..." Oliver swiveled slightly again and chewed in a thoughtful way on the edge of his lower lip. "I do see why he likes you. There's that whole 'please, Master, be dirty with me but don't tell anyone' thing about you, which Adam probably saw right away. Bet he knew from the get-go that you'd cream yourself at the first direct command he gave. Rune and Jackson were always too hard for him. Adam likes 'em to be secretly soft and whimpering, with a rough, macho exterior. It's hard to find that in a genuine way. Some guys are good at putting on the act, but Adam can tell a fake a mile away. It's one of the reasons he hasn't dated much or taken his own sub before. So, yeah. You're the whole package, Evelyn, and I mean that in a very literal way." Oliver smiled a shark's grin. "I mean, come on, he's been in there painting your cock for weeks, making shrines to it. And—funny thing—I bet he really did think that was all it was going to be—some sweaty, pressed against the glass pounding. But you really—and I mean really—fucked him over."

Ev bit his tongue and glanced up, his defenses rising.

Oliver just kept smirking. "What, you don't think so? After what he's gone through? He still doesn't have his head on straight about his past."

"I know about his parents," Ev interjected.

"Good. Then you know what I mean. So here comes you— thick, juicy ass, huge cock, cock-sucking mouth and begging eyes— and you fucking got him to fall in love with you." Oliver laughed, shaking his head. "And now look at him." He angled his head toward the door. "Falling all over himself to keep you safe and trying not to imagine what they did to you in that place night and fucking day."

Ev's chest felt tight. He sat motionless and kept silent.

"I was there, you know, through that whole fucking ordeal. He shut down when they died. But he never lost it like he did when he woke up in that hospital, wondering where you were, if you were okay. And when he heard?" Oliver gave a cold chuckle. "When he put the timeline together and realized how long they'd had you?" A bitter anger slipped behind Oliver's eyes, curling his lip. "It's a lucky thing you're so sweet and unassuming, and that I can tell you love him back, because if anyone else had put him through that kind of hellish mind-fuck, they'd be in pieces right now."

Ev had never gotten a clear idea of what had happened when Adam had woken up. He could only guess, though he didn't like to. "So, it was bad?"

"Yes. It was bad. As in, he could practically see you in there, on your knees, knife to your throat, the light going out of your eyes. But it got worse after he found out what actually happened to you," Oliver told him levelly. "It wasn't just that you'd suffered. They had you. You were buying it. If Rune and Max hadn't pulled you out..." Oliver shook his head.

"I'd be a basket case, like my cousin," Ev guessed.

"Are you in this with him?"

"Yes," Ev answered without any doubt. "I am. The reasons why I let them..." his voice faltered. "Hurt me, was because I thought I'd gotten Adam killed. That's the only reason why."

"You craved punishment."

Ev couldn't voice his answer, so he nodded, wincing at the movement.

"And now you know it's solely your Master's job to decide on punishment?"

"Yes, sir."

Oliver considered Ev's expression, then said, "I bet he's too soft on you."

"Probably."

Pointing a finger, Oliver jabbed it at the air between them and said with plenty of authority, "No one but him touches you. No one."

"Yes, sir."

"Next time you crave some punishment, tell him. In the meantime, I'm happy to help make sure that rule gets followed. Over my dead body will his heart get broken again."

It was enough. Ev knew it. Something eased in him, and helped him breathe a little better.

"Does he seem happier now, to you?"

Losing his anger and the smile, wearing a look that lived somewhere halfway between those two extremes, Oliver said, "Dangerously so."

"Are you going to buy one of the paintings?"

Oliver smiled. It widened and turned into a laugh that filled with heat. "He's very giving with his subs. Always has been. And he's good. Very good. I know subs who've begged for one scene with him. *Begged*. So I was… pleasantly surprised… to see how *giving* you are as well. You're a good match."

"That was a yes, wasn't it?"

"Very arousing to see you again, Evelyn," Oliver said in dismissal.

Ev stood from his chair and, with a tight nod and some assuaged worries, left the room.

Chapter 33

Submissive's Surrender

Later that night, after Adam's several-hours-long absence from the apartment, Ev was ready and eager for his return. He'd finished his school work. His thoughts and heart were calm, but he needed something desperately. After the talk with Oliver, Ev knew it. Adam still hesitated to press Ev for sex, so it was up to Ev to ask for what he required.

He waited in the bedroom for Adam's return. Oliver knew he was in there, had seen him go in, so it was no surprise that Adam came in directly once he was back, before he'd even taken his coat off.

They locked eyes silently. Adam shut the door behind himself, then locked it.

Ev turned his back, facing the bed. He pushed down his jeans and briefs, bent sharply at the waist and planted his hands on the bed.

"Please fuck me, Master."

There was a slightly breathless chuckle. Heavy booted footsteps trailed right up to Ev's back. The lube waited right in grabbing range—Ev had made sure. Adam picked up the bottle and squirted some out. Only a moment later, Ev felt steady pressure as his hole was fed two fingers that pressed in hard to the last knuckle.

Letting out a complete breath, Ev hid a smile. "Thank you. Please more, sir," he said roughly. Adam's other hand reached around to find Ev's cock fully erect and dripping wet.

"Mmm. A little pent up, are we?" Fingertips ghosted over the sensitive crown, barely touching, skimming through warm fluid. The fingers up Ev's ass twisted, seeking his prostate. Finding it and pressing at it, Adam drew a gruff cry from Ev, who thrust, trying to get friction with the hand playing over his dick. "No moving." He rubbed across Ev's gland again, drawing a whimper this time. "Open your mouth. No self-censoring." The jolt came again, and Ev's cry was louder, sharper. "Bend more sharply. Let your shoulders take your weight. Good. Now, reach back here with both hands and spread your hole."

Adam kept working him, and Ev had no choice but to vocalize his torment. Each drag of Adam's fingers over that spot caused more fluid to drip down his cock, which strained and jumped, petting Adam's fingers cradled loosely below it.

Ev complied, spreading his cheeks. Adam removed his fingers and stepped back, as if to admire the view. He began to undress, tossing his coat onto the bed, then his shirts. He opened his buckle, the zipper of his fly pulled down.

Wanting it, imagining the way Adam's cock looked when hard, heavy and red, remembering the taste of it on his tongue, the softness of the taut skin sliding over his lips and the scent of it getting in his head, Ev begged, "Please, sir, give it hard."

With a curious hum, Adam stepped forward again, until Ev could feel the unmistakable heat and softness of his lover's skin against his own. The rigidity of his cock nudged at Ev's spread hole.

"How hard?" Adam whispered dangerously, just as he gave a firm thrust. The broad head of his dick popped through Ev's rim. Shouting, gasping, Ev closed his eyes and relaxed his muscles as much as he could. The skin of his opening stretched wide around the intrusion, his hole wrapping the blunt column. A shiver worked its way through Ev's body from his head to his toes. His dick jumped happily and Adam's fingertip swiped over the end, through the dampness there.

But he stopped once barely inside, so Ev beseeched, "More, Master," his voice cracking.

Palming Ev's pelvis, Adam drove into him with a continuous, demanding thrust that saw most of his length sheathed. Gasping for air, throbbing with ache, Ev struggled to bear it, but pushed back into Adam's next inward movement. The rest of Adam sank into Ev. Cringing, gritting his teeth, Ev grunted and whimpered.

"Mouth open," Adam said sharply.

Ev wrenched his jaws apart and all the sounds he'd been holding inside spilled out, describing all of his anguish.

Ev had let go of his cheeks as Adam had pressed too close to permit it any longer, so instead, Ev braced himself against the bed, his blood pulsing around the thick cock buried in him to the beat of his heart. Glad the door was shut and that they had privacy, Ev let it all out. The physical pain and mental struggle with the submission, as well as the acceptance of how much he needed to feel taken and claimed, no matter what it implied about him as a man—it was all there.

Adam gently arranged Ev's arms on the bed, and adjusted the curve of Ev's back. Straightening up, Adam withdrew, then slowly thrust back in, provoking a low moan as the friction lit Ev up. The pleasure washed over pain.

"More," Ev rasped. "More, Master."

Adam kept giving it to him, going steadily faster, each stroke long and mind-melting. He took his time, letting Ev feel well and truly fucked. When he was sliding easily, pounding Ev's ass, their bodies slapping together, Ev made breathy little gasps. Adam caressed the side of Ev's ass and the heavy weight of Ev's balls.

"Do you love it?" Adam asked in a wicked whisper.

"Fuck yes," Ev sighed.

"Does it hurt?"

"Not enough."

Adam instantly started going even harder. Ev yelped and had to hold on even more tightly to the bed. The force of it drove his breath from him along with pleading cries. It went on and on, then almost suddenly slowed way down as Adam slid in and out through the wet squelch of his come. Ev trembled.

"Arms behind your back."

He clasped his wrists together behind his lower back, leaning more sharply into the bed to support himself. The shift inside of Adam's dick made him groan.

Adam pulled slowly out, leaving Ev empty. A moment later, Ev gave a startled yelp of surprise as a kiss pressed to his rim.

After walking a few feet away to wipe himself off at the sink just inside the bathroom, Adam returned, dick softened but pants opened. He retrieved a phallus from a drawer and smeared it with lube. Closing his eyes, Ev focused on the way it felt as it fed into him, stuffing him full again, in a slightly less ideal way. Nothing felt quite as good as Adam, but he'd take what he could get.

With the toy lodged in place, Adam worked to remove Ev's pants and underwear completely, guiding him to step out of the legs one at a time, until he was bare.

"Good. Crawl up onto the bed on your knees. Head down."

Ev climbed up, glad for a shift in position. Then, Adam guided him to roll onto his side and pushed the undersides of Ev's feet so that his legs were curled up tightly to his chest. Kneeling over him, Adam worked the phallus in and out of him in a smooth, constant motion.

"Good?"

"Yes, thank you," Ev breathed.

Adam spread Ev's legs and reached for Ev's aching, neglected cock. He began massaging it, rubbing over the head and down the shaft. Letting out a hard moan, Ev fought to be still and simply enjoy it, though the need to rock and rut was strong.

"I can't take my eyes off of you sometimes," Adam said with something like awe.

Ev convulsed, whining quietly as Adam continued working him inside and out. It eased, then his whole body tensed as his orgasm crashed into him. The force of it wrung a heavy load of come from him, his thighs clenched as Adam rubbed him through the aftershocks, moving the phallus in long, smooth thrusts.

Sheathing the toy completely, Adam lay down just as Ev's arm came up, beckoning. He let Ev draw him into an embrace, lying on his side to face Ev, sliding up between his legs as Ev wrapped the top one behind Adam's thighs.

Adam kissed him, brushing the hair back from Ev's forehead. "Better?"

"Mm. Thank you." Ev nuzzled at Adam's neck, his breath hot and coming quick. He caressed through Adam's chest hair, letting the curls slip through his fingers. "You're so good to me."

Adam sighed, drawing Ev even closer. He pressed a firm kiss to Ev's jaw and encircled him with his arms. His fingers clutched Ev and there was such passion in his small kisses. "I'm so proud of you."

Ev smiled, needing the acknowledgment of the struggle to surrender as much as the tenderness afterward. "If I can ever do something more for you, you'll let me know, right? I want to make you happy too."

With an aching exhale, Adam kissed him again and said, "You do make me happy. This makes me so happy. All of this sweetness? This is all I need."

"Mmm." Ev smiled against Adam's lips, then felt a tug. He realized Adam was drawing the toy out again. Once it was out, in a smooth movement, Adam rolled Ev to his stomach, then shifted on top of him and sank in deeply with a moan. With a shiver, holding on, Ev caught Adam's mouth in a kiss over his shoulder. He hoped it would never end.

Leading up to the show, Ev continued to keep his low profile. Schoolwork remained a solitary, online endeavor, managed through email and rare instances of live-streaming lectures via video. As far as his social life went, it was the part of himself he abandoned the most completely. Unable to imagine facing people who had no idea what hell he'd gone through, and the awkwardness that would surely be there, he chose instead to let Adam's world and school fulfill him.

Claustrophobia began to set in a little. He never left the apartment and, sprawling though it was, he craved expanding his personal universe. That's how the thought of visiting campus at night, in the dark, getting lost in small gatherings of arts' patrons and admiring his lover's hard work from the shadows began to have quite a strong allure. He imagined it often, how the paintings would look in their careful arrangements, caught in spotlights and decorated with little ID tags. The people there would be just like Adam and Ev's former, brief employer—arts professor, Günter Ahlm. Around open-minded folk like that, Ev would feel more comfortable to own his role as Arm Candy and Loving Admirer. Anyone going to see an exhibit meant to showcase vulnerability in male sexuality was likely to be of a generally tolerant mindset.

So, he let himself look forward to going. Adam and Oliver arranged for extra security at the venue. Rune got Max and the old gang to agree to act as their eyes on the grounds, looking out for any potential troublemakers or Bible thumpers.

Threats hovered in the air, though, like phantoms. They were mostly memories, but some potential future horrors manifested too. The funny thing about surviving one of your worst nightmares come true was that it left the door wide open for more nightmares to come on through to join the party.

This meant Ev avoided most conversations about the event. He tried not to listen to Adam making plans. He still avoided television, radio, or news in paper or digital form. When he received text messages from friends, more often than not he didn't read them. After seeing a few that had been sent mainly to relay gossip or shock over something that had been seen in the news regarding Ev or his father, it turned him off to them entirely. Avoid at all cost was his means of staying sane.

Maybe it wasn't healthy, but it was a tactic he'd grown up with and it had always worked just fine. Ev thought he'd grown a lot since meeting Adam, but that didn't mean he had become an entirely different person. His coping mechanisms remained the same.

This left him dressed in a button-down violet shirt and black pants with dress shoes, standing by the door to the terrace, avoiding the clump of people hovering near the apartment's exit as they prepared to go to the opening night celebrations.

Adam hurried to gather last minute notes for his speech and checked his messages. Oliver tried to keep Adam calm. Jackson waited patiently with his wife, both of them dressed nicely in a suit and cocktail dress. This left Rune to catch Ev's eye as he shifted uncertainly, biting at his thumbnail.

He signed a question, making a circle of his thumb and index finger, letting the other fingers stand up, his expression curious or concerned.

Ev shook his head, then stopped himself and shrugged instead.

So, Rune walked over, his concern becoming more apparent. Ev felt so frustrated, wishing he knew more signs than he did, resolving to take lessons from Adam once they all gotten through the momentous night.

Rune gripped Ev's shoulder, as if steadying him or showing support. Ev tried on a smile, but it wouldn't quite come. Rune gestured to Adam, then signed 'okay' again, and did the same thing after gesturing to Ev. Ev used one of the few signs he'd picked up and placed his flat right hand to his lips, then moved the hand away, forward and down. When Rune smiled and hooked an arm around Ev's shoulders companionably, Ev chuckled a little.

Adam caught sight of them, one eyebrow lifting. He looked so flustered, but Ev didn't know how to help when he was barely keeping it together himself. Thank goodness the others were there to pick up the slack.

"You two ready?" he asked, signing the inquiry as well.

Ev nodded and said, "Yeah."

Rune urged him forward and they headed to the door. It was showtime.

Chapter 34

Showtime

They were still several blocks away from the gallery when Ev had some hard evidence in front of him that he'd been a complete dumb-ass. He sat beside Rune in the backseat of Oliver's Range Rover. Oliver and Adam were in the front seats. Adam caught Ev's eye in the rearview mirror, then turned to look directly at him. On both sides of the car, people rushed to parallel park, coincidentally walking in exactly the same direction they were headed. The sidewalks were packed with pedestrians. As they coasted slowly through an intersection, a police officer waved them on, their squad car parked nearby with the lights flashing.

"Oh, goddamnit," Ev said with soft reverence. "You've gotta be shitting me. Tell me there's a stadium or concert venue near the gallery, please? Please?"

"I'll have Oliver drive you back home," Adam said, not looking nearly as shocked and suddenly panicked as Ev felt. "Max and everyone are already there. I'll get out with Rune. Olly will keep you safe."

"You knew?"

"We all knew, Evelyn," Oliver interjected, turning the wheel as they tried to carve a path down a completely jammed street. Cars and people crowded in on all sides, fighting for a spot in the tiny gallery parking lot. Several groups of local news teams perched like vultures in front of the gallery entrance, all set up with their cameramen positioned to get some of the gallery and crowd in the background of their shots. Their reporters stood in spotlights, microphones in hand.

Nauseated, his expression blank out of practice rather than honesty, Ev felt glued to the car. Nothing in him wanted to go out there and face those people.

It wasn't just the reporters that intimidated him, it was the people. Some Ev recognized, but many if not most were students from the university. The crowd was also composed of families, elderly couples, and people from all walks of life. Thankfully, he didn't see any children, but that didn't exactly help put him at ease.

"The word got out," Adam told Ev, with such stunning calm, Ev found he didn't want to look at anything else. "Which is good for the show, good for me, but bad for you. They have a pair of metal detectors set up at the gallery entrance and the police are working with the detectives and agents investigating Pathway to ensure no one dangerous or suspicious gains entry."

"Why didn't you tell me?"

"We've been talking about it around you constantly. You didn't hear any of it?"

"Well.... No. I've kind of been in my own head a lot lately."

"We didn't know how big the crowds were going to be, but I've made sure preparations were made, just in case. This is a good thing, Evelyn. But keeping you comfortable is more important than having you with me for this. Olly will take you home. When you get there, you should celebrate. I want you happy, not worried. This is all for you."

"Bullshit," Ev replied. "This is for you. Your talent."

Adam raised an eyebrow. "I'm flattered you think so, but you're wrong. These people came to see you. The real you. The one I fell for so hard, and who's been standing up for himself against disturbed but powerful people."

Ev managed to tear his gaze away from Adam's blue eyes. He scanned the crowd. The windows were tinted, but some people pointed at the Range Rover, calling to each other and gawking.

Rubbing a hand over his mouth, Ev groaned. "I don't know if I want to hear what all of these people think about the way I look in those paintings."

"It would be commentary about me, not you. It's a showcase of how I see you, not how you are."

"Adam, I can't just turn around and leave you here alone."

Adam laughed. He caught Oliver's eye and Oliver laughed too. "I'm far from alone. I can handle this. Trust me."

"Of course I trust you." Ev took a deep breath. He thought of all of those times he'd been brought along as a window decoration, standing up on behalf of his father rather than himself. For how many years had he wished he could just stay in the car and head back home instead of getting out with flashbulbs blinding his eyes and dread sinking his stomach? Here was his out. He didn't have to stay. He could keep avoiding everyone and pretend it all away.

"I'm staying," he told them. "I need to be here."

"Why?"

Ev smiled, loving the way Adam tried to draw him out, even now. "I need to stand up for myself for once. I'm proud of this. Of me. Of you. This is us. These people all came here," he laughed at the thought of it, "for us."

Adam seemed to struggle to allow it. Ev realized then that Adam had already assumed Ev would go back to the apartment, and he wouldn't actually want to stay. He glanced uncertainly at Oliver, who had pulled up close to the gallery. Some of the security had waved them in and kept the crowd back. Reporters tried to lunge forward anyway, bellowing questions and trying to get a shot of them through the tinted windows.

"It's your call," Oliver told Adam with a half-shrug.

"I'll be distracted in there, so he doesn't leave your sight for a second. Not even to take a fucking piss," Adam warned Oliver. "And keep an officer with you."

"Got it, boss."

Ev felt on edge. The old, familiar adrenaline rush that always hit before doing something intimidating or downright scary now had his blood surging and body tensed. The urge to look everywhere at once kept him wide-eyed and tight-lipped. He realized he was actually going through with this.

Rune gripped Ev's shoulder and gave him a strengthening look. After he signed something, Oliver translated. "You can do this."

Ev gave a tight nod in reply.

Looking to Oliver, both of their hands on their door handles, Adam said, "I'll get him inside. Watch our backs."

"Will do."

From the moment Adam's door opened, the roar crashed into them as a soaking wave of sound. It swept around and initiated the mad confusion of trying to get from point A to B while humanity swept in from all sides. Ev tracked Adam circling the car, letting police push reporters back as he got to Ev's door. Oliver got Rune and Ev glimpsed the submissive's face, fully focused. It made Ev strangely glad the clamor wasn't touching one of them, at least. Instead, Rune's gaze mapped faces, scanned bodies like he was checking for weapons amongst the outstretched microphones.

"Evelyn Myers, what do you have to say for yourself?!"

"Mr. Myers, why did you model for Adam Buchanan?"

"Did you do this as an attack on your father?"

"What do you think Senator Myers would say about your participation in this show?"

Noise, lights, people pushing, surging toward them only to be stopped by the outstretched arms of the uniformed security team.

Adam brought an arm around Ev's shoulders and led him toward the entrance. After only a moment, Oliver and Rune were right at their backs. They closed in around Ev, making a human wall to protect him with their bodies. But they were his friends, his lover, and he wished he could do this alone, to show he was capable and not put them at risk for him. Adam needed to be allowed to set the rules and run the show. If seeing Ev maintain a submissive role kept Adam comfortable during one of the biggest nights of his life, Ev was happy to obey.

The big glass eyes of the cameras stared. The glow of smart phones held aloft shone down at him, recording everything. The questions and commentary swirled together, nothing indistinguishable other than a word here and there—things like "Myers," "statement," and "thoughts," which only gave him flashbacks of so many other public appearances, for a wildly different reason. He pulled the cloak of composure around himself, masking his expression, giving away nothing. He set his sights on the door and leaned into Adam, giving him a kiss on the cheek that had camera lights flashing all around them. The questions grew suddenly louder, more forceful. The door loomed near; the crowd's collective body heat pressed close and the firm touch of several hands moved him.

They poured through the entrance as a guard held it for them, standing aside to let them through. The reporters were kept back.

Everything suddenly got much quieter, the glass door pulled closed behind them.

"Maybe I should say something to them," Ev said in Adam's ear, uncertainly.

"You're here. It's enough. Let the art speak for you."

Smiling, Ev knew it was an elegant solution. The paintings explained things much more gracefully than he ever could, anyway.

Directly in front of them, on the wall right at the front of the gallery space, was the key piece of the whole show. He stood blindfolded in Damhan's garden in a fight stance, his expression mirroring his readiness and acceptance. Pale pink petals fell all around him, set delicately on his tan skin. A strange tension filled the strokes, giving a frantic energy to clash with the careful precision of his hands, face and broad shoulders. Just looking at the painting, Ev sensed men in the brush, nearby, carrying weapons, creeping closer. At the painting's side, the name of the show was stenciled on the wall in white, lowercase letters: *bare*.

Ev couldn't stop staring at the painting, wondering how Adam had captured the feel of that day so perfectly. The label with the name of the painting said it all—*Helpless*. There was Ev, all of his strength and power on display, ready to fight, and intimidating, a confident, masculine force, but in the end, none of that meant anything. He'd still been taken, moments after this image had been captured. It was how Adam saw Ev, with all of his fear for his lover's vulnerability, crying out for others to understand, respect their truths, and allow them some peace.

It showed the clash of how Ev knew he could fight for himself, but didn't want to always have to. Sometimes giving in to a loved one's need to protect was a blessing rather than a curse. Adam saw the real Ev, where his family had only saw the vision of a young man crafted in their own image.

A glass of champagne was set into his hand. Tearing his attention from the painting with some effort, Ev saw the others had retreated, giving him and Adam a moment. The show was about to open, but first they had this—a breath together.

Adam smiled, looking wickedly happy and handsome in his dark blue suit and partially unbuttoned black shit beneath. Just a few curls of red chest hair could be seen, covering a muscular, impressive chest.

"You look great," Ev confessed, letting his fingers caress the lapel, his knuckles skimming down the firm expanse of Adam's torso. "I'm so proud of you. These paintings, your talent—it's magic. It's changed my whole life."

Adam's expression twisted with some urgency as he came in for a soft, lingering kiss. One hand wrapped behind the nape of Ev's neck. The press of his lips, the taste of champagne on him, it made Ev need to pull closer, to get lost there for a while, if only he could.

"Love you, my muse," Adam whispered against his lips.

Ev felt it—how he really was Adam's, and always would be, no matter what else happened. Part of him belonged to Adam, claimed and utterly unable to be relinquished. The whole world knew it.

With a joyful grin, Ev kissed him back a little. Then they clinked the edges of their glasses together and took a sip.

"Let's do this," Ev told him. He was ready.

Chapter 35

Honesty's Reward

Standing in the farthest corner of the gallery, champagne in hand, flanked by two armed police officers and Oliver, who was scarier than both the cops combined, Ev watched people take in the show. Adam's natural charm mesmerized as he moved from person to person, diving into conversation, saying hello, shaking hands. He embodied the mysterious man Ev had first seen that night in the art studio on campus who had affected him right from the start as no other man ever had.

It startled Ev to discover how many people were there that he knew. Because the brazen, fearless paintings displayed him—nude, exposed, coming or crying, pleading or hiding, relaxed or rigid. There were other subjects besides him, but the sheer quantity and variety of the ways Ev was exposed made him shy.

Professors, school administrators, classmates and friends surrounded him. The police scared off many, though stares continued to come and most were brave enough to at least say hello as they moved past.

Oliver appeared to recognize people as well. When a handsome young couple passed by, flanked by a few private security guards whose intimidating appearance caught Ev's attention, Oliver called out to them. He motioned to the officers to allow the group past. "Master David. Shea." Oliver smiled. "So glad you could come."

"Well, we are in the neighborhood and wouldn't dare miss one of Adam's shows," the dark-haired, elegantly attired gentleman replied. "Or the chance to acquire some new decorations for the Manse. You owe us a visit, you know. All four of you."

"We'll be there soon. Been busy lately with lending Adam some support," Oliver told him. Indicating Ev, Oliver said, "This is Adam's muse, Evelyn. Evelyn, Master David and Shea are good friends of ours."

"Thought I recognized you," David winked. Ev shook with him, feeling a little flustered without knowing why. "Nice to meet you, Evelyn. I see why Adam was so inspired."

Ev spotted a collar around Shea's neck and noted his downturned gaze. A few things mentally clicked into place and he fought back a rising blush.

"We won't keep you," David said, excusing himself. "There are a few pieces I need to inquire about."

"Understood. Enjoy the evening," Oliver replied as they headed back into the crowds. "See you both soon."

When Damhan arrived, Ev noticed right away, his face heating again as Adam's grandfather gazed around at the work on display. After giving his grandson a peck on the cheek without drawing him from the current conversation he was wrapped up in, Damhan headed over to Ev in the corner.

With a word from Oliver to the police, Damhan was allowed past.

"Good to see you again, Mr. Ciar."

"Damhan, please," he asked with a warm grin. He gave Ev's cheek a pat, then drew him in for a brief hug. "How are you doing?"

"I'm good," Ev assured him.

Damhan gave him the same sort of doubtful glare he was used to getting from Adam, which only made Ev smile wider.

"I really am. I'm glad I'm here for him. He's just amazing, isn't he?"

"He really is," Damhan agreed. "But he'll be at this all night, you know. You should have a chair at least. Oliver?"

"I'll take care of it," Oliver complied with a nod, drawing out his phone and pressing it to his ear. "We need a chair for Evelyn," he began to say. "Ask a member of gallery staff and have them bring it to…"

Ev's attention drifted as he spotted Leo and some of the track team enter the gallery together. His nervousness rising, Ev fought the instinct to be embarrassed as his friends got an eyeful of things he never expected them to see.

Damhan sensed it and gripped Ev's shoulder. With a sheepish look, Ev covered his mouth with a hand and mustered his courage. Leo pointed to a few of the paintings of Ev, making commentary to the other guys. Ev wasn't sure he wanted to hear it or not. They gazed at Ev's likeness, draped in cloth, everything from his chin to his upper thighs exposed, his cock stiff and red, his body tensed with either extreme torment or pleasure. And nearby, glass reflected his body as Ev pushed against himself, not budging an inch. On the wall opposite, he curled up on a bed, wearing a skirt, his face hidden in shadow. Behind him, embracing him tenderly, laid Adam with his unmistakable shock of red hair.

Leo and the guys came over. The police stepped slightly forward, blocking the way.

"It's okay. They're friends," Ev spoke up.

Oliver glanced between Ev and Leo, then nodded. Leo came through, shaking Ev's hand and clapping him on the back.

"Can't imagine why you'd be blushing like that, man," Leo said.

Ev laughed.

"You've seen all the stickers, right? That's what I was showing the guys," Leo said, raising his voice a little to be heard. Ev smiled in hello to the others gathered around.

"Stickers?"

"Yeah. The yellow ones. See?" Leo pointed to some of the same paintings Ev had seen him gesture to when they'd first walked into that section of the gallery. Then Ev did notice neon yellow stickers on some of the painting labels.

"Oh yeah. What are they?"

"Those are the ones sold already."

"What?!"

The closest painting with a sticker was a small twelve-inch square canvas depicting a cropped-in view of Ev's mouth. His lips were parted as if crying out. It bore a price of five thousand dollars. And it was sold.

"Holy shit." His mind whirled. "I hadn't really noticed the prices or... oh my god. He's sold a lot of these."

Imagining these images of himself hanging in other people's homes or businesses sent his mind whirling. The self-consciousness and wonder he felt, of sharing these private parts of himself with the last people he'd ever wanted to, would go on now indefinitely. Those glimpses would always be out there, being seen, capturing attention.

"Well, that's the whole point," Leo reminded him, elbowing him good-naturedly.

"Yeah, but..."

"You thought he was just going to take these home and put 'em in storage or something?"

Ev bit his lip with embarrassment. "Maybe? I mean, I get why I like them, and why Adam does. And Oliver said he was buying one, but that's... Hey, Oliver, which painting did you buy?"

Oliver winked at him.

"Oh, come on, please? Just tell me."

He appeared to consider it, giving Ev a look that made butterflies flutter in his stomach. Leaning in, Oliver whispered in Ev's ear, "Beg me again."

Ev rolled his eyes, his face heating even more. He shoved his hands down into his pockets and saw Max walking over with a chair. Biting at his lip, Ev turned his back on Leo and the guys, who'd fallen back into conversation. He lowered his eyes and said quietly, "Please, Master Oliver?"

Wearing his amusement mostly in the darkness of his eyes, Oliver pulled out his phone and brought up a picture on the screen. He tilted it to show Ev.

Embarrassment twisted up Ev's insides—making his balls draw up and his throat close, a shivery sort of nausea connecting the two. "Jesus fuck," Ev sighed, pushing down hard on the sense of raw humiliation.

"I had him set it aside for me. It's not here."

"Thank you," Ev said with more than a little relief, adding "sir" as an afterthought.

"You're welcome, slave."

"Ev, we're gonna keep walking around, okay?" Leo called. Ev waved to show he understood, then shifted so Oliver blocked him from view.

"You can put it away," Ev told Oliver softly, through gritted teeth. When Oliver's lips twisted up on one side, the phone still held out, Ev said, "Please put it away, sir?"

The screen showed Ev on his back, in the cheerleader skirt and stockings, legs spread, his dick in the chastity device but obviously red and swelling against the constraints, and his hole looked equally swollen and used, a gleam suggesting he'd just been fucked and come was leaking out.

"I forgot about that one," Ev admitted, wishing he could melt into a puddle and slip away, out of sight.

Oliver leaned in again, since people were all around, nearby, and told him quietly enough that no one else could hear, "So, tell me, Evelyn, how did he get that wetness effect on your caged cock? Was it a special type of varnish, or…"

Remembering the paintbrush that had pet his dripping cock, which Adam had then used on the painting in progress—the one Oliver had just purchased—Ev bit the tip of his tongue and struggled to overcome his mortification. "He told you, didn't he?"

"I do know him *really* well. And after seeing all of that? I feel like I know you pretty well, too."

"Yeah, guess so," Ev answered.

He settled into the chair, saying thank you to Max. A couple of hours slipped by with an endless stream of people sifting through the gallery. Soon, though, Ev did start to feel tired, and was ready to head home again.

He gave the word to Oliver, who called Adam rather than leave his post. A moment later, Adam appeared.

"I'll take him home," Oliver offered.

"Okay. I'll come with you out to the car to make sure you get there safely."

"Adam, I'm fine, really," Ev protested. "Enjoy your accomplishments."

Adam gave him a kiss on the lips, holding him by the jaw, "I am, and you're not in charge, slave. I do what I want, and you do what I want."

"Yes, sir," Ev replied, wishing they were both headed home, rather than just him. "Please don't be too long, and be careful."

"Okay." Adam's thumb caressed the swell of Ev's lower lip before kissing it again.

They were shepherded out to the entrance. Oliver had gone ahead to get the car, which waited only a few steps from the doorway. Some reporters still waited there, and they surged awake upon seeing them appear.

"Ev, a statement, please?!"

A microphone lunged toward his mouth, an eager blonde in a power-suit holding it out. Adam moved to block the woman and pull Ev ahead, but Ev stopped him with a hand and said, "I'm here to support Adam, and his beautiful work. It's what brought us together and I just hope that in sharing it with everyone, you'll be able to see why. He's pretty irresistible."

Adam chuckled and said, looking only at Ev, "So are you." They kissed and cameras flashed.

Ignoring the follow-up questions and demands to talk, to explain or share more secrets, they instead pushed to the car and Ev got inside, waving to Adam in farewell.

Ev knew he wouldn't sleep until Adam was home. He paced restlessly. Once in a while, he texted Adam to check in, but didn't want to seem clingy or paranoid, so in addition he also wandered out to the office, giving Oliver a pleading sort of look that prompted him to say, "He's fine. Things are wrapping up soon."

Ev nodded and wandered away again.

Adam finally returned at almost two in the morning. Exhausted, Ev jogged out to the door when he heard it rattle. Throwing himself into Adam's arms as soon as he was in sight, Ev groaned in relief, burying his face against the side of Adam's neck.

"I missed you too," Adam chuckled, embracing him.

Oliver had followed Ev out, and Adam glanced at him over Ev's shoulder.

"Let me take care of one thing, then I'll meet you in the bedroom. Go lie down."

"Yes, sir," Ev replied, hesitant to let go.

Happy to have Adam home, almost giddy to be alone together again, Ev pushed his hands into his pants pockets and, head bowed, hurried to bed. He passed Oliver and left the two alone.

A few minutes later, Adam finally came into the bedroom, his jacket off and shirt unbuttoned the rest of the way. Ev waited, naked, and sitting on the edge of the bed, his spine straight and head lowered.

"Mm," Adam hummed, walking up to him and tossing the jacket aside. He hooked a finger under Ev's chin to tilt his head up. Ev kept his eyes down. "Perfect."

Reaching into his back pocket, Adam pulled something out and extended it to Ev. "For you."

It was a small folded paper. A check.

"Adam, I don't…"

Ev unfolded it. His gaze snagged on the amount—fifty thousand dollars.

"Whoa. Adam…"

"Your share from the show proceeds, for you to save for when you're ready to open your flower shop. You'll be able to make that dream come true, and I'd like to help. You earned this."

"I can't. I can't take this," Ev protested. "You worked so hard on those paintings, and have done so much to protect me."

Adam stepped up between Ev's spread knees and cradled his face in his hands. "I realize how much you gave up to be with me, and you've given me so much, Evelyn. This is just the beginning, to get you started. I believe in you, too, the same way you've shown that you believe in me."

"Thank you," Ev said, his heart full of gratitude and devotion as he turned to kiss one of Adam's wrists. He felt it then, how there wasn't just the heavy past or the complicated present, but a bright and hopeful future waiting for him, too. It hadn't taken shape yet, but if he kept being honest and following his dreams, the path would lead him there.

Ev gazed out on the snow-covered campus, seeing some green poking through the white, here and there. Spring was coming. It was close.

"How's the new roommate?"

"So boring, dude. He studies all the time, never goes out, doesn't get into sports at all."

"So he's just like me," Ev said.

"Exactly like you," Leo agreed. "Only there's no sign he's into letting the male professors seduce him for butt-sex."

"That's a shame. He doesn't know what he's missing."

Leo laughed heartily and nudged Ev's shoulder.

Ev's car waited only a few feet away as they walked toward the parking lot. "Glad he's letting you out on your own again."

"Yeah," Ev agreed, digging out his car keys. "Things have been good. Quiet. After my dad resigned from his position and the charges against Pathway were filed, things settled down a lot. No more media attention. It's just been kind of normal."

"Ev, I'm pretty sure your life will never be normal."

"Eh, normal's boring anyway. Like your roommate."

"I hear that."

"You still coming over for dinner tomorrow? I'm cooking," Ev said eagerly.

"He's letting you cook?"

"Dude, he lets me do things. It's not a big deal. It's not like he's the boss of everything I do."

"That's actually kind of exactly what he is," Leo countered.

Ev sighed and shook his head. "I should never have told you the Master/slave stuff. You're actually never going to let it go, are you?"

"No worries. I'll be there tomorrow. Is he going to let you wear clothes this time?"

"I wasn't naked in front of you. I was modeling and I put on a robe when you got there."

"That doesn't really answer the question."

"I'll be wearing clothes. Let it go."

"I mean, it's not like I haven't seen you naked anyway, so it wouldn't even matter. Just might upset my appetite or something."

"Dicks don't make you hungry?"

"Not like they do with you."

Ev unlocked the car and threw his backpack into the passenger seat, then shut the door again.

"Good talk. I'll see you later," he said with a wave.

"Hey, so what's the deal with the school? They ever confirm the housing and meal charges were cancelled? I thought you were looking into the paperwork or something?"

"Oh, yeah, I did finally talk to someone," Ev told him, leaning on the roof of the car. Sunlight glistened on all of the melting snow and shining car roofs. A few students walked past, chatting softly, books clutched to their chests. "They're refunding me for the second half of the year."

"Wait. What?" Leo sputtered, shifting his bag's strap. "You said the money was gone."

"Yeah, all I know is they're refunding me the money paid for room and board and the meal plan. It's not usual, but the administrator I spoke with said an exception was made at the request of the account holder."

Leo said nothing at first, looking like he was working it out in his head. "That doesn't make sense."

Ev shrugged.

"So your dad asked them to refund you the money, even though he's the one that paid up?"

"Guess so."

"But what does that mean?"

"Means one less thing to worry about," Ev smiled. "Later, Leo."

"Later, Ev. Be well."

"You too."

Feeling like he had more going for him than working against him for the first time in his whole life, with a light heart and excitement for the future, Ev sat behind the wheel. He waved to his best friend, pulled out into the road and began the trip home where the man he loved was busy painting miracles, and where Ev felt like absolutely anything was possible.

The bridge stretched out before them. The wind whipped off the water, far below, and swirling up through the walkway's thick railings to catch their clasped hands. Ev kept glancing over at Adam, looking for hurt or heartache in his eyes. So far, he hadn't found any.

"You okay?"

Adam caught his gaze, seeming to climb out of deep thoughts and distant worlds of imagination. He opened his mouth as if to answer, then closed it again. Instead, a slow smile spread across his lips. He gave Ev's hand a tighter squeeze and tugged him closer just as a shiver raced up Ev's back. The forget-me-nots in Ev's hand danced in the gusts. He pulled them more snugly against his chest, and tucked them inside his partially opened coat to protect them.

"I never thought," Adam began, "I could ever be in this place and feel lucky. But I do."

They were almost at the mid-way point on the bridge's huge span across the gaping river which had claimed the lives of his parents, Darian and Ceit Buchanan. Adam pulled Ev to a stop, then moved around behind him, embracing him with his arms hugging Ev's shoulders, his lips pressed in a kiss to Ev's cheek. The view of the sprawling city, gleaming with the possibility of a bright, blue, beautiful sky, bathed in sunlight, took Ev's breath away. His school waited there, buried in the fertile maze of streets laced with hopes and fears, innocence and guilt, lost in the crowded rush of too-busy lives. Adam's home—their home—waited there too. To step back and admire it all from a distance helped Ev breathe more easily. The new perspective was a good one, taking him out of reach of things that couldn't hurt him any longer.

With traffic rushing back and forth behind them, and the glistening current rippling far below, Ev savored the peace of a picturesque moment in an important place with the man who had so drastically changed his life.

But Ev's life wasn't the only one that had endured the growing pains of change, and that particular day, that moment, wasn't about him at all.

The blustery day tugged at his coat, prying at it, so he moved to further shield the fragile flowers in any way he could.

Adam's hand slid over Ev's, grasping the stems. After another kiss to his jaw, Ev was urged, "It's okay. Let them go."

"I wish I could have met them."

"Me too," Adam admitted, "They would have loved you, though if they were still here, none of this might have happened. I'd have been a lawyer, and a miserable one at that. Ridiculously successful, most likely, but bored of it all very quickly."

"How modest of you," Ev chuckled.

"I thought you'd think so. But it's true. I wouldn't have my art, my freedom, or you. I really hate the idea of fate, especially if it implies they were meant to die that way, so young, and yet…"

Adam sighed, the warmth of it a caress over Ev's skin.

Ev imagined that alternate world, and found he didn't care for it, even if a different outcome spared Adam such awful grief. Guilt from the realization drew him closer into Adam's embrace, wanting more of the press of that firm body against his back. So, instead, he imagined the reality they did have, and all of its implications. He thought of his parents, and how they'd surprised him after all. Love had triumphed over fear. Their relationship was likely permanently scarred, but it persevered nonetheless. His parents were out there, right now, and were they thinking about him? Worrying about him? If so, he might tell them of his happiness, of the way all of the knots woven by terror had been coming loose, of the goodness of having someone he loved so much hold him and keep him safe.

But then he wondered about Adam's parents, and if they worried about him too. With a flush of surprise, he asked, "You don't… think they watch us, do you?"

Adam laughed, the flowers now firmly in his possession.

"I'm sure they're respectful of your privacy," Adam assured him. "Not that you have much of that left."

"Yeah. Likewise."

The wind at their backs gusted harder, pushing them up against the thick metal double-layered railing that lined the open side of the fortified walkway. Adam relaxed his hold and let the invisible force take their offering. The blue buds flew upwards and out over the sparkling, gentle waves.

"Love you," Adam said, almost too softly for Ev to hear. "Miss you."

Ev drew Adam's arms around him, covering his hands with his own to shield Adam's blessed warmth.

"I promise to take good care of him for you," Ev added as they watched the blossoms tumble down, scattering in a wild shower.

"Yeah. Likewise," Adam said.

Ev gave him a nudge, felt the brush of another kiss and was promptly turned around. Seeing the tangled emotions in the vibrant shimmer of Adam's eyes, Ev gave him the hug he knew he needed. His nose buried in the side of Adam's neck and he drew in a deep breath of the good, complicated, cherished scent that marked him as Ev's to have and adore.

Never before had everything felt as right as it did then, with Adam in his arms and a few rogue petals dancing on air around them. Ev finally found his truth. He'd fought hard for it and had no plans to stop.

Brushing his lips against Adam's neck, Ev whispered, "This is everything that matters."

Author's Notes

The initial idea for this story came while wondering what the most (pleasant) sexually awkward situation I could think of might be. Of course, if you've read this far you know I came up with a vision of a profoundly repressed and closeted young man being quickly convinced to act as a nude model for a handsome, charismatic painter whom he secretly desires. But it wasn't quite enough. The missing piece was Adam's fiery personality, which revealed itself naturally as I wrote and the scenes played out through Ev's eyes. Adam brought the tense, squirm-in-your-seat dynamics to life. The two men are at odds right from the start, because while Ev tries so hard in understandable ways to conceal many secrets, Adam is the devil prying open all of Ev's weaknesses with wicked lust and pure-hearted intent. Adam's non-stop pursuit of vulnerability in his new model is the fire that burns right through Ev's willpower. I couldn't have done it without him. Poor Ev didn't stand a chance.

There are plenty of twists in the unveiling, though, and I loved simultaneously giving Adam exactly what he wanted in exposing Ev, and blowing right past each and every one of Adam's expectations in order to leave him as emotionally thrown as Ev. The intensity of the psychological battles they engage in, working to jab, duck and weave without daring to pause long to rest, too enraptured to dare stop, made this one of the most enjoyable stories I've had the pleasure to write.

I intentionally named them after the Bible's first lovers for a couple of reasons. First off, in the context of this story, religion is what establishes the true problem by creating a vicious, judgmental atmosphere among families, with whom which children should feel safe, not threatened. By identifying Adam and Evelyn with recognizably biblical names, the religious theme begins to underscore everything in subtle ways.

This is Ev's story. In his mind his relationship with Adam is the beginning of it all. It reshapes his entire world and reality. He didn't really exist until Adam initiates his rebirth. I also love the symbolism behind having Evelyn play the role of Eve, and all of the complex implications therein which Adam exploits through his art in striving to expose the feminine in the masculine. Ev is the one taking a bite of the fruit of the tree of knowledge. He's the one taking the risks. He's on a quest to determine what is good and what is evil. And once he finds out, there is no going back. Adam, meanwhile, is the provider and the unwavering, confident masculine presence.

I actually identify with both men. Evelyn closely resembles aspects of who I was in college—doubting everything and trusting nothing while trying haphazardly to carve a new path away from where family expected me to go—whereas Adam is my present, tearing apart the foolish ideals and missteps of the past while speaking desperately through his art. I understand the enormous task Ev faces in shattering rigid, cruel confines and breaking through the lies that defined his identity since childhood. But I also feel every bit of Adam's passion for his art and the message he wants to scream to a world that doesn't always listen. They're both just trying to live the most authentic lives they possibly can, and not waste a second if they have the ability, willingness, and energy to keep fighting.

This is the headspace I occupied while writing this book. It's an entire world created around the notion of, "Let's cut the bullshit and talk about what really matters, no matter how much it scares us." It's my sincere hope that this message inspires my readers to enact positive change in their own lives, to never stop fighting for what they need and what they believe.

I also need to touch on the conversion therapy aspect to this book. All of the rumors and details incorporated here were directly pulled from my research into current and past, actual, functioning organizations who set out to do these things to vulnerable people in their midst. Nothing is embellished for dramatic effect. These things have been and are being done— and much worse—on a grand scale. These dangerous practices are still legal in most places and are terrifyingly widespread. We all need to be aware of this. Knowledge is the best defense. We need to do our best to help victims recover and understand what they've been through, to speak about their experiences when they are able, and to do whatever is in their power to move on in healthy ways.

I need to thank absolutely everyone who has helped encourage my writing over the past year and a half, specifically. This book was born during the roughest period of my life. It was my joy and escape while healing after the untimely and sudden passing of my brother, and in breaking free of the tightly woven, toxic environment of my past. It's my proof that good can come of bad. My husband and kids, all of the lovely people at ForbiddenFiction, all of the generous reviewers who have been kind enough to take on my stories, all of my readers, colleagues, cherished friends, and inspirational fellow authors are blessings in my life I couldn't do without. I'm right there with Ev feeling like this is only the beginning, and happily anticipate everything still to come. I expect to stumble along the way, but I'll do my best to keep putting one foot in front of the other.

Much love and gratitude, from the bottom of my heart,

Lynn

About the Author

Website: lynnkelling.com

Lynn Kelling began writing in order to tell stories that weren't afraid of the dark, didn't hold anything back and always strived to be memorable, forging lasting attachments between character and reader. Her inspiration comes from taking a closer look at behaviors and ideas lurking at the fringes of life—basically anything that people may hesitate to speak of in mixed company, but everyone wonders about anyway. Her work is driven by the taboo in order to expose the humanity within it. Lynn is an artist, designer and lover of any form of creative self-expression that comes from a place of honesty and emotion, whether it's body art or opera. She has had multiple novels published, has written over fifty works of erotic fiction of varying lengths, and always has several novels in progress.

Works by Lynn Kelling:

Deliver Us series:
Deliver Us (Book 1)
From Temptation (Book 2)
Forgive Us (Book 3)

Twin Ties series:
My Brother's Lover (Book 1)
Dual Affairs (Book 2)
Double Heat (Book 3)

The Manse series:
Loving the Master
Learning from the Master
Bound by Lies

Arctic Absolution series:
Arctic Absolution
Caged Jaye

Other Works:
Whatever the Cost
Song of the Lonesome Cowboy

Cursed Blessings (short story)

About the Publisher

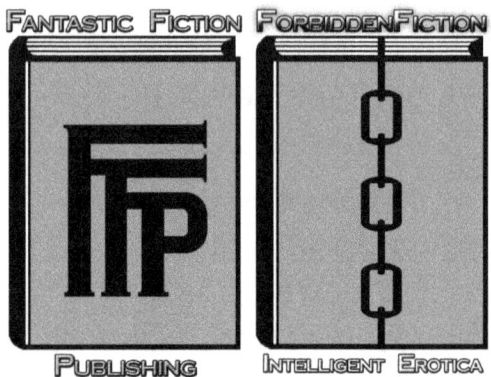

ForbiddenFiction.com is a publisher devoted to writing that breaks the boundaries of original erotic fiction. Our stories combine intense sexuality with quality writing. Stories at Forbidden Fiction.com not only arouse readers through sensations, but also engage them emotionally and mentally through storytelling as well-crafted as the sex is hot.

ForbiddenFiction.com is also designed to be a social reading environment. You'll have fun even if just reading the latest post each day, yet you will have the chance for so much more. Readers and authors can be part of ongoing discussions of specific works and individual authors as well as more general topics.

Sign up for a FREE Membership today at ForbiddenFiction.com